Spectral

Analysis

Seeking Lost Souls

Joanne Alain Cook

Cover art by Joanne Alain Cook
This 2nd edition the deleted prologue at the end.
This is a work of fiction. All the characters and events in
this tale are fictitious. Except, of course, the ghost. The
ghost is a ghost.

Dedication

For Jonna, to remind her of home

Chapter 1

Old Town Sacramento

Emerging from the depths of Old Town Sacramento, Janine took a grateful breath upon reaching fresh oxygen. Below, on the original street level, a stagnant atmosphere saturated the tunnels. Stale, cold, and acrid in places, the underground section of the capitol city reeked with the stench of rat droppings and moist soil. Rumors of a haunted Old Town had lured the ghost-hunting team of *Spectral Analysis* to the Golden State, and most of the hauntings lurked in that dank darkness.

Old Town is considered the riverfront district of the California Capitol with Gold Rush era buildings, streets paved in cobblestones from the 1800s, horse drawn carriages, and fun novelty shops. Foot-worn wooden planks formed walkways along each block, except in the back alleys where the ground dipped to the original level. Over a hundred years ago, the streets had been raised to combat against periodic flooding from the Sacramento River. *Spectral Analysis*, a team that filmed paranormal investigations, chose Pioneer Park as their entry point into the underground. The park sat on the lower level and provided easy access through the simple removal of a wood wall. They could pass directly into the tunnels and explore.

Scattered across the park, broken pieces of metal ironwork lay rusting and half buried. The technical crew, Carlos and Janine, waited patiently as the special talent for *Spectral Analysis* traipsed out of the opening and into bright sunlight.

"Can you believe the smell?" Carlos whispered. "We'll need gas masks."

Janine watched the tall scientist, Doctor Ian McNally, as he helped the petite Kiki Mellow out of the dark. Kiki ran her hands up and down her arms to warm up. The doctor scratched his head and gave the crew a little wave. Janine's attention was drawn to his eyes as they squinted in the bright sunlight.

The doctor meandered toward their Sacramento guide to the underground, a short bald man from the Old Town Discovery Museum by the name of Jeff Lang. Lang sat on the edge of the wooden walkway wearing extremely dark sunglasses. His head tilted toward Kiki, giving the impression that he stared at her.

Kiki did not follow the doctor toward Lang. Instead, she gazed back into the tunnel. Kiki Mellow was a self-proclaimed witch and medium and stood just shy of five and a half feet tall. She was blessed with a curvaceous but slender build. Her naturally dark eyelashes framed bright green eyes, but the natural color of her smooth hair remained an enigma. Kiki's mane altered from dark brown to chestnut to strawberry blond on a rotating basis. She could appear anywhere from mixed West Asian to European depending on how she dressed and what she did with her hair. She had a flair for fashion and constantly changed her style. Steve rushed across the debris to cover her with a light coat.

"My hero," she gazed at him. His face broke into a smile.

By far, Kiki was the most famous asset on the show. Her colorful personality and very sexy persona kept the public wanting more. Sponsors always vied for Kiki Mellow to be their spokesperson. Following their first season, talk shows and speaking events begged Kiki to appear. She resisted over showing at outside engagements and often declined the invitations. Kiki obviously enjoyed keeping a more mysterious image. At the moment, Kiki studied the makeshift entrance to the underground with a puzzled expression on her face. Ian McNally strolled toward her, whispered something, and they nodded agreement with each other.

Ian towered over Kiki at about six-foot-three. As usual, his dark-brown hair was in a bit of a mess over his brow and his pretty blue eyes sparkled. He actually had a doctorate degree, so the crew felt justified in calling him *the Doctor* instead of just Ian. He earned his PhD at the University of Edinberg's Koestler Parapsychology Unit (KPU) and spoke in a fading Scottish accent that Kiki mimicked perfectly on occasion. Janine easily imagined what inspired the many fan letters from female viewers regarding the doctor. It was those pretty blue eyes, masculine jawline, and broad shoulders.

Ian could also be very funny and his dry humor worked well with Kiki's over-the-top personality. Their dynamic, more so than the ghost stories, provided the driving force behind a very popular first season. They easily bantered on almost any topic and they looked good together. On several episodes, Kiki got herself into a situation that called for the doctor to rescue, catch, or pull her to safety. A couple of times, they almost, just about, but didn't, kiss. The rescues began accidentally, but everyone knew the audience loved it. The doctor and Kiki came round to where the crew stood waiting.

"All right everybody," the doctor announced. "Our guide, Mr. Lang, tells me we're having lunch on the Delta King, our other destination. There are two ghosts on the boat, one of a little girl and one of an older man, so, it'll be a working lunch. We'll grab what we can on SBT voice, maybe a small portable EM box and also the camcorder. Then we'll come back to this underground entrance at nightfall."

"Ion detector?" Carlos suggested.

"Aye, good thinking. We'll just walk ahead."

The doctor and Kiki strolled ahead of the crew. They usually developed a rough game plan while Janine and Carlos gathered the needed equipment and followed.

Spectral Analysis just entered into a second season. Their breakthrough episode occurred in Providence Rhode Island at the very gaudy Biltmore Hotel. It was the first episode with a Kiki-Doctor romantic tease. Kiki had managed to lose her footing in the dark basement where animal sacrifices were once performed and the doctor caught her quite spontaneously, saving her from a nasty fall. Kiki then proceeded to faint languidly into his arms. Upon recovering, Kiki insisted the basement held the spirits of more than just animal sacrifices. She insisted that one angry entity caused her fainting spell, and then it invited her to a party in room 1404. After that episode aired, room 1404 at the Biltmore in Providence became booked out for months in advance. Viewers also began to speculate if the doctor and Kiki were an item.

Each episode started and ended with a lessor ghost story near their feature investigation, which they called bookends. They were short snips of a tale meant to capture audience attention. The bookends for the Biltmore episode revolved around a library near Brown University, the historic Providence Athenaeum. People claimed it was haunted by both H. P. Lovecraft and Edgar Allen Poe.

Kiki didn't agree. But she did insist that the Biltmore was haunted, extremely so, and Janine almost believed her.

That hotel had spooked her more than any other film site. In the grand ballroom, her thermal-panger, a fancy thermometer, had plummeted to subzero temperatures, then, just as instantaneously, the temperature rose back to normal levels. Everyone felt the dramatic cold rush of air, and though it was snowing outside, not a single window or door to the ballroom had popped open.

"Unhappy spirits bring in the cold," Kiki had uttered through chattering teeth.

Spectral Analysis consisted of a very minimal and basic crew. Steve Hanks managed the computers, tape storage, and data-conversion software. He spliced the image and audio media, and took care of the computer equipment. He acted as their executive producer/director, as well as the editor/art director. He spooked easily and kept a safe distance from the action. Janine got the sense that his interest fell into creating a successful indie television show, not so much on their paranormal discoveries.

Ted operated the main camera. He trained his lens on the talent, the doctor and Kiki. He set up lights for the shoots and remote cameras for the angles they offered. Ted gave very little input to any of the events he filmed. He managed to stay quiet and almost completely off camera, much like Steve.

Carlos and Janine carried and operated the sensors, recorders, and other gadgets needed to document paranormal evidence. They trailed Kiki and the doctor and assisted as needed. They served as extra witnesses to unexplained spectral activity and offered nonexpert commentary. Carlos mostly provided wisecracks. They acted as onscreen receptors for the doctor or Kiki to analyze an interesting event to. The doctor kept his discussions on the measurable data they collected, while Kiki rambled about her psychic feelings and the stories behind the ghosts. A few times, she spontaneously pulled Janine and Carlos into an impromptu séance. No one ever knew when Kiki Mellow would whip out a candle, or tarot cards, or a crystal ball.

During lunch on the Delta King, Kiki pulled out a small, translucent orb. She polished it with a blood red cloth.

The Delta King was a 285-foot riverboat permanently docked at the pier in Old Town. A giant, bright-red, immobile water wheel dominated the stern, and the main deck felt slightly tilted and warped. The manager opened up the Pilothouse Restaurant for the crew to gather and investigate the local ghosts. He offered them a free meal. Airtime on their show translated into free advertising for his boat.

The *Spectral Analysis* team gathered around a table in the center of the dining room. Out the back window, a spectacular view of the Sacramento River and the gold-painted Tower Bridge loomed. The operational drawbridge rose during their short lunch and a tall boat passed underneath. The metallic paint scattered beams of afternoon sunlight onto the water.

When their lunch had been cleared, Kiki centered her orb on the table. She used her red scarf to make a base and balanced the ball in the folds. She glanced at Janine.

"Perhaps us girls should stay in here to try to draw the spirits," she said.

Doctor McNally rose. "Carlos, let's hit the deck. Ted is going to tape Kiki and Janine inside while we try to get what we can on camcorder out there."

He gave Kiki a little nod, then smiled at Janine. His eyes lingered a moment. Did she imagine it, or did his eyes become a tad deeper blue? Every so often, Janine caught him gazing at her like that, like he wanted to say something but thought twice about it. His attention caused her nerves to buzz. Janine once told Carlos that she thought the doctor was making "eyes" at her, but Carlos just laughed. Carlos claimed the doctor often gave girls that same wrong impression. *He's a Scotsman,* Carlos said, *every girl thinks he's making eyes at them.* Carlos grabbed a portable LED electromagnetic field box and camera before moving out to the deck.

Kiki readjusted the crystal ball as Ted set up a tripod. The empty dining room fell quiet. Janine retrieved her thermal-panger and registered a micro-temperature rise. Kiki leaned into the table.

"Janine, I've got something to tell you." Kiki's eyes slowly swept the empty room. "This boat is not haunted."

"Really?" Janine let out a startled laugh.

"Really, there's nothing here. I don't feel a thing." Kiki reached across the table and took Janine's hands. "But we'll give it a major-league try. A little show to get those book ends." Kiki smiled sweetly at Ted. "Ready? We are going to call on the spirit of the little girl. Rumor has it, the girl is often heard singing *Ring Around the Roses*. We should call to her with her song." Kiki glanced at the door the server disappeared through. She looked back at Ted. "Do you think we could get some water?"

"Am I a waiter?" he snarled. Ted often snarled, so they were used to it. He turned toward the doorway and redirected his booming voice. "Hey! Can we get some water in here?"

"Better order a whisky sour too. Two if you want one," Kiki advised. She smiled at Janine. "I know you won't touch one, Janine, but we," she tilted her head toward Ted, "will be glad of them in that tunnel tonight."

"What do you mean?" Ted aimed the camera on Kiki.

Kiki put on her game face. "Main Street Sacramento is buried in a tunnel underground. On those streets six feet under, I felt panic, sorrow, anger, and greed. Desperation too. It is a gold strike on the original streets of Sacramento. A California gold strike of spectral energy."

"Nice," Ted said.

Kiki turned back to Janine and grabbed her hands.

"Now let's give this the old college try," Kiki said. "We'll need something for the bookends. It's a sure thing that Ian and Carlos will turn up empty handed out there, so we need to get something usable in here. Then, I want to catch a long nap. It's going to be an exciting night."

The doors to the *Spectral Analysis* van were splayed open exposing several blinking monitors. Steve Hanks lounged on the back bumper with a large drink in one hand and a double burger in the other. He often worked and munched at the same time and had a little pudge to show for it. His command console glowed and hummed behind him.

"Everything is ready to go. I set up a fan to air out some of the smell. Lang assured me that the stench is only near your opening. That's where the rodents and such will hang out. The further in, the less stench," Steve told them.

Floodlights created a bright circle that illuminated their gear. Two air cases sat side by side on the curb. On a makeshift miniature sawhorse, headsets were lined up with decals to identify them so no one would mix them up. Doctor Who for the doctor, Patriots for Ted, Captain America shield for Carlos, and a Wonder Woman "W" for Janine. Steve recently added two small lamps to the top band of each headset for emergency purposes: a red light to keep their night vision, and a white light for total illumination. Carlos called the white one "the scared little investigator" lamp and no one had used it yet.

Kiki refused to wear a headset. She clipped a small microphone onto her shirt instead. She required unencumbered senses to receive paranormal energy.

Ted, Carlos, and Janine geared up. For feature segments, they wore violet-colored coveralls topped with red vests and black work boots. Their color choice represented the two ends of the visible electromagnetic spectrum. The red fishing vest provided pockets for tools, random gadgets, and ponytail bands for Janine's long, auburn hair. Carlos loaded his pockets with gum, candy, and treats of different sorts. As the riverfront town drew a cool evening breeze, Janine was happy for the jumpsuits.

The doctor wore a button-down shirt under a lab coat to identity himself as a scientific doctor and the leader of their investigation. He topped it with a multicolored *Spectral Analysis* tie. Kiki wore whatever she wanted, which usually turned out to be an outrageous ensemble designed to tantalize the audience. Although Kiki was a very serious spiritual seeker, she realized their program involved show business. Plus, she loved attracting male attention and didn't appear shy in the least.

For the Old Town Sacramento segment, Kiki chose dangly gold jewelry and a Western-themed outfit. She strutted into their circle in red cowboy boots, black lace gloves, tight denim jeans, and a rhinestone-studded blood-red shirt unbuttoned to reveal her deep cleavage. She probably couldn't button it properly if she tried, Janine observed. Kiki had pulled her hair into a tight bun and wore an old cameo pendant which fell into the V of her shirt, drawing eyes to her shapely breasts. Her grab-bag of items resembled a leather saddle bag right off a Pony Express horse. Kiki paused to flirt with their guide, Mr. Lang, for several minutes.

Carlos didn't conceal his amusement. He laughed loudly and flashed his dimples at them.

"No one told me we were headed to a rodeo later."

Ted and Steve chuckled. Kiki blew them a kiss then promptly ignored them.

Janine popped open an air case and retrieved a small electromagnetic field reader with five LED lamps. She secured it to her vest with a carabiner. Set to automatic mode, the EMF recorded sixty minutes of wave activity in any section of the lower-than-visual-frequency range of her choice. Her recharged temperature reader, which they called a thermal-panger, was dropped into her front right pocket for quick access. Specifically designed by the doctor, the silver meter resembled a phallic device, as Carlos loved to point out. It stored thirty minutes of temperature fluctuations to the nearest one thousandth of a degree. Her headset hung snuggly around her neck while the transmitter-receiver was zipped securely into her arm pocket. Only the stubby antenna poked out between the zippered teeth.

Steve finished his burger, stood up, and climbed into the van with a big bag of french fries.

"I'm firing up!" he announced before shutting the doors.

The crew strolled down the street to Pioneer Park and Janine clumped down the steep steps in her heavy work boots. They formed a semicircle just outside the tunnel entrance. Pitched blackness loomed in front of them. It represented a doorway into a dark and forgotten era. The ultralow wattage bulbs on the remote camera's would give them little respite from that darkness. Adrenaline jumpstarted her heart as she recalled Kiki's "gold strike of ghostly energy" declaration.

Ted planted himself a few feet apart from the crew and panned his camera over their semicircle. Showtime.

As they invaded the blackness, Kiki rattled on about the charged feel of the atmosphere. Her voice level dropped as they rounded the first corner in their route. She mentioned heading toward the basement floor of the BF Hastings building under Second Street. The dim light from Ted's camera provided just enough luminosity for the crew to be aware of each other. Janine's heart beat loudly in her ears and she wished her night vision would show up to quiet that drum.

Kiki led the pack. Her cowboy boot heels clicked rhythmically, echoing against the tunnel walls and giving them something to follow. Kiki said the Hastings ghost story seemed to be the most credible of all the tales in Old Town Sacramento. Earlier that day, she sensed a very strong energy in the building directly under front foyer floor. According to sources, three ghosts haunted that area: a cowboy, a former saloon girl, and a small child. They caused lights to flicker, footsteps to echo, and pockets of negative energy to manifest. Kiki had detected a lingering presence hovering in the building, perhaps even two. She felt certain one of those entities was a cowboy.

Steve's voice filtered into Janine's headset, clear as a bell.

"Ted, go down all the way on your luminosity input. I'm barely getting outlines." They paused for a moment. "And your sub IR settings, one step up on your lamp. Okay, that's beautiful. Now, I see you."

Kiki's boots began clicking again and the crew followed the sound. The stench in the tunnels altered from an organic acrid to earthy damp. It became more bearable with each step away from their escape door.

"*We seek yon souls of near to there, we call on you to us appear, reveal yourself for us to see, so I command, so mote it be,*" Kiki whispered. "I am starting to feel something. Something is in this tunnel. Do you hear that?"

During an investigative shoot, Kiki often vocalized her stream of thought for the camera and crew. Her tone became sharper and her volume changed slightly when she addressed a spirit.

"*I hear you, cowboy.*"

Janine pulled out her audio recorder and turned it to super slow motion by feel, then slipped it back into her pocket. She glanced toward Carlos and could just detect his outline in the darkness. She didn't need to see his face to know Carlos wore a wide grin.

Eerily, the air did feel strange. A stagnant wall of cold seemed lodged inside the tunnel. If they were going to find a ghost, the underground of Old Town Sacramento seemed like a good place.

"Do you feel it?" Kiki whispered to the crew. "The tingle? All along your skin. There is definitely something lingering down here. It's stronger in this direction." The tone of her voice changed again, "*I'm here, cowboy. Talk to me.*"

The clicking of her boots slowed to a halt. She shuffled on the hard ground and it sounded like she turned around. In the darkness, it was near impossible to tell who Kiki addressed. She whispered.

"Do you hear him? *What's that, cowboy?* He doesn't seem to be a very happy fellow."

Kiki stood with her arms out as if she were an antenna trying to pick up a signal. Janine's eyes were quite adjusted and she could see Kiki's outline perfectly. The doctor circled Kiki, studying one of his smaller gadgets. He turned toward Carlos.

"I'm getting thermo-layers at that wall," the doctor said quietly. "High to low."

"I'll go ultralow band red, just below visible on video," Carlos said.

"He's saying something," Kiki whispered excitedly. "I think he's laughing. He feels like a crude fellow. Angry and accusatory."

Kiki's boots clicked right up to the wall and stopped. A sudden spike flashed on the main EMF box making them jump. Any night vision they developed was severely reduced in that flash. Kiki began breathing harder, hyperventilating. Janine's own heart beat faster as she listened to Kiki gasp in a frightening way. Janine did not like that sound and felt her tummy tighten.

Relax, relax, she told herself, but her tummy clenched into a severe cramp. The air molecules seemed to crowd around her and she began to feel claustrophobic. Did she feel a hand on her back? Janine spun around, but nothing was there.

"*No. No. What?*" Kiki gasped again. "I am really feeling something awful here. Does anyone else feel this dark energy? I feel like he's grabbing me. Oh my god, my stomach…"

Carlos panned his camera and suddenly stopped. "Geezus! What's that!" He squeaked. "Doc, Doc, take a look at this!"

Janine glanced at the infrared camera. A definite blotch pulsed against the far wall near the thermal image of Kiki. It showed clearly on Carlos's camera display. It roughly resembled the shape of a small human body. Yet the thermal blotch was not uniform like a human heat signature would be. Parts of it moved randomly and independently flared at times. Good grief! What in the world could it be? Cool cracks appeared throughout the shape. It moved and twisted in different directions.

Janine peered into the darkness but saw nothing, just the darker figure of Kiki bent over and clutching her tummy. Was her own cramping abs sympathy pain? Did any of the guys feel a tummy ache? She tried to breathe easy. Janine definitely felt a pressure bearing down on her, squeezing parts of her body. She began to break out in a sweat.

"He's very angry. I sense terrible rage. This is not a happy spirit. *I'm not lying. I am not lying to you!*" Kiki panted. "My stomach… *I am not lying to you, cowboy!*" Kiki's boots shuffled in the dark.

"There is an enormous level of ionized air popping off in here?" the doctor whispered. "Kiki, what do you say?"

"I'm feeling manhandled, literally. Like he's trying to rip out my guts," Kiki gasped.

Quite suddenly two red spots appeared, like tiny eyes.

Janine startled, and she instinctively stepped backward. She glanced to Carlos's infrared camera display. The heat signature near Kiki flare up once before bursting into fragments that shot out in every direction. Carlos yelped and dropped his camera.

At that moment, Kiki ran to the opposite corner of the tunnel and proceeded to dry heave. Alternatively, Janine felt her own abdominal muscles flex before loosening in relief. Her breathing eased as she swallowed down the bile. Could that have been a ghost she felt? The hair on the back of her neck stood on end and it took a lot of discipline to stand calmly.

"Christ!" The curse came under Ted's breath as he stumbled a bit.

Someone flipped on their red headset lamp, Carlos. He crouched over to look for his dropped camera. The doctor spoke calmly into his headset microphone and moved toward Kiki.

"Steve, confirm that you got all that," the doctor said. "Kiki, are you okay?"

Janine also moved toward Kiki, but the doctor got there first. His hand dropped to Kiki's back and he whispered something to her. Janine felt her own hands shaking. She took a deep breath and then let it out. She told herself it was nothing, only the power of suggestion.

"Just give me air." Kiki, breathing heavily, clutched the doctor's arm. "I need to get somewhere to breath. I need fresh air."

The doctor turned toward the crew and fixed on Carlos.

"I can get her," Carlos stepped forward and scooped Kiki up as if she were a child. She whimpered against his chest as he started shuffling down the dark tunnel toward the entrance. "What the heck!"

Janine watched him stumble, banging against the wall, almost dropping Kiki. Rats. Lots of rats ran past. They crisscrossed and scurried around. Where did they come from? The pitter-patter of rat feet echoed everywhere. Janine felt ready to pee her pants. At least the rats were running away from them.

"Are you two okay?" Excitement hovered just below the calm, cool of the doctor's voice. "Are we ready to move toward the Dingle's Coffee and Mill? We should get whatever we can down here. This is quite exciting. Did you see that flash of energy on the EMF box?"

After a moment, Janine nodded and squeaked out an affirmative.

"Christ!" Ted cursed. He hoisted the camera on his shoulders. "Give the recap as we walk. Walk and talk."

Their second destination lay under the Dingle Steam Coffee and Mill building. People cited a bad haunting with inexplicable moaning sounds and the random opening and closing of doors. An old legend blamed the spirit of Nathaniel Dingle, a rough pioneer of early Sacramento, known to be a harsh and dangerous man and who committed one of his daughters to a lunatic asylum out of spite. Dingle was found mysteriously dead in his basement workshop in 1897. The current owners still used his old workshop as a storeroom of sorts. A large picture window allowed them to spy into Dingle's old basement. Before Sacramento raised the streets in 1862, the basement door and window would have been the storefront. Janine tried the door and found it locked, or blocked rather. The knob turned just fine, but the door didn't budge. Kiki's sixth sense wasn't needed to hear the noise. A loud clacking and scraping increased in volume nearer the Dingle basement.

At the doctor's orders, Janine set up a low intensity electromagnetic wave boosting antenna in the forty to fifty Hertz range. The doctor pulled out a rather large coil of copper wire from the pack he carried.

"Instead of electric oscillations, we'll try to tap into the magnetic part of the wave. Boost the receiver to full throttle."

They instantly picked up super low frequency electromagnetic signals. Janine proceeded to clamp the extra leads onto the large copper coil.

"Next, I want to do a heat sig on those pipes," the doctor pointed to the plumbing running in and out of the Dingle basement. "They might be a clue to these phantom noises."

"Uh, Doc?" Ted spoke.

The doctor turned slowly to face Janine. His eyes grew wide and his brow furrowed with concern. Ted's camera, which usually points at Kiki or the doctor, was aimed directly at Janine. She straightened up slowly, wondering why they were staring at her.

"What?"

"You're glowing," Ted blurted.

"Aye, you are glowing," the doctor confirmed with his eyes glued to her. Her heart began to pound again. "And your lovely hair is standing on end. It's static electricity or something. Don't touch anything," the doctor warned. His eyes blinked rapidly as he glanced around.

"What are you talking about?" She felt nothing out of the ordinary but then noticed her hand. To her astonishment, a soft yellow/green halo radiated from her skin. She reached up and felt stray strands of hair from outside her pony tail floating.

"Somebody is going to get one hell of an electric shock when they ground you," Ted said. "You're getting brighter."

"Are you connected to something? The antenna? Are you stepping on something?" The doctor moved cautiously near, looking everywhere. His handheld lamp blinded her as the beam swept the floor. "Don't touch anything. Don't move," he repeated, fanning the light slowly, systematically. Janine raised her hands in surrender.

"Tell us how you feel." Ted kept filming her.

"I feel fine," she spoke calmly to the camera. "I feel like, nothing. Nothing."

"Do you hear the buzz?" he asked.

"The buzz?"

"You seem to be buzzing as well as glowing," the doctor made a second slow circle around her. "Crikes. What could be causing this?"

Janine turned ever so slightly and barely lifted one foot. A sudden flash of light, coupled with searing heat, rushed up her legs, through her body, and out her fingertips. From a faraway place, she spied the doctor lunging forward before she blacked out.

"Janine!" His voice sounded desperate in the blackness. "Steve, we need EMT. Steve, do you copy? Steve, come in… Ted, I think the com is out."

"Shit! Shit! Shit!" Ted spat out in the dark.

"Janine? Ja…" The doctor stopped suddenly.

Janine saw a bright light. Her fluttering eyes allowed the light in. She noticed the doctor staring right at her. He was bent down so close that he was practically nose to nose with her. As her vision cleared, his soft blue eyes locked right onto hers and they appeared worried. Her heart melted under his gaze. She watched the emotions in his eyes slowly dissolve into relief. Ian McNally had very expressive eyes. She felt her heart begin to flutter and wondered if she was still glowing. It dawned on her that she lay limp in his arms, staring at his eyes and lips, hands casually on his shoulders; not unlike a Doctor-Kiki encounter. She felt him shift as his hands moved along her back sending tingles down her spine.

"Hello there, lass," he said tenderly, in almost a whisper. "Can you speak?"

She wriggled out of his grasp and stood on her own. Her heart still raced and she could feel a flush rushing up her neck. She was embarrassment at having a Kiki-like moment with the doctor. It wasn't in her job description to play the damsel in distress. She took a step away from him.

Ted had illuminated the "scared investigator" lamp on the top of his headset so the tunnel glowed bright. Janine pretended to dusk off invisible particles to avoid the concerned eyes boring into her. *Just give me a minute*, she silently demanded. Other than feeling very warm physically, she felt just fine.

"Are we done here?" Ted sounded anxious.

The men exchanged glances.

Janine noticed that somehow the door to the Dingle Steam Coffee and Mills basement had cracked open. When did that happen? The doctor also noticed the door. The loud creaking noises had mysteriously stopped. The tunnel was stone cold silent and the air stagnant with a burnt smell.

"We should get you out of here and checked out." The doctor blinked at Janine.

"We should check out what's in there first." Janine defiantly indicated the open door. She stared down his concern and started to move toward the basement door.

The doctor took in a sharp breath.

"Shit," Ted mumbled. "Christ. Okay, I'm still rolling."

After the paramedics cleared her, Janine opted out of going straight to bed as they advised and instead joined the crew in Steve's hotel suite to debrief the night's events. The others always drank whisky and watched the film clips, discussing which parts would work best for the show. Sometimes they recorded a little narration, or voice-over, while the experience was still fresh in their minds. Janine rarely stayed longer than necessary, but this time she was eager to see the extra information on their static sensors and cameras. There must be a reasonable explanation for what happened to her in underground Sacramento.

As they congregated around the coffee table with shots of single malt whisky, the doctor came up behind Janine with a steaming cup of tea. He passed it over slowly, taking care not to spill. He used two Styrofoam cups to protect against the heat.

"Careful, it's a wee bit hot." Ian smiled at her. "Remember, the paramedic said to keep hydrated. I'm glad you're staying up a bit longer. We want to keep an eye on you. Just give that a bit of a blow before you try it."

Well, that made her feel about five years old.

They viewed the video of Janine's experience under the Dingle building several times. Everyone was curious to discover where and when the glow of electricity originated. It appeared spontaneously and spread along her perimeter from the feet up. Her ponytail levitated a bit, and red/gold highlights appeared in her hair. When she suddenly flared up, Janine cringed as her body stretch tensely before collapsing. It appeared much more painful on video.

Then, the doctor swooped in to catch her and cradled her tenderly in his arms. The way he gazed at her fluttering eyes caused her pulse to thump. She especially enjoyed that playback in slow motion. It was more tender than his Kiki moments and exactly how Janine fantasized such an event. She kept rooting for the doctor to lean all the way down and kiss her, but it never happened.

24

She glanced automatically toward the doctor and caught him staring at her. He immediately began blinking and turned his attention back to the monitor. Carlos was right, the doctor definitely sent mixed messages. She blew on her tea and took a careful sip. It was extremely sweet. Apparently, the doctor added lots of honey to it.

Steve made a comment that perhaps they might infuse a little rivalry for the doctor's attention into the current season. Who will win the doctor's affections, tomboy science geek or sexy ESP vixen? The audience would surely eat it up. The look Kiki kicked out made very clear her opinion on the subject, but Steve sounded pretty set on the idea.

"I think your new antenna malfunctioned?" Kiki purred, lounging like a cat on the sofa.

"The antenna is a receiver, not a transmitter," the doctor countered. "That energy did not originate from our devices. The battery in that EM box could not pump out that kind of power." He looked a bit embarrassed. "I guess, I should take another look at it."

"Janine. You got pretty pink when you first came to." Carlos chuckled. "You were either totally fried, or… you were hoping the doctor would lay one on you."

She could kick him. Carlos, the world-class teaser, knew how she blushed beet red in certain situations. He also knew she had developed a little crush on the doctor. Did he need to call her out like that? Luckily, no one ever paid attention to his off-color comments.

The rest of the Dingle film led to nothing of consequence. For all their adrenaline, the Dingle basement turned out to be just a dusty and quiet room. Not even a mouse scurried about. The noise recorded in the hall had ceased during her blackout and they attributed the racket to the pipes of fluxing temperature.

On the other hand, the first encounter came with hidden gems. The super slowed down audio from Janine's recorder revealed actual words. A distorted but understandable *swallow nails and spit corkscrews* emanated from the recorder. Steve set it to repeat over and over again. The group laughed at the creepy voice. Was it real? What did it mean? Sounds can often be warped into words when they are sped up, slowed down, or played backward, but this voice sounded very real and clear.

Kiki insisted they caught a clip the cowboy speaking. The cowboy said those words in her ear, with that voice, at the moment Kiki began to feel ill. She insisted that he attacked her and manhandled her. The spirit of a cowboy desired to harm her in a painful way.

"In life," Kiki sipped her single malt whisky, "The cowboy was likely an outlaw who died in the great flood, probably at the very spot his spirit lingers. I sensed that he killed someone. Maybe even enjoyed it. I sensed a particularly strong hatred of women. He doesn't trust women. He called me a liar more than once. I felt him pulling at my hair. Evidently, he was trying to rip out my guts. He felt animosity towards you too, Janine. Did you feel it?"

"Come on now, Kiki," Ted called from his corner of the room. His eyes were still closed. "It wasn't that whisky sour mixed with oysters at lunch you were feeling?"

Kiki threw a small square pillow at his balding head.

"Speaking of the lunch. We need something better to bookend the show. The Delta King was a total bust." Steve played with his computers, all three of them, moving as he spliced clips together. "My lord, those rats had me freaked. They still have me freaked. They are just freaking crazy. Do you think rats were pulling your hair?"

They reviewed the low infrared playback of the man shaped rat mass, a greenish glob that moved like an amoeba across the screen. Red blotches shot out rapidly in every direction as the rats suddenly dispersed. Odd behavior, even for rats.

"I'll bet they were outlining the cowboy on the very spot he died," Kiki mused.

General agreement trickled around the room. Kiki put a hand on Steve's shoulder, not an uncommon thing for her to do. Kiki had a flirty nature around all the men.

"Are you sure our little crystal calling can't be good filler? The look on our faces when the waiter joined in on Ring Around the Roses is priceless."

"It looks forced." Steve nixed it. "The underground stuff is sure to be audience pleasers. Inconclusive, but entertaining stuff. We need something with a little more appeal for the bookends."

"He's right," the doctor added. "We can have a bit of fun entertainment," he meant the little fainting dramas. "But not too much. We want to be the show that delivers the real goods. We don't want to muck up what we discover with forced intrigue or useless comedy. I know part of all this is show business, but our main goal is pinpointing real paranormal activity. Let's brainstorm. Where can we get a quick little side story?"

"F Street house," Ted said. "Dorothy Puente lived there. Remember that story? Little old lady luring her victims with cookies."

"Wasn't there a vampire of Sacramento?" Carlos added. The doctor shook his head.

"No, no. We do not want serial killers. Not unless there's paranormal activity involved. And we want something relatively unknown, near here, near the capitol. I don't want to drive out to that deserted Bodie again. There has to be something good close by. That place is overdone."

"We could hit Rio Linda," Janine suggested softly.

"What's Rio Linda?" The doctor asked.

"A little town about ten minutes away," she told them. "It has hauntings. Out at Dreyer Road. A tractor trailer specter. The river too. Apparently, a little girl ghost lures kids into the water. Yearly drownings are blamed on the ghost by the locals."

"People believe this?" The doctor asked, "How do you know?"

"My gram lives in Rio Linda. I'm visiting over my break. The Dreyer Road ghost and the river ghost are well known tales in Rio Linda. When a kid plays all alone, people say they must be playing with the river ghost. People scare kids about the ghost. In fact, when I used to visit my gram, I had an imaginary friend, normal, like most kids, my gram became convinced it was the river ghost and sent us away that summer. She refused to let us visit until I grew older. She believed it that much."

Ted snorted. Steve Hanks appeared riveted.

"That is fantastic!" Steve said. "We have to check it out and reconnect you with that girl spirit. This is perfect. Seriously, with your glowing segment in the tunnel it will be the perfect side story for this episode. Kiki, think about it. You specialize in child spirits. Janine used to see a child spirit. You both had encounters, fantastic encounters, in this episode."

Enthusiasm grew in all corners of the room. Even Ted sat up to give the room a good positive glare with his thumbs up. Janine began to rethink opening her big mouth and offering up Gram's ghost story. Did she really want this extra attention?

"Do you think your grandmother would fancy a visit?" the doctor asked.

"She'd love it. This is her new favorite show and she actually begged me to bring you guys over."

Everyone agreed, they would head out to Rio Linda for a simple rural ghost story to bookend the Sacramento adventure. Janine needed to give Gram a heads up.

Chapter 2

Rio Linda

ram, aka Martha Williams Stinger, welcomed the *Spectral Analysis* team with open arms. She hugged every member of the crew as if they were each a grandchild of hers. Gram surprised Janine when she whipped out Doctor McNally's rare book on paranormal electromagnetic spectroscopy and requested his autograph. Gram further established her superfan status by showing off Kiki Mellow designer earrings. They dangled flamboyantly from her lobes as she poured the tea. She offered cookies and coffee cake in honor of their visit. Gram lamented the crew for failing to wear their *Spectral Analysis* uniforms. She really thought they looked cool. She raved on and on about the show, and at one point, she inferred that much of the show's excitement must be directly connected to Janine's efforts. If Janine could sink into the earth, that was the moment she hoped it would happen. Yet the crew appeared to genuinely adore Gram, and everyone agreed that Janine played a vital role in their success.

Until recently, Janine managed to keep a private, businesslike relationship with her coworkers, but Gram dashed it all in a matter of minutes. She blatantly exposed a more intimate side to Janine. She gossiped about their family and relayed tales of Janine's childhood antics. She bragged about Janine's perfect student record and sports accomplishments. Gram seemed determined to systematically help Janine dismantle her carefully constructed wall, brick by brick, a wall Janine built to obscure a painfully damaged past. Gram realized that she was ready for that wall to be demolished, and Gram knew that she needed help doing it.

After everyone felt completely at home, Gram embraced Janine for a very long time and whispered into her ear, "I love you, girl."

Even after their reconnection over the long weekend at Sammy's birthday, Gram treated her like she might disappear again. Janine felt ignominy about shutting her grandma out of her life for so long. It took until recently for her to feel recovered enough to face her family again. Her heart ached thinking of the ties she nearly severed during her depression. She vowed never to go into that dark place again.

Ted attempted to charm Gram by kissing her hand and noticing the decor. He asked where he could set up the camera.

"Really? I thought Jaja was joking with this old lady when she said you wanted to interview me."

"Jaja?" Carlos chuckled at Janine. "Jaja, did you not explain to the lovely Mrs. Gram that we are on an important mission? Jaja. I love that. I'm going to start calling you Jaja."

The doctor interrupted him, "Here's the plan. Ted and Steve will remain here and film Kiki interviewing Mrs. Stinger about the river ghost, and her memories of Janine. The rest of us will make ourselves scarce, so, maybe we'll ask around a local pub or someplace, about the local ghosts. Then, later tonight, we'll head out to Dreyer Road."

Ted gave his standard thumbs up and started setting up his camera.

"Is there a local hangout we could visit?" the doctor inquired.

Janine, Carlos, and the doctor found themselves at the Old Rio Linda Bar, a hole-in-the-wall worn-out building with frosted glass windows taped over with cardboard. Dubious of entering, they were pleasantly surprised to find the dark room was clean and well maintained with cushy bar stools and a nice pool table. For early afternoon in a small town, the bar already welcomed a sizable collection of older drinkers. Couples played board games at small tables and a few old men sat at the bar. Gram certainly sent them to the right place.

Janine imagined they were unassuming to that older crowd, so it was surprising when people recognized the doctor. Admittedly, his foreign accent and intellectual aura clashed with the local surroundings. The fans waited about three minutes before pouncing on the oak table to say hello. A waiter delivered beer on tap in frosted mugs.

"Are you investigating Rio Linda?" After the first sip, questions started flying at them.

People inquired about the Providence episode and asked if there actually was something in that old hotel. The New Orleans episode also sparked questions. Did the voodoo priest really make a zombie? Where did the zombie boy go? No one knew.

Janine studied the doctor as he smiled at each person who spoke. He took every question seriously and treated everyone with regard. No quick, witty responses from Ian McNally; he formulated his answers in a thoughtful way, indicating that there were no stupid questions. Janine decided that he must have been a very pleasant professor. She could listen to him babble all day. She quickly shifted her seat slightly away because she realized she was staring at him.

Other women also found the doctor attractive. In spite of the nerdy, kind-of-stiff quality he projected, his good looks and slight Scottish accent created an alluring image. His rough hands and muscular forearms gave the impression of a powerful physique hidden underneath his proper shirt.

Janine flashed on that moment in the tunnel when she woke staring into his eyes. She recalled the pleasant warmth of those overlarge hands holding her up and wondered how a real embrace from Ian McNally would feel. Her pulse ticked up just thinking about it.

From the corner of her eye, she watched him interact with a woman who obviously flirted with him. The doctor somehow made her feel noticed without acknowledging the forward behavior. Was he giving her the wrong impression? The doctor caught her watching him and smiled pleasantly at her. She glanced away, annoyed with herself.

Her psychiatrist warned her that an increased libido might be an after effect of weaning off medication. Was that what was happening? How? The weaning ended months ago. Whatever it was, she really wished her little crush would go away. Her out-of-control daydreaming was getting her all worked up.

People asked after Kiki. Where was she? Would she join them at the pub? The Old Rio Linda Bar packed in a bit more since they arrived. Janine got the distinct impression that friends were calling friends to come see the paranormal investigators.

"Kiki's interviewing someone right now," the doctor told them. "We're looking into your River Girl Ghost and the Dreyer Road Specter."

Lots of folks put in their two cents.

"We once went out to Dreyer Road after the football game," a middle-aged woman confessed. "I saw a guy driving a tractor, just inching along, and I thought it was funny, him driving out there at night. I laughed so hard I dropped my beer. When I went to pick it up, I look up again and he's gone. There was nowhere for him to go."

"We saw him in the evening clear as day. In the rearview mirror, behind us. When I turned around to look for him, he wasn't there. Vanished!" A man in a plaid shirt added.

"I saw him in the rearview mirror too. I'm not kidding about this. We never passed a guy in a tracker, but he magically appeared in the rearview mirror anyway. I'm not kidding," a woman gave.

"That river bend is spooky. You can hear a little girl crying whenever there's a soft breeze," a man in a different plaid shirt told them.

"She only speaks to children. People say, if your little sister or brother sees her, they are required to drown in that river. The river ghost always takes children who play at the water edge, out near the bend, close to the rocks," a woman sitting very close to the doctor rasped, without a doubt, a serious smoker.

"Kids drown at that river bend all the time. Half the streets in this town are named for kids that drowned at the river bend. Everyone insists the river ghost lures them, or marks them, or some other nonsense. Some folks even call her Linda after the river," an old man in a red baseball cap sat at the bar. He turned full around and stared directly at Janine.

"Linda?" Janine asked him. "People say the river ghost is named Linda?"

"Sure." He took a slow sip of his draft beer and scowled. "You're Martha's granddaughter, ain't cha? I remember when she told me that you saw the ghost. You called her Linda too. Damn near gave Martha a heart attack, you seeing that ghost. Especially since she kept the river off limits to you and your sister. Insisted the ghost would never try anything with *her* granddaughters. 'Course, others have called the ghost Mary."

Janine silently considered the old man: salt-and pepper beard with thick, grey-patched brown hair on his head, light-brown eyes behind his scowl. He seemed familiar. Did she know him?

"Keep in mind, there's plenty of kids who never said anything about no ghost and went ahead and drowned in that river," he continued. "Certain times of year, after the snow melt begins, there's nasty currents, and the water runs pretty wild. Freezing cold too. There's a natural trap at the bend where a body can get stuck under the rocks."

"You say the streets are named for kids who drowned in the river?" The doctor's interest was piqued.

"Everybody knows that," a raspy voice next to the doctor said. She had luscious red hair, but wrinkled, cracked skin. "Some people say each little child ghost can be spotted on their namesake street from time to time. I've encountered the ghost of Eloise on Eloise Street more than once."

The man at the bar let out a gruff laugh. Clearly, he thought that bit of information was rubbish.

Janine eyed the old man. He turned his back to them and didn't offer any more information. Who was he?

They returned to Gram's house to retrieve Kiki for the drive out to Dreyer Road. Steve and the doctor took off in the *Spectral Analysis* van and the others followed in a rental car after Kiki finished getting ready. Kiki said that Martha Williams Stinger insisted on putting the entire crew up in her rather-large house that night. Gram pushed the offer numerous times. Janine's grandmother lived in one of the original farm houses in Rio Linda. Although the house was huge, sections of the house were in dire need of repair: faded paint inside and out, chipped moldings, and areas of the wood floor were slightly warped. But Gram's beautiful antique furniture, refurbished and cozy, were all the rage of fashion again. The recently remodeled kitchen was filled with modern energy-saving appliances and finished with solid granite countertops. Best of all, the house offered plenty of room to spread out and relax.

In the interview, Gram told Kiki that most of the furniture came handmade from Europe over one hundred years ago. Antiques delivered during the main reconstruction phase in the early 1890s, after the great valley flood. As the first structure in town, the Williams house once hosted important visitors to Rio Linda. Janine was surprised to learn that Gram's house had such history and was filled with such old heirlooms. The Williams "mansion" boasted two wings, which were added to the original one-room structure during the Gold Rush era. Gram only used one bedroom in the main wing, while her roommate Misty used another bedroom in the smaller wing. Gram's roommate doubled as a cook and a maid.

Janine recalled Misty from childhood, always in the house but hardly ever seen. Gram always said that Misty feared crowds and detested being around people. Misty diligently kept the rooms dusted and aired for guests, even though guests rarely visited in Gram's old age.

Kiki agreed to spend the night. Not to worry, Kiki was actually very excited at the prospect. She looked forward to sleeping in the old farmhouse that once founded the town. Kiki said that she caught a tremor of a presence in Gram's backyard, and wondered if she would sense any other Rio Linda ghosts in Gram's old "mansion."

"Your gram is a treasure trove of history," Kiki gushed.

Sometime after the interview, Kiki changed clothes for the Dreyer Road excursion. She teased her hair into a bob, and she wore a shimmery pink jacket that shouted Pink Lady's. Kiki's kohl-lined green eyes bore into her.

"Your grandmother is totally tapped in, like me. Only, she doesn't know it, or admit it. Extrasensory perceptions like ours are genetic, Janine."

Carlos followed the GPS directions to Dreyer Road. They drove toward farmland and horse pastures. Very little traffic went past in the early evening.

"Your story chilled me," Kiki said. "Chilled me. Hey, Ted, was the story about Janine and her imaginary friend chilling or what?"

"Chilling," Ted agreed flatly. His eyes remained closed.

"What was so chilling about it?" Janine asked.

"You'll have to watch the interview to see how Gram tells it." Kiki reached out to cover her hand. "But the main gist of it is, you were targeted, by the River Girl Ghost. Targeted for death. Children who see that ghost are meant to drown. Oh, don't worry. You're safe now. Martha, Gram, insists that only small children are in danger of the ghost, because they don't understand and can be lured into the water. As a child, you were on her death list. Your Gram is sure of it. Everybody thought so, she says. You spoke to the ghost regularly. She was your best friend. You repeated things she said, things other drowning victims also repeated."

"Like what? What did I say?"

"Weird stuff, like *seek redemption, fill an empty spot*, but with no context or explanation. Crazy talk, your grandma said. She didn't know what it meant."

"Dreyer Road!" Carlos interrupted.

"We'll talk about it later." Her soft touch turned into a brief reassuring squeeze, then Kiki let go of Janine's hand. *When did Kiki find time to change the color of her fingernails*, Janine wondered. Tan last night, hot pink today. Kiki slipped into her quiet moment of meditation. She always did. Kiki claimed it centered her and opened her psyche to the other side.

The *Spectral Analysis* van idled on the shoulder of the pavement. Somewhere on that lonely rural road, they hoped to see the farmer and his tractor.

Experiencing actual paranormal activity is rare. Recording scientific evidence, practically impossible. On Dreyer Road, they ditched the EMF box because the power lines on both sides of the road provided too much close electrical interference. Water pipes poked up 15 yards off the shoulder of the asphalt, rare and unfortunate. Piped water often caused phantom noises. Carlos pulled out his handheld infrared camera. Luckily, the camera only took a scratch from the fall in the tunnel. Janine grabbed both an audio recorder and her thermal-panger, two meager gadgets used in the hopes of backing up their primary paranormal receptor; Kiki.

Kiki and the doctor set out on a casual stroll down the deserted road. They walked toward Ted, who held the main camera. Ted slowly moved backward while he filmed. A boom microphone stuck out on a short telescoping pole attached to the camera.

The doctor recounted several tales of the Dreyer Road ghost to Kiki and they discussed their authenticity. Kiki once said that viewers desired a rich ghost story more than anything else. They yearned for the lives behind the ghosts, more so than any blip on a box. Carlos and Janine followed about ten feet behind. Temperature readings on her thermal-panger jumped from the positive hundreds to the negative fifties.

Crap! Temperature fluctuated dramatically in natural settings, but this jumping around was impossible. Janine shook it; no change. She knocked it against her leg with a tap, tap, tap; nothing. She hit it hard with her open palm; still wild readings. An amused expression broke out on Carlos's face as he watched her abuse of the silver phallic-shaped device. She checked the battery level; good. She slipped it into her back jeans pocket with a frown and shrugged.

"I hope you're nicer to your boyfriends," Carlos snickered.

"In op," Janine ignored his comment. "I don't know what's wrong with it."

"Maybe it got fried. It was on you when you got fried in the tunnel."

An inoperative thermal device was bad news. Making a big deal out of changes in temperature was a huge part of her onscreen job. Janine definitely checked the silver panger the previous night and it seemed fine. Perhaps she should have run a reset on it. Hopefully, the doctor would not ask about temperature readings on their stroll down Dreyer Road. She focused on the visual display of her audio recorder instead. The needle jumped with Kiki and the doctor's conversation.

She played around with the tuning to hit sounds beyond the sonic range.

"Take a look." The doctor waved Janine and Carlos forward. "We see something out there in the field, just off the road."

"I don't see anything," Carlos said.

"Look at the air above the ground," Kiki told him, "Close to that tree."

"It looks a little blurry," Janine offered.

"A bit like convection currents over hot asphalt? But at this time of evening, and in the grass?" the doctor offered back.

"Or maybe it's the start of a spectral mass—wait!" Kiki stopped and rotated around. She searched up and down the street. From out of a pink mushy bag, she pulled a tortoiseshell compact out and opened it. She peered into the oval mirror while slowly pivoting. She stopped. Her eyes squinted into the small mirror purposely. She frowned before snapping the compact closed. "I'm not getting anything."

Kiki often claimed that spirits were more easily seen reflected in mirrors than with direct observation. Carlos fondly pointed out that it was the exact opposite for vampires. Janine recalled that the man on the tractor often appeared in rearview mirrors, according to folks at that bar.

"Do you feel this?" Kiki bent down and put her hand on the ground. The doctor did the same. The two spoke about the ground vibrations while Ted slowly circled and filmed the conversation. Janine pulled out the thermal-panger. It still fluctuated wildly.

"Vibrations. Like a truck on the road," the doctor said. He looked up and down the street. "Yet, there's nothing out here."

Kiki's eyes widened. "It's stopped. No, it's still there. Stronger?"

A train whistle echoed in in the dark distance. They chuckled. Then the doctor shook his head and stood up. He offered a hand to Kiki and helped her rise.

At that moment, Janine noticed her thermal-panger blinking a constant 20.5 degrees Celsius. The gauge miraculously fixed itself. Janine glanced at Carlos and he winked.

The group moved forward, toward the tree. Upon closer inspection, the blurry spot turned out to be right over a drainage hole. The thermal-panger confirmed a temperature rise above the drain and Carlos's camera picked up warm thermal currents emanating from the opening. They hung out for another half hour before calling it a night. Any ghosts on Dreyer Road did not come out for *Spectral Analysis*.

The guys headed back to the hotel in the van while Kiki and Janine drove the rental car to Gram's house.

The next morning, Janine interrupted Gram and Kiki at the kitchen nook table. They were speaking intimately with their heads bent together. An enormous breakfast spread of bacon, biscuits, jams, butter, and fruit lay across the counter. Gram beckoned Janine over and directed her to sit in her normal place at the table, the same spot she always took as a little girl. She noticed that Kiki sat at Juliana's spot. Gram had placed Kiki in the superior big sister chair.

The early morning in that familiar kitchen had an odd effect on Janine, a feeling similar to being on too much cold medication. She felt slightly sluggish and laden down with images she couldn't quite remember. The aromas, colors, the very density of the air provoked a flicker of feeling from her distant childhood. Gram's wallpaper of small stenciled flowers unsettled her.

Kiki's hands were wrapped around an empty teacup. Her lips pursed as she stared into the delicate porcelain dish. Kiki poured a little more tea into the cup, swirled it around, and gave it back to Gram. Then she stood up.

"It needs a little more sediment in there," Kiki said. "Sip that slowly and I'll be right back." Kiki left the kitchen.

"Kiki is reading my tea leaves," Gram daintily sipped her tea.

Of course. Reading tea leaves turned out to be a very popular blip on the show during the first season. To date, Kiki only read leaves once on camera, but fans still wrote in about it. Even so, Kiki rarely agreed to do a tea leaf reading. She avoided it because she said she wasn't any good at prophecy. Also, if she sensed anything frightful, she wouldn't want to look at the leaves and that left people upset at her.

To demonstrate, Kiki read Ted and Carlos's leaves but stopped short when she got to Janine's cup. She didn't even glance at Janine's cup. Obviously, Kiki's message to Janine was ominous. Carlos laughed it off later that night. He said that Kiki was just flexing her feminine muscles. Kiki was a showboat. Look at her outrageous camera outfits. She was clearly defining the pecking order. Kiki wanted it very clear that she was the alpha female and wanted to be sure Janine got that message. *Ignore her*, he advised.

Janine poured cream into her own coffee mug and watched it swirl into a light brown soup. She helped herself to the biscuits and fruit. Gram loved rich creamy butter and the smooth spread made everything quite tasty. Janine stared at Gram's teacup.

"What kind of tea is that?" she asked.

"A red raspberry and green tea mix. Want some?" Gram offered the cup. Janine took a mouthful of Gram's tea.

Ugh, quite sour. She shook her head.

Gram laughed and finished the last bit as Kiki returned and sat down. Kiki retrieved the cup and tilted it around, studying the interior. She set the cup aside and smiled at Gram.

"You're definitely in for a turn of fortune," Kiki told Gram. "Major wealth is coming your way. That sounds so cliché, but the leaves say what they say. One sour note, I'm not quite sure how to put it. The return may not be worth the investment?" She shook her head and laughed.

Kiki poured more coffee into her own mug, an old University of Chicago cup, then took it as she made her way back to her room. Off to shower and get dressed, she announced. The guys were due to pick them up in a little less than an hour.

Gram beamed at Janine.

"Jaja, I'm so glad you came to visit. But does Juju need to come too? Does she need to bring the kids right now?"

"Oh Gram, you should let everyone visit more often," Janine chided her. "Juliana's kids have never seen this house, and it's a part of our family history! Juliana and I used to beg for a visit. We loved coming to California and sleeping on your back porch. Remember taking us to the ocean? Fisherman's Warf in San Francisco? Horse-riding at Gold Country? Remember taking us to ski at Homewood in Tahoe? Juliana wants the kids to experience some of those places."

A look of concern crossed Gram's eyes.

Janine continued, "Plus, you're getting a little old to tramp to Texas every year, let Juju bring the kids to you."

That sounded a little off from center, but thankfully, Gram didn't notice. Gram nervously tapped her forefinger on the nook table, deep in thought. Janine evened out the tone of her voice.

"You seem to be getting along with Kiki. Kiki never read my tea leaves. You two are really hitting it off." Gram grinned and nodded. "What exactly did you tell her yesterday? She was very hyped about your interview."

"I just told her the truth."

"You mean about my imaginary friend?" Janine asked. "Did you tell her my imaginary friend was a ghost?"

Gram poured coffee into her cup. She drank it black.

"There goes your fortune."

"Oh, that's just a bunch of nonsense. Fun nonsense," Gram said. Her mood changed to nervous. She rearranged the plate of biscuits. "Do you think those boys will be hungry?"

"I don't know, maybe. What did you tell Kiki?"

Gram's eyes met hers, "Don't you remember anything about your imaginary friend? Do you remember anything at all? That summer, you constantly rambled about her."

Janine considered that question. Yes, of course she remembered her imaginary friend. Her name was Linda, she had a funny accent, she had blond hair…but did she really remember those things? The true answer was, no. Janine did not have a single memory of that part of the summer. Anything she knew about her imaginary friend came from her older sister, Juliana. Juliana fed her the details long after Janine grew older. Juliana teased her about once having an imaginary friend. She claimed that Janine insisted Linda spoke in a funny way. Juliana said that Janine swore the girl had yellow hair and sky-blue eyes. When Janine ruminated over things, she had no personal recollection of her imaginary friend at all.

Except, trapped in the back of her mind, she did have those memories. Late the previous night, she dreamt about her phantom friend and an image of that girl hovered just below the surface of her subconscious. Maybe the house was playing tricks on her. The house definitely stirred up feelings of childhood. The atmosphere teased her memories in the dark of night, but in the light of day, she could not recall a single detail of any of them.

"I don't remember," Janine confessed. "I was too young. What, was I, five or six?"

"You were barely five that summer," Gram told her. "You drew a hundred pictures of her."

"I did?"

"Of course," Gram said. "Kiki asked me to find them, and I'm going to set about doing that later today. I kept every drawing you made. I have piles and piles of paper and such in the attic. I'm certain I saved the pictures you made of…of your imaginary friend. I wouldn't throw those away."

The doorbell rang. Janine jumped up to answer it, but Gram's maid Misty already held the door open and the guys filed in. They came early and hungry. Gram loved feeding people. She did not let them refuse her the right to cook each man eggs made to order. Fresh eggs from her free-range hens, she told them. The hens roamed all over her hill during the day and respectfully laid eggs in a coop right outside the side door. Then, they disappeared into the brush to sleep at night. There were over twenty hens in that brood. At one time, Rio Linda was famous for poultry farming.

The doctor grinned openly at Janine making her feel a bit uncomfortable. She ignored him by turning to Carlos. Carlos winked and chuckled, so she left to change into her jeans and a *Spectral Analysis* T-shirt. When she returned to the kitchen, everyone held a plate full of eggs, bacon, fruit, and a biscuit. Scrambled with cheese for Carlos, sunny side up for Ted, not enough left to tell for Steve, and over easy for the doctor. By the time the guys finished breakfast, Kiki waltzed down the stairs ready to go.

They set off toward the bend in the Rio Linda River. Steve and Ted drove the van down a gravel path ferrying the big camera and bulky equipment. Everyone else walked. While the river access road was no more than a short drive from Gram's house, the river itself was much closer by foot. They only needed to cross over a small hill before reaching the edge of the water. A constant babble could be heard quite clearly right outside the back kitchen door.

The doctor and Kiki walked ahead, discussing last-minute details of the upcoming segment. Gram's hens clucked comically away in a large gaggle toward the brush. Kiki and the doctor spoke easily together and Janine felt something very similar to envy. Kiki seemed to chat and flirt so effortlessly with practically everyone. Janine wondered when she would excise her demons enough to flirt again.

Carlos strolled alongside her, fiddling with his portable ion wand. He had it in a plastic bag and obviously wanted to seal it with the duct tape hanging from his mouth. His eyes inquired if she'd like a similar setup for her device. Janine flipped her thermal-panger over and showed him the placard. Good for ten meters submerged. He rolled his light brown eyes.

"That's not going to work in a plastic bag." She smiled at him.

A narrow beach of pebbles came into view. Further up river, Janine spied the blackberry brambles she had forgotten about. Back there, somewhere, a narrow path led to more houses. Gram's little portion of beach had always been a popular path for the neighborhood dog walkers, but that particular morning, the river was deserted. Even though the water ran smooth and slow, manmade signs warned of a deeper, faster current hidden beneath the surface. The air progressively grew cooler as they neared the water. Janine registered the temperature drop on her gage. Even on a nice sunny day, the water could be freezing. River water in the valley came from snowmelt runoff from the mountains.

At the bend in the river, the infamous boulders glistened in the morning light. Someone had spread out a blanket where the pebbly beach met the sparse grass and put the fancy EMF box in the center of it. The big coil antenna was nowhere in sight. The doctor motioned for Carlos and Janine to stay near the blanket with the big box. At the van,

Ted pulled out large, overall-looking pants from the open rear door.

"What are those?" Janine asked.

"Fishing bibs." Carlos said. "The doctor had them delivered to the hotel. It's why he didn't want to stay at your Gram's last night."

"Gram was okay with that."

"That's good," Carlos told her. "He was worried that she, you, both of you, might be insulted that we didn't stay at the house. He didn't want anyone upset that he declined the invitation."

That explained the funny look this morning, she thought. And here she imagined she may have caught the doctor's eye. Wow, Janine felt pretty stupid. She fiddled quietly with the EMF box as the doctor and Kiki slipped into the overlarge, rubber fishing bibs.

The farmer johns came with built-in boots and suspenders. Kiki and the doctor would not get wet unless they let the water rise above chest level. Kiki must have known the cut of those fishing bibs. Under the sweatshirt she ditched, she wore just the right clingy top to make her ensemble fall just this side of decent. The doctor and Kiki chuckled together as Ted joined them in tall rubber rain boots near the shoreline. The doctor's head swiveled toward Janine and Carlos.

"We're going to get started," he called to them. "Tune in at the forty to eighty Hertz range on the box and focus on the lower end. Other than that, just soak up the ambience as we venture toward the center of the bend."

"Want the thermal-panger?" Janine called to the doctor. "It's waterproof."

She jumped up as he nodded and made her way to the rocky shore. She held the thermal-panger out to the doctor. As he searched his ensemble for a place to put it, she found herself fixating on the stubble along his chin. She resisted a sudden urge to touch that roughness. He smelled nice. One of his hands fiddled unsuccessfully with the zipper pocket on the bib. He had very large hands, she noticed. Janine suddenly snapped the carabiner onto his right suspender. Then she took the silver probe and pushed it firmly into one of the belt loops on his bib. Before she could turn around, the doctor gentle grabbed her arm. There was that look of concern again and her heart skipped a beat as she gazed into his soft blue eyes. Then her eyes drifted to his lips.

Why was she reacting this way with the doctor, it couldn't just be weaning from the meds? Way back at the start of season one, when she was still a little foggy from the drugs, Carlos and Janine used to joke that Ian was a bit of a dweeb. His female fan club made them laugh. If they only knew how nerdy he was. Definitely a nervous Clark Kent hid behind his suave TV image. Now, with her mind cleared up, Janine found herself becoming one with the fans.

"Kiki says she's already feeling a tingle about this place." She zoned in on his jaw as he talked. "Just take it easy over there. According to the interview, you are linked to the spirit that haunts this river. Just concentrate on what you feel. Don't worry too much about the EM box. Just see if you feel anything."

I'm certainly feeling something, the blood pounded in her ears. *Stop it!* Her juvenile crush was beginning to get the better of her. He patted the temperature gauge.

"Thanks for the panger."

She nodded and turned. The big eye of Ted's camera lens focused directly on her as he filmed their exchange. Janine bit back a comment at the intrusion. Of course, in this episode, she was meant to be a major part of the storyline. She brushed past Ted, annoyed at him. She was not going to be part of a simulated rivalry for the doctor's attention.

Back near Carlos, she plopped down and put the EMF display tablet on her lap. They watched as the doctor and Kiki slowly waded into the river while conversing with each other, and to the camera. Kiki pointed toward the center of the river and her voice carried through the crisp air. Janine nudged Carlos.

"Did she just say baptisms?" she asked. "That this is where the early townsfolk performed baptisms?"

"Yep."

Kiki and the doctor moved out of earshot into deeper water. Janine watched as the two moved around, circling each other, smiling and chatting. Kiki said something funny, and the doctor laughed, throwing his head back. He grinned at Kiki in a pleasing way. Wouldn't it be funny if Kiki slipped under that cold surface? *Come on, little ghost, if you're out there, get her a little wet, so I command, so mote it be,* Janine joked silently to herself, mimicking Kiki's witch talk.

Kiki and the doctor turned their attention to the boulders at the bend. The rocks reflected a beautiful metallic luster. The doctor pulled out the thermal-panger and put it in the water. His large hand moved the temperature reader around, making swirls. The ends of his rolled sleeves got wet. Janine wondered if his arms and shoulders were very muscular beneath that dark blue button-down shirt. Of course they were, and she could just make out the line of his pecs against the material. *Ugh!* She should just accept that she found Ian McNally a very attractive man.

A rush of cool air blew across her neck. It felt like someone brushing her hair aside with a light touch. She instinctively shifted around, expecting to see someone, maybe Steve. No one was there. Carlos noticed her movement and gave her a questioning look before turning back to the ion detector. He adjusted the gain as he began picking up odd ticks. The cool breeze hit her neck again. Janine turned to survey the trees and tall grass. Nothing moved. There wasn't a breeze. Her vision began to tunnel and a sudden heaviness poured into her veins. Every cell in her body pinged on high alert. Her heart sped up. For whatever reason, her body began to escalate into panic mode.

She tried to focus on the action in the water but her body systems distracted her. She squinted her eyes and strained to hear. She felt something, or someone, trying to say something to her. Kiki's head suddenly snapped up and her green cat's eyes narrowed. Kiki sensed something too. Kiki's head swiveled to look around before her eyes halted on Janine. Kiki began moving toward the shore, fighting the resistance of the moving water.

A soft tickle developed deep in her ear and became a faint whistle. The whistle increased in volume and began to sound like a distant child's voice. Janine's body felt heavy, like lead, and she began to tilt over. Time decelerated into ultraslow motion. Her eyelids drooped heavily. She concentrated on Kiki and the doctor.

She watched Kiki flail, slip, and fall deeper into the river. Water crossed Kiki's bib line and her eyes registered the shock of freezing snowmelt by becoming large and round. Kiki's shirt soaked up water and started to darken and cling to her skin. At one point, the shirt passed the line into indecent. As usual, the doctor swooped in to catch her in a perfect Doctor-Kiki encounter. *So very romantic.* In that moment, Janine's eyelids slammed shut and the voice in her ear became clear.

Why did you leave me?

"Janine! Janine!" Carlos shook her.

Voices echoed in the far distance, mixed with the splashing of water. Carlos helped her sit back up. Janine blinked and opened her eyes. She felt perfectly fine; no more tunnel vision, no more leaden weight, just a bit of breathlessness. The doctor and Kiki squeaked up in wet rubber suits.

Ted pointed the big camera directly at Janine. The doctor bent down to grab her hand while Kiki shivered in front of her. Kiki's teeth chattered loudly and water dripped down her rubber suit as she bent forward.

"She was here, wasn't she? The ghost. I felt her and saw the air wavering near you. Did you see her? Did you feel her? Did you hear her? What happened over here?"

Both Kiki and Janine were shaking.

"She said something," Janine whispered.

"What? What did she say?" Kiki's green, hypnotic eyes urged her.

"She said, why did you leave me?" Janine's voice was soft.

At that moment, Steve appeared with a large towel and wrapped the top of Kiki as he helped her out of the bib. Cold water saturated the pebbles making them shine deeper colors. Kiki's voice ran a mile a minute but Janine didn't register any of it. The doctor still held her hand and she gently pulled it away, embarrassed. A blackout and a fainting. What was going on with her?

"I'm fine," she told him, avoiding his eyes.

Ian nodded and stood. He took a few steps away to remove his wet bib. He stepped toward Kiki and Ted as they set up for a parting shot with the boulders in the background.

Kiki stood wrapped in the thick towel, decent again, but cozy in the one-armed embrace of the doctor.

On the walk back to Gram's house, Janine realized that they spontaneously decided to do a feature in Rio Linda. Kiki believed that the river ghost story could be flushed out more. They could be the first investigators to put it on the paranormal activity map. Excited voices brainstormed how they'd run it; as a two-part story on the Sacramento area or a standalone episode based on Rio Linda? They needed to discover the complete back story for the ghost and interview more people. There were loads of folks in that bar who wanted to help.

With their two-week break about to start, everyone discussed how to best adjust the schedule. Steve would fly back to the Texas studio to put finishing touches on the Old Town clips, then return as soon as possible, and Ian and Kiki would stay in town to research the area. They needed to develop an origin story for the ghost. The next episode in the *Spectral Analysis* lineup could easily be pushed back to make room for a closer examination of Rio Linda.

Chapter 3

Sierra Nevada, 1839

Only four families remained from the dozen that forged a trail from Missouri to the top of the world. Strength comes in numbers, people said, and many advised them to travel in a later, larger group. It would be safer and easier to share supplies and share burdens. They could better help one another across the open country for the California coast and the port settlement of Yerba Buena. But they believed a larger number would prove too ripe with human disagreements and didn't listen. Also, they wanted to arrive first to the new coast and have the first pick of the land.

They set out with a count of fifty-six wagons, a small party, but full of hope with their carefully selected provisions. Now their supplies had dwindled down to three rickety wagons stripped bare of all but meager tools, a Bible, a ledger diary, and a weakened old man. Twenty souls huddled together under a frayed and sagging canvas cover. Twenty souls sat on top of a large mountain range staring at the ice-blue water of the most beautiful lake imaginable, humbled. The oldest soul being the dying old man in the wagon, and youngest being the little girl, Linda, so vivaciously alive at five years old.

A recent storm drove home the name of their jagged mountain range, the Sierra Nevada. The wind blew freezing cold over their heads making the canvas cover dance precariously between the trees. From under that cover, Helen watched Mr. Frederick Stauch limp toward the blue lake. He appeared in terrible pain. The wound he acquired during the Indian attack in the Forty Mile Desert, festered. Everyone feared he might not be able to keep that leg unless things changed for the better. Still, he got off easier than most. His wound was the only physical ail his family suffered. He could have avoided that wound altogether, had he run away from the Hansen encampment instead of toward it. Frederick only managed to save the old man by carrying the strongbox for him. The wrong box. Oh, the ire on Frederick's red face when he discovered the box was not the one safeguarding the tinder but the box with Hansen's ledger and a bottle of spirits. At least the foul liquid served to cleanse the many wounds suffered in their midst.

Helen noticed her husband, Nick, trudging into the wind toward the minister, Frederick. The two men conferred quietly as they queried the sky. Certainly, the men were afraid to tarry because the weather threatened to change. But moving forward would put a strain on the wounded. Not one of them doubted the old man in the wagon, Oscar Hansen, would die if jostled further. And the younger Miller man suffered an arrow through the arm while his wife laid miserable with the beginnings of a pregnancy. And her dear friend Irene would surely pass before the end of the night.

Thick animosity toward the dying old man streamed constantly from every circle, because the old man's sons had been their guides and led them astray. Oscar Hansen's sons were both taken in the blink of an eye and rotted in the same meadow where they had been butchered. The burden now fell on her husband and the minister to lead them to the coast. The only remaining item of the Hansen's family was the ledger book his son Stanley kept as a diary of their journey. This item passed into Helen's care. Nick and Frederick both insisted she keep up the daily record because she made very handsome letters. Some authority may ask for it as a testament to the trials of their journey.

Helen took the small bottle of black ink Mr. Hansen prized and placed it in her shirt next to her heart. It badly needed warming from the cold air.

Nicholas glanced toward her, and his gaze skirted their huddled mass. His eyes met hers for a brief moment before settling on Peter Webber. Peter recognized the summons. He and his boys stood wearily and left the protective cover to shuffle toward Frederick and Nick. The men stood close together, conferring. The wind blew their voices away, but their postures revealed tension. White flurries fluttered around them. Gustoff, who was not yet a man, stood shivering and clutched his blackened paw close to his chest.

Peter Webber became more agitated. The minister, Frederick, stretched to his full height in response. Helen's husband, Nick, stepped between them, the peacemaker. His full head of sandy-brown hair blew about. It made him appear like his younger self for a moment, causing her breath to catch. Suddenly the men split up. Each moving quickly as the snow flurries grew. Nicholas entered the shelter and moved toward her.

"Grant, Ethan." Nick shook their sons awake. "Hurry now. You'll need to help Rolf and Gustoff. They are breaking down what's left of the Hansen wagon for lumber and parts. A wheel might be fit for ours."

"Are we staying another night?" Grant jumped to his feet.

"We are," Nick told him.

"The Webber boys need assistance moving Oscar Hansen and we will be erecting a more sturdy shelter. We need to better place the fire for tending."

Helen's sons, Grant and Ethan, went off quickly. Helen reached out to grab her husband before he also departed. His eyes found hers, and she noted his furrowed brow.

"It's too early for winter. Surely this flurry will cease by tomorrow," he assured her. "The old man will die soon. Moving him would unduly hasten his death, and if we rest here, Mrs. Lumen might make a recovery, if God wills it. John Miller and his wife also need the respite, and Peter Webber's own daughter is not fit to travel. I think this is best."

"What did Peter say?" she whispered.

"He urges us to keep moving. He wants to leave Hansen's father here to die and move down the pass quickly. He blames Hansen for all our troubles, but he has no means to travel. The red wagon is beyond repair and the Webbers must rely on ours, and Stauch. The oxen are near exhaustion. Peter would continue alone but knows he cannot. He believes Hansen's curse will follow us if we dally. He now believes Whitaker spoke the truth, that Hansen purposely led us astray on the trail. He believes we should have left with the Whitaker group."

Helen pressed her lips together. Deep down, she also harbored a foul feeling for their complicity with Hansen. The ledger diary was not written for eyes other than himself, and he was a devil of a man, but she did not say as much to Nicholas. The men did not bother to read the diary contents and she would not burden them with those words now, words that confirmed everything. Nicholas took her hand.

"A few days rest will give our numbers strength," he told her. "We found this rough pass and beautiful lake by the favor of God. It is not the Great Valley we hoped for, but here there are charms. With no guide, the storm fooled us in our direction. Not to fear Helen, we will likely be in the Great Valley soon."

She gazed over the blue lake. The surface acted like a perfect mirror and clouds drifted rapidly in the reflection. Tall conifers grew thick all around the lake, framing the blue waters with a luxurious green ring. Surely, they were very near to heaven. Perhaps they needed to pause and reflect on their inactions under Hansen.

The young girl, Linda, ran up as Helen prepared to write in the ledger. The child's wide and curious eyes knew not the severity of their circumstances and sparkled with amusement.

"I want to watch," Linda said.

"Of course." Helen smiled at the young girl.

Then she pulled the small vial of ink from her shirt and the turkey quill Stanley Hansen had used daily. The warmth brought the dark ink back to life and she proceeded to add her first entry into the diary. Linda smiled, fascinated.

Chapter 4
Research

Spectral Analysis began with funding from Steve Hanks. Hanks, along with Ian McNally, devised a rough outline of the show the summer the doctor guest lectured at NYU. Steve became the executive producer while Ian became the main character. How Kiki came on board, Janine could only guess, but she definitely entered during the beginning stages of concept development. The three of them knew each other fairly well and envisioned the different aspects of *Spectral Analysis* as a team. Ted was a NYU film classmate of Steve's. He signed on before any recruitment went out. Carlos and Janine applied online and underwent an extensive interview process in Texas. Their actual job title was technical assistant to paranormal research doctor. Knowledge of electronics and the electromagnetic spectrum was a requirement, as well as having an open mind.

At first, Janine didn't realize she would be on camera. She thought it was a behind the scenes science gig, but Steve said there might be a tiny bit of camera time, so, just in case, they wanted a science woman to balance out the crew. Because of Kiki, they needed a "neutral female." Janine was the neutral female, whatever that meant. She guessed it meant boring and plain.

Spectral Analysis operated out of a two-room studio and a small office in Austin, Texas. Both Carlos and Janine were Austin locals, while the others moved from New York City to work on the show. Their location stemmed from the fact that Steve Hanks was originally an Austin boy. Other people involved with *Spectral Analysis* included a guy in promotions, a money manager, a lawyer, and one office person named Cheryl. It was a very low-key operation. Other than Cheryl, the main receptionist, Janine only ever dealt with Steve, Ted, Carlos, Kiki, and the doctor.

At the end of the first season, there was a little after-party, but Janine opted out. Having the job actually helped her gain enough confidence to reconnect with her family. For a long time, she alienated them through avoidance, ashamed of being on psychiatric medication and of the events that occurred during college. At the conclusion of that first season, she forced herself to attend a potentially very stressful event, her niece Sammy's fourth birthday party. It was during Sammy's party when the show's lawyer called about a second season.

Originally, she applied for the job on a lark, believing the show wouldn't really pan out. She planned to use the sign-on money to pay for her next semester at Texas A&M. But Janine didn't realize how much fun the show would be, or how well paying and popular. In fact, no one imagined *Spectral Analysis* would last past three episodes and result in the longer time commitment.

Getting a regular paycheck was nice. The college money her father set aside had been eaten away by medical bills, and Janine had no intention of asking her sister if there was anything left. For the second season, the show made her an offer she couldn't refuse. The extra season would take care of tuition for the rest of her education, if she budgeted smart. Of course, keeping the job meant delaying that very education again. Thankfully, Gram, her sister, nieces and nephew helped make the decision. As huge fans of the show, they listened when she got the call and unanimously voted for her to continue ghost hunting. Janine could see the relief in her sister's eyes, relief that she finally worked far enough past the events that landed her in the mental ward to make a solid connection with something.

Janine needed Juliana's approval to keep her momentum going. She owed it to her family to make a full recovery, and she wanted to please her young nieces and nephew. Meeting the giggling four-year-old Sammy completely melted her. She came extremely close to missing that little girl's entire childhood. So, she decided to continue with the show.

Between film locations, Carlos and Janine took a break while the others finalized plans for the next episode. For this particular break, Janine agreed to visit family in Rio Linda. She didn't anticipate visiting with her ghost-hunting coworkers, but when they switched the focus to Rio Linda, Kiki and the doctor decided to stay in town with her. They needed to conduct major research on the river ghost and develop a plausible story from scratch. Janine's Grandma insisted that they stay in her large house.

Why did you leave me? Janine tossed and turned with a mixture of vivid dreams of love wrapped inside dark nightmares of fear. In the dream, someone followed her and she was happy about it, but when he closed in behind her, fear took over. She tried to run, but the air became thick, like water. She tried to look behind her, but there was only darkness. First, she ran across the pebbly beach on a bright, sunny morning. Then the ground altered into dark woods of leaves and rocks and twisted tree roots. She stumbled through the umbrage, barefoot and fearing for her life. *Why did you leave me?*

Janine sat up in bed, breathing hard. Parts of that nightmare always crept into her dreams. An image of her niece Sammy lingered in her head. Sammy, who she only just met on her fourth birthday. Then she recalled the little girl's voice in her head saying, *why did you leave me?*

She threw a pillow across the room in frustration and guilt, then dropped her head into her hands, exhausted from all the running.

Gram and Janine shifted through old papers and photos as they pulled them out of a dusty attic box. It was very slow going because Gram felt the need to exclaim over almost every print. Between the photos, she pulled other useless items from the box: old bills, menus, and random advertisements. Gram insisted they would soon find the drawings Janine created of her imaginary friend. Gram saved every memento from the summers their father sent Juliana and Janine to California. Dust bunnies from the box caused Janine to sneeze uncontrollably.

"Gram," she flipped through a pile of black and white photographs of the thirties or forties. "This isn't the only box, right? Why didn't you bring down more? Or, we could go up there."

Gram gave her a look.

"It's dusty up there. Dusty and dark. I'm an old woman. Carrying down one box just about cleared me out yesterday afternoon. Want more boxes, we need to get one of those young men to carry them out. That handsome Doctor McNally will be back soon, won't he?"

The doctor was due back all right, with Kiki. The previous night, everyone except Janine gathered at the hotel to pack up. Kiki and the doctor planned to drop the crew off at the airport then drive the van to Gram's house. No sense in driving it back to Texas just to turn around and come right back. Gram graciously offered her garage to store the *Spectral Analysis* van. She probably planned on letting friends pose for pictures next to it.

"Kiki and the doctor are due back this afternoon, I suppose," Janine said.

"The doctor? Don't you call him Ian? Why so formal?"

"I don't know." There was nothing in the box after the year 1953 and Janine pushed it aside.

"Don't you think Doctor Ian McNally is a handsome fellow?" Gram smiled.

Janine grimaced at Gram.

"Now, now," Gram chastised. "Don't get into a huff. Nothing wrong with your grandma asking about you know what. Is there a man back in Austin? Maybe that cute Carlos fellow?"

"Gram," she groaned. "Carlos is happily married with twins. There is no man."

"And I don't believe that doctor-Kiki nonsense you push on the show. I have seen how everyone interacts here. Everyone agrees that there's a little something brewing between *you* and the doctor. What is he, about thirty?"

"Everyone? Who is this everyone?"

"Me and the gals. We analyze every show." She grinned excitedly. "Remember the graveyard show, the one in Savannah, where you and Doctor McNally did the lab sample thing. You know, the glowing chemical thing."

"Phospholuminescence."

"Yes, along that trail. It was very clear he was quite taken with you. I saw sparks."

"He didn't want me to start a fire," Janine told her. "Some of the stuff we were using is very flammable. Maybe those were the sparks you saw."

Gram shook her head in denial and chuckled.

Janine would chuckle too, if Gram hadn't actually hit a nerve. Truthfully, after that Savannah shoot, she also imagined something might develop with the doctor. During that shoot, they talked and laughed easily for the first time and they connected briefly on a different level. The doctor couldn't know their banter was a breakthrough event for her. Opening up to him a little bit was a huge step in her recovery.

Yet, nothing ever came from that encounter beyond Janine developing a little crush on the doctor. That, and the self-realization that she actually wanted a relationship again. Thankfully, only Carlos suspected her change in demeanor, and no one ever took anything Carlos said seriously.

"Hey, Gram, I wanted to ask you, the things you told Kiki about my imaginary friend? Did you make any of it up? Like, embellish it a bit?"

Not the right thing to say. Gram's amusement dissipated quickly. She opened her mouth to apologize, but Gram held up her hand.

"Look here, Jaja. I don't joke about that ghost girl. What you don't know is, she is a real spirit, restless, one that seeks out children. When you told me about her, described her and repeated her words, I about died of fright. Why do you think I stopped letting your father send you here? That ghost lured more than one child into the river and she was trying to lure you too. Thank goodness your sister Juliana stuck to you like glue."

Clearly, Gram believed a real spirit haunted Rio Linda.

"Did you ever see her?" Janine asked.

Gram shook her head.

"Never. Never. But I tell you, my own second cousin's sister saw her. Maple. Ma, your great-grandmother, always warned us about the little girl ghost that Maple met at the river. If I were ever to see her, I was to tell Ma immediately and nobody else. Nobody."

"You mean great-cousin Maple who died tragically in childhood?" Janine asked.

Gram nodded, "And my older brother, John. He told us the story of the mystery lady and her two daughters. Those two little girls just walked right into the river like they were following someone. The poor mother couldn't do a thing."

Gram shuffled through the box and picked up a large group photo. It was an extended family picture of about twenty people gathered together on the front lawn. The big oak tree with the tire swing was just a skinny sapling in the photograph. Gram pointed to a dark-haired woman and a baby.

"That baby is Maple. I'd like to find another picture of her. Older, near when she died. I am sure there's one somewhere in this box."

"Did she drown?"

"Of course," Gram said. "In the river."

"Did your mom ever see the ghost?"

"Oh no, not that ghost. But she did see the other one. A girl she called Mary."

"Another one! You mean there's another ghost? How many ghosts do you think are in Rio Linda?"

Gram ignored the little laugh Janine gave.

"Don't believe everything you hear," she told Janine. "Lots of folks will say there's a ghost on every street corner. That's just fantasy. There aren't any spirits except your little friend, the River Girl, and the other, Mary. Just the two of them. That old man driving a tractor out on Dreyer Road, I can't say about him, but he has nothing to do with Rio Linda. We don't generally go advertising about such things, about our ghosts. But that man from Dreyer Road has got a lot of advertising."

"Did you tell Kiki about the other ghost? Mary?"

"She didn't ask," Gram told her. "Plus, I thought it would make me look a bit looney, believing ghosts are everywhere. But she is real. Doesn't come around much. But every so often, you'll hear of a sighting different than the river ghost. It's Mary. Mary stays away from the river. She's mainly the orchard ghost. Anything else you hear, rubbish."

"Have you seen her? Any of these ghosts?"

Gram pressed her lips together and looked away.

"I won't say, so you can stop teasing me. But there is a very long history of sightings. Many have seen her." Gram found another photo. "Here she is." She held up an old black-and-white photo of a little girl.

"Maple?"

"No, your great-grandma, my mother. Looks just like Juliana, don't you think?"

Certainly. Janine trudged up to the attic for another box. Oh, the attic. Dark, dusty, and crammed with junk. Gram's description of her stacks of boxes did not do them justice. Sneezing, Janine picked the nearest, newest-looking box and headed downstairs. When she got back to the living room, Kiki had taken her spot on the couch and the doctor lounged in the recliner with a drink in his hand. He flashed a dreamy smile at her. Oh, let the fun begin, Janine thought.

They searched three more boxes of paper before finding the drawings from the summer of Janine's imaginary friend. Kiki sat cross-legged on the floor, slowly shuffling through piles of old photographs. She created three piles: one pile for people she believed saw the ghost, one pile for people she believed did not, and one undecided. Apparently, Kiki's sixth sense told her these things. *Carlos, my friend*, Janine mused silently, *you are missing some nice wisecracks here.*

The doctor departed hours earlier to take care of business. Permits and permissions were required to film in certain locations, especially if they required exclusive access to the river. Ian planned to swing by the town hall records department and copy information on river drownings and early Rio Linda history.

Janine examined the artwork she made as a child. They were simplistic drawings of a girl with a very large head, blue dress, yellow hair, with a big ribbon, or band, on top of her head. The drawings had stick arms and legs. Scribbly blue lines surrounded the girl, suggesting a windy sky or water. Unfortunately, Janine sorely lacked artistic ability at five years old.

"Here are a few better ones." Gram delivered drawings still attached to a sketchbook. "These drawings were made after you really took a shine to her. You were obsessed with your imaginary friend and drew a picture almost every day. You said you were going to be an artist someday. I didn't realize who you were drawing until a friend told me it was the river ghost. I was surprised, because everyone always agreed that the ghost only appeared at the river. Your sightings occurred in the backyard. That's why I didn't worry about the ghost at first."

There were at least twenty drawings of the same girl. The twig body didn't alter much, but the details in the face increased with each new depiction; the girl had blue eyes and red lips, her hair was quite wavy, she wore a decorative headband, her smile was lopsided and she had a mark on her chin.

"Look at the headband you drew," Kiki said. "Is that a simple three petaled flower or an attempt at a Celtic knot?"

Janine had no clue.

Suddenly, Janine flashed on a memory of her phantom friend. An image of a girl standing near the back lawn flooded her brain. She stood right along the edge of Gram's manicured yard in the middle of the day. Janine clutched her crude drawing and peered at the Crayola lines.

"What is it?" Kiki asked softly. "Do you feel her here?"

"No," Janine remembered more details. "She can't come into the house."

"She can't come into the house?"

"She's not allowed inside the house," Janine mumbled. "She can't come in."

Kiki gently took hold of her hand, "Then what is it? What just happened?"

"I remember her, as clear as day," Janine said. "I know what she looks like."

Other than the soothing hum of the river over the mound, and the random clucks from hens in the brush, the night surrounding Gram's house remained quiet. Gram and Kiki ran off to visit Gram's old friends. When Gram announced that her gals always gathered for tea and cards, but wouldn't it be nice to have a tea-reading too, Kiki retrieved her signature Kiki Mellow tarot cards and suggested they do it all: tea leaves, cards, and gossip. It was Kiki's way of cleverly conducting research in Rio Linda.

After several awkward portraits of her imaginary friend, a long hot shower sounded more pleasing to Janine. Sadly, her artistic ability had not improved much in the past twenty years. She decided to relax and take in the stars on the glassed covered back porch. Being a fair distance from city lights, Gram's night sky often resembled a black star-filled universe map. Janine could even make out the faint band of the Milky Way.

Gram's home and land separated the business portion of Rio Linda from the river. At one point in history, the family property stretched to the opposite side of town and ended at I-80, the road that connects the Sierra Nevada to San Francisco. Two hundred years ago, before California's Gold Rush era, an old trail followed that same path. Janine didn't venture outside because her memories of the ghost still spooked her. She knew the imaginary girl couldn't possibly be a real ghost, but it didn't hurt to avoid the yard.

During her art session, Janine remembered other details about that girl. Very clear and definite in her mind, the girl was not allowed to enter Gram's house. She always walked at the edge of the yard, but not in the cut lawn area or near the house. Very different from most spooks. Most spirits attached themselves to a solid object, according to her experiences with *Spectral Analysis*. Janine's imaginary friend also avoided grown-ups, she didn't trust them and would disappear whenever Janine ran off to find Gram or Juliana.

A shooting star flicked across the sky. Milky Way, Big Dipper, Man skiing, Flying squirrel. Her older sister pointed out those constellations on that back porch. Janine chuckled, remembering her sister weave imaginative tales at bedtime. Juliana always created detailed stories for the amusement her baby sister, and Janine really was a baby sister. She was more than ten years younger than Juliana.

Her sister agreed to delay her visit to avoid interfering with the *Spectral Analysis* investigation. Janine wasn't sure if she felt disappointed or slightly relieved. She was eager to see her sister and the kids again, but she was also a bit nervous. Even though she missed many years in Ashley's young life, her older niece behaved as if she hadn't disappeared at all. Would Ashley finally ask Janine why she had been so totally absent the past four years?

A slight movement in the shadows made her jump. The shadow kept moving and Janine bit back a yelp as she tensed. Then she saw the shape a little better.

"I saw the picture you drew of the ghost," Doctor McNally shifted in his seat. He cradled a tumbler as he lounged in one of Gram's wine barrel Adirondack chairs in a dark corner. He raised his glass and grinned. "I stocked your gram's bar with some nice single malt. Want a little snort?"

"How long have you been sitting there?"

"I don't know, about half an hour, maybe longer. I may have dozed off a wee bit." He yawned and stretched. "I think you were in the shower when I got back. No one else was around."

The entire time she stood musing at the stars, thinking she was all alone. He fought his way up from the deep chair and took a couple of steps toward her. His jawline fell at her eye level and she could just detect the musky aftershave he used. The top two buttons of his shirt were undone and her eyes were drawn to the indent of his jugular notch. Heat radiated from his body, drawing her to lean closer.

Janine suddenly realized that they had never been alone together besides that night in Savannah. She felt the intimacy of that fact in interesting parts of her body and the nerves along her skin woke up. Her pulse ticked faster and faster flooding her chest and torso with warmth. She hoped it was dark enough to cover the blush that must be spreading across her face. She became distinctly conscious of her flimsy outfit: thin sleeping T-shirt, no bra, short shorts, and no shoes— very underdressed for a work meeting. She resisted an urge to hug her arms to her body in a defensive stance. She didn't want the doctor to think she felt uncomfortable around him.

"Your gram has a very nice setup out here." He admired the sky view.

"Yes, it's pretty special." She made a slight move to escape into the house.

"Are you recovered then, from the river incident?" He pulled her back with the question.

"Ugh," she said, "I'm embarrassed, about fainting. I've never fainted before. I don't know what that's all about. I feel fine now. No need to worry."

"It's normal." He smiled at her. "According to Kiki. Kiki faints fairly often when she experiences a strong spirit. Nothing to be embarrassed about." He drained his glass and set it aside. "Kiki believes your gram and you are…how does she put it? Tuned in. Closet mediums. Maybe that's what attracted you to our show in the first place."

"Kiki thinks it's genetic," Janine gave him.

"It probably is. At least on the female side. Runs mostly in girls, I hear," he said.

"Well, that sounds a little sexist, don't you think?"

He smiled slowly at her, "Aye, I always thought so. Very sexist. Looks like you were having a few nice memories."

His eyes drifted down her body and she wished her shirt was tad thicker. Oh no, where was the stiff work relationship she always counted on? Her deep intake of air drew his attention and her breasts reacted when his eyes paused there, tingling from his attention. He corrected himself and his eyes snapped back to her face. His pupils were hyper dilated in the dark.

"It's not often seeing you with your hair down, smiling so sweetly. Your eyes are very golden in this light and…" He suddenly stiffened and stepped back. "Crikes. I, I'm sorry. I've had a few on an empty stomach. I get a bit buckled. I didn't mean anything by that. I just meant, you look very pleasant, enjoying the night air and all. Very, very pleasant, and even in this dim light… Crikes, am I messing up again?"

"No, no. No worries. I know what you mean." Janine smiled. How very amusing. It felt pleasantly intimate standing on the glass patio with Ian McNally in his tipsy condition. He was very cute flailing in conversation. His flustered expression was quite charming and she couldn't take her eyes off of him.

"You do? You know what I mean?" Ian's voice was low.

"Umm, yes. I do. Of course, I do. I know exactly what you mean." Not really sure what they were talking about at this point. But he looked a little apologetic, so she softly added, "It's okay, really. I don't mind at all. Really. You're not messing up."

He considered her awkwardly for a moment. In the next moment, he stepped forward and scooped her into his arms. She was overwhelmed with the contact, and the smell of him. Her body begin to melt into his. Surprisingly, her arms wrapped around Ian's neck and pulled him closer. Her brain lost all command of her physical responses. Her body ignored her request for decorum as she soaked him in, welcoming and surprisingly eager. She felt a spark as their lips brushed. Then her lips parted for a deeper kiss, hungry for more. She detected a taste of his Scottish whisky as the kiss escalated. His hands moved all over her body tantalizingly bold. She was on fire! She was spinning.

In the muffled distance, her name echoed. Janine heard rustling and laughter. Ian moved away and she heard audible breathing. Every nerve pinged. The doctor's hand lingered on her shoulder as they began to realize the loud bang had been the front door slamming. Gram and Kiki called out from the living room. They must think Janine was upstairs. The doctor stared at her for a second longer.

"Crikes, lassie, all right then." His voice was low and breathless. Ian turned tail and dashed into the house.

Janine heard him greet Kiki and Gram. He offered them whisky and talked about the town records. They each sounded very excited. Janine heard Kiki say she acquired a long list of potentials and then something about Steve and Ted. Janine didn't know how to get past them without being seen. She waited a bit, felt silly for hiding, then went into the house. Ian had his back to her as he held up a folder full of paper.

"The recorded deaths go back to the start of the town. Before there even was a town," he told them. "Guess whose name is written on the very first page. You are going to shite your pants, Kiki. A five-year-old child drowned in the river during a baptism. Guess what her name was…"

But Ian no longer had their attention. Gram and Kiki both watched Janine slink into the room from the same door Ian entered not five minutes prior. Janine still felt pink from that kiss. She felt another rush of blood at the sight of him. Ian turned and slowly trained his eyes on her. He definitely appeared embarrassed. Did she really just jump him a moment ago?

"Linda," his volume diminished suddenly. "Her name was Linda Mae Stauch…" His eyes were blinking rapidly. "Janine." His voice bounced back. "Will you join us? We were just talking about…"

"Oh no," Janine cut him off rather rudely. She softened her tone and managed to look him in the eye. Her throat was dry and her voice came out odd, husky. "It was a long day and I'm going to go up to bed." She walked over and gave Gram a nice hug then buggered out of there as fast as she could.

The town of Rio Linda kept meticulous records dating from the very beginning of the settlement in the 1800s. The death of Linda Mae Stauch was noted as a back entry in a handwritten book kept by the town leaders. She died during a baptism in the *valley river* that they took as a reference to the Rio Linda River. Another line stated that *she is released from her ailments and illness*, implying that Linda had been close to death when she drowned. The doctor photocopied everything available in the city archives. Perhaps they would find more clues in the large pile of papers he stacked on the coffee table.

"Seems odd that she wasn't baptized till five years old. Wouldn't she have been baptized as an infant?" Kiki perused the stack of papers. "Some of this is unreadable. The ink is washed out."

"Perhaps her family were converts," Gram suggested. "Protestant religions don't baptize infants. They wait until a body is old enough to ask for baptism."

The doctor ordered copies of a diary from a museum in San Francisco. He discovered that the original Rio Linda settlers came off two wagon trains. The first group left the diary. The doctor put a rush request on the copy and spared no expense to have it sent to Grams house.

Gram insisted that they continue to use her home as their base of operations until Juliana's visit. The house offered plenty of space and Gram wanted to help. She even lent them her Ford F-150 with the covered bed. Gram was no fool. She hoped the house would be featured in the *Spectral Analysis* episode about the river ghost. Gram often bragged about having a historic house, now she wanted it famous too. She probably shored away bragging rights to use with her card girls. Kiki and the doctor were happy with the arrangement and made themselves right at home, choosing the rustic sitting room as a central planning area. Kiki referred to Gram as their local Rio Linda expert, their go-to guide for all things Rio Linda.

But really, Janine suspected, Gram's motives had more to do with helping Janine forge personal bonds and establish trust again.

For the next couple of days, Kiki and the doctor kept busy with interviews in town while Janine spent time with Gram. Technically, she was on her two-week break. Gram dragged her to visit friends around Rio Linda and then to different farmers markets. They went to the boarding stables at Gold Country to brushed down the patched mare Gram owned. They fed the free-range hens and delivered a flat of extra eggs to the local feed store. Gram knew just about everyone in Rio Linda and bragged to everyone about the television show being filmed from her house. Each day, Janine just missed Kiki and the doctor. She could hear them walking down the hall late at night or in the early morning, but their paths never crossed beyond that.

She finally came face-to-face with Ian two nights after their porch kiss. Gram and Janine stumbled in from a local honey vender to find Ian and Kiki lounging in the rustic sitting room. Kiki had obtained a large dry-erase board and propped it against the far wall. The doctor lounged in the recliner with the big EMF box at his feet. He glanced up quickly and Janine got the distinct feeling that he was waiting for her.

"Janine." he sprang to a standing position. "I was just about to do another low-frequency EM survey. I could use a bit of help if you care to lend a hand. Of course, it's okay if you don't, but maybe you do. Maybe you'd like to get out… I mean, come out with me, on an official errand, of course. That's what I mean. We've been running at full throttle and maybe you're thinking we're leaving you out of the loop. I just thought, you know, since you're around and about for this phase, you might want to come along. Help me with a little tech stuff. I don't know, what do you say?" He was rambling and his eyes were blinking.

"I've never seen you so smooth," Kiki smirked softly, and the doctor gave her a sour look.

Gram nudged her, "Of course she wants to go. Run along, go on, girl. I'm to bed early tonight."

In the truck, the doctor filled her in on some of the leads they were chasing. Kiki wanted to interview Janine on camera right away, before she learned too much about what they were finding out. Janine being on the crew, and in the story, could compromise things.

Ian wore a button-down, light-blue shirt with the collar open at the neck and Janine watched his Adam's apple bob. He recently shaved and smelled very nice. The muscles in his neck flexed as he turned his head and spoke. His coloring was rich, deep brown hair with bright blue eyes, *not haunting blond locks with silver eyes*. She liked it. She realized that she was staring at him and looked away.

"She wants to get your unbiased perspective. You know, not cross-pollinate your experiences with too much information from other sources. Maybe even use a little hypnosis. We're taking your story as the authentic one, your portrait of the ghost as the actual one. We will authenticate other information by what we learn from you and Gram. We're going to get your clip first off before taping anyone else."

Janine already knew all that information. His rambling voice was a far cry from the usual Doctor McNally analytical tone he used.

"Where are we going anyway?"

The doctor had steered the truck out of Rio Linda and they were heading toward Sacramento.

"Oh." He glanced nervously at her. "That was a wee ruse back there, didn't you guess? Ha-ha, I confess, I just wanted to get you out and away from everyone. You know, take you to a private dinner. Go somewhere we could be a little less, observed."

That explained the shave and cologne.

"You're taking me out to dinner?"

"That's my plan. Crikes! Is that okay?" His eyes rounded. "We could go back. I don't know. Did I cross the line? Is this unprofessional? I thought you were…I thought we were…I hope we are on the same page and about things." He appeared just as nerdy as when they first met. But somehow, she found his blinking eyes and pressed lips incredibly charming. Even quite irresistible.

He pulled the truck off the road and began navigating through a parking lot. The Malabar Restaurant appeared to be their destination.

"So, this is a date?"

"Aye. Yes, this is a date. Bollocks, I should have asked you first, right? I mean, I thought you'd want to go. But maybe you have plans. Maybe there's something I don't know. This is a bit, I don't know. I mean, I can't stop thinking about that…the moment on the porch." He parked the truck and faced her. "Tell me I haven't made a brutal mistake."

"It's just. I'm not dressed for a dinner date." She felt disappointed to be in jeans and a T-shirt and not something more girly or sexy for their first date. She imagined her hair was a total mess. That thought process definitely confused her. When in the past five years had she wanted to dress more girly or sexy, be noticed? Not once, never. How surprising. Doctor McNally looked her over. His eyes ran down her body and Janine felt every inch of his gaze.

"You look dressed just fine to me," he said. "You look fantastic." He moved toward her.

Thank you, Gram, for having a full bench seat in her F-150, she thought. They met in the middle and resumed the kiss interrupted two nights before. She went from zero to one hundred in less than a second and surprised herself at how unbashful her response was. After a bit, Ian moved away. The engine still idled and he turned off the truck.

"So, will you have dinner with me then?" He grinned at her.

"Yes," she said. "Yes."

"We need to get something straight though." Suddenly he looked serious. "You need to make me a small promise."

Panic swept in. *The last time a man asked her for a promise, bad things happened.* She tapped it back down.

"I want to go slow, you know. This is something I've been thinking about for quite a bit of time and I don't want to make any mistakes. Plus, we have the professional side of our relationship to consider."

"Are you saying, you want to keep this, thing, a secret?"

Ian looked her in the eye. "I'll leave that part up to you. You seem pretty private, reserved, and so maybe you don't want everyone to know your business. I'll follow your lead on that."

"Then what promise is this about?"

He began to blink rather rapidly again. "That you won't let me push things too quickly," he said.

"What do you mean?"

He shook his head and looked out the front windshield.

"I confess. I almost knocked on your door the past two nights. I was a bit off my head and imagined you wouldn't mind at all, that maybe you were expecting it... All because of that kiss." His voice took on a rambling tone again, and his slight accent thickened. "When you said you were to bed the other night, looking at me with those eyes of yours, I practically convinced myself it was an invitation. I've been a bit mad because we've done all these shows together, and, it's like we know each other, we're familiar, and, I guess…I admit it, I've been imagining kissing you for quite some time. But really, we know very little about each other, personally." He finally looked at her. "How do you know you even want to have a go, with me, I mean? Did you give it any thought before the other night?"

Her panic morphed into a relief of sorts.

"What I mean is, let's make an agreement."

"An agreement?"

"Let's take things slow. Not cross any major lines until the Rio Linda segment is wrapped, promise to stay a bit professional here. If we agree to this, I can concentrate and not read into things and muck things up. That way our relationship can develop more rationally over time."

"Rational sounds good."

"All right then, good." He nodded. A small smile cracked his serious expression. "So, will you have dinner with me, right now?"

She considered that nice square jaw of his, "Yes. Okay, I'll have dinner with you."

The Malabar steak house was just off highway 99 halfway between Old Town Sacramento and the international airport. The top floor consisted of a trendy bar that overlooked a dimly lit dining area. Ian requested a corner booth in the back, away from the main traffic. The young hostess instantly recognized him. After she showed them to a table, Janine heard a buzz of excitement permeate the restaurant.

They ignored the buzz and focused on their date. Ian became interested in paranormal activity at an early age. His mother, who passed away when he was a teen, saw spirits in her youth, and at one point his dad had his mum committed over her beliefs. Ian never forgave his father. Ian said he always believed in his mum. As he grew older, he wanted to obtain proof of the paranormal and found a proof of sorts; mysterious energy at the ultralow end of the electromagnetic spectrum always bounced around the more believable hauntings. But people still had doubts. Steve Hanks came along at the just right time, and had just the right proposal, to take his study to the next level.

Ian also shared past relationship history with her. He had one serious girlfriend from high school to college, a few interesting women during his graduate years, and a couple of girlfriends in the past few years, but nobody serious. Most of the brainy women he dated laughed at his paranormal beliefs. The women who were attracted to his profession tended to fall on the irrational side. He admitted that most mediums were a little off their heads.

"You think Kiki is off her head?"

"Oh no." Ian shook his head. "Kiki is the real deal. Sometimes she plays stuff up, for fun and show business, but she has a real connective link going on." He paused and opened his mouth like he wanted to say more, but didn't.

"Do you believe there's a real ghost in Rio Linda?" Janine asked. "Do you think I've seen her?"

Ian nodded, "Yes. Something real is going on in Rio Linda. The EM vortex around that river bend is enough to convince me. Plenty of high-frequency waves, perfect for misleading folks into thinking they've experienced something. That's part of the trouble. But hidden in that noise, there was unexplainable, distinct patterns in the lower than fifty Hertz range. We only detected it during your faint out, just a wee bit. It had to come from something."

Ian drank his wine. Her eyes were drawn to his very large and powerful-looking hands. Large knuckles, broad palms and long fingers. He held his glass delicately, absently caressing the curve of the bowl with his thumb. She liked how carefully he handled objects. Janine found everything about him attractive. Capable, handsome, and intelligent—a winning combination.

"I also believe you had a legitimate paranormal experience as a child. You named the ghost. You called her Linda. You drew a picture of her. Other reports, other old sightings, tell of the same spirit. We're certain it's the same Linda who died in the river in the 1800s. How would you know to call her Linda, Janine? How would you know about that?"

"Maybe I heard people talk about it," she countered. "You know, kids tell each other scary stories all the time. The river ghost is a common enough legend. People tell it to kids to scare them away from the water. The river has a real undercurrent around that bend and things get stuck in the rocks all the time. You heard that old man. People blame it on the ghost but it's just a natural trap."

"Yes, but what you may not realize is; other people have also seen your phantom friend. It's been reported and recorded. You weren't the only child to draw a picture of

Linda," he told her. "We visited the old man from the pub, Henry Webber. He had a lot to say about the ghost of Linda Mae Stauch. One of his own relatives encountered the ghost many years ago and drew pictures of her. Henry Webber saved one of those pictures. Just like your portrait, her Linda had blue eyes, curly blond hair, and a clef in her chin. We're going to do a camera interview with him sometime after yours."

The waitress brought their calamari plate. Anytime Ian smiled, his eyes became blue sparkling gems. He smiled easily and often. It was contagious. He gazed at her and she felt herself melt.

"Don't take this the wrong way, but his young relative was a much better artist than you were. Her drawing at five years old looks closer to the one you made the other day. Anyway, she immediately drowned in the river after creating her portraits. Her own spirit is said to haunt one of the smaller streets in town, a Lara Lane."

"Are you supposed to be telling me all this?" she asked. "You're not afraid you might be cross-pollinating ideas or something?"

"Crikes! You're right." He knocked himself in the head. He emptied the wine bottle into both their glasses and leaned toward her. "How about you tell me more about you. I know you're from Texas. What was it, biochemistry at A&M, right? I know your parents have passed. I know your family originates from out here in California. I know you have at least one sister, with kids, in Texas. You prefer sweet tea and you read mystery novels. You like to run. And I've seen you kicking the football with Carlos. Pretty impressive moves. Gram said you played sports competitively. Any old beaus I need to worry about?" He chuckled nervously.

Oh boy. Oh brother, now she remembered why she avoided this sort of thing. Full disclosure would surely doom this new beginning with the doctor. Did she really need to answer that question right away?

At that moment, two women popped up to their table. They rudely interrupted and Janine felt relief at the pause in the conversation. She needed to think for a moment. If the date happened with a guy she barely knew, then maybe she could blow off that question. But this was Doctor McNally. They've known each other for a quite a while, not personally, but professionally. Was it okay to lie, fib a little bit, or slightly mislead him? Could Ian have at least waited a week before asking point-blank about past boyfriends?

The two women continued to chat at Ian, gushing about the show while sharing their spooky experiences. They asked for autographs and to take selfies. Ian smiled politely but kept glancing at Janine with concern.

If she couldn't just blow him off, should she tell him everything, all at once? Maybe it was better to get it out in the open sooner rather than later. But, she carried a lot of baggage, scary baggage, and most people might think her mind was messed up, broken, and her body ruined. If the truth changed his intentions with her, she'd rather it happen before she got too involved. Could she do it, tell him about her past? How would she word it? Panic bubbled under her composure. Perhaps she should just leave it and halt things right away. She probably wasn't ready to start a relationship, not if she still couldn't verbalize a little of what happened to her.

The women barely glanced at Janine. They gushed a bit more and then reluctantly slunk away when Ian reached across the table for her hand. Ian shook his head apologetically and Janine knew that she didn't want to halt whatever was brewing between them. She really liked Ian McNally and was very interested in kissing him again.

"Sorry. I still don't know how to handle that sort of thing. It's a bit like students running up after a lecture, but much more. Well, much more…"

"I get it," she said softly. "I think you handled it fine."

"Thanks," he said. "You're very easy to be with. Funny and intelligent. Delightful. You always seem so levelheaded. Reserved but also nice, open, very grounded. I love it. No games or weird hang-ups with you, just a breath of fresh air."

She suddenly blurted, "I was stabbed."

He appeared confused.

"I got involved with a psychopath."

He stared at her blankly.

"An old boyfriend tried to kill me." *He kidnapped me. He stabbed me. He left me for dead in a deserted area of woods*, she didn't add. Most of it was still hard to say out loud, even to herself.

"He's currently serving a twenty-year sentence in the Illinois state pen, and I am terrified he will be released early for good behavior." *Because he's very good at pretending to be a normal person.* "I was in my fourth semester of college, the University of Chicago, when it happened."

Ian shifted uncomfortably.

"There's more." She hesitated, gripping her napkin. *Why didn't she practice saying these things out loud?* "Afterward, well, I spent some time in a hospital. A hospital for people who… It was a mental facility. It took a while getting through what happened and I only recently weaned off all my medication. It's why I didn't drink whisky with the crew the first season. It's why I kept to myself."

Ian sat frozen, eyes wide.

"And there's something else," she said. Could she really tell him? She gave birth to a baby, her niece Sammy. Her sister adopted Sammy right after she was born because Janine refused to have anything to do with the child or what happened to her. Janine had actually been infuriated with her sister for taking Sammy. Janine wanted the baby lost and forgotten in the system, forever. No, she couldn't say that. Not without becoming a blubbering idiot. She killed her wine instead.

The doctor's eyes grew serious and he fidgeted a bit.

At that moment, a different waitress came with coffee and two more fans for the doctor. The three women chatted him up, giving Janine very little notice. She almost took a sip of her coffee but stopped because there was a perfect lipstick stain on it. Did the restaurant not clean their cups properly, or had that cup been meant for the doctor as a silent message? *The doctor.* In her mind, he was the doctor again. He actually looked relieved with the interruption. *Okay*, Janine thought, *a little disappointing but survivable. Kudos for going on a date again.* That short dinner was her longest relationship in the last five years. At least she took a step. The doctor shooed the women away in a hasty way.

"All right then." His eyes met hers. "Shall we get on?"

They left quickly and silently. Outside, he stopped right in front of Gram's truck and turned to face her. He gripped her hand and stared into her eyes.

"That was a lot to take in and I don't know how to ask you about it yet," he said quietly. "I'm a bit of an idiot at saying the correct thing, and I don't want to you to get the wrong idea because I'm so lousy at expressing myself. What I mean to say is, what I want to say…"

His eyes were deep blue and just as concerned as they were in the tunnel after that electrostatic shock. Ian pulled her into a soft slow embrace and leaned toward her. He kissed her tenderly on the forehead. He felt so large and strong and safe.

"Aye, that's what I want you to know. I just want to be clear about my feelings," Ian whispered.

Chapter 5
The Ledger Diary

A bulky express mail envelope sat on the front porch alongside the morning paper addressed to *Spectral Analysis*, attention Dr. Ian McNally. It came from the California History Group in San Francisco. The wagon train diary!

Janine carried the package into the house and set it on the coffee table on top of a pile of research. Kiki snatched it up and ripped open the package. She began shuffling through the pages rapidly. Gram brought Kiki and Janine mugs of coffee and sat down with multicolored yarn and thick needles. Gram settled comfortably into her chair, ready to knit, watch, and eavesdrop.

Ian McNally skipped down the stairs still damp from a morning shower, grinning from ear to ear. His intense eyes sought Janine out. Good grief, Janine thought, could he be more obvious? If they really wanted to keep their budding romance unadvertised, his huge grin was not helping matters. Janine looked away, but couldn't help smiling as she recalled their date.

"Here's a clue to our little ghost!" Kiki exclaimed. "Right here on page one. Stauch!"

From the first page of the ledger Diary of Stanley Hansen; May 22, 1839

85 souls in the Hansen virgin train from Independence, Missouri, to Yerba Buena in the Mexican territory of California.

Investing families include:

Hansen Leaders; Oscar, Stanley, Earl (2 wagons).

Stauch Group; Frederick, minster (6 wagons in this group).

Webber Family; Peter, woodworker (3 wagons).

Williams Family; Nicholas, pastor (5 wagons).

Lumen Family; Marcus, blacksmith (4 wagons).

Whitaker Family; John, farmer (6 wagons).

Miller Family; Andrew, famer (2 wagons).

Note: The Whitaker family and followers (8 wagons lost) departed our train before the desert plains. John and I were unable to come to a resolution to our disagreement and our numbers are now 63.

Signed *Stanley Hansen*

Ian sank into the easy chair with a mug of coffee. Instinctively, the girls left that seat open for him. The musky aroma of his aftershave filled the room and Janine felt him gazing in her direction again. His smug smile appeared much more conspicuous than he must imagine and she tried to ignore him. After their restaurant dinner, they drove down Marysville Boulevard with his electromagnetic energy receiver. They planned to mark distinct bands of wave energy across the old Miller almond orchard. Ian wanted a baseline of the area at night. Instead, they ended up having an old-fashioned parking session behind the trees. The memory of his large hands running over her body made him very hard to ignore.

Kiki arranged and divvied up the pages between herself, Ian, and Janine. Kiki tore blank paper out of a spiral-bound notebook for each of them. She pointed out a long list of names on her whiteboard, some already crossed off, some underlined. She asked them to cross-check connections between drowning victims and the original settlers.

"This is a list of people confirmed drowned in the river, crossed-checked with local street names. We should confirm if the streets were indeed named for the victims. Let's see if we can find any more links for my list."

"These surnames are pretty much all linked. Stauch, Miller, Webber. Here's the Williams link." Ian handed the page to Gram. Gram nodded as she surveyed the names.

"Yes, yes. These are our relatives. Great-Grandpa Nicholas Williams built this very house. There are tin types in the attic somewhere, taken when he was very old, and also one of the little boy Christopher. I remember that one well. They've mostly gone to grey and are hard to see. Old photographs of the family too, I'm sure of it. But Nicholas isn't in those pictures."

"Where is Yerba Buena?" Kiki asked. "Is that near here? Where exactly did they want to go?"

Gram laughed, "Oh, that's San Francisco." She nodded at her face. "Back before California was a state, it was part of the Mexican territories. There are missions all up and down the California coast, built by the Spanish out of Mexico. Twenty-one, I believe. The area around San Francisco is still called Yerba Buena." Gram settled into her knitting. She seemed very pleased with the flowing script of her ancestors in the historic museum diary and glanced down at it fondly.

They spent the better part of the day sifting through the diary. The beautiful artistic script turned out to be hard to read in places. Smudged lines and random scribbles confused much of the information. Imbedded in the daily log they found crude hand-drawn maps and personal notes regarding the Hansen's digestive processes.

The most fun were the scandalous sections of gossipy rantings interspersed between the regular entries. Stanley Hansen clearly disliked most of the men in his wagon train and lusted after a few of the women. He pulled no punches when writing out his personal feelings. He barely tolerated his "feeble-minded" brother, Earl, and detested his own father. Janine gasped at the bold, crude remarks regarding some of the women. Ironically, those crude words were written in dramatic cursive handwriting. They had a terrific time reading Hansen's more outrageous musings out loud to each other.

"My goodness." Kiki laughed. "He calls Mikael Stauch a whining she-goat and wonders if the little girl is really his. He's talking about Linda! Our little ghost, Linda, and her father."

"In my section, he writes that he would like to cut Mikael's throat in his sleep," Janine added. "Hansen thinks he would be doing the man's wife a favor."

"Here he claims the Webber group is hoarding the salted pork and wants to whip somebody. He's convinced someone in the Webber party is stealing food." Ian shuffled through his share of pages, attempting to put them back in order.

"Stanley wanted to knock someone else in the head, but doesn't name him. He just refers to him as that old gristle idiot far," Janine said. "Do you think he's just venting with this violent talk?"

Ian looked up, "Far? Like F-A-R? That's Danish for father. Do you think they were Danes then?"

"He wants to fine the Whitakers for disobedience. Doesn't say how they're disobedient," Janine informed them. "Did he have that kind of authority over the others? He sounds like a tyrant."

"Not sure," Ian said.

"He spied on Ingrid Stauch bathing!" Kiki looked up. "They found a pond of water and the women were washing. This occurs in an early section, and, apparently, Ingrid has the smoothest most flawless skin and very well-shaped breasts and buttocks. He writes a nice, very graphic description of how he'd like to get better acquainted with her." Kiki gave the passage to Ian. "I'm not going to say that out loud. It's no wonder they kept this diary hidden in the back room of the museum."

Ian took the passage and raised his eyebrows.

"Here's more about Ingrid." Kiki read out loud, "He writes that she is the prettiest woman he has ever seen, flaxen hair, blue eyes, tall and shapely, milky smooth skin. He wants to save her from her lazy husband. He definitely fancies Mrs. Ingrid Stauch. He actually spies on them and describes the husbands' unimaginative performance. He writes a bit of details about it." She handed it to Ian, then found another one. "He's a total peeper, now watching Mary Webber. Apparently, she was just starting to bud and quite nubile."

"He spied on all the women in this entry, where they came upon an interesting spiked rock on their journey. He tried to draw it." Janine held the drawing up for them to look at. "The Whitaker family was still part of the group and Hansen had his sights on the daughter, Elizabeth. He didn't think people would read this diary, or he didn't care. He actually describes her father as a jackass."

Kiki laughed and reached for the passage. Janine delivered the pages, then added,

"He offered to marry the daughter after kissing her, and the father refused. So, he was spurned."

"Unbelievable." Kiki scanned the section. "But don't feel sorry for him. He accuses the father of keeping him from his rightful urges by refusing a union. He offered to release her from the arrangement at the coast. He requested a handvest at the suggestion of Irene Lumen. I believe he means a handfasting, a temporary marriage. Now, that is very interesting."

"It was a hard, cruel world back then," Gram simply said. She made terrific progress in her netting. "But you say a temporary marriage, not an engagement?"

Kiki nodded. "I believe so. It's very pagan, not Christian at all, and at the suggestion of an Irene Lumen. Might we assume Irene followed a bit of the pagan ways? She is the healer of the group, and I don't believe there were many female doctors back then."

Ian blinked rather rapidly, "I guess we know what the Whitaker disagreement was about. Here's another nice comment about the Lumens. He admires Mrs. Irene Lumen as a fine woman and great cook. Apparently, Ingrid Stauch and Irene were cousins. Irene got the brains and Ingrid the beauty, it seems. Hansen also respects the Lumen men, Finn especially. Apparently, Finn is a natural blacksmith and has repaired a broken wagon wheel effortlessly." Ian looked up and chuckled.

"He disliked Frederick Stauch for praying and giving sermons all the time, said the minister felt his soul was dark. I can't say I disagree with the minister." Janine restacked her pages.

"Have you found any gossip about the Williams family?" Gram asked from her rocker and yarn ball.

"He seemed neutral on the Williams family. He just mentions them in passing in my pages," Janine conveyed. "Just notes about their wagon obligations. They carried most of the water barrels and camp supplies. Others in their group carried dry goods."

"There's a line about Nick Williams being reliable for advice and a steady voice in the masses. He calls them good, solid folk," Kiki told her.

"I'm relieved." Gram chuckled. "But coming from this rough fellow…"

"The Lumens, the Millers, and the Williams are mentioned by their workload and wagon cargo." Ian told her. "His ire seems more focused on the Stauch, Webber, and Whitaker clans. He had his eye on a female from each of those groups. He clashed the most with Frederick Stauch, a church leader. There are hints of a power struggle between them."

The diary entries end before the wagon train reached California. The last entry was dated September 6, 1839, and described a luminous red sun retiring behind the majestic Sierra Nevada Mountain chain.

"He called it the shortcut to Yerba Buena." Kiki said, "The California History Group added a note stating that the diary was delivered to San Francisco in a later group that arrived to the port city in1842." Kiki read the note out loud.

"The Hansen Party was not considered an official train of the Oregon trail. They were a small collection of people who traveled before the larger migration of the Gold Rush era. A later group encountered survivors of the Hansen Party in the Great Valley. They reported that Hansen died in an Indian attack along with most of the original travelers. The survivors preserved Hansen's ledger diary out of respect for the dead, and sent it to the proper authorities in San Francisco. A section of pages were removed from the book, nobody knows why, perhaps the paper was used for kindling. The Smith Party did not leave a diary, but did create a large map of their travels instead."

The museum included a copy of the map, reproduced as a nice poster.

"Looks like a gift store item." Kiki spread the map out on the coffee table.

"So, what did we learn?" Ian asked out loud.

"Stanley Hansen was a Peeping Tom," Gram called out, initiating a laugh.

Kiki stood and stretched her legs and arms, "I'd wager it wasn't an Indian attack that led to the demise of Stanley Hansen. I'd wager one of those men killed him after he tried to seduce one of their wives. My money's on Ingrid, who happens to be Linda's mother. Do you think it was mutual? The ghost story thickens." Kiki grinned excitedly.

"That could explain why they stopped here before reaching San Francisco. Perhaps they needed to get their story straight. Perhaps someone killed him right here, next to the river." Ian added.

"Why would he stop writing in the journal before going over the pass? Maybe they killed him on the pass. Or maybe those missing pages would tell us more," Janine said. "The family surnames in the train, Webber, Stauch, and Williams all show up on the list of drowning victims. We should cross-check the other names on the wagon train with the complete city records to see if more of these people settled here. See if a Hansen stayed or left."

"You are a terrific investigative partner." Kiki flashed pleased green eyes at her. "Also, there is a Mary mentioned in the diary, Mary Webber," Kiki added. "Some folks mentioned a ghost in the orchard called Mary. Linda and Mary were the two most popular names for a little girl ghost."

"Was Mary Webber a little girl?" Janine pointed out, "If she was budding, wouldn't that make her a tween at least. Is the Mary ghost older, or younger like Linda?"

"I get the impression she's pretty young, like Linda." Kiki shuffled through the diary again. "But who knows?"

Janine glanced at her grandmother and Gram winked at her.

"I'll get the city records." Ian jumped up. "Perhaps we can develop a solid story before Steve arrives tomorrow morning. We'll want to put a few interviews on film right away." He turned his eyes on Janine. "Starting with you, Janine, okay."

She nodded.

"You know," Gram said from her knitting. "There is a pile of old books and things in the attic. Most of it stowed long before I was born and never moved an inch. Like I said before, there's an old tin plate of Great-Great-Grandpa Williams somewhere up there. You are welcome to look through it all. There might be photos of some of these other folks too."

That left them with plenty more to do. After delivering the city records to Kiki, Ian went outside to make a few phone calls to Texas. Kiki began drawing lineage trees for each of the founding families of Rio Linda. She used a very dramatic and artistic script. Gram observed her work, nodding and helping. Gram knew many of the old families and told Kiki which people in town might have old tales and even historic documents hidden away.

Janine tramped upstairs to Gram's dusty attic. She hunted for a particular box which stored tin-plated photos from the 1800s. The attic bulb was bright, but with so many boxes and furniture in the way, the light didn't do much good. Gram kept a handheld flashlight next to the door and a quick test told Janine the batteries were still good.

Gram described a specific paisley-patterned heavy-duty cardboard tub that should be near the east dove window. Janine scanned the room. There were hundreds of paisley boxes scattered everywhere, and the attic had six small oval windows. Sunlight streamed into one window which meant the opposite wall had to be east, the most cluttered and cramped side of the unfinished room. Large boxes sat trapped behind a covered desk or table. Janine managed to push the desk out a few inches and then transferred boxes one by one to the top of the covered surface. Dust bunnies leaped into the air. She felt a sneezing fit coming. A motion at the door distracted her and she discovered Ian standing there with a big grin on his face.

"Your gram sent me up to carry boxes," he said.

Ian took a quick look over his shoulder, then closed the short distance between them. Ian McNally felt like a drug to her. The moment they touched her muscles turned to Jell-O. His kiss sent a flood of fire to every private sector in her body. Then, she started to sneeze.

"Are you becoming allergic to me?" He smiled.

"It's the dust."

"Stanley Hansen and his lurid descriptions. Sorry, but my mind kept drifting to you during those diary entries. That man should have gone into the X-rated novel-writing business. I've been thinking about our agreement, that promise," he said. "Maybe it's a stupid idea. I mean, do you think it's still a good idea? Maybe Kiki and your gram already know something's up. Your gram sent me straight away up here to help you. You looked pretty cool down there, but me, they must have noticed me ogling you from across the room."

Did he imagine smooth milky-white skin under her T-shirt? Flawless skin, like the description of Ingrid? Is that what he was imagining? Janine thought about her scars, seven knife wounds across her stomach and back. *Ruined.* She could never be what he imagined. She didn't want to think about his reaction when he finally saw those marks. She pushed Ian away.

"No. No one knows anything yet. Nobody noticed. My gram just thinks I need help carrying boxes." She picked up one of the paisley boxes and put it in his hands. "I think our plan is still a good idea. We should take it slow. Slow and quiet. Keep things light while we're out here. You were right as usual."

She added a second box to his stack. She picked up a third box and turned to go.

"Have I mucked something up?" He brow had lined.

She leaned in and initiated the kiss this time. That made him very happy. She loved the way his lips moved across hers. She liked that he was so attracted to her.

"No. I just want to stick to the plan. We're in my gram's house after all. We should definitely wait until we're clear of Rio Linda and on our own time before jumping into something more serious. When we can have more privacy, don't you think?"

He nodded and followed close behind. Janine hit the light switch and stowed the flashlight on the way out the door.

"I've crossed checked all the city documents." Kiki stood at the whiteboard like a school teacher and used a dry erase pen as a pointer. "Here's what I found. Of the Hansen wagon train, only the following people remained to populate the area." Kiki read them out as she pointed to the names on her board.

Janine barely paid attention as Kiki rambled off the names, she kept glancing at Ian from the corner of her eye. Would he still find her attractive when he got a good look at her mangled body? She was afraid to find out.

"No mention of Mikael, Ingrid's husband, or the three families in the minister's flock. The Millers that remained include John, Susan and a newborn baby they named Mary Elsa Miller. Nobody else."

Janine took in that information.

"What happened to the Lumens and Hansens?" Ian asked. "Where did they go?"

"No mention," Kiki said. "Most likely, they continued to San Francisco, or maybe Sacramento. There are references to a fort being built by Sutter. Although, based on the marriage list, I'm guessing Mikael died sometime between the last diary entry and the settling of Rio Linda."

"Maybe in the same Indian attack that got Stanley Hansen," Janine suggested.

"If it really was an Indian attack that got him," Kiki responded, "Perhaps they fought and mortally wounded each other over Ingrid. That's where I put my money." She

"It's this house, isn't it?" Ian pointed out something to Gram. "Look here. This area is the kitchen and back porch."

"It must be when Great-Great-Grandpa Christopher built up the house. He added the first large wing and the second story. These are some of his designs. Yes, yes. See here, on the bottom, River House. That's what he called it."

"Did they build the house around a small structure?" Ian studied the rustic sitting room. "It's this room, isn't it? The original house consisted of just this room?"

"I suppose so." Gram passed him the plans.

Ian crossed to where Janine sat near Kiki. He spread the plans out in front of them and then squeezed between them on the sofa. Three pages of plans, along with a sketch of the original house, lay before them. The front porch appeared the same, but now much more house existed on either side of that porch.

"Is that a cross on top of the original building?" Kiki pointed to the sketch.

Gram spoke from across the room. "Probably. Gramma used to say the whole town started out of this very room. It was the first structure in Rio Linda. That's why Great-Great-Grandpa Christopher did not want to tear it down. He wanted to add to it and live in it."

"But why the cross?" Kiki asked.

"Why? Well, they would likely meet here for prayer on Sundays, wouldn't they? Before an actual church was built. They say the town business was executed here too. Some of those pages in the city archives probably got their start in this very room."

"This is a very historic room." Kiki mused. Her hand dropped lazily and landed against Ian. "No wonder I pick up a powerful vibe in this house."

Janine noticed Kiki's hand and fought an urge to reach over and knock it away. Kiki always flirted with whichever male happened to be around and she did not want Kiki to start flirting with Ian. Janine stared her down.

"Aha," Kiki winked and retrieved her hand.

"Aha, what?" Ian still examined the plans, oblivious to their interaction. "What?"

"Just, aha," Kiki said and stood up. "I'm going to call it a night. Steve's comes tomorrow morning and Janine and I have a date in the study with the camera, where I will ask all these little questions that are dying to pop out but need to wait. I should probably get some beauty rest."

Chapter 6
The Ghost

Janine slept in. Well, it was more like hiding in. She cracked the code during a deep REM cycle and wanted to hide from her embarrassing psyche. Her shrink warned her that suppressed memories might reemerge while sleeping if triggered by daytime events or emotionally explosive stimuli. They were especially likely after weaning off the medication and her mind cleared up.

Janine was flustered, wondering what to do. She listened to the crew setting up for the interview downstairs. What would she say? She felt like a total fraud. She could honestly only affirm that she once had an imaginary friend. She no longer believed her experience at the river might be part of an actual ghost story. In fact, she felt certain it wasn't. The whisper in her ear, which felt so authentic at the river, was just more fallout from her wounded, fractured past. *Why did you leave me?* Those words had been locked away in a corner of her brain, waiting to ooze out at an inconvenient moment.

Janine hid under the covers, hoping to hide away from the demon determined to haunt her. *He* uttered those words when she completed her testimony and was forced to walk right past him. Very sternly, he said in a broken, betrayed voice, *why did you leave me?* He whispered it in the woods too, *didn't he*, after blaming her for everything and asking her to make that promise again. The memories, hazy in her mind, kept swimming to the surface. *Suppressed memories, lurking behind mentally protective layers, can spontaneously emerge if triggered,* Doctor Crisper warned her. How did Doctor Crisper instruct her to handle it? Find the trigger. *Identify the trigger, recognize it, and you'll be better able to control your responses.*

Could her new romantic feelings be the trigger? The emotions Ian stirred up when he turned the tap on her hot blood. Did that rush of passionate heat set her off. Her growing attraction to Ian McNally stirred up a flood of suppressed emotions, the exact emotions she felt with Rick when they first met, when she believed he was a normal person and fell catastrophically in love with him. Her psyche must believe it was happening all over again, and deep inside, she was scared to death.

She realized her fears were ludicrous. She knew Ian much better than she had known Richard Wilkens when she leapt into that passionate relationship. Perhaps she should call Doctor Crisper. The call was surely overdue. Almost a year passed since their last full conversation. Perhaps she shouldn't call him. How could he help anyway?

Bottom line, the river ghost was definite crap. Wasted time, wasted research, wasted money. Her little incident was nothing more than a fractured brain recalling a traumatic life experience. Should she confess her revelation to Ian? Kiki? Steve? How embarrassing. She wasn't nearly ready to tell everyone everything. The little bit she shared with Ian had been tough. Plus, the crew felt one hundred percent certain they stumbled upon an authentic, original ghost story. Janine the skeptic convinced them of that, and her wacky fun-loving grandma helped fuel that fire.

She debated coming clean or keeping quiet. Half the stories on the show turned out to be bunk and the audience still loved them. Even Kiki insisted that people wanted the stories more than the ghosts. But the team really believed in this one. Ian believed it. She could see it in his eyes. Would Kiki be able to see through her? Kiki debunked more than one fake story on camera, and not kindly. Janine lingered in bed a little longer, hiding from the world.

Steve and Ted rearranged Gram's study. They clamped the big camera to a large tripod and set it next to the piano. The winged chairs were no longer separated by Gram's country end tables, but face to face. Ted glanced up and grunted his hello. Steve greeted her with a huge hug. Both of them wore Marvel Universe shirts.

"Wow," Steve boomed. "The stuff you guys dug up, wow. We're going for a two-part episode on Sacramento now. It's the only way we can do it. Multiple camera interviews with witnesses, four or five streets to look at, and an orchard. All possibly haunted! We have a truly original, deeply rich ghost story to tell! I've even contacted my friend, Cheeky, from NYU about a reenactment segment."

He talked while attaching camera lights to a smaller tripod with a reflective umbrella. Ted hid chords and rearranged Gram's knickknacks on the piano. It looked like he wanted to get rid of some, but didn't know where to stash them. He laid a few photos flat. Steve showed her a silver sheet of metal with a faint picture of a boy on it.

"Your great-great, I don't know how many greats, but great-grandpa Christopher Williams. One of the founding fathers of Rio Linda! Your grandma found it this morning. There's another plate of the whole Williams family, but it's hard to make out the faces. This one is still nice."

Janine picked up the tin-type photo to study it. Grainy and grey, a startled boy stood in dress clothes stared at her.

"Not a father. According to research, he was a little boy when the town was founded," she told him.

"Close enough." Steve smiled. "We're floating the idea of staging a reenactment of the origin story for your river ghost. This is great stuff, really rich storytelling. Wagon trains, river baptisms, lust, murder. Religious undertones in a ghost story are always a major plus."

"Well, Sleeping Beauty awakes." Ian strolled into the room. He gave her a smile that sparkled to his eyes. "All set then? This'll be a snap," he said.

"Nervous about the interview?" Steve came round to massage her shoulders. "Don't worry, you come off very nice on camera. Very nice. I know it's imposing, having the camera pointed directly at you, but you're getting used to it, right? Not the monster you first imagined, that camera."

"Is it the hypnosis?" Ian asked her. "Kiki said you were hesitant but agreed to go under. Just relax, I've hypnotized lots of folks. If you really don't want to do it, we don't have to."

"She's fine." Kiki walked into the room. "Stop smothering her. You're going to make her nervous."

Kiki, channeling a sexy, gothic vampire, wore a tight, black, low-cut dress with a long slit up the skirt. A thick leather waistbelt with a small dagger formed the neck of her hourglass shape. Her outfit was bottomed with black spiked heels and topped with black spiked hair. Was it a wig? She was all black and white except for her blood red lips and brilliant green eyes. Ted whistled and Steve just gave her the up and down.

"Well," Ted grunted. "It's Elvira, Mistress of Darkness. Carlos is going to be very upset he missed this one."

"What if," Janine swallowed nervously, "What if I never really saw a ghost? My gram is a bit of an embellisher."

"Nonsense," Kiki told her. "You are connected to the spirit of Linda Mae Stauch."

Janine gave the doctor a worried look.

"Out at the river," Ted grunted again, "Can't fake that. I saw it. Something spooked you. Carlos was sitting right next to you and says he felt something too. He was totally spooked."

Janine left the room for the kitchen. Behind her, Kiki directed Ted to move the chairs back to their original positions. That entailed moving the camera and lights as well. Kiki insisted that direction was very important in an interview. Kiki needed to face west for this one. Kiki's voice carried into the kitchen.

"You know that, Ted! You too, Steve. Don't laugh, this is serious. A hypnosis subject should always face east, into the spin of the earth. I've told you plenty of times. It keeps a body from fainting, facing east. Think about Janine. What's wrong with you guys?"

Ian followed Janine into the kitchen. "Hey," he kept his voice very low. "Are you all right? Truly, hypnosis is nothing to be nervous about. Dinna worry, lass. I won't take advantage of you."

They stepped onto the back, glass-encased porch with mugs of coffee. Gram's backyard was riddled with hens. A single rooster with beautiful green and black tail feathers strutted in the center of the gaggle. Cocky Antonio strutting his stuff, Gram giggled the other day.

"What if I didn't see a ghost, Ian? What if I was just a kid with an imaginary friend?" Her voice was low. "What if that thing that happened at the river, what if that was just me fainting and hearing things? I'm nervous because everyone is so hyped about this being a real ghost story. Well, I never claimed that there was a real ghost out here. I'm worried that this story all depends on what I say, and I'm afraid I might disappoint you guys."

"Crikes." Ian set his mug aside and reached out to take hold of her shoulders. "It doesn't depend on you, Janine. You're too old to see this ghost anyway. And we're just hunting here, with this interview, like always. If you want to zero in on what happened in your childhood, let me hypnotize you. We could get a clearer picture. You could get a clearer picture of your imaginary friend. You never know, maybe we find something that links her to the historic Linda Stauch, maybe not. That's part of the fun."

In all fairness, Ian was right. They were hunting paranormal activity. They looked for evidence and clues. How could Janine rule out the ghost based on memories she could barely recall? This story was just as good as any of them. Bottom line, it was all just show business, no matter what Ian McNally studied in college or Kiki Mellow claimed to believe.

Kiki crossed one bare leg over the other as she lounged in an old-fashioned heirloom chair under the tempered beam of an umbrella lamp. She fired a series of questions at Janine regarding Gram's house and the surrounding area. Kiki urged Janine to reminisce out loud about her youthful experiences in Rio Linda. She asked specific questions about the imaginary friend, many of which Janine could not answer. Surprisingly, Kiki seemed pleased by the scant information Janine squeaked out. She leaned toward Janine with her breasts almost bursting from the deep-cut mistress of darkness dress.

"And now that you're back. How do you feel?" Kiki asked softly. "Have you seen your imaginary friend again?"

"No."

"The other day at the river, when we called for the river spirit to appear, you had an experience." Kiki drew in a breath, "Did you get the impression it was her, Linda?"

"I'm not sure." Janine glanced at Ian. "I don't know."

"You said that a voice whispered into your ear, do you still recall that voice?"

"Of course." Janine closed her eyes. "It asked, why did you leave me? It was very faint. Maybe I imagined it, but it did seem real."

"Maybe so." Kiki nodded in agreement. "Maybe yes, maybe no. Did it sound like a little girl?"

"It did."

Kiki acted very pleased with how tight-lipped Janine seemed to be. Janine appeared reluctant to participate. Well, she was, wasn't she? Kiki slowly rearranged her legs and leaned back in her chair, relaxing.

"Doctor McNally is now going to hypnotize you," Kiki dramatically extended her arm toward the doctor. "We will continue the interview shortly."

Ian wore his nerdy brown vest and rainbow *Spectral Analysis* tie. He settled into a cushiony chair and pulled a silver pen from his vest pocket. On a past show, the doctor hypnotized two different women with that silver pen. Carlos had insisted that people pretended to be hypnotized. Janine disagreed; she knew it often worked.

She followed every instruction. Ian raised the pen and she focused on the it, as directed. She began to visualize the backyard in her head, as directed. She closed her eyes, as directed. At first, she felt nothing, then her muscles relaxed and her thoughts sank into a comfortable place. It felt like someone placed a heavy blanket over her, anchoring her down, keeping her warm and protected. Her body let loose some tension. She saw bright colors in jumpy, uneven images similar to an old 8mm film played against a back wall. Janine did not register Kiki's exact words, only her voice murmuring in the background. Somehow, Kiki's murmurings spurred images into Janine's mind. She answered questions automatically and periodically became aware of her own voice as the images changed.

"It's unfair that I am not allowed to leave the yard, so, I skirt the very edge of the lawn, towing my doll, Samantha.

The grass men mowed and it smells very fresh. Just when I wish for someone to play with, I see another girl my age! Such bright-yellow hair, almost white. Her beautiful pearl headband makes her look like a princess, but her dress is very old and tattered. I am too shy to speak, so I walk right past, following the perimeter of Gram's yard. My boundary line is unfair! When I turn back, the girl is gone. She's free as a bird.

"Every day the girl with the pearl headband comes. All I do is wish her there, and she comes. It's a sunny day. I tell her we can be friends. I ask if she'd like to come inside, into the cool, air-conditioned house. But she is not allowed in our house or yard, so we walk along the outer edge of the boundary, back and forth, like caged animals. She asks if I found the necklace, but I don't know what she means. I never notice when she leaves. I just notice that she is gone.

"My friend comes again. Her name is Linda, and she talks funny. She's there whenever I go into the yard looking for her. She wants me to follow her home, but I am not allowed past the cut lawn, and she is not allowed into it. Juliana is always watching me, asking what I'm doing. When I go too far from the house, my sister yells at me to come back. Juliana is very bossy. Linda and I sit on the edge of the lawn until she must go home again.

"Linda wants me to follow her home. She knows where we can find wild blackberries. She wishes she had a doll like mine, like Sammy, but I will never give her my doll!"

Kiki's voice, in the distance, asks if the ghost ever encourages Janine to go to the river.

"Linda never mentions the river. She doesn't say anything about the river. She says I should not listen to the others. She knows where we can find blackberries and insists that we go back to where we belong. She says that we are forever friends and can do great things together. But I don't know how, if she can't come into my house and I can't go to hers.

"Linda refuses to meet Gram. Grown-ups get her into trouble, she says. And she isn't allowed into the house, so I shouldn't ask her to go in. I run to get Gram and Juliana so they can tell Linda that it is okay, but Linda is gone.

"Linda stays far away from the house. She always stands at the edge of Gram's yard asking if I will follow her home. She has been waiting a long time for a friend like me, but I don't go over there. Juliana tells me to stay close to the house, and Juliana is always watching. Juliana is wondering who I am always talking to."

Kiki's voice intertwines with the doctor's voice. They ask about the river.

"The voice at the river. Is it the same voice as Linda, the friend?"

The day at the river comes back. Images pop into her head of the boulders reflecting a metallic luster and breaking up the smooth surface of the water. Wavering ripples catch her attention as the doctor and Kiki wade in their rubber farmer johns.

"Kiki and the doctor are in the river, laughing again. Wouldn't it be funny if she fell into that water? Maybe the river ghost could knock her in for me. Then a voice whispers in my ear. I remember that voice. It is Linda, my funny friend. It is the same voice."

Janine opened her eyes to Kiki, the doctor, Steve, and Ted staring at her. Ian still held her hand. Kiki appeared thrilled.

"I wanted Kiki to fall into the water too," Ted said softly.

"That was a fantastic session." Kiki squeezed Janine's hand. Then Kiki suddenly rose. "I need to take this dress off and brush out of my hair. Janine, that was fantastic, just beautiful. Thank you. That was well worth the wait." Kiki flew off.

"We are going to debrief on the back patio," the doctor told the others. He helped Janine up. She felt a little heavy as he led her away.

Behind them, Ted and Steve began packing up the equipment while discussing dinner and picking up Carlos from the airport. Ian helped her into one of the deep Adirondack chairs. He knelt in front of her, holding her hand. He offered her a cool glass of ice water.

"How are you feeling?"

"I'm okay. That wasn't too bad. I think I remember some of it."

"You should," he said. "Kiki is right. You are a fantastic interview under hypnosis."

"How can you be sure I was really under?"

"You were under," he confirmed.

"Did I say anything besides my recollections of Linda? Was any of it useful?"

"You said she talked old-fashioned, dressed old-fashioned. That could be an 1840s wagon-train girl. You confirmed that her name was Linda."

Janine closed her eyes, still feeling a little dizzy.

"Why did you want the ghost to knock Kiki into the river?"

"What? Oh, that." She opened her eyes and gazed at him, thinking about it. She finally just admitted it, "I was jealous. You know, Kiki's always getting your attention. And you never noticed before; I've had a crush on you for a little while."

Ian grinned happily at her and tried kissing her, but it was awkward. Gram's wine-barrel lounge chairs were not shaped with two people kissing in mind.

"You were jealous? Let's get out of here," he whispered. "Obviously, we've both been sitting on our feelings for quite some time and we should explore it. Why wait? We should make a go of it. We could disappear for a little while and no one would miss us. The guys are going to the hotel and Kiki has her appointment. We don't have anything scheduled until tomorrow afternoon. We could find a private place and get to know each other better. A romantic getaway, alone, on our own time. You can break your promise to me." He swallowed, eyes blinking. "I'll forgive you."

Was Ian McNally the trigger? Under hypnosis, the voice at the river sounded exactly like the voice of her imaginary friend. Could the ghost story in Rio Linda have possibilities after all? The more-reasonable explanation pointed to Janine manifesting delusions because of her growing feelings for Ian, the anxiety she harbored at where it might lead physically, mentally, and emotionally; anxiety at making a terrible mistake again. Perhaps Janine needed to face her fear and follow through with Ian, it could defuse that trigger for good. Doctor Crisper said the key to her recovery would be when she finally trusted someone with everything. That someone could be the nice, considerate man she's been crushing on for months.

Gram always played cards with her girls on Wednesday night, so it was a given that she would be up late. Janine called to tell Gram not to wait up or worry. Gram didn't ask any questions, but her pause and tone of voice let Janine know that Gram suspected what she was up to.

They took the red F-150 and cruised up the granite infused mountains toward Lake Tahoe. Ian was curious to get a closer view of the mountain pass Linda crossed two hundred years ago. Ian rambled about the Sierra Nevada range. It resulted from a fault block uplifting of a gigantic igneous batholith over one hundred million years ago. Some of the giant chunks of exposed granite made up Yosemite

National Park, creating the half dome monolith among other peaks. He used his lecture voice as he talked and she found him extremely cute trying to impress her.

The drive provided plenty of time to fill in the blanks of the sketchy pasts they shared. Ian finally asked the question he was afraid to voice. In the privacy of the truck, with his eyes focused on the road, she might be able to tell him everything.

"So, the bloke that's in prison…" He was hesitant. "You met him in college? So, were you young?"

"I was twenty. Young, but not too young," Janine told him. "I thought it was… I was very taken with him." She found it hard to admit that she fell head over heels for Rick and actually wanted to marry him.

"Was he a university student?"

"I thought so, at first. But then he had a house in River Forest, a small place. He never went to class." Rick seemed perfect: Easy on the eyes, athletic, considerate, funny, smart. And charming, so very charming. He drew her attention easily and filled her up with bubbly excitement. She remembered falling in love, the tumbling toward him and feeling safe in his arms. How lucky she felt. She remembered telling her roommate that it was true love, how could it be anything else? "It's still unbelievable that he is the same guy that…" her voice faltered.

Ian just drove. He let her tell the story slowly.

"It was like a switch flipped one day."

Ian nodded, then shook his head.

"Someone warned me. I don't know who. But I got a note." *Three notes that I ignored because I thought someone was jealous. I was stupid, stupid, stupid.*

Ian glanced over, and she continued,

"The note said that his last girlfriend went missing." *She disappeared from school, never to return. Someone thought I should know that. Someone thought he was dangerous. Someone I ignored.*

"She's gone?"

Janine nodded. The note writer believed Rick did something to her.

"Did the police look into it? Check him out?" Ian asked.

"She left messages to friends. She wrote a letter to her parents saying she was going to Turkey to join some mystery group. That's what people thought. That's what she wrote in the letter. That's what he said." *Rick couldn't persuade her against it. He seemed very upset that he was being unfairly blamed for her reckless behavior. People always assume the guy is at fault when women run away.*

"Is that what he told you?"

"Yes," Janine said. *And I believed him. Why wouldn't I? He seemed so normal. He was very upset that someone would write those notes. He claimed to be a victim of malicious gossip, reverse sexism. It was cruel, because she left him brokenhearted and he was blamed. Of course, I believed him. I loved him.* "When I asked about it…"

"He became violent?"

"No, not yet," she said. "Not until I broke it off." *But I didn't really break it off. Not completely. I only wanted a small break.*

Janine instinctively hugged herself, reaching underneath her shirt to trace the scar near her navel. "I want to warn you. I have…I have a couple of scars." *Like seven. Seven knife marks. Mostly small, insignificant lines across her skin. But a couple of very distinct grooves, near-fatal gash marks on her back and one on her stomach. Ruined, some might say. So don't expect smooth, milky skin like Ingrid Stauch. Maybe they should turn back.*

"Dinna worry about that," Ian said. "I'm attracted to you because of you. You are so gutsy. You really make us all step up. I loved the way you just shook off that whole thing in the underground of Sacramento, like it was nothing. Ted about pissed his pants, more than once! You stay so cool, and are incredibly smart. Funny. You're always joking with Carlos. And you're a very nice person, always considering everyone's feelings." He looked back to the road. "And I bet you don't know how alluring your eyes are, lassie, bonnie golden and bright. Plus, you look spectacular in your Spectral uniform. I can tell you're smoking hot underneath. I got lots of tactile evidence to back that up. Whoops, sorry. Crikes, did I step in it?" There was a sheepish expression in his eyes. "Really, Janine, I've seen a scar, or two, before, it's okay. Don't worry about a couple of wee scars."

"There may be more than a couple," Janine said quietly. *And not so wee.*

"Dinna worry about that," he said again. "I think you're beautiful." Then after a time, "What happened?"

"I got caught up in the romance and I let things go. My grades began to slip and I needed to study. My sister became concerned about the time I spent with him. She pressed to meet him. She was wary of him. That's when the switch flipped. He turned into another guy." *He was angry. Rick did not want Juliana interfering in the relationship or influencing things. He detested anyone that questioned the time he demanded.* "I just wanted to have a little space to study, and go home for a visit. Just a break, for exams and the holidays." She stopped.

The memory overwhelmed her. She did not want to break down, but that happened to be the exact moment her bright and wonderful life altered into a nightmare. She felt a little of the love she had felt, the betrayal, and the disbelief. All those feelings were still lodged somewhere inside.

"Hey, I'm sorry. We can stop…"

"No. I want to tell you." She insisted. "I have to be able to talk about this."

"I don't want you to feel pressured and I also don't want…" He knocked himself in the head. "Crikes, I blew it, didn't I. I was hoping for full-blown romance, you know, a nice dinner, dancing, a fancy hotel, maybe bubbly. But I had to start asking these questions. I'm sorry."

"Ian, there can't be any romance if I don't tell you about this first," she said. "You need to know before we can move on, before we can go any further. So let me get it out, because, I want that romance too. Ask any questions you need right now."

He didn't say anything, just blinked at the road ahead.

"He switched personalities in a fraction of a second," Janine told him. "The man I knew was replaced by…that guy. He told me, no. No space, no break, no outside interference." *In fact, Rick would not let me leave his house until he was satisfied with my attitude. He would not let me go back to the school or anywhere.* "I tried to leave, but he stopped me."

"He struck you?"

"He beat me until I passed out."

Ian pressed his lips together.

"I woke up attached to a long chain."

Ian's brow furrowed.

"He, he…it wasn't consensual anymore. And he beat me again, when I tried to stop him. I don't know how many times because I still have a lot of missing time." *And in between those rages, Rick spoke sweetly, like everything was normal and I wasn't on a leash confined to the second story of his house. That we were just having a little tiff, a small difference of opinion, and all his actions were going to help change my mind. Make me see his point of view better.*

"Janine…"

But she cut Ian off, "I was trapped for over a week. People were looking for me. He wanted to take us on a trip, for privacy, a change of scene, to get back the romance. Back the way it was." *But maybe Rick just wanted to get me out of his house so he could kill me.* "When he unlocked the handcuffs, I ran away. Somehow, I escaped and ran into the woods. He came after me and stabbed me…a few times. He buried me with leaves." *I couldn't move. I couldn't talk. I was dying.*

Ian swallowed hard.

"A rock stymied the flow of blood. It saved me." *I lay in those leaves for what felt like hours until a guy walking his dog found me. Well, the dog found me.* "It took days until I was coherent enough to speak. I was scared out of my mind because he was in the hospital, holding my hand, acting normal." *I was confused. My brain was fuzzy. I was confused and terrified.*

"Blimey, what? How?"

"Everyone believed the story he concocted." *Even me. Even I thought it sounded reasonable and doubted my flashes of memory.* "He was actually the one to report me missing. He called my dorm, asking for me. He left messages asking me to call him while I was still chained in his house. My roommate said he was frantic. They arrested a homeless guy camping on the edge of the woods because there were handcuffs hidden in his stuff. Handcuffs that matched the marks on my wrist. I doubted my own mind at first."

Through the meds and fuzzy haze, I thought maybe I mixed everything up. The real truth, I wanted to be mixed up. It was nicer to believe he was the Rick that I first met, the first man I ever loved, the one I fantasized about and hoped to marry. I couldn't wrap my head around what had happened. She could not admit any of that to Ian.

"That's just unbelievable. How'd they get him?"

"At the hospital. He had a disagreement with Juliana." *Rick told her that I wanted to live with him, so she shouldn't worry about me. He planned to take me home from the hospital to care for me. Juliana did not like that idea and said as much. They argued about it.*

"At one point Juliana left the room, and…" *Rick flipped the switch.* "I saw the monster again, the look in his eyes, his mumbled ranting. There was no question about it, it all happened. I was afraid he would do something to Juliana if she kept resisting him."

"Blimey. What'd you do?"

"I could barely speak, but managed to tell a nurse. I don't remember how." *She was great. She didn't even blink when Rick came back into the room.* "She told the police."

One investigator never trusted Richard Wilkens. He thought Rick's truck was suspect. He had a shovel, a pick, and a tarp in the back bed. Based on that, Detective Anderson concluded that Rick planned to move my body to a more-secure location and bury me.

"They arrested him right away, right out of the hospital room. It stunned everyone: Juliana, the nurses, everyone. That's when I finally managed to give a statement. I—I still have a bit of missing time, so I don't know everything. They used that against me in court, having so many blanks. Called me unreliable, irrational, and hysterical."

"I just… It's just…"

"I know, it's a lot. But there's more. I pretty much cracked after that. You know, total mental breakdown."

"No one would blame you," Ian said.

"I cracked." *And had his baby,* she didn't add. *Abandoned the newborn and went back to hide in the mental ward because I feared the father. But more accurately, because I hated the mother for being so easily fooled and so completely stupid, and mostly, for still feeling in love with him. I wanted to pretend none of it ever happened and that the baby didn't exist. I couldn't look in that baby's eyes. They looked like his eyes. I worried the baby would make me go back and forgive him.* Maybe she should save that part for another day. Saying the other stuff out loud just about wiped her out.

"Anyone would crack. It's a lot to digest," Ian said.

"You'll have the rest of the drive to digest it," Janine told him. "It's a lot, I know. Does this change how you feel about me, romance wise? I'll understand if you want to turn around? Mental issues, emotional issues, relationship issues. I've got them all. This is your chance to escape. I wouldn't blame you. No harm done."

"No," he insisted. He reached over and took her hand. "No, I want this to happen. I want us to make a go of it. But are you ready? I mean, that's a lot to digest. That is a pretty heavy conversation. I suddenly feel like I'm rushing you."

"Just take the drive to digest it," she said. "I told you because I'm ready for the next step too, with you, but you should know what you're getting yourself into. I've been thinking about you for months, Ian, quite a bit. We've known each other long enough, don't you think? Already friends. There's trust, and I'm definitely attracted to you."

She watched the tree line thicken on each side of the road. Tall pines sped by in silence. They were above the cloud layer and the sun shone very bright.

They stopped at Donner Lake and checked into the resort. Patched snow still lay on the ground and the air was crisp. Beyond the pines, Janine could see the tall pole of a ski lift.

"This is on the trail the Hansen party took," was the only thing relating to the ghosts said between check-in that night and breakfast the next morning.

The aroma of coffee mixed with bacon and eggs wafted through the air. Sunlight broke through a tiny slit in the curtains and drew a bright line across the bed. Did it really happen? Did she actually begin an intimate relationship with Ian McNally? Janine kept her head down and eyes mostly closed to hold onto the feeling a while longer, but it wasn't a dream. She did it. She took a chance. Nothing in the way he looked at her changed after she told him that story, and he didn't flinch once at any of her scars. Underneath the sheet, Ian's hand caressed her lower back, right about where the near fatal wound that grazed her kidney would be. Janine tensed automatically, wondering if the deep mark repulsed him. Did he think she was ruined?

"I'm just admiring your bum," he whispered. "I've been eyeing this bum for very long time. You have no idea how long I was trying to get your attention. Hum, let's see, what would I write about this in my diary for future generations? Smooth. Aye, Janine has very nice, silky skin, very beautiful and lovely to touch. Let's not forget her ample, well-shaped breasts and buttocks, to plagiarize a phrase from Mr. Hansen. Sorry, lass, but I love the shape of you."

She playfully slapped his hand away. Then, she pulled the covers further up and firmly tucked them around her body as she turned to him. She felt a little bashful in the light of day, whereas Ian lay in all his glory on top of the bedsheets.

"How did you let room service in dressed like that?" she asked.

He just laughed and kissed her. He jumped from the bed.

"Let me fetch you a cuppa coffee, my lovely lass," he said. Ian McNally was nicely put together. His Scottish ancestry created his tall, muscular, manly build. Ripples along his abdomen drew her eyes to very well-defined obliques. She turned away, aware of the burning red blush forming on her cheeks. Did he have to look so perfect?

"I can't believe I thought you were nerdy," she said out loud.

"You thought I was nerdy?" He brought coffee and a plate of food. "Me? I'm nerdy?"

"Not anymore," she said as he slowly fed her. "Now, you're just...you're just, very, very sexy." More kissing.

"I'd like to stay here all day," Ian said. "But...we've got two interviews and a plan to shoot on a few streets tonight. Plus, I want to get pebble and soil samples from the river bed. Everyone will be at your gram's house in a couple of hours, so we should get going if we don't want to be late."

"Pebble samples from the river?"

"I want to see what's in the soil and rock," he said. "I wasn't kidding about the field lines out there. It's like a transmitter sending signals, or some sort of reflector. Maybe there's an ore or deposit picking up energy signals. I've got a theory about ghostly energy that I'm working on and want an analysis of the rocks."

He fed her the last of the toast then kissed the crumbs away. He said something softly that she couldn't quite hear, but it sounded sweet. Finally, he moved to take the breakfast plate back to the small round table with the other dishes. Janine shifted around to put her coffee mug on the nightstand and check the time. If they got moving soon, they could definitely beat the crew to Gram's house.

She sat up and quickly wound her long tresses about her hand to obtain control of the mess. Her cover suddenly slipped. She had to grab the sheet before becoming completely exposed but wasn't fast enough.

"Crikes." Ian stared at her, completely entranced. His voice was very soft. "You are going to think I'm a total animal."

Her eyes were drawn to the unmistakable fact that Ian was becoming quite aroused. As his eyes ran over her curves, they ignited every nerve imaginable. The heat spread like wildfire into her breasts and groin, teasing her. How did he manage to do that with only his eyes? He stood poised and ready to pounce, waiting for her to give him a signal.

"Let's be late," she managed to say. That was all the encouragement he needed.

On the drive back to Rio Linda they agreed to keep a low profile on their budding relationship. Janine wasn't ready to field the scrutiny, especially with her sister's family visiting so soon. Would Juliana think she was being careless? Plus, she wasn't ready to deal with ribbing from Carlos.

They found the *Spectral Analysis* crew waiting in the rustic sitting room. They were definitely late for the briefing. Every face scrutinized them when they burst through the door. Luckily, Kiki drew the attention back to her whiteboard.

"Oh, hey," Ian, a total coward in the face of his coworkers, went straight up the stairs. "Let me run up for my tie."

Gram waved Janine into the kitchen. Janine nodded to everyone before hurrying to meet Gram.

"I covered for you," Gram whispered.

"What?"

"I told everyone that you two took off early this morning to run an errand and would be back presently."

"Oh, thanks, Gram," Janine said.

"Not a problem, girl." She patted Janine's back. "Did you have a good time?"

Janine gave Gram the eye.

"Well, you look absolutely radiant, girl, absolutely radiant. Whatever you got up to, I'm going to tell you, I'm all for it."

Janine cracked a smile and hugged her grandma.

Back in the living room, Ian returned wearing his *Spectral Analysis* tie and a vest. He glanced at her and smiled conspicuously, absolutely beaming. He loitered across the room restacking Kiki's papers while shooting glances at her. *Good grief,* Janine thought, *everyone is going to guess.* Even so, she couldn't look away from his deep blue eyes, nor keep herself from smiling back and wondering when they would be alone again.

"What did you find out this morning?" Steve turned his attention from Kiki.

"Oh, well, you know," Ian uttered, "the mountain pass, rough, but nice. Very nice. Absolutely beautiful."

Steve glanced toward Janine and Carlos. "We don't need you guys until tonight, but you're welcome to come for the interviews if you want. Janine, you're probably interested in hearing what other people have to say about the ghost. Or, you can hang out with Carlos and charge up all the gear for the street shoots."

"Everything is plugged in." Carlos lounged in the easy chair, looking quite comfortable. "But I'll hang out here, I guess. I can read through Kiki's pile of stuff. Cram the info about which ghost is on which street." He tapped his head.

continued, "There are marriages listed in the first few years. Ready for more gossip? Linda's mother married her brother-in-law! And the Whitaker family must have caught up with them, because the name Elizabeth Whitaker shows up in the Rio Linda archives. She married Ethan Williams."

Kiki set her notes aside and stretched out like a kitten on the sofa. Sometime in the recent past, she acquired a big glass of wine, and so did Gram. Kiki nodded to no one in particular.

"I may have developed a nice backstory for our ghost. Of course, I'll see what Janine here has to say first." Kiki saluted the air with her wine. "Did you know, you are the only person who has seen the ghost of Linda Stauch and lived?"

"That can't be true," Janine said. "All kinds of people say they've seen her."

Kiki shook her head, "All kinds of people know of someone who has seen her. Those eyewitnesses were kids who unfortunately drowned in the river. Have you seen her again? No, don't answer any questions or tell me anything. We're going to wait for the interview."

"Kiki means authentic sightings." Ian sat next to Gram as she rummaged through one of the paisley boxes. "Lots of times, we can rule out stories that don't fit or that are obvious rubbish. What's that?"

A map, or a blueprint, came out of the box. Gram turned it around.

"I'll give you a big hint, my dear. The streets are named for the ghosts that haunt them." Kiki winked at him.

"I'll go to the interviews," Janine said.

"Maybe you can grab some samples while we're out." Ian turned to Carlos. He retrieved four collection tubes from his pocket. "I've been meaning to get to it."

A little old lady who lived on the other side of the orchard was their first interview of the day, Mrs. Caroline Govant. Several people claimed a ghost haunted her orchard and that her family kept a log of the sightings dating back almost one hundred years. Caroline's maiden name happened to be Miller. Kiki confirmed that Caroline was a direct descendant of John and Maggie Miller from the diary of wagon-train settlers. John and Maggie produced five offspring. Mary, who died very young from drowning in the river, and four boys who all lived into adulthood and sired children of their own. Only one of the boys stayed in Rio Linda, George Miller.

"Caroline is a direct descendant of George, the son that inherited the land and holdings of the Miller clan." That was as far into the history that Kiki rehashed for them.

As usual, Kiki dressed for the camera. Her hair was back to light brown and was tied into a high braided ponytail that exposed her tiny neck tattoo. Kiki wore a tight collegiate cashmere sweater from Brown University, pearls, and a shimmery skirt with a slit all the way up her thigh.

Janine took charge of the big boom microphone. It projected from a telescoping pole. Caroline spoke very softly, so Janine would need her headset to listen in and grabbed them from the box. The Wonder Woman sticker was replaced with a Captain Marvel sticker. Janine glanced at Steve.

"After those glowing hands in the tunnel, I thought Captain Marvel was more appropriate." He chuckled.

Janine nodded and wrapped them round her neck. She had no idea what he was talking about.

Caroline Govant allowed them to prop up the camera in her living room. She was a slight old woman with snow-white hair and an unusual array of wrinkles. Although she appeared very frail, she moved easily for a woman of her advanced years. Spritely even. Caroline sank into her seat and watched them with small beady eyes.

Kiki browsed the room studying the many framed photographs along the mantel and on a small table. Kiki directed Steve to snap pictures of some of the images. Janine stood silently, holding the boom microphone and watched Caroline Govant carefully observe Kiki Mellow.

"Is this you?" Kiki held a framed photo of a young, dark-haired girl standing in the orchard.

Caroline gave a slight nod.

The doctor walked in with a mid-size electromagnetic reader and set it on the floor. He returned from conducting a perimeter check of the house. There was a chair reserved for him and also one for Kiki. After a bit more browsing, Kiki sat settled next to Caroline and the doctor joined them. Ted gave Janine the signal and she adjusted the boom mic.

"Tell us about your first experience with the spirit," Kiki began the interview.

It took a moment for Janine to realize Caroline was speaking. She moved the boom mic closer and adjusted the gain. The woman's voice became more pronounced in her headset.

"About the time my father died," she said. "We have always known about the spirit in the orchard. She is said to be a long-lost Miller from the olden days. Mary Miller, the lone daughter of John Miller, the founder of the Miller General and the bank. The M.G. Bank still does business over on Fifth Street, but our family no longer owns it." Caroline's quiet voice was little more than a rasp.

"Are you certain of her identity? Of who the spirit was in life?" Kiki asked.

"Positive." Caroline said. "Her father settled this land and is responsible for the orchard. Hers was the first life born in Rio Linda, and she helped plant some of those trees as a small child. We've always known about our Mary. Hers is a kindred spirit. She lingers to protects us from that other one."

"Which other spirit are you referring to?" the doctor asked.

"Why, I told you the other day." She widened her eyes at Kiki. "The one they call the River Girl. The one who preys on children."

"Yes, I remember," Kiki said gently. "We would like to record the story on camera from your lips."

"Oh my, yes, of course." Caroline nodded.

"Tell us, in your own words, how do you know of Mary?" Kiki asked.

"She watches over us," Caroline said. "My grandfather reminded us of that fact every year. We must not fear Mary. She's one of us, a Miller, and protects our bloodline. She keeps the dark spirit from seeking the Miller clan. The main road is named for her, you know. Marysville Boulevard was the first road paved in town. Rio Linda was very nearly called Marysville."

"The dark spirit being the River Girl ghost?"

"Yes."

"Have you seen the river ghost?"

"No, not her. I told you, Mary keeps her away from us Millers. We are protected."

"Of course," Kiki said. "And have you seen Mary?"

"Many times," Caroline said. "She wanders the orchard at night. Not everyone that goes out there will see her, but some do. Mostly family, and also those that…"

"And who else?" Kiki asked. "Who else can see her?"

"Those that need to." Caroline Govant shifted in her chair so that her beady eyes bore directly into Janine. "You,

you would be able to see her." Her wrinkles increased with her grin.

Janine felt a chill run down her spine. She fumbled with the boom microphone and almost dropped it. The doctor jumped up and helped her steady the pole. She felt like a total idiot. Caroline's voice filtered into her headset.

"Oh, my word," the sound of the old woman's breath flowed into her ears.

"And why do you believe Janine would be able to see the spirit of Mary?" Kiki asked.

Janine got her footing back and took a firm grip of the boom microphone pole. She gave the doctor a very stern look. She hoped he realized that she was annoyed with him. What did he think, jumping up like that? He would not have done that last season. He would not have done that before last night. Do the others wonder why he ran to her rescue so quickly? The doctor gave her a little nod then stepped back toward his seat. She was instantly upset at herself for giving him that stern look. When he glanced back toward her, she offered him a little smile and watched his eyes soften again.

"She could have been the last one," Caroline Govant stared at Janine.

"The last one? What does that mean?" Kiki asked.

"I don't know what it means," Caroline mumbled. "Mary said that to me a long time ago."

"Do you know who Janine is? Do you know Janine?" Kiki asked.

"I believe she is Martha's granddaughter." Caroline smiled at Janine. "That is right, isn't it? I haven't spoken to Martha in ages, but you are the granddaughter who used to play with the river spirit, aren't you? You and Martha have the same doe-shaped brown eyes. You two look alike."

Ted swiveled the camera and trained it on Janine. Janine relaxed the boom microphone. She glanced each at Kiki, the doctor, Steve, and then Caroline. Did they plan this? No, at first Steve had told her she wasn't needed. Janine made her voice as neutral as possible.

"Yes, I'm Janine. Martha is my gram." She nodded to Caroline.

A few moments passed as she shook a very cold, fragile hand. Then Janine hoisted the boom microphone again. She glanced at Kiki and hoped she'd get the hint to continue.

"Tell us," Kiki asked, "when exactly did Mary say that to you? That she, Janine, was the last one? Did she say this directly to you?"

"Yes. Yes," Caroline said. "She revealed it in the orchard ages ago, after Henry told me about the artwork. That's a sign of seeing the river spirit, you know, making artwork of her. I went to Martha right away and she got very upset. I believe Martha eventually sent her granddaughters away, after she realized the truth."

Kiki leaned forward and crossed her legs. She gave the camera a spectacular view of one whole leg as it slipped from the slit in her skirt. Kiki teased the camera as often as she flirted with men.

"And when was the last time you spoke to Martha. Was it recently? Did you discuss this story, or anything about either the river ghost or the spirit of Mary Miller?"

"Oh no," Caroline said. "Martha refuses to speak with me since the day I shared what Mary said. She was livid. Martha does not like to hear anything I have to say about Mary. She refuses to listen anymore."

"I see." Kiki straightened up and uncrossed her legs. "At this time, would you consent to having Doctor McNally hypnotize you? We find that under hypnosis, the details of an experience are much more vivid. We would like to take you back to one of your past encounters with the ghost of Mary Miller."

Caroline consented and Doctor McNally moved forward. He reached under his vest and pulled out his silver pen. Janine closed her eyes as his hypnotic voice spoke to Caroline Govant. His instructions filtered into her headset and she reached up to take them off. She noticed Steve watching her. She gave a slight nod to let him know she was fine. Janine turned her attention back to the doctor and Caroline Govant. She moved the boom microphone closer when it was clear the old woman was under.

"Tell us about Mary." Kiki asked, "What does she look like?"

"Mary looks like me," Caroline answered, "me as a girl. Only, she plaits her hair in a single strand and has freckles across her nose. But we could be twins, her and I, that's what everyone says. The first time I saw her, it was like looking into a mirror and wondering at my new freckles."

"How does it feel when you see Mary?"

"It feels wonderful. She does not tarry long. She does not waste words. At times, she only nods. She roams the orchard, always. Sometimes she watches from very far away."

"Can you repeat anything the spirit of Mary has said?"

"She assures me that am safe. She presses me to ensure the others heed the dictum."

"The what?" Kiki whispered, looking to Ian. He shook his head.

Caroline continued, "She said that Martha's granddaughter could be the last one." Caroline became silent.

"Did she say anything else?" Kiki asked.

"Nothing. She does not waste words." Caroline's voice dropped to a very low volume.

"What do you think she meant by, *the last one?*" Kiki asked.

"I do not know," barely a whisper.

"I'd better bring her back," the doctor said out loud. "Okay, Caroline, I'm going to count back from ten. When I get to one, you are going to wake up. You will have a total recollection of our discussion and will feel very refreshed.

Ten, nine, eight, seven, six, five, four, three, two, one." Ian held Caroline's hand. "Hello there. How do you feel?"

"I feel fine," she smiled with a face full of wrinkles.

"I have one final question," Kiki said.

"Yes, yes. What can I tell you?"

"Why are you speaking about the spirit now? It's my understanding that you stopped talking about this spirit a long time ago. That you refused to speak about any of it and once admitted it was a fabricated folk tale. Is that true? Is your orchard haunted, or is it a folk tale? Tell me. What's compelling you to spin this old ghost story again?"

Caroline visibly shrank into her chair. She was just a little old lady with snow-white hair and small dark eyes wearing way too much jewelry and two sweaters on a hot day. Would Caroline Govant invent a ghost story? If so, why? There didn't appear to be a reason in the world for Caroline to dream up a ghost for her orchard. Caroline turned her stone-cold eyes on Janine for a very long moment before facing Kiki.

"It's no folk tale," her voice was strong, angry. "I am the last Miller to accept and interact with the spirit of Mary and the responsibility hangs heavy on my shoulders. I didn't push the ghost on the younger generation because people now treat it like crazy talk. Things are not the way they once were. I speak to you now because the ghost must not be ignored."

Serious black eyes turned back to Janine.

"Somebody needs to accept her message and be responsible. I pass the responsibility to you. Whether you like it or not, you are a part of it."

Ted and Steve drove the van directly to Henry Webber's house while Kiki, Ian, and Janine took the truck back to Gram's. Kiki insisted on changing clothes for the next interview. Janine drove and Kiki sat in the middle of the bench seat between them. It wasn't a tight squeeze, so it irked Janine to see Kiki's bare leg pressed against Ian. Is she goading me, Janine wondered?

"So then," Kiki asked. "Was she faking it? Being under?"

"No eye flutter, no softening of facial muscles. I'd bet yes. She's a faker," Ian said.

That old woman was faking hypnosis? Janine had no idea she had been faking. No wonder they cut that session short. Why would she do that? More lying? She noticed Kiki reach up to pat Ian's forearm.

"What was that other thing she said?" Kiki asked him. "I think I missed it."

"She said dictum," Janine interjected sharply. "You know, like a pronouncement or something."

"Makes sense." Ian nodded.

"Speaking of pronouncements." Kiki's green eyes seemed irritated as they glanced briefly at Ian. "I hope nobody makes any pronouncements anytime soon."

"What are you trying to say?" Janine glared at Kiki.

"Not a thing," Kiki said sweetly. "Just being the voice of reason here. We need to focus on this job and not get distracted. We are putting together a ghost story, an original ghost story. There's something going on in this town and we need to be on high alert. Aware. Evidently, Caroline Govant believes that you are a part of it."

The drive was short and they soon pulled into Gram's driveway. Ian let Kiki out and she ran into the house to change. Janine glanced at Ian and he took her hand.

"Don't worry about her," he said, but looked a little concerned.

Kiki changed into jeans, the red cowboy boots and a tight vintage concert T-shirt. Had she really gone to a Duran Duran concert? Her hair flowed loose and wavy from her released braid. Janine could see that Kiki touched up her makeup and wore shimmery clear lip gloss. Good grief, did she take off her bra? Janine's cell phone chimed with a text from Carlos.

Kiki going on an 80s date? Followed by a winking emoji. That put her back in a good mood.

Kiki climbed into the truck and sat between them again. She took out a handwritten, folded piece of paper with directions. It was another short drive. Henry Webber lived three doors down from the Old Rio Linda Bar.

Steve and Ted already had the camera on a tripod in the small living area of Henry Webber's house. Henry was not a housekeeper. Steve quickly moved around, tidying up. Janine jumped in to help him. She gave Henry Webber a nod, but he just scowled at her.

His entire demeanor changed when Kiki Mellow walked in. He broke into a gigantic grin as he took in Kiki's appearance. He eagerly stepped forward to shake her hand. For an older man, he certainly could turn on the charm. His interest in Kiki Mellow did not seem grandfatherly in the least. His behavior was very close to being creepy.

"It is nice to see you again, Miss Mellow," he said gently. Henry guided Kiki to the chair he reserved for her and helped her settle into it. "Would you like a refreshment? A Pepsi Cola? I have beer. I bought some of that brown ale you liked. It's in the cooler."

"How very sweet," Kiki gushed. "But let's get that drink after the interview. I get a little nervous and need to be on my toes."

"Of course, of course." Henry reassured her, patting her knee. "Don't you worry at all. I'm sure we'll do just fine."

Ted waved Janine over to take the boom microphone again, then he gave Kiki a ten second signal. The doctor stood behind Janine, far out of camera shot. He carried a thermal-panger, taking readings, but Janine could tell he was just milling about. Janine tried to tune him out. His nearness distracted her. She tried to concentrated on Kiki and Henry Webber. Janine got unnerved at how Henry Webber openly leered at Kiki. His eyes seemed fixated on Kiki's tight concert T-shirt and Kiki didn't seem to care at all.

"We are here with Mr. Henry Webber of Rio Linda, California," Kiki spoke to the camera. "Mr. Webber is a direct descendant of a family who braved the Oregon-California trail in the early 1800s and settled this fertile valley just north of Sacramento. Tell us, Mr. Webber, are the stories of a haunted river relatively new, or are they as old as the town?"

"As we discussed the other day, Miss Mellow, the ghost story is as old as the town."

"Can you give us a little background on the ghost story from your perspective?"

"Well, as everyone well knows, the bend in the Rio Linda River can become a very dangerous place at certain times of the year. When the snow melt begins, the river runs deep and quick. At our bend, there are natural rock layers with crevices that feet, legs, and arms get stuck in during a fast current, a cold current. Bodies have gotten trapped underneath a small ledge. It's always been that way. Worse since farmers built the levies and redirected more water to the main channel. They did it to keep the intermittent creeks dry."

Kiki fluttered her eye lashes at Henry Webber and urged him on. He grinned at her.

"So, there are drownings. Of course, there are. People pay no mind to the warnings and take their little ones to cool off from the heat. Mainly out of towners these days, but most every year, we get drownings. It's a shame. This is well recorded information, as you no doubt discovered, since the beginning of our town. The stories go back generations. Kids are lured into the river to drown. Lured by the little river girl. She's named after the river, you know. Linda is her name. I suspect people don't want to blame kids for misbehaving when they've drowned. They'd rather blame it on a ghost. So, the ghost became a real thing around here."

"Have you ever seen the River Girl Ghost?" Kiki asked.

"I'm not sure what I saw." Henry's eyes darkened.

"Do you believe you may have seen the ghost?" Kiki asked.

Henry closed his eyes, "No. But I think I saw someone see her. Or rather, someone who thought they saw her. Or people thought she saw the ghost."

"Tell us about that."

"It was back in '71, a couple of years before the big railyard explosion. I was a young man back from my year in Nam. I come home. This house is my family home. My ma was still quite young back then. She always had my little kin, nieces and nephews, my cousin's kids running around in the summer. She always warned them to stay away from that river. She feared what people said about that ghost, that if you see the girl at the river, you are supposed to drown in the river. When I came back, she asked me to keep a look out and keep the kids away from the river. Kids love swimming in the river in the summer. It gets very hot here. They were always asking to go. Always sneaking away."

He rubbed his furrowed forehead, "I took the boys, Jim and Todd. Then little Lara wanted to go, so, I took her out too. Didn't think no harm. The river was mild. That spot at the bend, the churches will go out and do the summer baptism on that shore. It's not always dangerous."

Henry rubbed his freshly shaved chin, "I heard all the stories when I was a kid. The river ghost wanted you to drown and so on, and so forth. I was scared to go near the bend when I was a kid, but not after coming back, grown up from a war. A little ghost story wasn't going to scare me. It seemed ridiculous, my ma still trying to scare me about that. A person shouldn't be afraid of anything that isn't real, right? I didn't want to feed the nonsense."

Kiki nodded her head, "That's understandable."

"But then I saw Lara talking to herself," Henry Webber said. "Out at the river, she was talking to herself. Said she had a new friend. I watched her standing there and she was talking to the air. Never saw nothing like that in a normal girl."

"She had an imaginary friend?" Kiki asked.

Henry nodded, "She drew pictures, beautiful pictures. I showed one to you. She gave it to me. She said it was all because of me that she met her friend and she was so thankful to me. That's when my mother realized that Lara was meant to…"

Henry Webber suddenly lost his composure and his head fell into his hands. For an old guy, his head full of hair was as thick as thieves. He sobbed softly into his rough, wrinkled hands. Kiki shimmied over and touched his shoulder in a comforting way. Henry Webber pulled himself together. He sat up and leaned toward Kiki.

"Sorry about that."

"That is quite all right," Kiki said, returning to her place.

"To get to it," Henry said sternly, "she drowned in the river not too long after that. Broke my mother's heart that she had to be the one. Couldn't live with it after it happened. And my cousin couldn't bear to stay on the farm either. He blamed me. When he left, we turned his land into the bottling company. The trees had all rotted anyway and it turned things around for us." He closed his eyes again.

"I'm sorry," Kiki said, "for your loss."

Henry nodded slowly.

"Believe whatever you want," he said. "I'm not sure why she went back to the river on her own, but I don't believe in no ghosts, not no more. She was just a strange little girl talking to herself, and there's a terrible undertow with traps at that river bend."

"Of course," Kiki said. "The undertow and rocks are well documented. There are plenty of warning signs posted near the river."

"They named Lara Lane after her. A little dead end over there off Front Street. Don't quite know why. A few crazy folks say she haunts the lane." He glanced at the doctor. "You met some of them at the bar. Don't believe a bit of it. I went out there plenty of times, and there ain't no ghost. It's all just a bunch of nonsense. Every bit of it is nonsense passed down from one crazy to the next."

Henry Webber turned around and glowered at Janine.

"Course, every old woman around here pushes those ghost stories and such. Don't think I didn't have to live it down all these years. Even so, a body can be fooled once in a bit. That picture. The one Martha had on her refrigerator, the one years ago that you drew, that was a bit like what Lara made. Martha was angry at me for saying it because, well, it was quite a coincidence. She was angry at me."

Janine didn't know how to respond. Kiki calmly reached over to take his hand.

"The doctor would like to try a little hypnosis," Kiki said. "It could help you remember more clearly and—"

"I remember things just fine," Henry Webber snapped. "I think I've said all I need to say." He suddenly stood up. "I'm gonna find my way to the old bar now, if you'd like to join me. You fellows are welcome to come along. Pack up now, or later, I don't care. We don't lock our doors around here. You're welcome to take your time. But no hypnosis, and no more talk about ghosts for me. Well, Miss Mellow, are you game for that drink?"

Henry Webber held out his arm. After a moment, Kiki took it and turned to give Steve and the doctor an urgent eye so they would tag along. Ted and Janine watched them leave in a group. Janine shrugged at Ted and they began to pack up the equipment.

The entire crew met after dinner on Bradley Road. Despite Henry Webber poo-pooing the notion, they decided to investigate four streets named for drowning victims. Kiki narrowed down which streets after carefully vetting all of them.

"I chose roads named for kids documented as drowning victims who also left artwork of the ghost," Kiki told the crew. "Not real streets at all, just little stretches of road. Maybe one or two blocks at most. The street-naming system in Rio Linda mainly followed letters and numbers. But when a short, secondary street was created, the Miller family insisted they use the name of a child who died in the river. Of course, Marysville Boulevard is extremely long, which we know is named for Mary Miller, and…"

"Hold on there," Steve stopped her. "Let's get the camera rolling. Storytelling looks much better with the backdrop of ghost-hunting. Tell it again with Ted filming." Steve jumped back into the van.

The doctor lugged his big EMF box onto the back of the F-150 tailgate. He hooked it to a portable tablet monitor. He stood up and slipped into his white lab coat. As usual, Janine, Carlos, and Ted wore their purple coveralls. Ted carried the big camera on his shoulder and filmed Kiki retelling the research and justification for the streets she selected. Kiki wore a black beret on her dark-brown hair and a mustard-yellow scarf tied loosely around her neck. Her black leather boots reached to her knees and covered the bottom of her tight fit jeans.

Carlos leaned toward Janine and whispered, "If she's dressed for the French revolution, she's missing the French accent."

Janine cracked a grin and lightly punched his arm. The doctor waved them to the tailgate of the F-150. His monitor showed four indicators blinking, all potential feed-ins for his EMF box.

"These streets are short enough that I'm hoping to do a canvass cover for low-frequency electromagnetic pulses. Four channels, set to twenty, thirty, forty, and fifty hertz." The doctor adjusted the gain on his box as he spoke, "I'll need someone to set up the receiver-transmitters at four spots down the street. I'm going to monitor here so I can make minor adjustments for frequency."

"I can set them up," Janine agreed quickly, "and record thermal changes as I go."

The doctor smiled at her. "That sounds fantastic. We'll communicate on com-2. Carlos, you should trail along with Kiki so she has someone to talk to."

"Je ne parle pas francais, amigo," Carlos said in a terrible fake accent.

"What?" Ian blinked quickly.

"I'll take the ion meter and point it where she might sense something," Carlos amended. "No problem."

"Yes. Yes, excellent." The doctor stood up as Ted came around with the big camera.

"What's the set up here, Doc?" Ted asked as he filmed.

Janine and Carlos strolled away as the doctor explained the EMF box and the canvas cover he hoped to create. Carlos headed toward Kiki while Janine strolled down the block with the small receiver-transmitters. They resembled mini old-fashioned transistor radios. She reached into her sleeve pocket to reset her headset for sound from com-2. Their audio headsets operated on four communication frequencies. They could select "all" to hear all four frequencies or tune into one specific frequency on their headset. They could set their microphone to "hot" so everything they said would be transmitted or use the push to talk button to transmit intermittent messages. Kiki always used a clip-on microphone set to "hot" on com-1 and she never wore a headset. The doctor transmitted voice on com-2, occasionally using hot mic. The rest of them only used push to talk. Steve transmitted on com-4, and Ted, Carlos, and Janine shared com-3. Janine often set her speakers to "all" but decided to tune out everyone but the doctor, so set her headset to receive on com-2.

She didn't say it out loud, but she was tired of hearing Kiki prattle on about the Rio Linda ghost. Mostly, she was still a bit miffed at Kiki's earlier attitude in the truck. Could there really a rivalry for the doctor's attention on her horizon?

About a fourth of the way down the street, she flipped the switch on one of the transmitters and checked the blinking power light. She flipped open the small pudgy antenna and set it on the curb. Janine hit her push to talk button.

"Got that, Doc?"

"Affirmative."

Janine checked her thermal-panger. It registered a stable air temperature. She continued down the street activating the final three transmitters and checking the temperature. She peered down the three blocks to where the truck and van were parked. Steve shut off the van lamps, so the night turned dark. But with the moon, Janine could clearly see Kiki, Carlos, and Ted strolling toward her on the street.

When would she be able to tell Ian about Sammy? She should do it soon. It was the main thing she was most ashamed of, rejecting her own baby. She recalled sitting with Sammy as they worked out a puzzle during the visit for Sammy's birthday. She had not seen Sammy since a brief glimpse after giving birth. That small red baby had miraculously morphed into the cutest little girl. Sammy giggled constantly, and offered "tips" and advice sounding exactly like Juliana. *Look at the colors, find a nice shape*, Sammy repeated Juliana's words. *You can do it. You can find the right one.* Janine remembered her sister coaching her with the same words many years ago.

"This is just a toy," Sammy suddenly announced, pointing at the puzzle pieces. Then she pointed upward, swirling her finger and said quite seriously, "All of this is the real puzzle."

"What? What's the real puzzle?" Janine had been very surprised, mesmerized.

"Life, Aunt Jaja, life is the real puzzle." Sammy nodded very seriously. Then she melted into her giggly face again and tossed her tangled hair over her shoulder.

Janine smiled at the memory and felt her heart swell up. She was going to get a second chance with Sammy. Maybe even with everything. The doctor's voice interrupted her thoughts,

"I got a nice canvas cover over the street showing nothing of interest so far."

Janine focused back on the street. The quiet of being tuned only to Ian was nice. Kiki appeared to be rambling. Carlos laughed and said something that made Kiki pause and stare at him. Janine chuckled to herself, wondering what he said. She could tell Carlos was amused even from that distance in the dark. She watched the trio move slowly toward her. The doctor spoke through the headset again.

"Not a flicker," he said, obviously responding to a question Janine could not hear. His voice continued, "I agree, we should move on to Lara Lane."

At that point, Kiki, Ted, and Carlos reached her end of the little dead-end road. Kiki turned to talk into the camera as Carlos wandered over to stand next to Janine.

"Did you hear all that?" He pulled one of his speakers off an ear. Janine did the same thing.

"I'm just tuned into the doctor," she told him. "Did something happen?"

He shook his head slowly. "Just Kiki saying this street was a waste of time in ten different ways."

Janine nodded. "I better pick up the transmitters."

"Oh, oh," Carlos touched his headset. "Steve's calling in a plan. You and me to ride with the doctor in the truck and everyone else in the van."

"Janine…" the doctor's voice came over her headset. She hit her press to talk button.

"I'll just pick up the transmitters on the walk back toward you."

"Brilliant," he said. "I'm shutting it all down here."

The crew repeated the same basic procedures on the next three streets. Jesse Street, Lara Lane, and Eloise Way were all very short, paved, dead-end roads. Kiki had higher hopes for those sites, as several people reported ghostly encounters on them, especially Eloise Way. Seven separate witnesses reported a specter on that small stretch of pavement. Unfortunately, zero indications of ghostly activity occurred for *Spectral Analysis*.

Kiki and Carlos completed walking down Eloise Way at around 3:30 a.m. The crew was disappointed and very tired. Kiki shook her head, clearly upset.

"I felt absolutely nothing, anywhere," she said. "Not one trace of any ghostly essence."

"We're going to run back to the hotel and download the footage," Steve told them. "Maybe sleep well into the afternoon. I'm beat. We'll meet at the orchard tomorrow night."

"Okay." The doctor nodded. "Don't forget the mag coil. It's in the purple case if I get tied up. We'll just head back to Gram's in the truck and see you tomorrow evening."

Gram stood anxiously on the porch waiting for them to arrive. She seemed very excited, or agitated. Janine jumped out of the truck to see what could cause her to hop about like that in the small hours of the day.

"I found something," Gram told them, "In an old book that was falling apart. A Bible with the cover torn half off. All wrapped together and buckled with a thin leather belt."

"What, what is it?" Janine asked.

"Pages," Gram said. "Pages from the diary."

"What diary?" Kiki asked, but her eyes were wide open and she already knew.

"The wagon-train diary!" Gram exclaimed. "The pages that were torn out of the wagon-train diary. I read them. I can't believe it. You have to see them. They're in the living room on the coffee table. Oh, my lord, Janine, you will never guess about Great-Great-Grandpa Christopher Williams. And that's not the most startling part."

Chapter 7
The Lost Pages

These are ledger entries made by Helen Williams. They were found hidden in a split, cracked, leather-back Bible in a cardboard box stashed in Ms. Martha Williams Stinger's attic.

September 28, 1839 Henceforth, daily entries into this ledger diary will be made by others than Mr. Stanley Hansen, as his untimely demise rendered his soul to Christ. It is now my duty to document the travails of our group. I have not the will, nor been given the leave, to recount the exact details and will simply list the restful souls that have left our numbers in the meadow of blood, fire, and death.

A long list of names followed, starting with Stanley Hansen.

September 30, 1939- The men altered our campsite. Mikael and Niels Stauch found a copse of trees that acts as a natural shelter from the elements. This, and the canvas cover from two lost wagons, make a cozy enclosure in which to shelter us from the elements. The men erected walls of fallen timber to block against winds. A sigh of relief fell over us, as this little circle of trees keeps us warmer than imagined. It is a beautiful camp, as we have sight of the deep blue lake that mirrors the blue skies. Resting was, perhaps, the better choice after all. Several of the wounded are still alive, including my friend Irene Lumen and the man, Oscar Hansen. *Gustoff Webber's burnt hand has begun to green, and we fear it may need to come off. *We lost an ox in the night. Frederick blamed the Webber boy, Rolf, for not securing the animal well and Peter Webber banished the boy from a hot dinner, though no one of us had much of a dinner as the cooking pots are lost. Dinner consisted of meager rabbit meat, on stakes, in the fire. *Nickolas tells me, we will stay until Oscar Hansen passes or one week of time. As the ground hardens, it is not clear how we will properly care for the dead when the time comes.

October 1, 1839-Added to the list of dead, three poor souls. *Gustoff, aged 14 years, had his hand taken. It was a messy and tragic affair, but had to be done as his hand was clearly in decay. The ax was dull from use and Gustoff was not spared a bit of it. His father, Peter, blamed Frederick. But Fred was right, my Nicholas told him. Without the hand, he could survive. If he did not lose it quick, it would rot through the rest of him in due time. What we wouldn't give for Irene

Lumen to wake and tell us of her knowledge of healing. *Mary Webber found a way to bake bread in the ground, as all our cookware had been stolen away by the Indians. The young girl dug out a hole and covered it with a plank of wood. Everyone marveled at her ingenuity and warm biscuits. This is good news, as we had little thoughts on how to usefully prepare the flour without a pot or a pan. *The younger men were successful in their hunt and brought in two rabbits.

October 3- *Frederick Stauch lost his leg. Upon sight, it was further gone than the Webber boy's hand. I watched his wife, Gretel, hush him and whisper sharply to "take it like a man" when she believed no one else could hear. She used his own words against him as those were the very words he growled to Gustoff two days prior. Never have I admired her more. *Needless to say, we will reside by our lake for the ill to recover enough to travel. As the weather has turned to blue skies, we are enjoying our leisure. Our outlook is brightening. *The children, Christopher, George, and Linda laughed today. It was so startling a sound I was caught off guard. I take it as an omen of good times to come. *Oscar Hansen woke and spoke briefly. He asked of Gretel Stauch, and myself, to fetch his sons. I was dumbstruck, but Gretel just hushed him softly and said his boys were busy with the oxen and would be by presently. I was surprised at how easily the minister's wife told false. But it was the Christian thing to do. Oscar then eased back into a quiet slumber.

October 4, 1839- *Irene Lumen, wife of Finn, passed in the night. She went quietly, may she rest in peace. A beautiful girl who leaves a lone son. Meg will adopt him and we will gather around him closely. *Ingrid shows no sign that she realizes her cousin has died. Hers is a death as well. One in a living body. *Bears have been sighted in the mountains. Grant and Mikael Stauch happened upon a lair not a quarter mile from our camp. It is hibernation time for the beasts and Frederick says they should pose us no harm. The younger men were instructed to steer clear of all caves. Better to set traps for our meager meat instead of poking in the brush. *Frederick Stauch has insisted he be kept abreast of all discussions, even though he fights fatigue and blood loss. *Thank the Lord for our crystal blue lake. The purity of the water seems to have lent a healing touch to us all. Niels Stauch, and the two small boys Christopher and George, keep our barrels to the brim. Meg has done well by young George. She has kept her word and cuddles both youngsters each night, singing softly to them. *Mary Webber has made good use of her earthen oven, and the young wife Susan Miller has taken to helping forge tasty biscuits, though rough. It is Mary's biscuits that keep our bellies from growling. *The traps the young men have set yield barely a prize, split amongst us, amounts to nearly nothing. *Grant asked to take the rifle, but was set aside by Frederick. After the Indian event, it seems there is scant but 8 tried left. There was a bit of a disagreement about that with the men. When queried,

Nicholas just shook his head. *Several in the party have taken ill with a bit of the runs and fever.

October 5, 1839- The ink runs low, and the men have given leave for the upkeep of this ledger to one a week. I am to write sparingly. It seems my entries are too mired in women's concerns, though I know not where they lay. Signed, Helen Williams.

October 16, year of our Lord 1839, F. Stauch. The upkeep of this journal has been reassigned for the purpose of clarity and brevity. Oscar Hansen rests under a small stone pile. The ground is frozen and our efforts impotent for a proper burial. Our stores are down. The women overused supplies against better instruction. We lost another ox in the night through the delinquency of the Webbers.

October 23, the year of our Lord 1839, F. Stauch. A most unexpected storm delays our departure. The legions of snow drifts stand ten feet high. Mr. Webber is put on probation. His uncivilized tongue and acrimonious ways have made him an unpleasant companion. I have a mind to banish him from our mass, but not for the young girl, Mary, falling ill. Against my better judgement, I allowed the Webbers to stay. But only on the condition that the senior Mr. Webber aborts his tongue in all matters of decision.

October 30, the year of our Lord 1839, F. Stauch. The storm continues. Our stores shrink to alarming lows. Grant Williams and John Miller press to use the rifle for "game" of which they mean bear. They would bring wrath on us all for their young man's folly. We have not seen a live animal, except our lone ox, for days. The illness spreading through our mass has made travel impossible with but one wagon, even if the storm subsides.

November 5, the year of our Lord 1839, F. Stauch. My beloved son, Mikael Ernest Stauch, has gone to his maker. He used the fourth of our last lead bullets. Why? It is the woman he married, her family was not truly godly. Now his own brother has fallen to her bewitching. Where is the community outrage?

December 2, 1839- The care and burden of this ledger diary is entrusted to my care once more, Helen Williams. I will not attempt to recapture the many heartaches transpired. Failing this, Mr. Stauch kept scant records. My husband, Nicholas Williams, is now our leading voice on this miserable, freezing mountaintop and has tasked the book to my keeping. He keeps close counsel to Mr. Webber, as they are men still of able of mind and body. *We are starving. We are dying. We will surely perish if the tides do not change on our fortunes. In this past week, we have lost Gretel Stauch, Mary Webber, and my dear, dear grandson, little Christopher, among many others. Meg has taken to a grave illness which has protected her from the loss of her babe. She is delirious with fever, as is my son Ethan. Myself and Sue Miller tend to the infirm, with little George Lumen frantically watching over Meggie. He has taken to calling her mama, and she has called him Christopher more than once in her delirium. *Gustoff and John Miller toil day to night scavenging for wood. *Nicholas, Peter Webber, and Grant hunt the hillside for food and keep watch. Their traps yield nothing. Something dragged off the ox, Millie Mae, last week.

December 7, 1839- Peter Webber survived a bear attack, but two others did not. The men took the rifle and the last of the pellets to find meat. They went into the bear lair, as there was no other living creature to be found. The pellets did little more than anger the sleeping giant, and Peter Webber took a claw to the shoulder while Tom Merk and Carl Handling are gone. I pray Peter's wound does not infect. Daily, we melt the snow as the edges of the lake has frozen. John Miller is tireless in this task, as he knows well it is keeping our friends alive.

December 13, 1839- The last of our flour is used. We now have only a meager supply of coffee and sugar. I fear the sugar will be gone before three days. It is all I have to feed the sick. A cold sugar water mix, two teaspoons each day. The rest of us have taken to chewing pieces of the leather strap Frederick Stauch uses to fasten his Bible. It was hard to put that strap in my mouth at the first, but now I want it more and more. Our days are surely numbered. Each morning, I expect to find more of our numbers passed.

December 16, 1839- It is now clear that Frederick Stauch should have banished Peter Webber. He is a Godless man. Mr. Webber returned from a break in the storm after checking the traps. Grant asked if there was anything, dead or alive, to be found, and Mr. Webber fixed my eyes and said that the snow did preserve our dead friends well. He laughed as he took a knife to the leather cover of Frederick's Bible. He laughed as he chewed the good book until he started raining tears. When Nicholas returned, neither Grant nor I had the words to tell him why Peter Webber was crying in the corner. Nicholas crashed to the bed, exhausted and suffering a terrible cold. I fear it is turning to fever.

December 18, 1839- We have been four days without food of any kind. The last of the ill will die soon. I fear the young Stauch girl, Linda, has gone already, though no one dares to tell me and I resist adding her to the list to make it true. Webber has taken to Bible quotes. He is finally mad, I fear. I no longer have the strength to care for the infirm. This may be my last entry into this ledger journal. May God forgive us our sins and pride. This is our punishment. Whoever may find this, know that our fate is deserved for not standing against the devil when we had the chance.

December 21, 1839- It is the darkest day of the year, but there is light! Grant and Peter Webber found meat! They returned day before yesterday night with a catch and made a crude stew prepared in a wooden pot heated with rocks from the fire. They have nursed us all. I look around and see only Grant and Peter moving about, and also the child, Linda. She is alive! The child's sweet laughter woke me from a stupor. That and the food. Praise the Lord.

December 22, 1839- The infirm are making a grand recovery. The children are rays of light and Linda's giggling is a salve to our souls. The new trap Peter and Grant have set is our salvation. No rabbit, Grant tells me. He is unable to identify the animal they captured. It was mutilated before they recovered it. It spreads fear that the bear is shadowing our camp. I fear when Grant goes out again, but also hunger for the meat he brings. The rifle no longer has issue and lays useless.

December 24, 1839- The devil dwells in our house. Our fates are now destined for hell. Mine own son has damned us. Grant confessed to his father, and his father to me— There are no traps. Just the preserved flesh our dearly departed.

That is the final entry from the pages torn out of the ledger diary.

Chapter 8

Séance

Steve parked the *Spectral Analysis* van on the extended section of Marysville Road alongside the almond orchard. Caroline Govant granted them permission to investigate the southeast quad of her neglected trees, the area most frequently haunted by the spirit of Mary Miller. The doctor and Carlos already disappeared into the dark to set up motion sensors and a subsonic audio recorder in the hopes of picking up ghostly vibrations. Janine hung back at the house to give Kiki more time to get ready. Kiki had a very good feeling about the orchard.

Janine and Kiki arrived in Gram's F-150 dressed for the shoot. Janine wore her purple spectral suit, red vest, and clumpy boots. Kiki came dressed like a sexy ninja without a mask. She wore black stretch pants, a form-fitting long-sleeve shirt and dark gloves. Her hair was hidden inside a black watch cap, and the small tattoo on the back of her neck was exposed. The tattoo resembled a Celtic knot. Carlos strolled over and chuckled at her. Kiki winked at him.

"Hey there, kid." Carlos flashed his dimpled smirk at Janine. "Is Kiki planning to rob a bank later?"

Janine cracked a little grin.

"Don't worry about the coil antennae." Carlos joked. "We hung it in a tree, over there. Just give it a wide berth. Unless you need another jump start or something."

"Funny." Janine pocketed an audio recorder and the silver thermal-panger.

She glanced toward the doctor. He went mysteriously missing after reading the torn-out pages of the diary. Did he go to the hotel to download data all day? His head was down fiddling with his large electromagnetic receiver box.

"The doctor's been a bit quiet," Carlos said. "He's worried about something."

I'll bet, Janine thought. *Probably thinking about the over-the-top family secrets his new girlfriend has. Just the icing on the cake to her over-the-top personal past. Damaged goods. Ruined.* And she hasn't even told him about Sammy yet.

The doctor stood up. He moved hesitantly toward her, glancing into the overgrown trees. The past year's almond husks lay on the ground covering the dirt. They crunched when the doctor stepped on them. *Does he think they moved to fast? Is he regretting things?* Kiki strolled over as well.

"We are going to go down this center, what do you call this, row or aisle, of trees?" He pointed with a hand. "I'm thinking, maybe Carlos out front with Kiki, then me and Janine."

"Janine should be out front with me," Kiki countered. "You two guys can trail behind. Caroline insisted Janine will be able to see this spirit. Us two girls need to be out front. I'm also tired of Carlos and his doty wisecracks." She fluttered lovely, green eyes at Carlos and he grinned innocently in return.

"That could work," the doctor agreed flatly. "I'm just thinking…" His voice trailed off. He tapped Janine's arm and urged her follow him. They walked to the edge of the tree line. "I'm a little concerned about you," Ian looked worried. "Are you okay with going into the orchard tonight? We're already picking up loads of activity on the EM box and there is nothing out here to create it. It's not like those dead-end streets. I don't know why I'm anxious." He glanced at Kiki. "She says things feel extremely real here, you know. There's a big possibility you may see something and not expect to. She's very hyped, and she's had real experiences and knows—"

"Caroline told us that this spirit is friendly, so I have nothing to be afraid of," Janine said softly. Did he really think they would find an actual ghost in the trees? He knew Janine didn't really believe in ghosts. "You took off pretty quickly after the diary revelations."

Ian nodded. "I thought you'd want a little space with your gram. To talk about stuff."

"The Donner party had to do the same thing," Janine said. "They were just surviving."

"I meant about your great-great grandfather," Ian said. "For some people, a name doesn't matter. For others, it does quite a bit. Knowing who you are." He leaned in. "Are you upset?"

"Gram is still working that one out. It doesn't matter to me."

His hand slipped to the small of her back as he leaned in slowly.

"I don't care about Kiki's voice of reason," he whispered. "I'm concerned with all this stuff we're learning. Crikes, you are in deep with this story. I feel like we're being pushy and I don't want you to feel compromised or something. Are we invading your privacy? Or, am I being an arse here? I feel like I should be protecting you from something. From the show? From this story? Something else? And I don't want you to feel faint again. Authentic paranormal events can make people faint."

"I'm fine," she said, relieved. "Everything's good. This is my job and it's just show business, Ian. Don't worry about the history, the ghost story. That stuff doesn't worry me."

"Hey, you two, let's huddle up." Kiki rounded them up.

They made their semicircle on the outside edge of almond trees. Ted pointed his camera and boom microphone in their direction. They passed around new clip-on microphones, one for each of them. They were foregoing their headsets to test out the new system.

"This might give us better audio," Ted told her. "I bought a complete set, five total clip-ons. All the better to get your impressions, or anything. It'll free up your heads nicely, and everyone will be on hot mic so we won't miss any wisecracks from Carlos. I got a console in the van to manage individual input. We can have nice audio of everyone this way."

"A close-up audio of Janine fainting would be nice," Carlos joked.

"Where am I going to put this?" Janine finally just clipped it onto her vest.

Kiki turned to her. "Add as much commentary as you like. Be an active part of the conversation. If you feel anything, don't hold back. Like, I'm feeling something already. Electricity in the air. What about you?"

Janine raised her eyebrows.

"If anyone's interested, I'm feeling a slight breeze," Carlos said.

"Okay, all right. Camera's set," Ted said. "Lights, and go."

The *Spectral Analysis* crew slowly wandered the orchard while discussing their interview with Caroline Govant. Kiki described a young Caroline, as seen in the photographs displayed in her sitting room. Kiki and the doctor spoke of founding town members John and Maggie Miller. They recited tales from the diary of the wagon train and the reported loss of the elder Millers during the Indian attack.

Carlos and Janine remained quiet, taking thermal readings and pointing their meters in different directions. The rising, waning, gibbous moon cast enough light to see very clearly. Aside from an owl, there was not much activity in the endless rows of crooked trees.

As the night ticked past midnight, they stopped strolling and formed a small circle. Kiki pulled a thick black candle from her ninja backpack. She lit the three wicks and placed it on the ground. A thin swirl of smoke with a spicy scent emanated from the candle. Kiki directed Janine and Carlos to free themselves of their gadgets so they could hold hands and complete a connected circle.

"Let's close our eyes and center ourselves," Kiki instructed. "Take some cleansing breaths."

Hand in hand they stood quietly, breathing. A very slight breeze rustled the leaves overhead. In the far distance, the sound of the river emerged from the darkness. The air felt clean, fresh, and charged as Kiki mentioned earlier. The temperature was very pleasant, not too warm or cold. Ian's large hand engulfed hers. His skin felt dry, rough, and warm. His thumb gently caressed her wrist and she wondered what would happen next with them. Her heart beat a little faster as she recalled Ian's protective impulse. She squeezed his hand gently as warmth flooded her system.

Kiki abruptly broke the silence, "*We seek yon souls of near to there, we call on you to us appear, reveal yourself for us to see, so I command, so mote it be.*"

Janine heard that rhyme many times from Kiki. Out of habit, she said it silently to herself as Kiki repeated it.

"*We seek yon souls of near to there, we call on you to us appear, reveal yourself for us to see, so I command, so mote it be. Mary, Mary, can you hear us? Please, Mary, reveal yourself to us.*"

An obnoxious odor wafted by.

"Anyone else smell skunk?" Carlos gasped.

"Yes," Janine said. Was the air getting cooler?

"Shh," Kiki hushed softly. "Listen for her. *Mary, I can feel you drawing near. Mary, is that you?* Do you feel it? Does anyone feel this?"

"I feel a bit of a chill," the doctor said. A cold patch of air definitely descended on them.

Janine released Carlos's hand to reach for the thermal-panger, to ensure the record function was set. At that same moment, she opened her eyes instinctively.

An angry young girl stood front and center with wisps of the candle smoke swirling around her head. Janine froze stiff with fright. Deep, dark eyes drilled into her. An eerie sensation seeped into her head and a creepy tingle snaked up her arms before sinking into her pours. Irritation, vexation, and displeasure radiated from the girl. This spirit did not have kindred feelings for Janine.

The cold that descended in the air found its way around Janine's torso and wrapped her like a tight blanket. The girl reached out with a wavering hand. Her flesh wasn't flesh at all; it appeared more like a smoky, amorphous liquid. *Was it smoke from the candle?* Smoke swirled and clung to the girl, filling in the colors of her dress. Her sketchy arms continued to stretch out. Janine instinctively shrank from her, pulse thumping rapidly. Those wavering fingers inched closer and closer and Janine felt certain the girl wanted to reach into her chest and grab her heart.

No! Janine screamed inside her head. The thermal-panger slipped from her fingers and seemed to fall in slow motion. The young girl glared at her. The girl became motionless with clasped hands in front of her body. Her head titled shyly downward but her piercing eyes remained fixed on Janine. A raspy voice floated into Janine's ear but the ghostly lips did not move. *Heed the dictum.* It was not a suggestion.

The thermal-panger hit the ground with a loud thump! Janine jumped and yelped at the same time. The apparition grinned wickedly before swiftly dissipating in a swirl of smoke. The three candle flames fluttered out one after the other. Everyone moved at once.

The cold air lingered and Janine scooped up the thermal-panger with a racing heart. She watched the numbers rapidly rise. She took deep breaths to tap down her panic. *Just calm down, just calm down,* she told herself. She felt dizzy and tried to steady herself. Carlos and the doctor turned their heads right and left, looking all around. Ted with the camera slowly circled the group and then focused in on Janine. Kiki stared at her.

"Are you okay?" Ian put a supportive hand on her arm. He asked, "What happened? You shouted."

"The temperature plunged twelve degrees in two seconds," Janine reported evenly. "It's recovering now."

"Did you see something?" Kiki's green eyes glowed in the dark.

Janine nodded, silently watching the flash of numbers slowly tick upward on the thermal-panger gage. The hair on the back of her neck still stood on end. She felt like something might be lurking in the trees, watching them, and did not want to glance outside their small circle. She drew in another slow breath in an attempt to quiet her thundering pulse. *Was she losing her mind?*

Kiki turned to Ted. "Your eyes were open the whole time. Did you see anything?"

"I saw the candle go out," he said.

"Did anyone else see something?" Kiki asked. No one did. "Me neither, my eyes were closed," she gave. "But I heard her very clearly. I heard her speak directly into my ear."

Janine met Kiki's green eyes.

"What did you hear?"

"She said, *find the dictum*. Did you hear it too?"

Unbelievable. Maybe she wasn't losing her mind after all. Janine nodded.

"I heard, *heed the dictum.*"

"Let's regroup." Kiki held out her hands. "I can feel traces of her lingering around us."

Using a flip lighter, the doctor relit the candle and they reformed a linked circle. The doctor gripped her hand tightly now. Janine kept her eyes open this time, paranoid of closing them. Kiki called to the spirit. She urged Janine to call to the spirit but Janine's heart wasn't in it. Instead, she silently begged the spirit to stay away. *Stay away!*

They did not have a second encounter that evening, but they left pretty excited anyway. Janine finally verbalized exactly what she witnessed as they reached the flood lights near the van. No flashing lights or wavy, blurry air, but a full apparition. As she described the ghost on camera, their fervent jubilation could hardly be kept in check. Kiki said full apparitions were a very rare event. Usually, they only appeared to serve an important purpose, or, if called upon by a very talented witch, she smiled.

They drove to the hotel to debrief. Gram's house felt way too close for comfort and they didn't want to disturb her with their excitement. Plus, Steve's heavy software was located in the main computer in his hotel suite. Steve was eager to download and view the footage as soon as possible, in slow motion, backward, and zoomed in to catch anything they might have missed. He believed he saw something in the video. Ted, Steve, and the doctor zipped off quickly in the van, while Janine, Kiki, and Carlos followed in Gram's bright red truck.

Instead of the hotel back in Old Town, they booked rooms at the Holiday Inn Express, right off freeway 99 between downtown Sacramento and the airport. Janine gave the Malabar Restaurant a glimpse as they cruised past it and into the hotel parking lot. Carlos steered the truck around to the back lot, closer to the door they should use.

Steve sat at his computer console in the living room part of the suite working away. An open bottle of Glenmorangie single malt rested on the center coffee table and tumblers were filled. Everyone smacked Janine on the back as if seeing a ghost made her some sort of hero. Kiki took a tumbler for herself and offered one to Janine.

"No thanks," Janine said.

Janine picked up the thermal-panger to review the readings over the recorded half hour of their encounter. She watched the temperature numbers suddenly plunge, then rise. Impossible. She knew it wasn't a malfunction, or a false reading, because every person in that circle felt the cold patch that descended on them. Quite like that eerie, unexplainable encounter in Providence that spooked her. Something odd happened.

"If you see anything on video, anything at all, call me over," Kiki said from her comfortable spot on the sofa. Kiki removed her black watch cap and shook out her thick hair.

Carlos moved near Steve to watch the slowed-down action on the monitor. Kiki sipped her second whisky more leisurely, studying Janine with her striking green eyes.

"You're quite certain she said *heed the dictum* and not *find the dictum?*"

"The voice was pretty clear," Janine softly replied. "Heed the dictum."

"Was the spirit next to you, or was she next to me? I felt her essence beside me, like she was whispering in my ear." Kiki closed her eyes, remembering. "Did she whisper in your ear too? Where was she in relation to the circle?"

"The apparition stood right in front of me," Janine said, "in the center of the circle, over the candle. Her eyes held mine as she said *heed the dictum* in a very entreating way."

Kiki appeared to be thinking, "Interesting."

"What's interesting?" the doctor asked. "What did you notice?"

"The voice I heard," Kiki said. "The voice that spoke very distinctly for me too, whispered *find the dictum* directly into my ear. I felt her right next to me, her breath on my skin. Watch the clip, I actually turned sideways to look for her."

"Was that when Janine let out that, shelloch?" Ian asked. "When the temperature dropped."

"Yes." Kiki turned to Janine. "Was that shout before or after you saw her?"

"Pretty much at the same moment. Or very immediately after she spoke." Janine felt embarrassed about that yelp.

"That is interesting," Ian said. "Can we assume it was the same spirit in two places at once? Or, maybe she moved very quickly."

Kiki narrowed her eyes and sipped her drink. She stretched out and nestled further into the sofa cushions, getting comfortable.

"She said, *find the dictum*. There was a long *mm* on the end. Whew, I needed this after tonight. I was ready to faint out there. What about you, Janine, do you feel faint? Thanks for getting the eighteen-year batch." She blew a flirtatious kiss toward Steve.

Janine closed her eyes. Did she hear the same voice? What was the voice like for her?

"Mine had an *mm* too," Janine said quietly, thinking about the ghost. And she did feel weak, and in the orchard, she had felt woozy.

"Yo!" Steve pointed dramatically to the screen shot on the monitor where an odd glow hovered just above the candle. He put his finger on it. Janine could see her own startled face on the edge of the screen. Ted's camera had been focused on Kiki, but Janine's profile was clearly visible on the monitor. Her eyes were wide with terror as they stared at the light.

"Couldn't be a reflection on the lens. We used a low-contrasting polarized filter and Janine's staring right at it," Steve said. "The light pops up right at the time the temperature descends and ends when Janine shouts out and jumps. I knew I saw something. Too much of a coincidence?"

They watched the clip, a mere eight seconds, over and over. They watched Janine reach into her pocket and open her eyes as the mystery light appeared. Then, her doe-shaped eyes grew wide with fright as the light pulsed and the thermal-panger fell from her fingers. The light disappeared, along with the candle flames, as the loud thump of her panger hit the ground. Janine imagined that light hovered right about where the girl's ghostly heart would be.

"I heard a little whistling in my ear?" Carlos said. "Do you think the ghost said something to each of us? Maybe, there's a lot of stuff mixed into the tapes. I wonder if she said something to me?"

The doctor poured himself a generous portion of whisky and recharged Kiki's glass. He lounged cozily next to Kiki on the sofa, sinking comfortably into the cushions.

"She's very concerned about the dictum. She really wants us to find that dictum." He looked across the coffee table at Janine. "Or heed the dictum. Either way, we need to find out about that dictum."

"We need to go back to the orchard," Kiki enthusiastically declared, directing her attention at Ian. "We need to execute a proper séance. Maybe bring in the old girls, people with a strong connection to this place. Carol Miller believes that only certain people can see that spirit. We need to round up those people. There is a real spirit in that orchard and we've got a good shot at getting some real definitive, concrete evidence. That ghost wants to talk to somebody."

"You're right. We may already have the evidence." Ian grinned big at Kiki. They seemed positively giddy with each other. They clinked cups. "This is brilliant. Exactly what we always talked about. You should see the low frequency spikes around midnight. I'm going to check the peaks for the exact time against that little light in the video. I also need to cross-check the time on the ion detector. Apparently, a cascade of ionized oxygen moved in."

Kiki and Ian put their heads together and discussed some of the plans that drove the idea for *Spectral Analysis*. Janine watched them giggle and high five like two kids. Kiki's beautiful green eyes fell so easily on Ian and he returned her attention without reserve. Kiki poured them another round and Janine realized that the friendship between the doctor and Kiki ran deep. It was something very old, older than *Spectral Analysis*.

Carlos joined them at the coffee table and poured himself another whisky, laughing. When he set the bottle down, Janine snatched it up and poured herself one. Why not, she no longer took medication. The three of them gave her a startled look as she gulped it down. She coughed a little as she gave Ian McNally a bit of a glare.

"Whoa there, girl. Take it easy." Carlos chuckled. "I thought you didn't drink hard liquor."

"I've had a few here and there," she said simply and poured another generous helping.

"Seeing a ghost? I guess you earned it," Carlos broke out the dimples. "Hey guys, I understand what a dumb-dick is, but what the heck is a dick-dumb? Do people even use words like that? I admit it, I'm dim. But what is it?"

"Some kind of a short, little—oh, stop it, Carlos." Janine could tell he was on the verge of another rude comment. Janine put her empty glass down with a clunk. "Look, everyone, I'm going home. To Gram's house. I need to get some sleep and I'm done thinking about the ghost for the night. Does anyone want a ride?" Janine glanced at Kiki and the doctor.

The doctor's brow creased with a concerned expression, like he was trying to solve a problem. He stood up and looked around, like he still had a hundred things to do, such as check electromagnetic wave peaks against the mystery light. It would be very unusual for the doctor to leave after such an exciting, eventful investigation. Ian moved toward her. He didn't want her to go, but could see that she didn't want to stay.

"It's late, maybe we should get you a room here. You had a big night."

"She can crash out in my room," Carlos told them. "I'm not moved in yet." He indicated his suitcase on the floor next to the door.

Kiki remained lounged on the sofa like a cat, an amused expression remained fixed on her feline face as she studied their interaction. She said,

"I'm going to wait and see what else is on that video. I couldn't sleep now if you paid me. Go on, Janine. We'll Uber back when we're done."

"It's very late," Ian said again. "We really shouldn't be driving, and there are still a few things for me to do here. Go sleep in Carlos's room for now. It's right next door, right? Don't go driving back when you're tired and wired up like this. We'll take the truck back later in the morning. Also, the whisky, you don't want to drive after all that. And there's an extra bed in here for Carlos, if he needs it. He won't mind."

"That's right, no problem," Carlos gave her his plastic key card. "I'll probably fall asleep on Steve's sofa anyway. I always do."

Ian stood in the doorway of the suite to watch that she made it into the next room. Janine went inside the small room and sat on the bed, agitated and angry. She could hear murmuring through the wall. It sounded more like a party than anything else, laughing and celebrating. Why not? They were hunting paranormal activity and seemed to find just what they were looking for. Janine stayed for about three minutes before she left for Gram's house.

She found Gram, the night owl, shifting through the papers scattered in the rustic sitting room. The extra diary pages still lay on the coffee table atop the tattered Bible. Fresh photo copies of those pages lay on the very top of the pile. Gram lit up and beckoned Janine to sit next to her.

"I saw the ghost of Mary Miller in the orchard," Janine whispered. Gram nodded and patted her knee. Maybe she didn't hear. "Are you looking for more stuff?" Janine asked.

"There's nothing else here," Gram told her. "Just old bills and such. Doctor McNally asked for copies of these pages at the tear marks. See how they were torn out? He wants the museum to see if the tear patterns match the real diary." She picked up the battered Bible. "Do you think these are bite marks on this Bible?"

"He wants proof that they come from the same diary. Standard procedure, always backing things up. It usually leads to a lot of disappointment." She turned the old Bible upside down. The marks did look like bite marks; bites from someone with very uneven teeth. She handed the Bible back to Gram.

"Are you upset about Christopher Williams?" Janine asked softly.

Gram closed her eyes, then started to laugh, which turned into a fit of giggles.

"Oh my, oh my." Gram raised her hand for a moment, trying to catch her breath. Her eyes twinkled in amusement. "I tell you, I'm completely relieved."

"Relieved?" Janine was confused.

"Oh yes. I am very relieved," Gram said. "And a little ashamed."

"It isn't your fault, Gram."

"Oh no, no, you don't know what I mean." Gram patted her on the knee again. "I've been so upset at my mother. Thank God she was long passed by the time I did that DNA test. We called the company and they assured me everything was correct. Even did it a second time. I wanted to confront her, as you can imagine, but thank goodness Ma had passed away. Twenty-three and Me, how I hated those genealogy people. Leone bought me the test a couple of years ago, you know my third cousin Leone. Kiki traced her great-greats to Ethan and Elisabeth Williams." Gram chuckled as she shuffled papers and tidied up. "I swear, Leone keeps asking if I did the test and I keep saying that I didn't. She wants to share results. But not after what happened with Bertha."

"What happened with Bertha? Who's Bertha?" Janine asked.

"You know Bertha. That old gal who used to give you pennies. You called her Bertie. Leone gave Bertha a DNA test too. Leone pretty much made DNA her theme that Christmas. Everyone got one."

Janine recalled Bertha and Leone. Bertha was short and wide while Leone was tall and thin. They both went to the same Lutheran Church on Third Street with Gram. Janine imagined that they were occasionally part of the card gals too. She remembers the raucous gossip sessions when Gram's gals came to the River House. Juliana and Janine used to listen-in late at night and get quite scandalized.

"Bertha is a Williams from Christopher's side, like us, and her tests were all wrong. Leone never lets her forget that her mother was a cheating whore. Oh, she's slick about it, but I've seen her get a dig in here or there. Oh, she's backed off a bit, now that poor Bertha is not doing too well these days. Cancer."

"Gram, you took a DNA test?"

"Yep," she said. "And I really believed my mother cheated on my wonderful father. For two whole years, I believed I was the illegitimate love child of a man my mother kept a secret to her grave! It about tortured my heart thinking my mother was so thoughtless. I wanted to know who my real father was. Oh, my goodness, the anger I directed at my mother's memory!"

"Gram, what did the test show?"

"Obviously that I'm not remotely related to Leone. She was nowhere in my relatives list. Kind of another nice surprise, ha ha. Anyway, she's a true Williams and I am not. None of us are. Christopher Williams was really a Lumen. He was really George Lumen, must be. There were Lumens all over my DNA report."

"And you're not upset about that?"

"No. I'm just happy I finally have it resolved. My DNA test was not a mix-up, nor did my mother— My DNA doesn't remotely match Leone because Christopher Williams was really George Lumen, not because my mother committed the sin of adultery and kept it a secret my entire life. My poor father is my own real father and thank goodness he was never cheated on. Oh, thank goodness! I am so sorry I thought poorly of my own mother! She's likely laughing at me from heaven instead of crying from hell."

Janine didn't know what to say. They hugged and tidied up a bit more.

"Don't let me forget, I need to tell Bertha about George Lumen. I need to do it right away because she is not going to make it. She is really sitting there at the end of it all. She can go to her grave happy now." Gram closed her eyes and took a deep breath. She reached out and took Janine's face between her hands. She said, "I love you, girl."

Gram went upstairs to sleep. Janine shut off all the lights and followed her lead. But Janine couldn't sleep. The reason she left the hotel was to be alone to think. She needed to reexamine the orchard events in private. The crew had buzzed with excitement about their ghostly encounter, so thrilled they were celebrating. Janine should be excited with them, but she couldn't help feeling dread. Did she really see a little girl out there? Did she really hear a voice? *Heed the dictum.* What in the world did it mean? And the serious, ireful eyes on the girl, as if Janine had done something wrong, terribly wrong, but what? Did she break or go against the dictum, whatever the dictum was? The image of that girl, standing for only a few seconds, was worrisome. Was she going crazy, or was it conceivable that she actual saw a spirit?

The old people, Caroline and Henry, came to mind. She had a nagging feeling those two knew something more than they were letting on.

Kiki and Ian laughing together popped into her head, another nice image to keep her awake. A sour feeling welled up inside her. What was it? Jealousy? She never should have left them at the hotel drinking whisky together, flirtatious Kiki sitting cozily with Ian. Kiki with her extra-long lashes and beautiful, jade-green eyes and touchy-feely hands… And wasn't there an undercurrent of attraction between them? The show capitalized on it. *They looked good together.* Janine did not put it past Kiki to try something with the doctor, if for no other reasons than to establish the pecking order, as Carlos would say. Crap! Loads of men found Kiki Mellow totally irresistible with her voluptuous curves and startling eyes. All Kiki had to do was glance at a guy and he'd come running to do her bidding. She's seen that play out plenty of times.

Janine opened her gripe journal, a habit Doctor Crisper encouraged during her time at the hospital. A journal makes a very good listener. It can help a person work through important issues. She pushed away the image of Kiki and Ian to jot down a description of the ghost. Dark hair in a single braid resting over her shoulder. Dark round eyes, most likely brown or even black. A simple dress with a wide sash in the middle, most likely tied in the back. Protruding ears that stuck straight out, but small, without lobes. Red and pouty lips. Red cheeks, a patch of red completely covered each cheek as if the child spent time in the cold wind. *Or the cold water?* Mary came off a little sinister and her beady eyes seemed serious and angry. She was older than five, but definitely below ten years of age. Not a kindred spirit; Janine underlined it with a heavy pen.

Janine threw the journal aside and turned out the light. She started running through her checklist of things to be grateful for, another tip from Doctor Crisper. Janine needed to do something to block out the image of Kiki and Ian laughing on that sofa. She resisted reaching for her phone to call him. What if she caught him doing something she didn't want to know about? Just because her heart had open up on that mountain doesn't mean that his did too. And wasn't Janine classically terrible at reading men and their intentions?

She kept running through her checklist hoping she would fall asleep, but she couldn't and went downstairs to find something warm to drink. She found Gram awake at the kitchen nook table with coffee and the Sacramento Bee. Janine filled a mug and took her regular seat next to Gram. The gleam streaming in the window told her it was just prior to dawn. The quiet house told her Ian and Kiki were still out.

"You don't need much sleep," Janine said.

"I've never been a good sleeper," Gram said. "What about you?"

Janine shrugged. "You didn't ask me about the ghost."

Gram glanced over her reading spectacles.

"I know all about that ghost, Janine. You aren't going to tell me something I don't already know. I just don't like to talk about it much."

"Then you have seen her?"

"Oh, yes. Lots of us have seen her, long ago. I don't like to admit it, and probably won't ever again, so don't tell your friends. But Bertha and I used to sneak into that orchard, you know. We were much more friendly with the Govants back then, with Caroline even. But seeing that ghost led to our falling out, you know. Some folks think the Miller family is cursed. Lots of us stayed away from the Millers because of that ghost. They have funny ideas about their ghost."

"Don't you want to know what the ghost said to me?" Janine asked.

Gram just stared blankly at her.

"Heed the dictum," Janine said. "She told me to heed the dictum. What does that mean?"

Gram eyes darkened. Was that recognition? Fear?

"Do you know what the dictum is, Gram?"

Gram shifted her gaze to her coffee.

"No," Gram said firmly and stood up, "I'll think I'll go back to bed after all."

Janine thought that was a good idea. No one else was in the house yet. That meant everyone was still at the hotel, sleeping, planning, reviewing things, or whatever.

Janine woke from the sound of Gram speaking loudly, almost yelling. She flew down the staircase to see what was amiss. Gram stood with her back to Janine, speaking harshly into the landline telephone. It was attached to the wall with an extremely long cord. Gram slammed the phone down and turned to face Janine.

"That was Caroline Govant," Gram said calmly. Gram passed Janine a folded piece of paper. "This note was left on the coffee table for you. Kiki is upstairs, asleep."

"What was that all about? On the phone."

"Caroline has rummaged through her old rubbish for your group," Gram conveyed. "Apparently, she has some important finds for you guys. Has some story wrote about Mary Miller after she died."

"Like a short story?"

"I couldn't say. She insisted that I wake the lot of you. Convinced of her importance, as always," Gram chortled. "Do you think she'll be invited to the séance tonight? Kiki told me when she came in at noon. I'm sure Caroline will insist on it. She's very bossy. Kiki asked me to find someone else, a real Williams. I gotta go and find Leone. Oh now, look, there's some fresh lemonade in the cooler. I'm gonna run out to shop a bit. I want a nice shawl for tonight, for the camera, and I need to go get Leone and make sure she doesn't back out of this thing. I gave my assurances to Kiki. Imagine, a séance with Kiki Mellow!"

"Gram?"

"No, no, go on," Gram said as she fluttered out of the house.

Janine opened the folded note. It was from Ian. He wrote in all lowercase letters. It said, *missed you at the hotel—don't you know a ruse when you see one?* He was suddenly standing behind her on the last step of the stairs. His steady gaze was bright and cheerful.

"Got my note then?"

He strode quickly across the room. He gave off a fresh and clean aroma from a shower and shave. His skin still felt cool from the water. Somehow, he managed to wring out the sour feelings she had with a deep kiss.

"I can't believe you ran off like that. After I cleverly secured a nice private room for us."

He was not holding back. They were standing in the middle of the living room in full sight of the stairs and the front door. Yet, Janine did not push him away. She instead pulled him in. She realized she had been upset because she got jealous the night before. What had made her so jealous? Talking intimately with another woman, Kiki. Very ridiculous. She knew the crew drank whisky and stayed up late after an exciting shoot.

"Are you all right then? I was pretty worried when I found you flew the coop. That was a pretty eventful night and I wanted to check in with you, privately, to make sure you were okay. From the sound of it, your gram is going to be gone a while." Ian whispered in her ear, "Want to run upstairs and discuss things?"

He continued kissing her as they moved toward the stairs. Janine grabbed his hand and led him to her room.

Ian rested a hand on the nape of her neck gently caressing her skin with his fingertips. He lay naked atop the covers while Janine had modestly wrapped her afterglow and scars underneath a sheet. Ian possessed a smooth, muscular back and shoulders, she noticed, but his chest was quite hairy. *He looks like James Sean Connery Bond lounging at the pool in that old movie her grandma loves.*

Ian finally filled Janine in on the plan. They were returning to the orchard at midnight in an attempt to reconnect with the spirit of Mary Miller. This time Kiki planned to have a more formal séance. The crew would set up cameras at the same location as the previous evening, but they'd stay completely out of the trees. Kiki and five select others would form the séance circle. Kiki hoped for a blood descendant of each settler from the Hansen wagon train: a Stauch, a Miller, a Williams, a Webber, and a Lumen if possible. Janine might be asked to sit in if they couldn't find one of each to participate.

"So, my gram and Leone. A Williams and a Lumen."

Ian snuggled close to her on the bed. His body radiated warmth. He whispered in her ear. "Also, Mrs. Govant, a Miller, and Henry Webber. Kiki is pretty sure she can talk him into just about anything."

"Am I the only one who found that creepy?" Janine asked. "Isn't he's like sixty or seventy or something. Kiki is a terrific actress. She actually looked interested."

"Kiki's not serious there." Ian shrugged at her inquiring eyes. "Did you know, she found some history between Henry Webber and Caroline Govant. Apparently, he was the much-younger man she corrupted for several years. It was quite a scandal back in the day. Everyone except Caroline and Henry talked about it. We're also looking to find an available Stauch. We're cross-checking names against a few of the interviews we did on Tuesday. We're pretty sure most people will jump at the chance to participate."

Janine found the gossip about Henry and Caroline surprising. That must be why she put them together in the back of her mind.

"Steve pushed for you in the séance, but Kiki nixed it. Said something about six being an optimum number, divisible by three. She is set on using local folks. She'd rather have your gram at this stage. She believes the spirit of Mary Miller was vexed with you and may not appear to you again. Carlos thinks Kiki is a wee jealous of the attention you're getting?"

His hand slipped under her sheet and slowly ran down the length of her bare back, causing her to shiver. She became aware of her large scar and wondered what it felt like to him. Did he find it repulsive? She tried to ignore her marks and thought about what he just said; Kiki sensed that the spirit of Mary Miller was unhappy with her. Janine had felt the same way.

"Gram certainly wants to participate in the séance," Janine said. His warm hand became extremely distracting as he massaged her lower back and buttocks. Her pulse lurched as she felt his hand going there. "I wouldn't want to take that away from her. And I am more comfortable as a background person. I'm actually relieved to be behind the camera. Is this our final segment? Tonight?"

"Actually, actors are coming in. There's going to be a little baptism reenactment at the river to introduce characters of the ghost story through drama. Next week, a whole other group is coming. Another camera, a film crew, and a screen writer. We need to have our ghost story flushed out completely by then, for the screen writer. This story keeps getting bigger and bigger."

She wriggled away from his distracting hand and he started caressing her neck with his lips instead. Well, that was even more distracting.

"I don't know how it's going to fit into a one-hour time slot," she managed a bit breathlessly.

"We are now shooting for a two-hour special, just on Rio Linda," Ian whispered. His hand came round and found her breasts, cupping them in a warm caress, pinching the tips harshly, then kissing them soothingly. His lips left a slow trail of fire over her chest and shoulders.

"What?" She lost track of the conversation.

"A feature," Ian told her softly. "There's going to be a little kickback for everyone who participates tonight, plus for the interviewees. Steve's got it all worked out. Mike Dunn flew in this morning, prepared to create a lot of paperwork."

Mike Dunn was the show's lawyer. He drew up contracts and releases as needed. Usually, he created generically worded documents for the doctor to use, but on occasion he did a little more. Sometimes he went on location to negotiate their working conditions. If Mike Dunn came out to California, it could only mean a larger production was brewing. Ian tugged at the sheet covering her.

"My bonnie lass, I'm afraid this needs to come completely off." His eyes were very dark blue and not at all compromising. He pulled the sheet from her legs and gathered her against him. Janine could not get enough of his strong broad chest and powerful arms and legs. He kissed her deeply before turning his attention to the nape of her neck. "Let me know right away if I'm being too demanding. I know this is a quick turnaround but I can't help myself. You are too irresistible. Will you be okay?"

She rolled up to straddle him. "I think I'll be okay," she said.

Leone and Gram both wore new bright knit shawls and sported freshly styled hair with matching manicures. Angie Minnihan, the redheaded smoker from the bar, loitered in the living room, holding an iced refreshment. Apparently, they traced her lineage to Niels and Ingrid Stauch. Angie wore a ton of jewelry, and bright-red lipstick. Janine wondered if Angie or Leone knew much about their ancestors or why they were asked to participate in the séance.

The *Spectral Analysis* lawyer, Mike Dunn, walked into Gram's house to meet the players just as Janine, Ian, and Carlos departed in the truck. They were heading out to the orchard to set up remote equipment. Ted parked the van in the same spot as the previous night. He set out small cameras, audio equipment, and two large spools of coated copper wire. A big box of Kiki's séance paraphernalia sat off to the side. Carlos picked up a folded piece of paper with Kiki's handwritten instructions for the layout she required.

"She's very specific about the size of the circle." Carlos displayed the drawn plan. "She wants the candles placed on the edges with a circle radius of 126 centimeters exactly. She underlined that number two times. There's to be a candle in front of each person and three candles in the middle." Carlos held up a little bag of flour. "We're supposed to draw stuff on the ground with this." He looked around. "Is there a measuring tape somewhere? Do you think she's really going to measure and see if the radius is 126 centimeters exactly?"

The doctor disappeared into the trees to place his electromagnetic receiver-transmitters and ion detectors. Each camera could be controlled by wireless communication, but Steve insisted on two hardwired in case of interference. That meant laying down an awful lot of copper between the almond trees. Janine spooled it out right away to be sure the cables were long enough. One regular camera and one infrared were hardwired and propped on tripods. She also spooled out wire for one audio receiver. She placed a short microphone stand in the large circle Carlos chalked with the flour.

"Don't step on my lines!" Carlos warned.

Janine set up two extra cameras on tripods that swiveled by remote control. She communicated through her headset to Ted at the van and he gave her input on positioning the cameras. When she completed the setup, she went over to see how Carlos faired with the chalked circle.

Carlos drew perfect circles with flour. He spaced six candles on the larger circle and placed a little pillow behind each candle. Three thick candles were placed at each foot of a large tripod in the center of the circle. A suspended cone-shaped aqua quartz stone pointed downward from the center of the tripod. It formed a pendulum. Kiki used it on a past show. Under the pendulum bob, a smaller circle was divided into thirds with a Celtic knot design. Carlos wrote out yes in one sector, no in another sector, and nothing in the last sector. He stood over his creation with a compass in his hands. He glanced up at Janine.

"She didn't specify true north or magnetic north in the note. Think it matters?"

Janine shrugged. "I'm sure they're not too far off anyway."

"Are you kidding? Kiki will ream me. She's gotten her panties in a wad about a lot less than this. Maybe, true north. I guess I can google the variation for here. Do you add or subtract variation? That point there, that's supposed to be pointing north."

"Just go with the compass." Janine checked her watch. "We're running low on time anyway. Isn't everyone supposed to be here in, like, fifty-five minutes?"

"Think we have enough time for a Starbucks run?"

"Yes!" Janine said. "I actually saw one in Rio Linda yesterday. It's just down Marysville Boulevard a bit, five minutes. Across from a gas station with a big cow on the roof." She laughed. "I got gas there. Let's take the truck." She paused to take another look at the circle under the pendulum. "Didn't you say that point should be pointing north? Why is it pointing southeast?"

"What do you mean?" Carlos said. "That's north." He pulled out the compass. "Look, north. See."

Sure enough, the compass needle agreed with his assessment of direction. Janine shook her head.

"Carlos. The sun rises over there, toward the mountains. That's not north. It's east!" She pointed. "Earlier it set over there, west." She pointed north. "That way is north. Plus, the farmer must have planted these trees in north to south rows. Seriously, that direction is north."

Carlos shook the compass. "Crap! This compass is crap."

Janine nodded. "Come on, let's fix this quick. I really want a hot latte for tonight."

Janine and Carlos returned with fancy coffee drinks for the crew. Ted and Steve sat in the van testing the remote-control sticks where images of Kiki and the doctor walking around the séance site flashed on the main monitor. Kiki plopped down on a pillow and the doctor walked out of the camera shot.

"Looks like Kiki's checking your setup. Did I tell you, you make very well-shaped circles, not eccentric in the least," Janine complimented him.

Carlos winked as he wrapped his headset around his neck. He pulled out the old army compass and dropped it between them on the console. They watched the needle swing and twitch a moment before it stopped.

"Seems to be pointing in the right direction now," Carlos moved the compass around.

"Weird," Janine said.

Steve glanced over with a questioning expression on his face. He drank his venti hot latte in practically one gulp. He pointed at Janine.

"You may have to sit in tonight," he told Janine. "Kiki said Henry Webber did not sound receptive to participating."

Oh no, she was looking forward to a carefree time sipping coffee and watching the action on video monitor. Janine dreaded the possibility of encountering the spirit of Mary Miller with those furious eyes again. Until the orchard, she never truly believed they ever encountered a real spirit. Deep down, she always believed a rational, plausible explanation could account for every experience. The reason she could be so cool, as Ian put it, was because she didn't believe any of the stories they wove. Not until she came face-to-face with that little girl standing in the orchard. Unlike the whisper at the river, Janine couldn't fathom how she might imagine the girl in the orchard

"Wait, who is that?" Carlos pointed down the dusty road. A ghostly figure of a man emerged from the darkness. He appeared very spooky. He wore a denim jacket and a baseball cap. His hands were buried deep in his pockets and he wore a terrible scowl.

"That's Henry Webber!" Janine brightened as the old man closed the distance to the van.

The flood lights soon flushed out his features and Steve stepped out of the van to greet him. At about that same moment, Kiki and the doctor exited the trees. They both perked up at the sight of Henry. From the short distance, Janine heard Kiki gushing happily at Henry and watched as she reached out to take his hand.

"Don't know why you want a nonbeliever for your thing," Henry's voice carried. Kiki pulled him off to the side and their voices muffled out.

Kiki led a formal séance in the first season and she was dressed very similarly. She wore a flowing outfit like a movie gypsy: big hoop earrings, large jeweled rings, and a heavy chained necklace. Her wrists and hands were adorned with metals and pure minerals. *Minerals help bring out the spirits*, she claimed. The large stones in her rings included a big chunk of holly blue agate and another of white topaz. The black obsidian stone in her necklace fended against dark energy.

Ian McNally wore a thick plaid work shirt and jeans. He leaned against a tree and accepted the now-cooled coffee Janine offered. He gave her an appreciative look. They stood about three feet apart smiling surreptitiously at each other and Janine felt her pulse start to pick up. She glanced away, resisting the urge to move in closer and kiss him, only to see the spot where they "parked" after their dinner date. The flood of that memory engulfed her and she stole another wistful peek at the doctor. Carlos noticed something. He looked from Janine and back to the doctor with a puzzled, concerned expression on his face. Great, Janine thought, now Carlos has cracked the code. Teasing soon to come.

A silver Toyota Sienna rental rolled up with Mike Dunn driving. From the front passenger door, a redheaded chattering Angie Minnihan popped out. Steve hurried to open the back slider door and assisted Leone and Gram, always the gentleman, he offered his hand to steady them. Caroline Govant emerged last, springing out quite energetically. Kiki beckoned the group to form a little circle and began chatting excitedly to them.

"Better run out and give Kiki a clip mic before she says too much," Ted passed her a new blue air case. "Not sure who should have them. I only got five clip mics in there. I'll set the audio to tape everything."

Janine lugged the case to the group and stopped next to the doctor on the periphery of the circle. Ian helped Janine open and manage the electronics. Janine passed Kiki a microphone and then proceeded to clip small microphones and transmitters onto the other participants. Gram beamed with excitement and Janine just smiled at her.

"I only have five clip-on mics," Janine said out loud. "So, someone—"

"I don't need one," Henry Webber said gruffly. "Not like I'm going to say anything for this thing. I'm just here on a favor to Miss Mellow. She said my presence is all she needs."

Kiki spoke gently and put a hand on his arm. "That's right, Henry. I just need your strength and your male energy. You don't need to say, or do, anything. Thank you so much for being here. We'll all feel safer with a strong male in the circle."

Henry cleared his throat and fidgeted. Janine noticed Caroline Govant smirk as she glanced at him from the corner of her wrinkled eyes.

Just prior to eleven thirty, Kiki led her chatty group into the overgrown orchard. Low-level stratus clouds rolled in to blanket the sky. They obscured the moon causing the night to take a sudden turn to darkness. Steve worried that it might be too dark for good images on the remote cameras. He asked if they left a flashlight at the séance circle and Carlos assured him there were at least two out there. The doctor leaned against the outside of the van and glanced toward the truck.

"I'm going to monitor the EM box and my ion detectors from the truck. The van looks like a tight squeeze. I'll take the tablet and link into your main feed." He pointed to the big monitor. "I'll stay on headset if you need me. I have a little weather box sending signals, so, maybe Janine could join me in the truck." He glanced fleetingly Janine.

"Maybe Ted can join you for this one," Steve suggested. "I think we should have Janine watching the main screen on the big monitor. Maybe she sees something the rest of us can't. I want her to sit next to the control box and listen to the condenser microphone. Ted isn't an idiot. He can watch for fluctuations on your box, right?"

"Thanks for the vote of confidence," Ted said. "Maybe I'll go sit in the rental with Mike and catch a nap."

"Ted will work," the doctor said to Steve. He glanced up once more before heading to the truck.

Mike Dunn waved at them and went to sit in the rental van. He walked and tapped on his cell phone the whole way. He obviously did not believe anything of consequence was going to happen in the orchard.

Janine, Carlos, and Steve crowded into the back of the van. Steve donned his headset and pulled out the joystick controls. He flipped the feed from camera three to the large monitor and they received a nice shot of Kiki leading the group around the séance circle. Steve appeared relieved with the picture. The ambient light proved plenty adequate for clear black-and-white footage. Steve glanced at Carlos.

"You going to be able to listen to five mics?"

Carlos gave him a thumbs up.

"Janine, you focus on the condenser microphone in the circle. As long as they face it, it should pick up everyone. I want you to focus on the main monitor too. If you see anything funny, anything at all. Just watch and listen. Tap the tag as much as you need."

The tag function for their audio and video bookmarked a spot for easy reference. Steve flipped open the main switch as she donned her headset. She could hear background talk, but the group was still too far away to pick out many words. She gave Steve a thumbs up. Steve settled into his captain's chair with a big bag of potato chips and ripped it open. He leaned back balancing the bag of chips on his stomach.

On the monitor, Kiki led each person to a specific spot in the circle and explained the importance of directional placement in a séance. Janine shot Carlos a look and he shrugged. He removed one speaker pad from his ear and Janine did the same. They often wore their headsets half off so they could converse privately.

"Thanks again for pointing that out. I almost muffed that one up," Carlos said.

Kiki encouraged everyone to sit and get comfortable. Her flowing sleeves shimmered in a pleasing way on the black-and-white screen. Kiki leaned into the circle and lit the three wide candles near the pendulum. The illumination brought out the warm tones of Kiki's skin. Kiki was definitely a magnet for the eyes.

"Now, we are going to light our personal candles." The condenser microphone clearly picked up Kiki's voice. "Before lighting your candle, inhale and exhale very slowly, at least three times. Take cleansing breaths. Each time you exhale, imagine letting go of your inhibitions. Visualize letting go. Mindfully release any tension you feel. I will light my candle first, then we will go around the circle, clockwise, each taking a turn. We will use this taper stick to pass the flame. There's no rush here. We want to calm ourselves and center our cores."

Janine found herself taking three deep cleansing breaths with them, a force of habit after ghost hunting with Kiki for a year. Janine noticed Carlos taking his breaths too. They exchanged glances and giggled. Janine turned her attention back to the monitor as Kiki cleared her throat. Kiki faced Gram.

"Light the taper with the flame from my candle and then light your own candle. When you are done, blow out the taper and pass it along. It doesn't have to be exact. Just remember to take deep, cleansing breaths and relax. Steady your heart." Kiki turned to smile at Henry. "Is everybody ready?"

"Yes, yes." Henry's head bobbed.

The others also verbalized consent. Kiki lit her candle and seemed to meditate quietly. In the soft black-and-white glow of the monitor, she appeared very young and innocent. Even without the green color, her eyes stuck out as glowing orbs, drawing in attention. Maybe Kiki really was part cat.

Her gypsy scarf and big hoop earrings gave her a whimsical look. Janine wondered for the first time about Kiki's real age. How old was she? Kiki always projected so much confidence that Janine imagined Kiki to be closer in age to her older sister, Juliana. Could she be in her thirties? How much of her projected confidence was real and how much of it was acting? Kiki certainly appeared much younger than Juliana, more like twenty-five, Janine's age. Janine realized she knew very little about Kiki Mellow.

Janine watched the taper move around the circle. Gram, then Angie, then Caroline, then Leone. Leone fumbled a bit. She lit the taper, seemed to remember she didn't breathe, so blew it out and apologized.

"Take your time." Kiki used a calming voice. "Breath in and then out, and let it go. It's fine. We're all friends here. Take as long as you need."

Leone's deep breaths were visibly obvious on the monitor. Gram's eyes widened as she watched Leone and it made Janine chuckle. Carlos nudged Janine, grinning enough for his dimples to show.

"Sounds like she's blowing up balloons."

Leone finally lit her candle and passed the taper to Henry. Henry quickly ignited his candle and passed the taper back to Kiki. He skipped his cleansing breaths but Kiki let it go without a word. Kiki set the taper down slowly and reached for Henry Webber's hand. Kiki smiled sweetly at the old man and he visibly softened. Kiki's movements were slow and deliberate, quite alluring, and Janine wondered again if Kiki was interested in that old man. Kiki then turned toward Gram and took her hand as well. Soon, the entire circle was connected. Three full minutes of silence passed.

"We seek yon souls of near to there. We call on you to us appear. Reveal yourself for us to see, so I command, so mote it be. We reach out to you, Mary Elsa Miller. We reach to you. We are listening for you. We desire to heed your warning. Please, come to us, Mary. Tell us what we should know." Kiki used a soothing, silky voice. Another long silence passed as the group sat motionless.

The obnoxious crunch of Steve's potato chips filled the van. Janine and Carlos both shot him looks, but he was oblivious with his eyes glued to the screen. Carlos opened his mouth to make a wisecrack, but froze. He slipped his second headphone speaker over his ear and adjusted the volume knobs for one of the microphones.

"She's whispering something," Carlos said softly. "Caroline Govant."

Janine adjusted the gain on the condenser microphone, then the volume. Nothing.

"She's saying, one each for redemption." The moment Carlos verbalized that phrase, Janine heard it softly through the condenser microphone. But it was Angie Minnihan who spoke. Angie repeated it. Then Angie joined by Caroline. Then joined by Leone and even Henry. Each of them repeated it in unison, *one each for redemption*, over and over again. Gram's eyes darted around the circle before settling on Kiki.

"What's going on?" Gram asked softly.

"Is this the spirit of Mary Miller," Kiki addressed the center of the circle. "Is this Mary speaking?"

The others stopped chanting. Angie ventured hesitantly, "She wanted us to repeat it."

"Did you hear her say this?"

"I felt compelled to repeat it," Angie told Kiki.

Muttering agreement permeated the circle.

"Let's center our energy," Kiki said. "Let's all breathe. Slowly."

Kiki called for another moment of silence and Steve crunched loudly on his chips again. Janine blocked him out by putting her headset over both ears. On the main monitor, Kiki leaned forward and touched the pendulum bob. Janine noticed Steve zoom in on the crystal with the second camera. The pasty white *yes* and *no* were both clearly visible against the dark ground. Kiki's voice filtered into her headset.

"Are you here, Mary Elsa Miller? Did you, Mary Miller, send the message *one of each for redemption*? Is that message from you?"

Kiki set the pendulum in motion with a tap of her finger. Everyone in the circle watched the bob move rhythmically back and forth along the line separating yes from no.

"Move the pendulum to yes, Mary Elsa Miller. Let us know that it is you."

No apparent change in the pendulum motion.

"Tell us, Mary, what is the dictum? Are those words the dictum?" Kiki asked.

Nothing.

"Is one each for redemption the dictum?"

Nothing.

"What's that?" Kiki asked "What are you trying to say?"

"Four-lend-day?" Gram said suddenly. "I feel like she might be trying to say, for Linda."

The pendulum suddenly shifted to swing in the northwest sector, to the yes.

"Is this Linda then? Is this Linda Stauch? Are we speaking to Linda Stauch?"

The pendulum came to an abrupt stop.

"I don't like this." Leone's voice?

"Don't break the circle," Kiki stressed sternly. Kiki rose on her knees and scanned around like a river otter. Janine heard static begin to build in her headset.

"It's getting cold," Angie declared, and Janine felt it getting cold inside the van too.

"This is a load of crap!" Henry snapped very loudly.

In the next second, Caroline Govant released Leone's hand. She slowly stood and pointed dramatically toward Kiki. The candles flames began to waver, as if a breeze passed over the circle. Caroline calmly uttered in her scratchy voice,

"She's standing right behind you."

Every other person on the monitor turned in unison to look toward Kiki. Kiki spun and rose in the same movement. Her gypsy outfit flowed beautifully around her as the candles extinguished one by one. For a brief moment, the image on the screen went pitch black and the audio remained silent. In the crackling static of Janine's headset, very faintly, a child's voice said, *she can be the last one.*

Someone in the darkness screeched.

Someone repeated, "Oh my god, oh my god, oh my god."

Henry Webber cursed loudly.

Suddenly, Kiki waved a bright flashlight.

Everyone began talking at once. Gram and Leone gathered together in a huddle. Someone had kicked over the pendulum and a few of the candles. Caroline stood near Kiki and appeared as calm as a statue. Angie fidgeted behind them. Henry Webber found another flashlight and aimed it toward the trees behind Kiki.

"Who is that?" he shouted. "Someone is out there." Henry glowered toward Caroline Govant and Kiki. "I'll not participate in this nonsense anymore!"

"I can hear someone running," Angie said to no one in particular.

"What's that back there?" Leone pointed in the opposite direction, south.

Henry Webber turned and trained his light on the south end of the orchard. From the third camera, they saw a form running toward the séance circle.

"It's only the doctor," Kiki told them.

A bright light filled the séance clearing, followed by Doctor McNally. He stopped beside Gram and Leone. He politely asked if everyone was brilliant while putting a hand out to calm each of the ladies. He took Kiki's hand and leaned toward her.

"Had a bit of a scare?" he asked in an upbeat tone.

Henry redirected his flashlight back toward the north sector of trees. Janine couldn't hear him clearly, but he spoke in very harsh tones. Ian gave his camp light to Gram and the women started moving away. Ian said something to Kiki and then turned to step closer to Henry Webber.

"We're done here," Kiki announced. "She's gone."

Kiki led the ladies away from the circle. The condenser microphone did not pick up the conversation as everyone moved further away. Janine watched the ladies exit the main camera shot. Ian remained with Henry Webber, staring into the trees. Ian turned toward the circle and Janine heard him say,

"You are welcome to go have a look. Take the flashlight."

Mike Dunn suddenly appeared on the screen. He dropped a camp light and a big box in the circle, all while staring down at his cell phone. He turned and followed Kiki and the women. The doctor reached down for the condenser microphone and Janine swept off her headset as he handled it.

On the monitor, she watched Henry Webber suddenly turn and follow the others out. Janine and Carlos silently watched the black and-white scene of the abandoned séance circle.

Ted popped open the back door of the van and reached for his large camera. He hoisted it on his shoulder and quickly turned toward the line of trees. Janine could see light from a flashlight flicker on the ground and then the gaggle emerged from the orchard. Carlos sighed and looked at Janine. They both turned to Steve. Steve was holding his empty bag of chips with a strange expression on his face.

"Did it get extremely cold in here?" he asked.

It did feel extremely cold in the van. Very cold. Janine glanced at the newly open door. The night air was warmer than the inside of the van. The three of them exchanged glances and then they all shrugged. Carlos started to stand.

"Round up the gear?" he asked.

"Let's go," she said.

Janine was anxious to head directly to Gram's house after the equipment was stowed in the van. She knew that Kiki, Mike Dunn, and Ted with his camera were there, but she wanted to make sure the old gal was okay. She stood next to the truck wondering where Ian disappeared to. The keys to the F-150 were in his pocket.

Carlos meandered over and stood beside her. He surveyed the stars and moon in the rapidly clearing sky.

"We're about to take the van back to the hotel," Carlos told her. "The doctor called on walkie-talkie and said he'd ride with you in the truck."

"Does he know I'm going to Gram's?" Janine asked.

"He does. He said he'd debrief and download later, or catch a ride with Mike if they were still there."

Janine nodded and sat on the tailgate of the truck. Carlos stood with his hands in his pockets, facing her. He rubbed the top of his thick mop head.

"I can wait with you if you'd like," he said.

"I'm not afraid of the dark, Carlos," Janine told him. "Go on."

"Are you sure?" Carlos crossed his arms in front of his chest, not budging.

"What is it?"

"What was going on with the doctor earlier? That did not look like your little crush thing. I'm concerned that he might cross a line. You need to be careful, kid. Look, Janine, I've seen him give a girl the wrong impression and then get too embarrassed to admit it. Keep that in mind. He can give a girl the wrong impression. That last girl, he didn't want to hurt her feelings and it went on for a month because he couldn't tell her he wasn't interested."

Wow. Was Carlos really giving her the big-brother talk? She knew, for all his wisecracks, Carlos cared about her. He treated her like a little sister. He once tried to set her up with one of his brothers. Carlos also knew more than most people about her past. Not as informed as Ian, but Carlos knew an old boyfriend stabbed her at least once. She gave Carlos a little push.

"Don't worry about me. I'm not getting the wrong impression," she said. "Just go."

Carlos hesitated before returning to the *Spectral Analysis* van. Janine watched them drive away, waving and beeping. When the van disappeared from sight, the night became very dark and quiet.

She can be the last one. Did she really hear that wispy voice? Why did Janine think of Sammy in that moment? She pictured Sammy running, with her long hair trailing behind her.

When she met on Sammy at her fourth birthday party, Janine nearly fell over from the impact of her emotions. Sammy was a sweet and funny girl and could already dribble a soccer ball well. Then, there were those precious moments when she echoed Juliana, trying to be serious, like with the puzzle. Sammy resembled Juliana's other children so closely she could easily pass as their real sibling, except she inherited Rick's pale eyes, eyes that induced complicated feelings in her. Eyes that haunted her dreams. Janine wondered if she would ever stop thinking of them as Rick's eyes. He was sure to get out of prison, sooner rather than later, on good behavior. Would he try to find Sammy?

Ian McNally snuck up and engulfed her in his arms. The heat of his embrace was a welcome change from the cold. He kissed her, holding her head in the palm of his hands. Her mind flashed to images of him in the hotel on the mountain and then during their afternoon tryst. The memories caused a delightful flash of heat in her groin. She didn't want to get too caught up in the moment and pushed him aside.

"I'm worried about Gram," she told him. "I need to go home and check on her."

"Sorry, of course." He opened the door for her and she slid onto the bench seat. "I saw Carlos talking to you. I hid in the trees so I could drive with you. I couldn't think up an excuse not to go back to the hotel in the van. What were you talking about, with Carlos?"

"He was worried you might be giving me the wrong impression," Janine told him.

"Really? Crikes. Has he caught on then?" He started the truck and leaned over to kiss her. "Maybe we should come out with it, us, I don't think anyone would be upset. Then, I could kiss you all the time and not have to duck in the trees in order to ride in the truck with you. I could hold your hand whenever I want." He put the truck in gear and they headed off to Gram's house.

Kiki and Gram lounged in the sitting room with a box full of manila folders between them. Gram did not appear upset in the least. She actually seemed a bit excited. Janine noticed the near empty bottle of wine on the coffee table.

Kiki and Gram relaxed on the sofa sipping and chatting like old girlfriends.

"Where is everybody?" Janine asked.

"You just missed them," Kiki said. "Mike Dunn is running Leone and Angie home. We dropped Caroline off before coming back here. That Caroline Govant is one cool cucumber. She gave us this box. Apparently, it has a story about Mary Miller in here somewhere. Some old relative wrote down her history or something. Caroline insists there's something very interesting in this box."

"Why don't you two join us for a glass of wine," Gram invited.

"I thought you'd be upset about the séance," Janine said. "You look fine."

"Oh, it was loads of fun." Gram sipped her wine.

"What exactly happened out there? Did you see something?" Janine asked.

"Not me," Gram said. "I didn't see a thing. I just heard a tiny whispered voice say, *for Linda*, but with a very funny accent, like Lind-day."

Kiki lounged on the sofa like a cat again.

"I didn't see anything either, but the air was very thick with her presence. Very thick. Caroline swears the spirit was standing right behind me. Ted got her on tape describing what she saw; definitely Mary and not Linda. Dark hair in a braid, very like your description last night. Angie and Leone both saw something like a child shape just before the candles went out, but they never really described anything. They basically concurred with everything Caroline said."

"There was a cluster of ions in the area, just like the other night, I'd almost venture to say plasma but that'd be crazy." Ian told them. "Webber looked troubled. What'd he have to say?"

Kiki and Gram exchanged a look.

"That man needs to learn his age." Gram chuckled.

Kiki shook her head sadly.

"He saw something, but wouldn't admit it. He accused me of, how did he put it? Cheap-ass shenanigans and in cahoots with Caroline for attention. I don't know what that means. Says we rigged the pendulum to move and had something to blow out the candles. That we pumped in the voice of a child with a hidden speaker. He even accused us of hiding a little girl in the trees to spook people. I'm certain Henry saw her, the spirit."

"He mentioned something like that in the orchard," Ian said. "I suggested he go and look for himself, but he seemed too petrified to go out there. He definitely saw something."

Kiki drained her wine and appeared a little shaken, "He started yelling at me, cursing. Mike had to forcefully escort him outside."

"Crikes." Ian rushed over to Kiki and gave her a comforting hug. He rubbed her shoulder a little, very concerned. "He felt that strongly? Are you okay?"

Kiki nodded.

"And," Gram added, "Kiki has lost her chance with him. There's no way he could be involved with such a deceitful woman."

That lightened the mood a bit, but Janine also felt bad for Henry Webber. She witnessed how Kiki flirted with the old man. What was it he said out there? Janine thought back. Had he been speaking to Caroline or to Kiki? What nonsense did he believe he was participating in?

Gram poured both Ian and Janine a little wine and they toasted the success of the séance. Kiki felt eager to see the film, but she wasn't in a mad rush to get back to the hotel. She wanted to shuffle through Caroline Govant's box of papers first.

"Let's split this up and see what we can find," Kiki suggested. Ian took his standard place in the easy chair. Janine plopped next to Gram on the settee while Kiki stretched out on the sofa. Her green cat eyes bore into Janine. "We didn't get a chance to talk out there," Kiki said. "Did anyone see anything strange on the monitor? Any hovering lights?"

"No, nothing that I noticed."

"Any weird things on audio? Anything other than us talking? I heard a few things. All very faint. I felt her mostly."

"No." She thought about that little wisp of a voice at the end. "Well, I heard a little static," Janine said. "If there's anything mixed in there, the guys will find it on playback. I tagged it." Janine didn't want to own up to the wispy voice she might have heard. She wondered if she only imagined it. In fact, she was sure she only imagined it.

"Poor Leone," Gram said. "She is fit to be tied. Believes we should all go to church on Sunday and ask forgiveness for participating in the séance. Says we stirred up dark, sleeping forces. Don't you worry. She'll be bragging about it for years to come. And I'll go with her on Sunday. Which reminds me, Jaja, Juliana flies in Sunday morning. She insists on renting a car from the airport but I want her to use my Accord. Adam took off work and is coming with them. With the three kids, they want to rent a van. What do you think?"

"They're coming on Sunday, already? Just let them do whatever they want, Gram."

Kiki perked up and looked at Ian. "That means you and me better clear out so this young lady can get her house in order."

Gram laughed at the young-lady remark. Kiki shot a nice smile at her.

"You have been an incredible host, just brilliant Thank you so much for everything, Gram."

"It's been a wonderful adventure for me. An eye-opener on our ancestors. I never would have found out this important information if not for you." She must be thinking about George Lumen and the DNA test.

"If your family, or any of the séance players want to watch the reenactment shoot, that offer is still on the table," Kiki told her. "It's a sure bet Angie Minnihan will be there."

"Don't worry about us," Gram said. "We won't likely go down to the river." Gram found another bottle of wine and Ian opened it.

"Did you come to a consensus about what it all means? One each for redemption? Did people say what they thought it meant?" Janine asked. "Are the ghosts of Linda and Mary connected then?"

"Everybody must give something to be forgiven," Gram said. "That's what Leone thought. And Angie agreed."

"Bingo!" Kiki cheered. "That is exactly what I think too. The two spirits are most definitely connected. And that phrase, *one each for redemption*, that phrase has to be the dictum. Has to be. But what must they give for redemption? Both girls drowned in the river, right? It's in the city log. Maybe the spirit of Mary is angry because she died in the river? Something wasn't given and she went to her death, like Linda. She wants to warn others. But what needs to be given? I'm going to work it out soon."

"Another reason Leone insists we go to church," Gram said.

"Hey, look at this," Ian spoke up. "Apparently, there was an official group that kept track of ghostly sightings and drownings. Looks like it was part of an actual town council meeting. The local governing body discussed summoning the ghost to determine what it wanted."

"That must be a joke." Janine couldn't believe it and took the typed pages to have a look.

"Dated 1923," Ian added. "Ghosts, séances, and magic became quite popular during that era.

"Maybe that's why the Mary ghost began to appear." Kiki waited for her turn to look at the document. Janine handed it over.

"Here it is." Ian found a short story titled, The Story of Mary Miller. It fit on one side of a piece of thick white paper, typed. He handed it to Kiki and she read it out loud.

"The Story of Mary Miller. Mary Miller was the first child born in our settlement along the river and the first child born of John and Susan Miller. Her birth, long considered a blessing from God, gave our founder reason to pause near the river and test the fertility of the soil. As a child, Mary planted many of the trees that flourish along Marysvilles road, the path that led leads to the river. The river, giving both the blessings of salvation and the curse of danger, took Mary at the tender age of seven. Her life sparked a town in this unlikely place and her name must never be forgotten."

How disappointing. They sat silently, digesting the short story.

"That's the big story Caroline Govant wanted us to find?" Janine voiced out loud.

"I've seen that story before," Gram said. "Long ago. Caroline showed it to all of us. Her father was very set at changing the name of the town to Marysville, or even Millersville, instead of Rio Linda, back when the city of Sacramento required an official name for our area. He pressed hard and I think that story was written for the paper to persuade folks. The Govants had quite a little cult back then. Obviously, Caroline would like to press for the name change and hopes your show will help. Don't fall for it. She wants attention. Caroline always wants attention."

Gram gathered up the wine bottles and nodded at the group with a slight flush to her features.

"This old gal is going to bed. Don't stay up too late looking through that pile of nonsense from Caroline. Those Millers have always been a bit loose in the head. Ask anyone."

Kiki helped Gram ferry the wine glasses to the kitchen and begged off to bed as well. Kiki appeared dog tired. The adrenal excitement of the past two nights must have finally caught up to her.

As soon as Kiki and Gram disappeared at the top of the stairs, Ian grabbed Janine and guided her to the couch. They had a kissing session on her gram's sofa, just like a couple of teenagers, giggling. Then his kisses turned hungry and slow. His body crushed hers but she still wanted him closer. Janine became intensely aroused, but hesitant, because Gram and Kiki were right upstairs and Gram was a very light sleeper. Ian pulled himself to a sitting position.

"Maybe I should take the EM box to the hotel," he said. "They're probably wondering where I got to, and Carlos is probably worried I'm dishonoring your virtue."

"Really, you're thinking about Carlos right now?"

"You're thinking about your gram," he accused. "I know you are. So then, lass, are you going to sneak me upstairs or should I go to the hotel? I'm afraid it'll be tough sleeping here with you right down the hall. Imagining you on that bed, I wouldn't be able to stay away from your door. Are we still playing it quiet?"

"My sister comes this weekend," Janine whispered. "I still want to keep things quiet a little longer."

Ian kissed her grudgingly before standing up.

"Good night then, my sweet lass. Let's finish this after the thing on Saturday."

The next morning Janine crept down the stairs to peek at the driveway, hoping the truck with Ian was back. No. The house was still quiet. The aroma of coffee fresh in the pot wafted from the kitchen. Someone had been up and about already. Mysterious Misty, most likely. Janine found fresh homemade biscuits cooling on the stove. She grabbed a cup of coffee and smothered a biscuit in Gram's rich creamy butter, then went to sit on the recliner and muse about Ian.

The coffee table was still a mess with the old papers from Caroline Govant's box. Janine shift through them, organizing and putting them back into folders as she worked. Old photos of men in army uniforms, the Miller Bank front, aerial shots of the orchard and river. Letters from an APO address. Grade reports from the Rio Linda Elementary School. Pages of handwritten fluff Janine already skimmed the night before.

As she crammed the items into the box, she spotted a piece of paper against the side of the box. This one had not been in one of the manila folders and the paper looked similar to a brown paper bag. It blended in with the interior cardboard and was pressed flush along the inside wall. Janine felt a shiver run down her spine as she fished it out. It was written in beautiful old spidery script not unlike the writing and paper from the torn-out pages of the wagon diary. How did they miss it the previous night? Too much wine and not enough sleep. Tired eyes.

There was no date and no signature.

For days in her delirium, she spoke of a girl and urged me to write this down, and I do so to quiet her hysteria. The darkness will rest if one of each will go with her. Linda believes it unfair that she alone was tasked for this punishment. Everyone sat at the same table. Why did the elders blame only her? She was obedient. All must be redeemed together, or none will be. It will never stop until there is one of each for redemption. Then all can go into the house of God, together. Riches will be rewarded as each acquiesces. Resisting will bring despair and death.

Mary said she will go willingly to set the example. She will be the first. Better to settle this debt quickly else there be too many called.

There was a postscript, written in a shakier hand.

Everyone failed to grasp her meaning. After her fever broke, she went to the river. Her body was found between the rocks.

Her cell phone chimed.

"She can be the last one!" Steve's excited voice burst in her ear. "Did you hear that last night? You tagged it for review. Regular speed, very faint, from the condenser microphone, along with some static. We cross-checked it with the clip-on recordings and no one said anything like that. Unless Henry Webber can sound like a little girl."

"I don't know, maybe," Janine said. "There was a lot of static."

"Believe me, it's there. Sounds like a little girl saying, 'She can be the last one.'" Steve chuckled. "This is proof! Proof positive. Look, Kiki is not answering her phone. It might be dead, but I need you to wake her up and get down here. We want to run through it with both of you and then get the story straight. I've got a writer working on putting together some scenes."

"Yeah, okay, I'll wake her and bring her out."

"ASAP," Steve said. "ASAP. We've had zero sleep out here and I've got some calls to make. Lots of stuff going on. I want to punch this out for the writer."

"ASAP. We're on the way," Janine told him.

Chapter 9

Rio Linda, 1840

The Hansen wagon party survived the winter by committing a most atrocious sin. Her husband and her son tried to comfort her, but nothing could ease her shame. Helen would never confess the deepest despair resting in her heart; she eventually ate more than needed to survive. Her tastes adjusted and she closed her mind to the meal's origin. She ate to thrive. Other women, like Meg, weak Ingrid, and frail Nancy were forcefully fed throughout the entire winter. Less sinful women either died, or remained ill in their sunny valley below the mountain ridge.

Only one wagon with movable wheels remained, and the Webber boys pulled that wagon like oxen. Their father, Peter, acted as the leader. The minister and the infirm rode in the back buckboard. Sue Miller, large with her startling pregnancy, rode in the coach seat, radiant, like a queen. Helen wondered if that seed had been planted in the meadow during the last days of the Hansen rule. John Miller cared not, so neither did the rest of them. Susan's pregnancy was their only miracle, and when Sue's water broke, the travelers stopped moving for the birth of the baby.

They found a rather-large branch of the watershed snaking near their path. Beautiful boulders marked a gentle bend in the river and the stone glittered a rainbow of colors in a metallic luster. Surprisingly, almond trees and wild blackberry bushes populated the area. The past season's almonds lay on the ground in husks. The vegetation provided sustenance and the river provided water enough to make camp. After days of walking in silence, the group welcomed the respite. Not one of them desired to reach their original destination of the port city yet. Helen did not know what they would convey about their trials.

Collectively, they took the birth as a good reason to delay their journey. Helen's daughter-in-law, Meggie, still festered with a confusion from the fever she suffered, but she was able in body enough to help with the birthing. They gathered pregnant Susan to the edge of the flowing river, away from the others. A natural hill blocked the view of their camp from the pebbly shore. Helen tasked her son Grant with the keeping of Sue's husband, John Miller.

In all the birthings Helen had seen, Susan Miller's proved the easiest. After near starvation, trials of life and limb, want of shelter and comfort of cloth, her baby eased into the world with very little fuss. Susan herself made not a peep. Only the small baby squeaked when they cleansed her in the cool water, but quieted as they swaddled her in the cleanest blanket left in their supplies. When they placed the babe in Susan's arms, silent tears streamed down the mother's face.

"Do you think we are coming back into the light of God?" she asked.

Helen and Meg both nodded, they did.

John Miller and Grant discovered that the almond shells showed signs of cracking. They reasoned the husks would give good fruit in the next week or two. The young men sat together discussing the possibility of propagating the trees into an orchard. The land beyond the river proved flat and rich in dark minerals, and the wild trees looked plenty healthy. A positive glint in the eyes of her older son soothed Helen's fragile heart.

Further in their scavenging, the men made an interesting discovery; lumber. New, but a little weathered, a broken flatboat full of cut boards had run aground upstream. Their excitement, coupled with the easy birth of the baby, lifted the spirits of each member in the small group as they pondered what to do with the treasure.

Lately, they shared one large community fire. No more secrets lingered between them. The infirm, pulled from the wagon, thrived on the wild berries and rabbit meat. The new baby woke Ingrid and Meg from their melancholy stupor as they took an interest in the infant, and the men spoke amiably for once. Frederick found a water smooth log and he took the ax-head to try to fashion himself a new leg. Young Gustoff Webber hovered near, itching to help, but waiting to be asked.

In the western distance, along the flat line of the horizon, the sky glowed a beautiful burnt amber in the wake of the setting sun. The clear California sky rarely held a cloud in that direction. But the opposite view, in the east, grey water-filled shadows congregated over the mountains of their heartbreak. Helen kept her back to those mountains as much as possible, angry at the losses they endured and ashamed of what they had done.

Her daughter-in-law walked with young George Lumen over the mound toward the river. They took the water bucket. Meg still called the boy Christopher and not one of them had a heart to correct her. Not even George himself. Everyone called the boy Christopher near her ears.

"Fred," Grant spoke quietly across the fire to the minister. "We want to ask if it is possible. George does not want to be called George anymore. And we are going to raise him as our son. He has asked to be renamed before the eyes of God. Already, we each call him Christopher." Grant had tears running down his cheeks. "I'll never forget my son, but this would be for Meg and George, for their peace of mind. Can he be baptized again? Can we name him in honor of our Christopher?"

Murmuring went around the campfire. Everyone desired to be cleansed of sins. The prospect offered hope.

Little Linda abruptly stood up. She startled them with her announcement.

"I like the berries but I hate this kind of meat." She threw her rabbit piece back into the fire. Then, the little girl skipped down to the river to help Meg and George with the water. So young and innocent, Linda was free from the burdens of a grownup heart.

The next morning, the men dismantled the wagon for the spare parts and the metal. Grant decided to use scraps from the wagon and the scavenged lumber to erect a permanent structure. All the men wanted to help. It was her son's wagon, so perhaps it would become a William's structure, a house shared with the community. Both Grant and her husband Nicholas desired to stay in the area longer. Even John Miller wished to stay for the almonds. Each of them felt something positive growing in that valley near the river bend. The birth of a healthy baby girl delivered hope to all of them.

The Webber boys had been trained in woodwork by their grandfather and offered to make a sturdy frame by way of hewed, notched fittings. They could easily make the notches with the ax. Half dovetail ends on the boards would keep the walls firm. River rock might be used to help stabilize the base. It would hold well enough, they believed, until someone could go for more supplies.

Frederick Stauch prepared a big Sunday service. He retrieved his cover-chewed Bible and slowly turned the pages. Everyone would be invited to ask for redemption through a confession, and then the group would put all the foulness behind them for good. They would be free to move forward, unburdened by what they endured.

But did Frederick mean all of their sins? The collective sins that had rained the wrath of God on them in the high Sierras? By turning a blind eye, they condoned everything that transpired under the shadow of one Mr. Stanley Hansen. Not one of them stood up with the Whitakers when Hansen's true colors emerged. The lot of them kept their pact with that devil and followed their government notes. Whitaker and his group left empty-handed, invalidated, in the cloak of night.

Hanson had charmed them easily with his confident talk. When he finally took liberty with Ingrid, everyone quietly minded their own business. When he preyed upon young Mrs. Miller, no one said a thing because John enjoyed his new status with the leader, relishing the favors and power bestowed on him. They separated their wagons a little further after that, wondering who else might fall from grace.

Then came the native family. By not addressing the evil inclinations of Stanley Hansen, they each carried blame for the treatment of the Indians and the subsequent destruction of the Lumens the night the Indians sought revenge. Would Frederick allow any of them to admit those sins? If they acknowledged such things, each of them could never pretend ignorance again.

No, he was only interested in the one sin; breaking their fast by consuming flesh of the dead and forcing the meal on the sick without their full knowledge or consent. Little Linda continues to ask for it again and again even in their sunny valley. Frederick's furrowed brow creases deeply when he stares at his grandchild. His fear mirrors each of their hearts. They desperately need the girl to forget, so that they can forget. Helen fears that Linda might speak of their transgression near outsiders. Who, besides their group, could ever understand it?

After the first day of building, the size of the small structure became clear. It might be used as a small home or a small meeting place. The men worked day to night, happy for a positive project with results they could see. After two full days, the Webber boys, Nicholas, Grant, and John Miller completed a rough square building. The addition of a cross above the door was a sign of coming home. They completed that touch in time for Sunday morning. Frederick nodded his approval. The children, Linda and George, very much desired to go inside the structure, but Frederick stayed them with an outstretched hand.

"After we are cleansed of our sins, we will come to fellowship in this fine house of God," he announced. "But we must first be redeemed and reborn."

Everyone dressed as fine as they could muster. Torn clothes, but clean faces. Young Linda and George watched Susan feed her baby as they broke their own fast. The girl Linda was prone to giggles, and she adored the baby who would soon be christened Mary.

Then, the small group filed to the river as Frederick preached about redemption. He mentioned naught the trials with Stanley Hansen, and that worried Helen. He solely mentioned their unholy transgression to survive. Peter Webber quaked with fury. In his sermon, Fred directly blamed Peter for the unholy meals. Frederick grasped his staff in one hand, steadying himself. He refrained from moving about, as he was unpracticed with the wooden leg.

"Forgive us our unholy appetite." He shouted to the sky. "Rid Linda of this sickness!"

Linda giggled at the sound of her own name.

Frederick Stauch glared at the child. Ingrid pulled her daughter close, afraid of the minister. Niels Stauch hovered near Ingrid and her daughter, offering what scant protection he could offer. For all his holiness, Frederick Stauch proved a hard man to live with. He summoned the Millers first, to baptize the baby and then the parents.

"Mary Miller," Frederick announced. "The savior of our hope. Your birth signifies the redemption of this community. May God bless you and keep you."

He baptized each member of the community in the ice-cold water of the river. He pushed heads beneath the water with a strong, firm hand. Everyone accepted the watery renewal without fuss. Then, they each strolled over the mound to the small square meeting house. Their new church and home stood proudly in the small clearing. The fire, with their Sunday meal of duck, roasted several yards away. People tarried shyly outside the house, choosing to drip the river near the fire instead. The aroma informed them that the duck was ready to eat.

"Oh no, not that again," Little Linda's voice carried loudly. "Why can't we have the other food? Why do we no longer eat the other meat? I like it much better than this greasy duck!"

Frederick Stauch screeched in vexation. His uneven hopping on one leg startled each of them. He moved at top speed, finally dropping his staff to the ground. His face flushed a livid red of anger and his wood leg had dislodged in his scurrying about.

"Do not say such things!" he screamed and spittle flew from his lips. "You are baptized and cleansed of that foul event! Put it away from you!"

Linda giggled nervously at his red face. She half hid between her uncle and her mother. Frederick fidgeted. His unkind grimace stared down on Linda.

"Look at you!" he chastised the little girl. "You are plump with the unholy meals you've eaten. Where most only ate to survive, you ate for pleasure. I watched you!"

"Oh now." Helen ran over to stand beside a trembling Ingrid. She hugged the mother then reached out to cradle

Linda's head in the nook of her arm. "Look here, Frederick Stauch. This here is only a child. Children have plumpness in their cheeks naturally. She has not done anything anyone else has not done."

"There is a vast difference in our actions," Frederick insisted. He searched the lot of them. "Does any among us still hunger for that which we ate on the mountain? If so, do not enter that holy house. You will proceed to soil it."

One of the Webber boys, Rolf, retrieved the wooden leg. He offered it to Frederick then took a step back. Peter Webber stepped forward as Fred reattached the appendage.

"Here now, Fred, keep with your accusing eyes! We saved you on that mountain." Peter Webber spat on the ground. He might never agree with Frederick's ways. Peter helped his wife to a seat near the roasting duck, cussing under his breath. His sons followed. The Webbers all turned their backs to Frederick.

Niels Stauch began moving toward the house with Ingrid, but Fred hobbled in front of them. He spread his arms wide.

"No!" They flinched at his shout. "Mine will not go into that circle. Not yet. This family is still in need of reflection and acceptance of our sins. Saved us, Mr. Webber? Maybe our fleshly body, but our souls are condemned!" Frederick's gaze bore down at the small girl and she looked terrified. "You will not go into that house until you are redeemed. Until you rid yourself of your foul illness, you will not enter that house. Do you hear me! You and your mother! Not until you both truly repent for what you did. You are my burden now, and I will fix you!"

Linda ran away. She disappeared over the mound toward the river. Ingrid nearly fainted. Niels tried to hold her up but needed help. Grant stepped forward to help him and they carried Ingrid into the camp circle near the fire.

"Can you please attempt to control your temper," Nicholas whispered harshly to Fred. "We experienced a lovely gesture out in the river, but our day is now ruined. Each of us are trying to cope with the memory of our ordeal."

"Gesture?" Fred shoved his Bible into Nicholas's chest. "Take this book and pray. If I am ever free of my filial burdens, if my family ever repents, I will fetch it again. I vow to rid that child of her illness and our family of the evil stain brought by that woman!" Fred turned and began to carefully step away.

"Where do you go?" Nicholas called after him.

"We will set up a camp nearer the river. A camp for sinners." Frederick waved in the direction of the mound. He awkwardly hobbled away. He shouted to the circle, where his son Niels cradled Ingrid. Fred's voice carried crisply through the air. "Niels! You will bring what little is our own and join me," he ordered.

For two nights, Frederick Stauch kept his small family separated from the rest of the party. They spied him on their daily water run but gave him a wide berth. Shouted prayers could be heard over the hill, day and night, as well as his reprimands toward the poor child. Helen found it increasingly difficult to sit at the fire and do nothing for the child or her mother. Fred loudly accused Ingrid of being a witch and her daughter too.

Nancy Webber, still quite frail, lamented that someone should fetch Ingrid and Linda into safety. But the men urged the women not to meddle in the Stauch family affair. Nicholas fairly ordered Helen to let that family work through their problems in peace.

"They'll return," Nicholas said.

"He's a tyrant," Helen told him. "That poor woman and her child are being tortured."

"Niels will keep him at bay," Nicholas said. "Frederick speaks correctly about the illness. It is unnatural for the child to keep asking for the meat she ate. It is an unnatural illness and he is doing his best to correct it, and her mother is not helping. We must respect his efforts."

Peter Webber suggested that someone should continue to the coast. He wanted to go, but his wife refused to travel so soon and claimed he couldn't fetch supplies anyway, they had no money. All their tender had burned in the Hansen wagon. They had nothing to barter except the scant personal jewelry in Helen's small box, the silver rings and trinkets from the Lumens.

Helen strolled to the top of the mound to check on the girl and her mother. Linda stood facing her grandfather with her blond waves fluttering in the breeze. They each leaned toward the other with hands on hips. If it were not so heartbreaking, it would have been comical. The child definitely inherited Frederick's anger and stubborn attitude.

"I want to camp with the others. I want to go into the house," Linda demanded, stamping her foot.

"You are not allowed in that house or anywhere near it!" Fred shouted.

Niels and Ingrid remained huddled together under a tree, cowed by the girl and the old man. Helen decided something right then; she didn't care what her husband had commanded. The Stauch family needed help. Helen no longer cared that Fred was a man of God and delivered the wisdom they all needed to heed. She could no longer tolerate watching and hearing his unbridled anger at Ingrid and her child.

"You! You ate it too. You told me to eat it!" Linda stamped her little foot.

"And now I'm telling you not to speak of it!"

Helen marched down the slope. She waved and shouted a greeting.

"Here now! I'm coming down there!" She made haste toward their little camp.

Ingrid and Niels rose, expectant and hopeful.

"You mind your own business! This is a family matter." Frederick glared at her.

He was a frightful man, tall and powerful-looking, and more menacing with the wooden leg. He swooped down to grab Linda up and she railed in his arms. He hobbled into the river, spewing holy words in a vile tone. In contrast, the water ran smooth and kind behind him, murmuring quietly with a tinkling melody.

"You will be redeemed! You will repent! You will rid yourself of this sickness and your unholy appetite! Each of us must go willingly toward redemption!"

They splashed into the water disturbing the tranquil surface. Helen glanced at Niels and Ingrid. They were hopeless. The poor woman appeared ready to faint again. Her eyes were glassed over with grief. Where once there had been striking beauty, now lay an empty wasteland. She lost her virtue, her husband, her cousin, her vitality, and she was now trapped in the clutches of Frederick Stauch. He was almost as bad as Hansen, maybe worse. Helen gestured for Niels to take Ingrid over the mound. He did not need coaxing.

"Why are you in that freezing water, Fred?" Helen reached the river shore as Niels passed with Ingrid. The pebbles of the beach crunched under her feet.

"He baptizes her daily," Niels managed as they went by, "hoping to cleanse Linda of her sins."

"He's crazy," Helen mumbled mostly to herself.

Frederick waded waist deep with a squirming Linda wriggling in his grasp. He was growling and she was screaming. Her flailing arms hit him repeatedly and he slipped. They both plunged under the smooth surface of the water and the yelling and screaming suddenly halted. A momentary peaceful silence filled the air. Then, hands slapped the water surface. The old man's head popped out and swiveled all around. Linda popped to the surface once before smacking into the boulder at the bend in the river.

Helen waded into the frigid water seeking the girl under the surface. She could see the colors of Linda moving rhythmically with the current. Somehow, the girl got stuck in that beautiful rock. Frederick splashed up next to her and pushed her aside. He hurried to fetch his granddaughter. His hand pressed against the rock for support and he balanced on his one real leg. His arm reached out. His head bobbed under and over the water. From behind Helen, Niels splashed into the river. He went right past his father but the current instantly caught him and pushed him hard against the rock. He slipped around the outer edge and disappeared downstream followed by Fred's wooden leg. Frederick gasped for breath but kept bobbing back down.

Already, Linda was under water too long.

Frederick kept dipping back under the surface. Helen reached out to stop him but he shoved her hand away with a snarl. Niels came back, huffing and puffing, dripping from head to toe. As he reentered the water, Helen slowly backed completely out. She retreated toward Ingrid, who stood motionless on the slope of the hill. Ingrid's empty eyes certainly did not understand what was happening. Helen took Ingrid into her arms anyway, for her own comfort. Hot tears dribbled down her cheeks. From over the hill top, Nicholas and Peter Webber emerged to see what the fuss was about. They ran quickly down the hill.

"It's Linda. She's stuck in the rock," Helen managed to say.

Both men plunged into the icy river to help. Each grappled against the rock but were unable to free Linda. Webber called loudly for his sons and the younger men came down the hill. No one could free the child. After a time, the water-soaked shivering men huddled on the beach, defeated. Hours had passed and their efforts had been fruitless.

Frederick crouched alone, up river, under his tree. His hands covered his face and Helen thought he might be crying. Niels sat close to the water's edge, breathing loudly. His brother's widow, Ingrid, sat behind him, patting his back in a comforting manner. She did not seem to understand that her daughter remained underwater. She instead seemed relieved that the screaming had ended and the valley was peaceful.

The men were never able to free Linda's body. Sometime during the second night, she freed herself. Her body was no longer in the rock. Webber's sons walked the whole day downstream, hoping to find her washed on the shore, but she was gone, never to be seen again.

The second gathering in the small structure was a memorial for Linda. Her grandfather's Bible provided the words, but her grandfather steered clear of the camp. Frederick chose a place even further upstream to reside. He disappeared alone.

Peter Webber still wished to find supplies for the building of more structures, yet he was wary of Frederick Stauch. He feared the old man had gone mad in the head. Peter was torn between going for provisions and remaining to guard the fledgling settlement. Two days after their memorial for Linda, he no longer needed to fret. The supplies came to them.

Long before they met the group, they felt them, given away by vibrations on the earth. A very large train of wagons neared. Wagon after wagon after wagon passed on the main trail, much larger than their group had ever been. The men walked out to greet them. Their leader, a man named Archie Smith, halted his horse and jumped down as the entire train stopped to set up camp for the night.

A few ill people in their party needed tending, one of whom was Archie Smith's mother. Helen offered them respite in their small shelter. It was cool and pleasant in the house, protected from the dust, and comforting. Helen also led them to the river for fresh water and shared the wild blackberries. John Miller harvested early almonds from several trees and they proved good to eat. There were piles of fruit in their empty shelter that the travelers were welcome to taste. Their new friends were charmed with the small settled area and several folks were fascinated at the solid build of the cabin walls. Archie Smith knew the source of the found lumber.

"John Sutter sent men into the mountains to mill trees, way up river. This batch surely took a wrong turn at the fork. He built a saw mill up yonder. I'll have more lumber sent your way when I speak to him," he offered. Archie carried a supply of real nails which he used on their meager structure. He gave them a sturdy hammer and an ax.

"We can't pay for this metal," Peter Webber told him.

"No payment necessary," Archie said. "I'm grateful that you built this house and it's here. My mother has been ill for most a month and begged for a roof over her head before she dies. She is done with the natural elements. I believe, if these are her final days, you have provided her last wish. I am forever grateful."

The travelers shared many provisions, pots and dishes, cloth and clothes to spare. Every item on Peter Webber's wish list dropped into their laps. Throughout the day, different folks arrived to see the small square structure and brought a housewarming gift along with their curiosity. They donated old chairs, a clock, candle holders and an old iron stove.

Another miracle emerged from that large train. One early afternoon, a familiar family meandered near, the Whitakers. John and his wife walked hand in hand, followed by their daughter, Elizabeth. Helen watched her younger son Ethan rush to meet them. He stood fast in a mixture of happiness and disbelief. Elizabeth appeared just as stunned.

Then, the two young people sprang forward into each other's arms. Tears of joy streamed down Helen's face. The Whitakers! Delivered to their laps for them to seek amends. Nicholas stood beside her.

"Did you know of this?" he asked, watching their son embrace Elizabeth.

Only the men never saw it. "I suspect we may have a new daughter soon."

The next day, Archie Smith sent the bulk of his party ahead to the coast. He was delighted to see his mother return from the edge of death, but she refused to continue on his wagon train. She didn't want to leave the quaint house in the middle of nowhere. Their group agreed to welcome the elder Mrs. Smith indefinitely and Archie vowed to spare no expense in sending provisions to add to the house and build an entire community. Although the Whitaker family would press on with Smith, everyone realized Elizabeth wished to stay behind and a small wedding ceremony was planned for Etan and Elizabeth.

The morning of the ceremony, John Whitaker inquired about Hansen's ledger diary. He asked if it still existed. He wanted to take the extended Hansen family to task for his wagon-train losses and thought it was possible, if he could deliver proof of their investments. Nicholas informed him of its continued existence and said he was most welcome to take the diary. Nicholas only saved it as a document to release to authorities upon reaching the port city.

Helen went into the small house to retrieve the ledger. Nicholas never looked with his own eyes into the diary and did not know what had been written by Stanley, or Frederick, or Helen. As she fetched the book, Helen hesitated. Giving that diary would out them all for what transpired on the mountain. Would Whitaker still acquiesce to his daughter marrying Ethan? Whitaker was a hard, religious man. Ethan would not fare well in losing Elizabeth a second time. Most of all, Helen was ashamed and did not want the world to know what they ate to survive. Weren't they cleansed of that sin, in the river? Why did anyone else need to know of it?

Helen tore the pages out, each page back to Stanley Hansen's last entry. It was not a lie to take those pages from the book. In truth, the Hansen ledger dairy ended with Hansen's hand. Helen unbuckled Frederick's Bible and stowed the loose pages within, then fastened it up again. The Bible and her pages would wait in the house for Frederick to fetch. He could decide what should happen to them when he returned for his book. Hopefully, he'd never return and they could put that past to rest forever.

Chapter 10

The Curse

Janine couldn't wait for her sister to bring the kids to Rio Linda, but at the same time, she was anxious too. She wondered if the kids would feel free to ask her the questions they politely avoided at Sammy's birthday party. Such as, why has their aunt been missing all these years? Surely, Ashley must wonder why her aunt dropped out of their lives so completely. Did Ashley know what happened in Chicago, or did Juliana protect her daughter from that story? Janine imagined an easy visit with Juliana, but with her fledgling relationship with Ian included into the mix, her anxiety level rose astronomically. Juliana's radar would surely detect something and she didn't want to field the questions her sister might ask.

Then, there was Sammy. She still didn't know how to act around Sammy. In Texas, she found herself staring at Sammy with a mixture of yearning and guilt. Would Sammy begin to notice her aunt acting weird around her?

In the back of her mind, Janine also harbored fear that the spirits of Mary and Linda might actually be real. After everything she experienced, she was practically convinced something paranormal existed in Rio Linda. Surely, her post-traumatic brain couldn't conjure the girl she encountered in the orchard, could it? And although Caroline Govant might pretend to see a ghost, she wondered about the others chanting together. Did they really hear something in the trees, or did they get caught up in the excitement? Collective hysteria? Leone would never pretend like that, would she? And Henry Webber's rage pointed to him seeing something he did not want to admit. What nonsense did he think he was participating in? Janine found Gram in the kitchen with the Saturday edition of the newspaper and a pen. Gram smiled up from her crossword puzzle.

"Are you worried about Juliana's kids coming here?"

"Of course," Gram said. "For years you girls have poo-pooed me and called me a silly old woman. Of course, I'm worried."

"Shouldn't we warn Juliana about the ghost?"

Gram looked at her wryly. "Good luck, Jaja. Don't you think I've been warning her about that ghost for years? You yourself have chastised me about my warnings."

"I know." Janine sat down hard in her usual spot. "It's just, I might believe you now. Juliana should not bring those kids here. What if the River Girl Ghost tries to get one of them to go to the river?"

Gram set her Sacramento Bee down in a wrinkled pile. "Really, Jaja. No one has mentioned the river ghost in many years. Your imaginary friend was probably the last we saw of her. The more I think about it, she was probably just an imaginary friend, or an echo of the original ghost. Kiki and I had a long discussion about it and we believe the river ghost might be a faded spirit."

"A faded spirit?"

"One that used to haunt a place, but their purpose is gone, and so the spirit slowly fades away. Kiki says it often takes a very long time for a spirit to fade completely. Even today I get a little upset at Henry for scaring me like that. He had everyone convinced the river ghost wanted you to drown, but she never asked you to go to the river, did she?"

"No, she never asked me to go to the river."

"Well, that ghost is known for luring children into the river. We haven't heard of any drownings blamed on that ghost in over twenty years. No sightings. Henry's niece was the last drowning blamed on that ghost. Maybe all the signs and precautions have helped, or maybe the ghost has lost her purpose, which is what we think." Gram nodded to herself. "Fact is, drownings are not what they once were. Perhaps folks should just let that ghost rest. Also, you know Juliana as well as I do. Those children will not leave her sight for a second. The river has always been off limits to Williams kids, and I'm sure Juliana will put her foot down hard about that."

"I swear I saw a ghost the other night," Janine insisted. "In the orchard. You say your mother saw that same spirit and even you saw her once."

Gram's worried brow aged her.

Janine quietly added, "Maybe Juliana and the kids should stay in Sac, just to keep them away from the river."

Gram chuckled. "I'm not the one you have to convince, Jaja. Juliana would never hear of any such thing. If you want her to stay in a hotel in Sacramento, you need to be the one to convince her. She doesn't listen to me about my paranoia."

Gram was right, of course. When Janine was under ten, Juliana and Janine tried unsuccessfully to petitioned Gram into letting them visit Rio Linda. *Rio Linda is not for young children*, Gram would say. It was a miracle when Gram consented to the Rio Linda visit at Sammy's birthday party. Janine realized that it was probably her own fault. Gram and Juliana would consent to almost anything to keep Janine from disappearing from their lives again.

"I have to go shop." Gram began to gather up her large purse and new shawl. "I am going to make a large roast for dinner tomorrow night. Well, Misty is cooking it. I hope you don't mind, but I've invited Kiki and Doctor McNally to join us. Your niece is a huge fan of your show, you know."

"Gram!"

"This gets you off the hook," Gram told her. "I invited him, you didn't. You can keep your secret a little longer and still have your sister size him up for you. Now, don't rain on my parade, girl. And I know you have that thing tonight, so don't worry about me."

The "thing" was a cocktail party with the *Spectral Analysis* staff and the reenactment actors at the Malabar Restaurant. The entire upstairs area was reserved for the party. A few of the show sponsors would be there, as well as some other high-ups, whatever that meant. Steve told her that some very important people were interested in meeting her, and although Janine was technically on her break, she should come.

Janine had not seen anyone on the crew for days. Carlos flew home to Texas, Kiki and Ted were working closely with the reenactment crew, and Ian and Steve were analyzing the séance footage. Ian hadn't been able to break loose at all. They were working eighteen-hour days, cleaning up clips and putting together some sort of last-minute presentation for someone. Janine spent the time childproofing Gram's house for Juliana and the kids. Janine replaced a broken electrical outlet, a light fixture, plastered wall holes and oiled squeaky doors. She also swept out the henhouse. The yard men usually managed the henhouse, but it didn't hurt to sweep it out again if the kids were going to fetch eggs. Gram and Janine even went to the stables to brush down Gram's painted mare and polish the tack in case Juliana wanted to go riding. Juliana always wanted to go riding and always scrutinized the state of the saddle.

Cheryl, the *Spectral Analysis* office manager, planned the entire party from Texas. Cheryl called Janine to schedule her transportation to the party but Janine said she'd take the truck. A dress came to the house, by courier, from Kiki. Kiki wrote a short note that said she recommended Janine dress up a bit, as the party leaned on the semi-formal side. Kiki's note said there'd be many pretty wannabe actresses and they needed to exert their status as the real stars of the show.

Come confident, Kiki wrote.

Janine stared at the dress, which was definitely a Kiki choice. She didn't know how she could wear such a revealing, sexy dress and not look totally self-conscious. Come confident? In that dress? How? Most of her scars would be visible: the X graze mark near her breasts that he made to be cruel, the jagged scar under her right armpit that looked worse than it had been, the deep gash on her right shoulder blade, and just a peak of the near fatal kidney scar. People would definitely stare and wonder. Questions would fly around about those scars. Did she have time to shop for an alternate? Janine glanced at her own wardrobe, jeans, T-shirts, sweatshirts. Nothing there for a fancy cocktail party.

Her cell phone chimed. Ian.

"Hi, Janine, I've got a few moments here and just wanted to check base with you." There were a lot of voices in the background, so he was still in some sort of meeting.

"Check base?"

"I wanted to hear your voice again." He said softly, "I miss you. I really miss you. I cannot stop thinking about you and your lovely lips. You're coming tonight, right? Remember, we have unfinished business. I had a wonderful dream about you last night. Shall I come fetch you?"

"Don't you have to be out there extra early?"

"Yes, yes, but I can come now. In half an hour. We can get ready together at the hotel. I have a private room. We can have a preparty cocktail or… Hey, what…" Janine could hear Kiki speaking to Ian. She obviously took the phone away from him.

"Janine?" Kiki asked but didn't wait. "I think you should come to the hotel right now. Bring the dress. We'll get ready together. In my room. Ian and I will come get you, or, if you prefer, meet us there in half an hour. But come now, right now. We should get ready together."

"Kiki, that dress…"

"Is going to be gorgeous on you. Bring it."

"I don't know. You just don't realize…"

"I don't think you know what's happening out here," Kiki said. "Things are getting bigger than we expected. There's talk about a feature film documentary for the big screen, Janine, the silver screen. We had a terrific presentation and people are very interested. This party is extremely important. It's not just Ian and me people want to meet. Carlos flew back this afternoon and will be there too. Shall we come get you?"

"I'll come in the truck."

"Good, room 335." Ian said something behind her, but Kiki repeated, "Room 335. They'll give you a key at the front desk, but there should be someone there waiting. I hired a stylist to do our hair. Don't forget the dress."

Beatrice had lopsided pink and frost-colored hair. Her big bag of tools sat half open and three curling irons were lined up on the vanity. When Janine arrived, she smiled, introduced herself as the beautician and invited Janine into the chair in front of the mirror. Beatrice studied Janine in the mirror.

"Let's get started," Beatrice said. "Your hair is very nice, very long." She pulled the ponytail out. "Let's go with flowing ringlets. It looks like it'll take a curl easily. Kiki mentioned that she thought large ringlets would look nice and I agree." She started brushing Janine's hair. "Light on the makeup, just a bit of lips and lashes, although, I want to clean up your brows if that's okay?"

"Whatever you need to do. Where's Kiki?"

"She's in the shower."

Beatrice somehow made Janine look glamorous. All it took was pulling out a few overgrown brows, applying a light touch of color to her lips, and adding large soft waves to her hair. She resembled the old Janine, from long ago. The college girl. No, not quite. She was just a little more defined and harder around the edges. No baby fat lingering along her chin line.

Janine recalled the last time she wore lipstick, in Chicago, before going out on that last date. Kiki stood behind her, looking with approval at Janine's reflection. Kiki wore a blood-red ruffle and lace dress, which was even more revealing than the ice-blue sparkly dress lined up for Janine. But then, Kiki often wore over-the-top outfits. She easily morphed into whichever character she wished to create.

"If I can wear this," Kiki said to her reflection, "you can surely wear the lovely dress on that chair without complaint. We need to be as glamorous as possible without looking like we're trying too hard. The studio is coming to the party. We want to stamp the seal on this deal."

"Kiki, that dress, it's just too…sparse. I'm going to need more dress."

"Just put it on." Kiki took the hairdresser's seat as Janine stood up. "I'll come see it in a minute. Think of it this way, Janine. It's just a costume, and sex sells. Why do you think I dress the way I do on the show? Because I enjoy it? Because ghosts like it? No. To make the ratings and get the sponsors. It helps fund what we do. I chose that dress specifically for you. The color, the cut. And it really is kind of modest, you'll see. I thought about that for you. The least you can do is try it on."

Modest? Okay. Janine could see what Kiki meant. It was modest compared to some of the stuff Kiki wore. But Kiki did not know about the scars Janine needed to hide.

"Could you just try it and then we'll discuss it."

"Fine." Janine took the dress into the other room.

Might as well just come out with it. Let Kiki see for herself. That'll shut Kiki up for life when it comes to dressing her up again. Let Kiki see the scars and she'll want to cover them up herself. She kicked off her jeans and T-shirt and began pulling up the dress. There were two very thin satin straps and she could see there was no hiding her bra under there. Luckily, the dress was designed to support her with a reinforced spandex type of material. When she pulled it up, she clearly saw that Kiki was right. The dress was very sexy, but also kind of modest in a classy sort of way. Kiki chose a gorgeous dress for her. A perfect color against her skin. Where Kiki's red dressed screamed devil, this dress sang angel. Kiki must be going for that message, they're opposites. Surely, Kiki didn't expect the angel to have such deep, angry scars. Janine could not get the zipper up all the way. She was about to zip it back down when Kiki walked in. Kiki gasped and then stepped over.

"Let me do that." Kiki turned her around to face the mirror and finished zipping the dress. It fit perfectly to every curve of her body. Janine noticed Beatrice standing in the doorway, staring at her.

"You look incredible in that dress," Beatrice said.

"She's right," Kiki told her. "You must wear it."

Couldn't they see her scars? The knife marks? Janine turned and looked over her own shoulder. Yes, there they were, glaring gash marks across her shoulder blade and one down her back. The near-fatal mark peeked ominously over the edge of the dress near the zipper. Dark and ugly. Surely, Kiki saw that entire scar before she zipped up the dress.

"They just make you look more badass than ever." Kiki stared solemnly at her shoulder blade, then turned her jade-green eyes on Janine in the mirror. "They go with your badass image, it's so right. And they don't take away one ounce from how beautiful you are in this dress."

Beatrice at the door nodded her head. "You look incredible," she repeated.

Janine shook her head. "You think people want to see this? Those?"

"Let me tell you what people, our audience, see when they look at you, Janine. For the first few shows, you and Carlos were just kind of there, barely in the background. Then you guys started with the wisecracks. You were the voice of reason, keeping us honest. People see you as the calm, cool chick that doesn't quite believe all the nonsense. Nobody scripted that. It just happened."

Beatrice continued nodding. "That's right."

"Remember Sacramento, in the tunnel. You were glowing and didn't blink an eye. You just shoved the doctor aside. You practically dared Ian and Ted to go into the room with all those ominous noises. *You're a badass.* That's what people see. And what's better, the badass nonbeliever now seems to have seen and spoken with a real spirit. You are a major key to our being taken seriously with this story. If you're convinced, the audience is convinced. The studio is convinced. This thing is going to be big. Nobody planned it this way, but there it is."

Janine looked in the mirror. The dark angry X over her left breast stood out glaringly. How many times did people tell her the scars were barely noticeable and to ignore them, and she knew they were always lying. Her scars were startling and frightening.

"Wear them proudly," Kiki said softly. "They just confirm once again that you are a badass. Those scars are terrifying, and yet, you're still standing here looking absolutely beautiful. You don't fall for any nonsense. Really, Janine, just keep reminding yourself that you are a badass, and you'll be fine."

Kiki spontaneously hugged her tightly.

"I'm so sorry for what happened to you," Kiki whispered in her ear. "It all makes sense now, this dark aura. I was afraid to look at your fortune, your future, but it was your past I feared. I think I know who you are." Kiki peered into her eyes and said very softly, "You're Jane Doe from Chicago, aren't you?"

You are a badass, you are a badass, you are a badass. Janine repeated it over and over to herself as Kiki directed. Carlos showed up to escort her to the party, the two sidekicks. Kiki suggested they make an entrance together. Kiki said that if they played their cards right, they would not only be on the silver screen, but on every screen from sea to shining sea. And they were the authors of this little ghost story, with all the rights involved. Kiki said that the little taste of success they've had was about to overflow.

But for Kiki, the best part of the media attention was providing proof that the mysterious door to the spiritual world, once closed fast to the world, would be opened. Kiki insisted that they were on the cutting edge of revealing a new dimension. Good grief, Janine thought.

Janine opened the door of Kiki's hotel room and observed a very uncomfortable version of Carlos standing in a jacket and open collared shirt. His eyes popped open when he saw her.

"Oh my god," he exclaimed, "you really are a girl."

"Is it too much?"

"Depends on who's looking."

"What do you mean?"

"The other girls are going to hate you." He chuckled.

Carlos offered his arm, and they started walking. Out the back door of the hotel, the Malabar steak house was in the next building over. The parking lot overflowed with fancy cars. Two limousines parked side by side in the back told them they were fashionably late.

"Did your wife get upset that you got called back so soon?"

"Maria's a little excited about the possibility of us being backed by a big studio. She already calls me a TV star for walking around in the background, now she thinks I could be a movie star too. The bonus didn't hurt either." He chuckled.

Carlos opened the door for her and the hostess directed them toward the stairs. They moved past a jam-packed bar and a restaurant full of a glamorous-looking crowd. Excitement buzzed throughout the entire building. When they reached the top of the stairs, Janine could see that it was basically a cocktail party with a buffet. Carlos pointed to the bar.

"I'm going to need a drink to get through this," he said. "Want one?"

"Go on," she told him. "I'm going to stroll around."

What she really meant was search around for Ian or Kiki. Mike Dunn stood in the corner, talking to a small group of men in suits. Lawyers circle, Janine guessed. Ted sat uncomfortably at a far table, eating by himself and ignoring the people, introvert's circle of one. Pretty girls fluttered everywhere, pretty men too, most likely all actors. Janine spotted Steve at a table, speaking intimately with three men and an older woman. Kiki stood in the middle of the room surrounded by a small crowd. She chatted and laughed in a flirtatious way with the people around her, right at home being the center of attention. How did she do it? Doctor McNally stood in the center of his own small circle. Mostly women surrounded him. They all resembled models or actresses. Ian appeared very pleased with the attention and not at all concerned about finding her. She felt a little heat of anger well up that she realized was jealousy. You are a badass, she told herself.

"Hey there, miss. Can I get you a drink? You look like you might be a little thirsty." A nice-looking man moved up next to her. He wore black rimmed glasses and a nice suit and tie. "Are you an actress?"

Good question. Was she an actress? Maybe she was. She was wearing a costume. She worked on a TV show.

"I noticed your scar, is that a…"

"Knife wound," she said in a matter-of-fact voice.

She noticed his eyes staring at her cleavage. Her X. He glanced into her eyes. He was captivated, she realized. Weird. Another man came up and said hello to the first guy while sizing Janine up. Their little trio chatted about the *Spectral Analysis* show. They pondered if ghosts were truly real. By their conversation, the two men knew Kiki Mellow and Ian McNally pretty well. It dawned on her that they might be trying to impress her with their associations.

Holy crap, she thought, are these guys connected to the show? Janine knew there were people connected to *Spectral Analysis* that she had never met, like silent sponsors and producers. The black rimmed glasses guy apparently had connections to many of the people in the room. He flashed his nice even teeth and was not shy about flirting with her or touching her arm.

Janine glanced toward Ian's small group and noticed that he finally spotted her. He stared at her with a concerned expression. When she moved to face him, she watched his eyes grow wide as he realized who she was with. Janine turned to the man in glasses as he handed her a fruity cocktail that she didn't plan to drink. She thanked him nicely and was about to move away when Steve suddenly stepped up.

"Janine, I've been waiting for you." Steve nodded to the two men. "Guys, I see you've finally met our tech specialist, Janine Stinger." Why did Steve get to wear a T-shirt and jeans to this fancy party?

"Wait, this is Janine Stinger from the show?" Black Rims asked. He gave her another look up and down. "Wow, you're totally different out of that, what is it, a jumpsuit?"

"Sorry, I didn't recognize you." The other man smiled at her and shook her hand. Janine gave him a small nod. He seemed nice enough.

"Really." Black Rims grinned and felt free to touch her shoulder again. "You should think about wearing your hair like this on camera. I mean, you're cute in the uniform and all, and whatever it is you do with your hair."

"Ponytail."

"Ponytail, yes. But like this, wow. Very pretty. Sexy. I like it."

"Put a sock in it, Max," Steve told him. "Come on, Janine. Someone wants to meet you." Steve led her back toward his table. "Don't worry about those guys. They're old buddies. Contributing, silent partners. If they bug you, let me know. I want you to meet Mr. Dixon and Ms. Stammers.

They're with the studio. Don't worry, you just need to say hello for a minute."

"Okay," she said.

"You look awesome, by the way," Steve said.

"So do you. Awesomely comfortable," she said, and Steve laughed.

Mr. Dixon and Ms. Stammers rose slightly when Steve introduced her. She shook hands and smiled politely. They exchanged a few pleasantries. No, Janine told them, the X did not have a specific meaning. Then, their actual question came.

"You saw a ghost out there?" Ms. Stammers asked.

"I am almost certain of it," Janine said evenly.

"Just like that? Were you scared?" Ms. Stammers asked.

Steve cut in, "Why don't we have our little question-and-answer session now. We're all set up right over here." The other side of the table had reserve placards. Steve helped Janine to a chair. He turned to wave others over and then left suddenly to fetch them. Janine turned to Ms. Stammers on the other side of the table.

"I was scared," Janine said evenly. "In fact. I'm still a little scared."

A glimmer flashed in her eye and a small smile creased her lips. That was exactly what Mrs. Stammers wanted to hear.

Steve returned with Carlos and Ian and a few others, including Black Rimmed Glasses. Eventually Kiki strolled over and was helped to a seat. Mr. Dixon, Ms. Stammers, Black Rimmed Glasses, and two other men sat on one side of the table. Ted, Kiki, Ian, Janine, and finally Carlos sat on the other side. Most of the party people gathered around to watch. Steve introduced the crew and then the questioners; Dixon and Stammers from the studio, Black Rimmed Glasses was Max Colliers, then John Buckley and Guy Montague, all producers or sponsors, Janine didn't pay too close attention. Steve summoned a waiter to bring out tumblers and whisky. He poured for the crew and offered shots to the questioners.

"This how we debrief after a shoot," Steve spoke to the crowd. "With single malt whisky to cool our nerves." People laughed. "We review the material, analyze all the data, and discuss our findings. At this time, we'll take questions from the panel." Steve opened his hand, indicating they could start.

Mr. Dixon asked the first question. "How many unexplained encounters did you experience in, is it, Rio Linda, for this ghost story?"

Ian answered, "We investigated multiple sites, one site twice. At two of those locations, we believe we experienced true paranormal activity."

"With proof to back it up?"

"Yes," Ian confirmed.

"Can you elaborate on the proof," Ms. Stammers asked.

Steve spoke up, "We'd like to wait for the show to make those items public. But we are talking about undeniable recorded proof here. Backed by scientific evidence."

There was an elevated murmur from the crowd.

"Of course," Ms. Stammers said. "I was also told that you know the identity of the spirits you encountered. That there is a detailed story behind them. Is that true?"

Kiki answered, "Yes. We know the names of each spirit, there are two, and we know a little bit of their life story. The blood lines of the population in Rio Linda run deep. We have oral history passed down from generations. We found written notes saved in private homes as well as official documents and news clippings. Together, all of the information, and the very real psychic energy, helped us reveal a rich story line for these hauntings."

"Official documents?" one of the other men asked.

"The official city log and a vetted document from the California History Group in San Francisco. They each corroborate the history of the spirits we discovered," Ian told them.

Many questions flew at him about the science side of things. The doctor spoke about very low-frequency electromagnetic disturbances and what they could mean. He explained precautions he took to crosscheck possible causes, other than ghostly, for oddities of temperature and energy disturbances. Someone asked Carlos about the technical setup and if he believed they actually encountered a real spirit.

"Oh yes!" Carlos dramatically tugged on his collar and gulped down his whisky, drawing lots of laughter. He flashed his dimples at the crowd.

The panel was extremely curious about the ghosts. Beyond revealing that they were both young girls who lived in the 1800s, the crew didn't reveal much. Janine was encouraged to give a brief description of each apparition. She confirmed that she encountered the river ghost as a young child and mistook her for an imaginary friend. Kiki told them that several drawings by kids who drowned in the river matched Janine's description and artwork perfectly.

"As far as we know," Kiki said, "only children can see the river ghost, and every one of those children met a watery death. Except, Janine Stinger."

"Did the doctor hypnotize you?" someone asked.

"Yes, he did." Janine glanced at Ian. His eyes lingered on her and she felt an instant stirring. She hoped she wasn't beginning to blush at his smoky eyes. *You are a badass*, she told herself.

Kiki fielded questions about psychic energy and the séance in the orchard. She kept it strictly on séance setup and how best to orient a circle, only saying that the séance was a huge success but they would have to wait for the film. Janine learned that Kiki hailed from Scotland, like the doctor. Did the two go back that far? Nobody asked. Then the questions started to get more personal. Someone asked if the doctor and Kiki were secretly a couple, and everyone chuckled.

"I could never limit myself to just one fellow." Kiki purred, and that got a bigger laugh. Clearly, a few fellows were encouraged by her statement.

"I've got a question for Janine Stinger." Max with the black rimmed glassed peered directly at her. "Would you be free for a few quiet words later? I'm hoping so. I'm in town through Monday morning and hope we could have dinner tomorrow night?"

Before she could answer, Ian McNally cut in rather sharply, "Unfortunately, Janine's been called to a dinner engagement tomorrow night." As soon as he said it, he realized how he must look. He glanced at her and leaned back. "Sorry, I just know that she can't get out of it. Kiki, myself, and Janine. We're meeting with one of the main subjects for dinner. It's a pretty solid commitment." He made it sound all business.

Max was not put off, "Maybe before dinner then." He passed his card across the table confidently, clearly establishing his interest. He grinned in a charming way. His overconfidence made him very attractive. "Please, let me know if you're free. I'd love to hear more from you."

At that point, Steve stepped in and made a few toasts. The crowd closed in and random people asked their own question of the *Spectral Analysis* cast members. Carlos stood abruptly and went behind Janine to help with her chair.

Together Janine and Carlos headed out of the crowd to the far side of the room.

"That guy that wants to take you to dinner. That's Max Colliers, the oil guy."

Colliers Oil? Texas oil and petroleum? No way.

"He's like a billionaire or something. I heard they might buy the Spurs. Can you imagine that kind of money? Woohoo. Last season he was all about Kiki. He likes his pretty women. Dressing like a girl pays off, hey? I need to find me a dress like that. That kind of money, how can anyone say no? Think about the courtside seats you could get me."

"You are such a jerk, Carlos..." but she stopped immediately. Max Colliers appeared behind them, clearly hoping to take her away.

"I'm sorry to interrupt." He smiled and patted Carlos on the back. "I feel compelled to chat with Miss Stinger. Do you think we can we have a private word together?"

Max had very kind eyes behind his glasses, light brown with long lashes, and he carried himself like a gentleman. He glanced at Carlos, and Carlos looked at her, then shrugged and went away with a grin. Clearly, Carlos approved of Max.

But they weren't alone for long. Ian caught up to them. The two men seemed annoyed with each other and Janine guessed that she was the reason why. She felt guilty and thrilled at the same time. The flash of emotion in the doctor's eye tugged at her heart and the anticipation of a private reunion got her blood pumping. She glanced at his large hands and imagined a rough, warm exploration from them in the near future.

"Hi there," Ian said stiffly. "I'm going to steal Janine away for a moment."

"This is a party, Doctor. Save that work stuff for office hours. Miss Stinger, Janine and I, are just getting acquainted here. Plus, looks like you have a fan behind you."

Sure enough, there were a couple of girls standing right behind the doctor. When he turned, they instantly began chatting to him. Janine saw his flustered, blinking eyes. Ian didn't know how to be impolite. They insisted on taking a photo with him. Max leaned in to speak softly. He attempted to lead her away, but she didn't budge.

"Can we find a less busy spot? Downstairs. Or, I have a car out back. We could disappear somewhere quiet for a coffee, lose this crowd. I'm very interested in learning more about you." His eyes seemed very interested in her X knife scar.

Ian suddenly reached out and put his arm around Janine in a clearly protective embrace. He rudely ignored the fans. His sudden passionate hug was tantalizing.

"This can't wait." He glared at Max Colliers and whispered to Janine, "Come along with me."

Ian led her down the stairs, ignoring people as they went by. They snaked around the booths to the small L hallway that led them toward the facilities. As soon as they turned the corner, Ian kissed her full on. His hand went over her near naked shoulders and then lightly traced her X. Her body instantly reacted and she pressed herself against him. For a moment, the noise and activity in the restaurant ceased. She was breathless, happy, and extremely hot for him. She was right where she wanted to be. She had waited two long days for that kiss.

"Do you want to wear my jacket?" he asked.

"What? Why?"

"Well, you look absolutely beautiful, stunning. But you in that dress is getting a lot of attention. The way some of those guys were looking at you, especially that pretentious prick, Max. The nerve of him asking you for a date in front of that crowd. What did he expect you to say on the spot like that?" He looked down at her and drew in his breath. "This has to be Kiki's handiwork. I don't know whether to thank her or curse her." He caressed her shoulder again, then bent down and kissed it lightly. "Did you find Max interesting? I about had a panic attack seeing him and Dave swarm you. Those two are notorious playboys. You should stay away from them."

"You don't think I can handle myself? What about you? You have a lot of female fans flocking around you and they don't appear very shy." Her hands pressed against his chest, to push him away, but he didn't yield. He kept her solidly in his embrace, not letting her budge.

A sudden wave of ice-cold fear coarse through her veins.

"I like to get you out of here right now." He kissed her again. People walked past, clearly noticing, but Ian didn't seem to care. "Do you think we'll be missed? Probably. I'm afraid you might get propositioned if you stay. By more than just Max Colliers. Crikes, why aren't you sticking next to Carlos or Ted?"

"Why aren't you?" *Was it anger she felt developing?*

"Okay, fair. You're having a good time." Ian was a little upset. "But if you're not careful, you are going to make me clock some poor lout."

"I'm not making you do anything." *Or just fear?*

He considered her for a moment.

"I've got an idea," he said. "Let's go back upstairs together, like this." He held her hand up in his. "And maybe, some of the time, I can slip my hand around your waist, like this." His arm went down to pull her even closer. "And just to make sure nobody has a question about what it all means, perhaps I can kiss you once or twice, like this." He leaned in and pecked her lightly on the cheek and behind her ear. He whispered softly into her ear, "I want it to be crystal clear to everyone that you are taken, that you're mine."

This blood flow was different than the heated response to his kiss earlier. Something felt completely out of phase, lopsided. A familiar and very frightening feeling flooded her chest. She imagined Ian pulling her away and confining her somewhere until she agreed to behave the way he wanted. She knew that was crazy, but she couldn't get the thought out of her head or tamp down the panic building in her chest. *What would he do if she refused?*

Janine forcefully pushed Ian away and looked into his eyes. A worried expression crossed his face.

"I think you need to trust me," she said very softly, blood pounding, moving away. *Good grief, was she afraid of him?*

"I do. I do trust you," he countered quickly.

"Well then, Max Colliers or any of those other men upstairs shouldn't matter, should they? So what if I talk with any of them. It's a cocktail party." *She definitely felt fear.*

"I guess I'm a wee bit jealous," he said. "I did not enjoy seeing him ogle you like that, or pulling on your arm. Talking to a guy like Max encourages him. He's got a considerable reputation and, somehow, lots of women actually prefer him." His eyes began to blink, and he was clearly upset.

"I understand jealousy." Janine tried to suppress her growing emotions. "I get jealous watching girls flirt with you but I don't try to dictate your movements, or hide you away, or act like I own you."

"Blimey," he cursed. "That's not what I meant. I don't think I own you. I just don't want—"

"I won't have a controlling, possessive man in my life ever again. Never. I won't do it. Do you understand? As much as I really want you, I'm afraid to leave with you right now."

Immediately, she wanted to take it back. He appeared slapped in the face. And why wouldn't he? Didn't she just equate his possessive impulse with the man who made all the marks on her body?

He moved away from her. His eyes were blinking rapidly, his sign that he was trying to sort things out in his mind. He looked everywhere but at her.

"I didn't mean it the way it sounded," she said softly, slowly. "I'm sorry. I'm just…I just missed you, and I'm self-conscious in this dress, and I don't really drink, and I'm afraid of…I don't know what I'm afraid of."

Ian nodded. He still did not look her in the eye.

"No need to explain, we're just a little anxious, that's all. There's a lot going on, and this thing, with us, we got…interrupted." He gave her a stiff little smile, still blinking. "Let's just go up and finish out the party. We'll work this out later."

She nodded, "You go first. I'll meet you. I'm just going to step into the ladies room for a bit."

She watched him meander away before she beelined out the door. She found the truck in the lot between the hotel and the restaurant and pulled out her phone. She woke Doctor Crisper, she could tell by his groggy voice. But the good doctor always said to call day or night, rain or shine. So far, she managed to avoid calling Doctor Crisper for ten months.

Cool as always, the doctor did not act surprised at her phone call. He spoke as if their last conversation happened earlier that week. She told him about finally visiting her sister and Sammy. She told him about her job, the friends she made, and her plan to finish college. She told him about taking a chance with Ian McNally and then becoming frightened.

"Janine," he said over the phone, "you realize that the first relationship may not be the one that lasts. There's bound to be a minefield of these flashes of feelings and memories to work through. Just take it one day at a time. I am proud of you. You sound like you are doing great. But give yourself permission to make a mistake here or there and move on if needed."

Doctor Crisper asked her about Sammy and more about how that meeting went. The entire conversation lasted about half an hour. Mostly just Janine talking. She ended the call and stared at the restaurant. She debated whether she should go back inside. It didn't seem to be a good idea. She no longer felt like such a badass.

She noticed three new messages. All from Ian. *Where are you? Are you all right? I'm sorry, are you still downstairs?* Then he was there, standing outside the door of the Malabar, searching everywhere. His eyes, like heat seeking missiles, zeroed in on the truck. Spotted!

Janine quickly turned over the engine and drove out of the parking lot. She texted with one hand, I'm tired, it's late, my sis comes in the morning. See you tomorrow. Then she completely shut her phone down as she drove away.

Why did you leave me? One each for redemption. Where are you? Heed the dictum. She can be the last one. Are you all right? The first relationship may not be the one that lasts.

Voices echoed in her head and tumbled together in her sleep. Janine remained stuck in a vivid nightmare. Loads of kids frolicked along the river edge as the current raged dangerously behind them. A voice kept whispering, *why did you leave me?* She tried to call out, to warn the children, but only static emerged. A young Henry Webber stood on the shoreline encouraging everyone to play in the water. She began to panic. Suddenly, she was running through the dark woods, familiar woods, worried she'd turn wrong again. She felt his footsteps right behind her. Miraculously, she turned right and relief flooded her system, but only for a second, because she was back on the pebbly shore moving obediently toward the river.

"Wake up!" Someone shook her.

Janine opened her groggy eyes and felt dizzy. Jumbled images of Henry near the river remained behind her eyes. Was that a memory or a dream? Her heartbeat pounded in her ears. Juliana smiled down at her. Janine sat up in bed and hugged her sister. Beautiful, capable, levelheaded Juliana.

"We're all downstairs," Juliana said. "Gram told me not to wake you. You had some sort of big-deal party last night?" She noticed the shimmery blue dress slung over a chair. She walked over and picked it up, admiring it. "You wore this? Must have looked gorgeous."

Janine checked the time. Noon!

"Oh no, Gram should have woke me. When did you guys get in?"

"Don't worry about it, we were running late," Juliana said. "We've only been here for about half an hour. The kids are not going to let you sleep. They all want to go to Fairy Tale Town. Gram is feeding them a little snack right now and we're going to head out in about twenty minutes. Think you can be ready by then?"

"Of course."

They wandered around Fairy Tale Town, a little storybook village filled with playground equipment across from the Sacramento Zoo. Ashley was nearly a teenager but still had fun with her smaller siblings. Jack was eight, and Sammy just turned four. Janine watched the kids run into the crooked mile attraction, a short, raised, winding pathway painted bright yellow. It wound through a jungle of trees and bushes in a twisting, turning circuit. Janine remembered the fun she used to have with her older sister on that narrow trail.

"Juju, Jaja, Juju, Jaja," Sammy and Jack chanted together, taunting their mother and aunt.

Gram laughed with them. She followed the children into the crooked mile walk.

"Let me get this straight, your imaginary friend is now a ghost." Juliana said. It sounded ridiculous coming out of Juliana's mouth.

"So it seems," Janine said.

"Gram says you guys are digging up real ghosts out here," Juliana said. "She seems to think your show is going to make a movie out of her river ghost." Juliana was laughing. It sounded incredibly ridiculous when Juliana said it.

"Don't tease, Juju, it's my job. We really got some interesting stuff out here."

"Didn't you just tell me, at Sammy's birthday, that this show was all fun and games for you?" Juliana asked. "Now tell the truth, do you really think you've seen a ghost?"

Janine hugged her sister. "I'm not sure what I believe. But believe me, at least there's talk of a real movie here. And there's a good story for a ghost out here. And we've got some nice unexplainable footage that people are really going to love. Better than anything we've taped before."

"Gram says this is going to be big for you." Juliana hugged her back. "I'm just really happy that things have turned around, and you're doing so, so fantastic. I'm proud of you, Janine. Truthfully, the kids, Ashley especially, love the show. Ashley is always bragging about her aunt Janine. She loves having you back. And she's super excited to meet Kiki Mellow and that dreamy Scottish doctor tonight."

Just worry about one thing at a time, Janine told herself. They watched the kids emerge from the crocked mile then turn to go right back in again. Janine's eyes were drawn to Sammy.

Juliana called out, "Where's Gram?"

"We're going back in to get her," Ashley told her.

Sammy and Jack sang, "Juju, Jaja, Juju, Jaja."

Jack held Sammy's hand as they ran past, grinning wildly at Juliana and Janine. Sammy's hair flew all over the place. Her ringlets were probably a nightmare to detangle. Sammy's laughing bright eyes locked right onto Janine's, causing her heart to skip a beat. *Oh my god, she's so beautiful,* Janine thought.

"Juliana," Janine got her sister's attention. "I never thanked you properly for taking Sammy. After everything I said and did. How horrible I was. I'm so sorry. Thank you. I'm so grateful you took her. I can't believe how beautiful she is."

Juliana embraced her for a very long time. They both ended up crying a bit.

"She really is a terrific girl. She's a lot like you. She's the most adorable little imp imaginable."

"I wasn't kidding when I said I might be a believer. Gram may not totally be off her rocker about these ghosts. I think I've seen something?"

"Like a real ghost?" Juliana's eyes creased.

"It doesn't hurt to keep the kids in sight when we're so close to the river, right."

"Oh Janine, are you going to pull a Gram?" Juliana looked worried. Janine didn't like that distressed face. She caused more stress in Juliana's life than she cared to admit.

"Ghost or no ghost, my kids won't run around unsupervised. We'll restrict them to the cut lawn, like you were. Please don't press Gram's ghost on us, okay. We want a nice, no-nonsense visit. Gram already urged me to tell your Kiki about what happened way back then, and I'm not participating," Juliana said.

"Kiki wants an interview?"

"I don't think that request is coming from anyone but Gram." She turned her big sister, scrutiny eyes on her. "Look, Janine. You had an imaginary friend, okay. I watched you. You would get bored in the house and run around talking and singing to yourself. There was nothing there but you, Janine. It was broad daylight. I was too old to play kid games all the time, I'm sorry. I was a bit of a preoccupied teen."

"They say other kids saw the same girl I did. I knew her name."

"That may be my fault too." Juliana shook her head. "You always wanted to stay up and roast marshmallows when my friends came over. You heard plenty of tales about that river ghost. Me, Chrissy, and Tanya, we told you the stories. I was responsible for babysitting you, remember? Gram often ran off to play cards and put me in charge. I didn't want you running down to the river on my watch."

"But, I actually remember seeing her."

"Janine, the first time I asked you what your friend looked like, you couldn't tell me. I suggested blond hair. I suggested blue eyes because that's what the river ghost is supposed to look like. I didn't know it was so taboo for you to see that ghost. I didn't realize that Gram would take it so seriously."

Juliana nodded at her disbelief.

"You see, there is no ghost." Juliana said firmly, "There is only a ghost story."

Gram loved hosting large dinner parties created by her mysterious roommate, Misty. Janine realized that Misty must also be responsible for the biscuits and coffee each morning. Misty, who people hardly ever encountered, was like a ghost herself. When they got back from Sacramento, Janine noted that Misty prepared easy-to-serve food and set the table. Then Misty pulled her disappearing act and hid in her room from the commotion.

Adam, Juliana's husband, relaxed in the doctor's easy chair with the newspaper. He remained at the house to repair a rain gutter for Gram and must have completed his task quickly, as, he appeared pretty comfortable in the lounge chair. He also discovered Ian's single malt Scottish whisky and enjoyed an early cocktail. He smiled as Sammy ran over to jump on him. Sammy adored her father.

"Your Misty says it's all ready to go. She's done for the night and doesn't want to be disturbed." Adam managed to relay his message from under Sammy's little bear hug.

"Such an introvert," Gram said. "She abhors any type of socializing. Even when it's just the two of us. She refuses to eat or even watch TV with me sometimes. She's so sour."

"How long has Misty been here?" Adam asked.

Gram just waved the question away and hurried into the kitchen. Juliana and Ashley rushed upstairs to freshen up. Janine plopped on the couch and Sammy ran over to bear hug her next. Janine still felt overwhelmed around her little niece. She hugged the little body tightly, soaking her in. What did Juliana plan on telling Sammy about the past? Surely, Ashley knew something, but how much? She obviously knew Sammy was adopted, but did she know how that adoption came to pass? This was a subject Janine feared to bring up.

Sammy grabbed Janine's face with her little hands and looked directly into her eyes.

"I love you, girl," Sammy said, stunning her with an echo of Gram's voice. Then she jumped down and ran off.

"Jaja!" Gram called from the kitchen, "Are you setting up the cocktail bar?"

Janine jumped up, still a little touched from Sammy's spontaneous declaration. She felt very lucky to get a second chance with Sammy. She went to Gram's minibar area.

"I didn't know I was supposed to!" she yelled back, looking for the ice bucket.

Adam strolled over to help. Her brother-in-law was a Texas A&M grad who worked as an accountant in a large company. Adam and Juliana's relationship went back to their high school days and Janine first met Adam when she was Jack's age. Through the years, Adam always managed to stay out of the drama between the sisters. Janine knew that Adam harbored guilt for encouraging Janine to go so far away to college against Juliana's advice. He shouldn't. How could anyone know what would happen?

The doorbell rang. Both Adam and Janine looked toward the front door. Adam glanced her way but Janine remained frozen in place. This was it. What would she do? Doctor Crisper's wise words put things in perspective. Maybe she should just tell herself, *nice try*, and move on. Maybe Ian decided not to come after all and it was only Kiki. Crap, she wished she didn't have so many fears haunting her. Once upon a time, she had been the opposite of insecure.

"Should I get that? Or do you want to?"

"You go," she said quietly.

But Ashley leaped down the stairs and beat them to the door. She flung it open and instantly gasped and did a little jump.

"Oh my god! Hello, hello, come right in." Ashly's wide eyes were excited as she waved Kiki and Ian into the house. "Mom, Mom! Gram, they're here. The guests are here!" Ashley announced loudly.

Kiki was dressed like a normal person. She wore a simple, pretty, fairly modest, calf-length dress with low heeled, neutral-toned shoes. Her hair, now a dark-brown color, flowed naturally in a very feminine, conservative style.

But there was no way to tone down her striking green eyes, and she still drew all the attention in the room instantly.

Ian carried a bottle of wine, which Adam took off his hands. He also carried two bunches of flowers. He briefly nodded to Ashley and Adam before fixing his attention on Janine. He seemed on edge, and his eyes were blinking.

"Can I get a picture? Would you take a picture with me?" Ashly pulled her cell phone out. "Dad, Dad, take one with my camera."

"Ash. Let them come in and get settled a bit. Maybe they'd like a refreshment. We have a nice batch of single malt Scottish whisky," Adam told them.

Kiki smiled and winked at the teen. "Let's take a few now while we're fresh, and we'll take a few later when we're old friends."

She glided over to Ashley, took her phone, and passed it to Adam. Kiki and Ashley were very close to the same height. Adam appeared a bit bashful with Kiki. He probably imagined Kiki in one of her revealing show outfits. She did have a sex-symbol reputation and was striking no matter what she wore. Kiki passed Adam her own phone as well.

"Call me Kiki, by the way. And this fine fellow is Ian McNally."

Ian greeted Adam and joined Kiki and Ashley. Ian still clutched his two bunches of flowers. He gave Janine a brief smile under his blinking eyes. She instantly felt bad about turning her phone off to avoid talking to him. She really just wanted to walk over and embrace him. But Doctor Crisper's warning, *the first relationship may not be the one that lasts*, hovered in the back of her mind, keeping her frozen in place.

"I'm Ashley," the teen said a little meekly.

"We know who you are," Kiki told her. "I've heard a lot about you from your grandma, great-grandma, Gram." she corrected. "You remind me a bit of your Auntie Janine over there."

Gram entered the room, as did Juliana, Sammy, and Jack. Gram conducted formal introductions while Janine stood like a statue as quiet as a mouse. Ian and Kiki shook hands with each small child. Sammy stared into Kiki's eyes and wondered how they got so very green. Sammy giggled contagiously and Kiki fell into the giggles with her. Then, Kiki fixed those very green eyes directly on Janine and it was clear that she knew exactly who Sammy was. Thankfully, Adam began pouring drinks. Janine snapped out of it enough to help open the bottle of wine Ian brought. Kiki strolled over and gave her a very warm hug and accepted a glass of wine.

"These are for you," Ian presented Gram with one bunch of flowers. "A spring mix, to liven up the table." Gram smiled, very pleased. Ian turned to Janine, he hesitated a moment, unsure of himself with blinking eyes. "And these are for you." He passed her a bunch of red, long-stem roses. He gave her a nervous smile. Janine accepted them shyly, melting all over again. She managed not to leap into his arms and bashfully returned his smile instead.

"Thank you," she said. "They're beautiful."

Ian appeared very relieved. His eyes calmed down.

"Come on girl," Gram nudged her toward the kitchen. "Let's find a couple of vases for these beauties."

Misty prepared the perfect roast with stewed potatoes, steamed carrots, and a nice pumpkin soup to start. Juliana and Janine served. They were seated on the kitchen side of the table, facing Kiki, Ashley, and Ian. Adam carved the roast at the head of the table and Sammy and Jack were seated together at the tail. The kids were in their own little world, ignoring the grown-ups and giggling about something. Juliana, Ashley, and Adam asked loads of questions about ghosts and the show. Janine realized that though she knew much of the Rio Linda story, she did not know how they planned to tell the story.

"I'd like to read the wagon-train diary, if that's possible." Juliana cut roast and potatoes into very small pieces for Sammy. Sammy's eyes stared adoringly at her mother. "Are there copies here?"

"I've got a set in the office," Gram said, "as well as the pages found in the old Bible. The torn-out, secret pages. Although, Doctor McNally asked to borrow some of them for something, what was it, an authentication check?"

"I won't need them till Tuesday," Ian said across the table. "I'll bring them right back, of course. I'm afraid the history group will be interested in buying them, all the torn-out pages, eventually. They were pretty excited on the phone." He turned his pretty blue eyes on Janine and Juliana. "The tear marks on the pages found in your gram's old Bible appear to match tear marks in the wagon-train diary. They want to see a couple of actual pages to confirm and agreed to do a little low-key interview this week."

"If you can get away," Kiki spoke across the table toward Janine, "Maybe you can go and help the doctor with that. Take one of the handheld cameras. Better than a tripod. Everyone else is pretty booked with the river shoot. I'm sure Ian would love the help."

Was this another ruse? Was Kiki helping him now? Janine glanced between Kiki and Ian, suspicious. She changed the subject.

"Be careful reading that diary, Juju." Janine glanced at Gram. "It has some upsetting revelations in there."

"You mean the Donner Party type stuff?" Juliana asked. "I know about that."

"Ooh, a party!" Sammy perked up with bright eyes.

"Not that type of party, honey." Juliana stroked Sammy's wild hair. She chuckled and then Sammy and Jack went back to their private, quiet chatter.

Everyone focused on their meal for a few moments. Ashley told Kiki her friends in Texas tried to conjure a ghost during a slumber party. They used Kiki's summoning charm and freaked themselves out, but nothing happened.

"What's the Donner Party?" Ashley suddenly asked.

"The Donner Party," her father Adam grinned wickedly, "not the best dinner conversation, but you asked for it. Back in the Old West days, a group of travelers got stuck in the High Sierras during a snowstorm. They nearly starved to death at Donner Lake, right up Interstate 80. They survived by resorting to…" He looked around, then dramatically turned to Ashley. "Cannibalism!"

"That's so gross, Dad!" Ashley pushed her plate away.

"Cannon balls!" Sammy giggled across the table at her father. "Cannon balls!"

"Want me to take her to the glass patio to watch a movie?" Jack asked his mother.

Juliana nodded. "Are you two done here?"

The kids nodded and flew from the table, but not before running around and giving everyone a little hug and kiss or a handshake.

"That's not what I meant about the revelation. This one is a little more personal," Janine said.

"You mean about Great-Grandma Williams?" Juliana and Gram exchanged a glance with each other and then burst into laughter. "Gram already told me. How did you put it? Grandma Williams is no longer a sorry sinner. Gram has solid proof that exonerates her completely. What's the name again? Not Christopher but…" Juliana started snapping her fingers and looked to Gram.

"George Lumen," Gram said.

"You already know about this?" Janine asked Juliana.

"I called Juliana when you were out doing your street filming, as soon as I read that thing. What was I supposed to do?" Gram told Janine. "I had to tell somebody, and Juju has always known about my mistake blaming my mother. You know, thinking she was hiding that terrible secret."

"What secret?" Ashley asked.

"Juliana knows about the DNA test too?" Janine asked. Was Janine always the last to know everything?

"Who do you think helped me contact the DNA people?" Gram said. "I'm a little old lady. I can barely use a computer."

"What DNA test?" Ashley asked.

They spent the next several minutes reviewing their family lineage and how Leone, with her obsession with her online DNA family tree, opened up a whole can of worms. The real Christopher Williams was buried somewhere near Lake Tahoe, which meant half their ancestors were really not their ancestors at all. Gram proposed a road trip to see the lakes, Tahoe and Donner. They could check out the history museum at Donner Lake and get a better idea of what must have happened in 1840.

"Plus, it is really beautiful up there," Adam said.

"I agree." Ian stared directly at Janine. "Very bonnie landscape up there."

Janine felt that moment in the hotel at Donner Lake again. The moment when she woke up in bed with his hand caressing the scar on her back; when her past didn't seem to matter at all; when she no longer felt completely ruined. Ian's soft eyes warmed her heart.

"I got an idea," Ashley said. "When Aunt Jaja goes to San Francisco for work, we should do a day trip to Tahoe. I want to see some of the history stuff."

"That's a good idea," Gram said.

"I am up for that," Adam said.

"I still don't understand where the ghosts come in," Juliana said. "Who are they? Were they kids in the wagon train? Did they die on the wagon train? Where do the ghosts come in? Why would one haunt an orchard and one haunt the river? Are they connected in any way?"

Kiki leaned toward Ashley.

"I'm going to tell you the whole story. We didn't even tell the movie people, but I'm going to tell you, because you're family." Her green eyes flashed excitedly. "The Hansen wagon train was cursed. Terrible things happened, and they were cursed."

Ashley looked thrilled.

Kiki continued, "The River Girl Ghost is the spirit of Linda Stauch, the youngest survivor of a wagon train led by the Hansen brothers out of Missouri. In life, Linda had a sunny disposition and loved to giggle and play. She died of an unnamed illness on the same day they baptized her in that river over the hill. The baptism was likely a rushed event, in order to beat her impending death. Maybe they didn't do it in time, and thus, she is cursed to wander the surrounding area forever.

"As a spirit, Linda is a restless child, always hoping to find other children to keep her company. She lures them to the water in an attempt to get them to share her fate of drowning. She promises to be their friend forever. Unfortunately, the spirits of other children don't hang around long and she keeps searching for new friends."

"Linda was your imaginary friend, right?" Ashley peered at Janine.

"Apparently so." Janine nodded.

"Was she trying to lure Aunt Jaja to the river?" Ashley asked Kiki.

"I'm not absolutely sure," Kiki said. "You see, I believe Linda stopped luring children to the river around 1970. That's when the final part of the dictum was met and the curse was broken. Not many drownings since then, but her spirit still appears now and again because she became a part of this place. Her spirit has walked this area long enough for her essence to linger, but her original purpose, luring kids to drown, is complete."

"What's the dictum?" Adam asked.

"One each for redemption," Kiki told him. "I'll explain it in a moment."

Ashley appeared confused.

"In the first two years of the settlement, child drownings in the river were a common occurrence. People didn't realize the danger of the undertow or the catch in the rocks," Kiki continued. "In as early as the mid-1800s, many drownings were connected to the river ghost. We have those facts backed up with documentation. The town even had a special council that met about the ghost. Folks really took it seriously."

Gram brought out hot apple pie and steamy coffee; the aromas were sweet and enticing. Fresh from Apple Hill, Gram bragged. She informed Julianna and Adam that the kids appeared ready to fall asleep. With all the excitement and the time change, they were wiped out. She set up the sleeping roll outs on the back glassed-in porch for them. Juliana smiled gratefully.

"The second spirit is the essence of Mary Miller, a girl born very near the time Linda Stauch died. According to our sources, she was well aware of the River Girl Ghost. Perhaps she felt lured by the ghost or saw the ghost. It's very likely both happened. We found, or rather, your auntie found a little handwritten note buried in a collection of important documents from the ancestors of Mary Miller. A note that indicates Mary drowned herself, on purpose, at an extremely young age."

"Suicide?" Ashley gasped with wide scandalized eyes.

Kiki nodded, mirroring Ashley's shocked expression.

"We also discovered that Mary Miller is not buried in the consecrated grounds of the cemetery, but on the outside edge of the orchard."

"I didn't know that," Janine said. "Is there a family plot out there?"

Kiki shook her head. "Just Mary. The rest of the family is in the cemetery. Mary was banned from the cemetery because of her suicide. We're going to film a little clip at her grave marker with the actors this week."

"I bet that's why she haunts the orchard," Ashley said, and Kiki nodded agreement.

"Her headstone rock is flush with the ground," Ian added. "It's a chunk of river rock, similar to the big boulder in the water. I can't quite identify all of it, but it has a bit of magnetite and hematite, minerals with lots of iron, and maybe some other choice elements that I'm studying. It shows signs of magnetism, you know. A closer inspection of that river boulder suggests that a section was cut from it. Mary's marker is the right size for that missing piece."

"The Mary spirit warns people to follow the dictum," Kiki said.

"What was that again?" Ashley asked.

"One each for redemption," Kiki told her. "We're pretty sure those exact words are the dictum that she wants followed."

"What does it mean?" Juliana asked. "One each for redemption."

"It took a while to figure it all out," Kiki told her, "but, I think we've cracked the code." Kiki nodded toward Gram. "*One each*, refers to each of the original survivors of the wagon train. *For redemption*, means that the survivors must seek forgiveness for a grave sin. They want to be redeemed. But what grave sin has been committed? That's the fun part, guessing. Perhaps for killing their wagon-train leader and blaming it on the Indians. Or maybe for the cannibalism in the mountains. Or maybe something else. Either way, they're cursed until the dictum is fulfilled."

"Why would they kill the wagon-train leader?" Adam furrowed his brow.

"Read the diary." Ian patted him on the shoulder.

"What is it they must do for redemption? What do they give?" Juliana asked. "How is it tied to the river or the orchard?"

Kiki leaned in. "I think it means death. One descendent from each survivor in the wagon train must drown a watery death. Just like Linda during her baptism. That's how they will be saved. Perhaps it's some weird baptism of their lineage. Mary's written note states that riches will follow if they go willingly to their death. Hardship and death, senseless death, will occur if they resist. And that is exactly what happened here. Come on, let me show you the connections we've made."

They moved into Gram's old-fashioned rustic study. Much of the preliminary research still lay in large piles between the wingback, antique chairs. Kiki rummaged through the written notes she created. Her whiteboard still sat propped in the corner against the bookcase and Kiki retrieved it. She turned to her audience and waited as they settled into separate chairs. Kiki's eyes flashed excitedly as she spoke,

"Only a small group survived the Sierra Nevada winter of 1839 to 1840, maybe sixteen or so, a fraction of the original travelers listed in the Hansen wagon train. Parts of the Williams family, the Stauch, Miller, and Webber families made it. They decided to stop here, near the beautiful river bend instead of pushing to their final destination of San Francisco. Why? Maybe to get their story straight: To cover for the murder of Hansen, or the ordeal in the mountains, or because they have a few sick folks to care for. Linda, for instance. Or maybe something else. Whatever their reason, the cursed survivors must sacrifice one soul from each family to be redeemed. Death and struggle will befall them if they resist, riches awarded if they follow the dictum.

"The first to succumb is little Linda Stauch. Her death may have sparked the dictum, *one each for redemption*. Following her death, what happened? Riches appear. Practically overnight. The town surges in size and money drops on the vagabond survivors in the form of goods, tools, and all kinds of wealth. It's a mystery how they got it. The Millers and Webbers manage to build a successful hotel and store. The new outpost is touted as a stopping place for travelers on their way to San Francisco and the town thrives all through the1840's. But the wagon train survivors fail to feed another soul into the river.

"A whole slew of other people drown instead. An average of fifteen drownings the first few years. That's incredibly high. And we found documentation that tells of a ghostly girl haunting the river in 1843. The River Girl Ghost has made her debut. Linda is desperately seeking souls to share in her watery fate. Unfortunately, she requires souls from the wagon train, not the others, and she keeps hunting for the right victims. The town begins to falter due to a bad reputation and a better route over the mountains is created."

"The route near highway 50, on the other side of Sacramento?" Adam asked.

Kiki gave him an approving smile.

"Possibly. Mary Miller is the next link from the wagon train to drown. In a delirium, Mary dictates the secrets of the curse. She gives the guide book, so to speak, and explains the rewards and punishments of the dictum. Mary sneaks into the river willingly to set an example, to demonstrate the truth of her words. The year following her death is the first spectacular year for the new orchard. A local almond industry is born, creating the riches. Wealth from the orchard saves the community and the town grows exponentially. An added bonus, not a single child drowning for the next three years.

"But people fail to follow Mary's instructions, and the dictum is ignored. As a result, tree rot descends on Rio Linda with a fury. Much of the orchard is ruined, only the Miller trees are saved, and child drownings begin again. Four kids are swept away in 1851 alone. The River Girl Ghost is blamed for every one of them. People believe that any child who sees the ghost will surely find their way into the river. That belief stays with the town to this very day. That a death must follow an encounter with the ghost, and if it doesn't, a more terrible loss, like a disaster will happen."

"Wow. That is quite creepy," Adam said.

Kiki winked at him and flamboyantly wrote the name Sarah Williams on the board.

"Then Sarah Williams drowns in 1853. One of your relatives. I tracked her back to Ethan and Elizabeth Williams." Kiki turned to Ashley. "Sarah spoke of a girl named Linda before drowning in the river. It's reported from oral history. Almost immediately following her death, the Southern Pacific train company built a major junction a few miles from Rio Linda. It's a boom town all over again, and the hotel business flourishes. The economy thrives like never before and the local descendants of the wagon train reap the benefits, the riches. Then another kid, Bradley Monte, drowns. He descends from Ingrid and Niels Stauch. His death keeps the momentum going on the local growth of wealth. Plus, there are no child drownings for the next three years."

"All this is documented?" Juliana's brow was raised.

"City history on drowning victims and of the local economy," Ian told her. "Personal notes and letters cover the ghostly sightings. We even found two old articles from the local Herald mentioning a river ghost. One printed back in 1840 something, 1843, and another printed a couple of decades later. There are copies in those piles." He pointed to

Gram's copy of the research. "There is an implication that a committee once managed the ghost sightings and was tasked with authenticating them. There are actual meeting minutes from the early days that mention a river ghost task force."

Kiki wrote the name Bradley Monte and Eloise Webber on the board. She tapped the dry erase pen in her hand as she spoke.

"More drownings occur three years after the rail junction opened. Mostly kids without links to the wagon train. Child drownings increased drastically with the increased population. The River Girl Ghost is clearly an established myth by this time. Lots of oral history reports of her. Many of the victims make artwork right before their demise." Kiki glanced at Janine. "The dictum is not being fulfilled, so disaster hits again. Flood water covers the entire valley. Even downtown Sacramento near Sutter's Fort wallows in water. The lucrative train junction is completely destroyed and Rio Linda descends into ruins once more.

"That is, until 1865 when young Eloise Webber drowns. I traced Eloise back to Gustoff Webber, another founding member off the wagon train. Miraculously, Rio Linda recovers with poultry farms. Following the valley flood, thousands of chickens descended on Rio Linda. The new and very profitable poultry business saved Rio Linda for several years, more of the riches. The new upswing in wealth and downswing in drownings lasted almost a decade. There is only one new drowning during that entire time period, a small child named Timothy Williams, a descendant of Christopher Williams. No new wealth with this one, but the community didn't really need it as things were going well.

"Eventually more and more kids are lost to the river. More hard luck followed as well. Sometime in the early 1900s, a fowl illness, a chicken disease, wiped out the local poultry farms. The local economy suffered again."

Ashley glanced at Gram, "Do you think the free-range hens are related to those old chickens?"

Gram nodded, "I bet they are."

Kiki continued, "The population is riddled with ghostly sightings during this era. People are terrified of the ghost. The river ghost is blamed for any death near the water. At the same time, there are reports of a different ghost, one in the orchard. Each sighting mentions an urging to heed the dictum. Many believe the new ghost knows which children must be sent to the river. Perhaps the dictum was a known secret in certain circles. The Miller family has always had Mary's written instructions hidden away."

Kiki wrote Maple on the whiteboard and moved toward Gram's collection of photographs on the piano. She tapped a framed group photo.

"Next to drown is Maple Williams in 1931. Your gram has a picture of her over here. A direct descendent of Grant and Meg Williams. That's when the military base breathed life back into community. Between 1931 and the 1971 the river averaged one to two victims a year. The Mary spirit is very prominent during this period. The Miller family kept an extensive log of documented sightings of the orchard ghost." Kiki wrote the name Lara Webber and underlined it.

"The last significant victim was Lara Webber in 1972, directly linked to Rolf Webber, the last of the founding fathers on our list of survivors. Lara's death was followed by the erection of the Pepsi Bottling Company. Money pumped back into the economy and provided many of the remaining descendants the ability to make a good living, especially the Webber clan since the factory was built on their once barren plot of land. It happens to be where a section of the original orchard rotted away years ago. The most interesting fact to note, since 1972 there have been only two drownings in the river. A normal number for a river like Rio Linda. Actually, a pretty good number considering the rocks and undertow."

"Do you think the curse is broken?" Ashley asked.

"It's very likely." Kiki nodded. "The curse is fulfilled and the dictum is met. One descendant of each founding survivor has met their murky end."

"Then why would the ghost still haunt this place?" Ashley asked. "Why is she still around? Why did Aunt Janine see the river ghost?"

"Echoes. The spirit has been here for a very long time, as I mentioned earlier. Although her purpose is met, the spirit stays in a familiar spot. She lurks near the river, but no longer entices anyone into the water. Under hypnosis, your auntie said that the spirit never tried to lure her to the river. She never even mentioned the river. And your auntie was really the last one to see her. Perhaps the River Girl Ghost has finally faded away and now she is only a whisper on the wind. Soon, she'll be nothing at all."

They were interrupted by Sammy standing in the doorway.

"I need juice!" Juliana moved to rise, but Janine jumped to her feet first.

"I'll take care of this one," Janine told her sister. Janine took Sammy's hand and led her back toward the kitchen. Behind her, the conversation went on. It was a little disappointing to miss what came next, but Janine would hear it soon enough. She was more interested in tucking Sammy into bed; she hadn't got to do that yet.

"What happened to Jack?" Janine asked.

"He fell asleep," Sammy said.

Janine poured a small glass of apple juice and watched Sammy drink it down in one gulp. Sammy indicated she wanted more.

"Maybe you should drink a little water," Janine suggested. "That's a lot of juice."

"Juice!" Sammy ordered with an irresistible smile.

"Okay." She poured a little more for Sammy. "Did Jack fall asleep on the porch?"

"Gram is letting us sleep on the porch," Sammy told her. "We can see stars when we sleep. It's like we are outside but it's not outside. You can see every star in the world, Aunt Jaja. I have stars in my room, but Gram's stars are real. Really real. Real stars from outer space. I'm going to go to bed now. Thank you, Aunt Jaja."

Good grief, she was absolutely precious. Janine gave Sammy a tight hug. Little hands patted the back of her head in a comforting manner and Janine's breath caught in her throat. Little Sammy felt so nice. She had grown so much since their first brief meeting in the delivery room. She had turned away when they brought the baby over, because the grey eyes that locked onto hers were exactly like his. But not any longer. Janine could only see Sammy in those eyes now. *This is the baby I abandoned,* she thought. *Will she ever forgive me?*

She walked Sammy to the screened-in porch. Jack snored softly on one of the rollout cots and Sammy crawled into the other one. Janine tucked the blankets around the little girl and hummed softly. Janine was rewarded with one last smile. The kids slept in the rollouts Juliana and Janine used many years ago. Janine eased away and lingered at the propped open kitchen door to watch silently. She tried to resolve her tumbling emotions by breathing slowly. Sammy tossed a bit before settling in. After a moment, Sammy's breathing became slow and even.

Ian moved up behind her and her entire body felt his presence.

"That wee lassie is pretty cute. Looks just like her beautiful auntie," Ian whispered softly near her ear.

"I'm sorry about last night." Janine didn't turn around.

"Oh no, that was all me." He stepped closer, "I got stupid, jealous. I'm not used to feeling this way." His hand just barely touched hers, diffusing some of her nervous energy.

Janine glanced toward the den. Voices floated out in a lively discussion. Any one of them could come looking for her at any moment and she didn't know how to have the conversation they needed in a quiet way. Janine silently led him through the glass porch and out the back door. They stood in the fresh night air under a dark star-filled sky. *Every star in the world,* Janine silently chuckled. The river burbled in the distance. They shared a long hug. She felt herself start to breathe easier and relax, he fit her so perfectly. She debated what to say. Doctor Crisper's warning echoed in her ear, *the first relationship may not be the one that lasts.* The problem with Doctor Crisper and his friendly warning was; she wanted the relationship to last. Ian's voice broke their silence.

"Janine, I have to tell you something, about what I feel for you. Maybe we went a little too far, too fast, I don't know. I just got very swept away, overexcited. I was worried about that, you know, that I would push things too fast and scare you off. But I need to tell you…" Ian paused, and Janine could feel the anxious energy he emitted. She felt nervous too. He hesitated a moment longer, then inhaled a deep breath. "I'm pretty sure I may have fallen in love with you."

Why did you leave me?

She froze, suddenly frightened. Did she actually hear that whispered voice? Something caught her eye. In the distance, at the edge of the manicured lawn, where Linda used to stand, shadows moved in the darkness. Were her eyes playing tricks on her? Were the stories in the den catching up to her? She took a hesitant step toward the shadow.

"Crikes. Too fast again?"

"Shh." She grabbed his warm hand and hushed him. She pointed to the far lawn, heart thumping. "Something's out there. I just saw, or sensed, something out there."

Slowly, silently, they inched toward the far edge of the green. The ghost was not supposed to come out at night, Janine reassured herself. Linda was a daytime spirit. But the air temperature dipped as they moved farther from the house. The river flowed just beyond the small mound in front of them and the sounds of moving water grew louder. A very faint breeze stirred her hair and it felt like the whisper from the river that day. Did she detect another movement in the corner of her eye, in her periphery? Janine turned quickly but saw nothing.

Her heart hammered in her chest. She could hear herself breathing.

"Do you see something?" Ian whispered.

"No."

"Did you hear something?"

"Maybe."

"Does this feel familiar, like the ghost?" he asked.

"A little."

"Are you scared?" he whispered.

"Yes." But she wasn't sure what she was scared of. *Identify the trigger.*

"Should we go back inside?"

"Yes."

He stood very close, protectively close.

"About what I said a minute ago…" He hesitated again. *Identify the trigger.*

Her hand shot up to stop him from speaking.

Fixating on the firm line of his jaw, she realized the meaning behind her out of control pulse, the panic attacks, the sensations haunting her, everything. Like pieces of a jigsaw, they all snapped together dispelling the mystery. Beyond a shadow of a doubt, *he was the trigger!*

She felt like such an idiot.

"I may have fallen in love with you too." Her voice was barely a whisper.

He stopped moving.

She nodded. "And I'm a little scared about that."

His eyes stared at her in the darkness. He pulled her into a close embrace and they kissed passionately, then desperately. Janine entertained the idea of getting a bit indecent with him on Gram's back lawn. The yard was completely sheltered from the road and other houses, she reasoned. As long as everyone stayed inside, they could get away with it. It could work. It would be so nice. The voice of a little girl interrupted them. They both jumped at the same time.

"Is somebody out there?" Sammy's voice floated from the house. They could see her silhouette poking above the screened door window. "I see you!"

"It's just us, Sammy," Janine called to her, "Aunt Jaja and the doctor. We're coming in." Janine turned to Ian. "Let's not discuss what happened out here, with them in there. I don't want to freak anyone out tonight. After Kiki's story, poor Ashley is going to start seeing ghosts."

"Are you coming with me to San Francisco?"

"Yes."

"Good." He took a firm grip of her hand as they approached the porch door.

They entered into the little glass covered room as quietly as possible. Jack still snored in the corner. Sammy stood poised with her hands on her hips and a critical look in her eye. All Juliana, Janine thought.

"What were you doing out there?" Again, just like Juliana.

"Nothing," Janine told her. "Why are you still awake?"

"I heard somebody talking," Sammy critically sized up Doctor McNally then gave him the cutest smile. Sammy giggled a bit.

"Sorry Sammy, it was us," he said.

"Are you going back to sleep?" Janine asked.

"I need another kiss good night."

Janine urged Ian to go ahead to the den. Then she kissed Sammy on the forehead and tucked the small girl into the rollout bedding.

"I love you, girl." Sammy wriggled into her cot.

"I love *you*, girl," Janine said back softly, heart pounding.

Sammy closed her eyes instantly and settled into her pillow with her golden-brown hair splayed this way and that way. It will surely be a tangled mess in the morning, Janine thought. *He thinks she looks just like me.* Janine touched one of Sammy's curls before standing up. She made certain the back screen and the actual door were both locked and bolted shut. Linda is not allowed to enter the house. She glanced toward the edge of Gram's yard and only saw a quiet night. Definitely her mind playing tricks out there. That shadow was likely one of Gram's hens. *There is no ghost. There is just a ghost story.* And she didn't care what Doctor Crisper said.

Apparently, Kiki, Juliana, Gram, Ashley, and Adam had gotten into a nice discussion on the differences between pagan practices, wiccan belief, and witchcraft. Kiki had her signature tarot cards spread out on the table and was in the process of explaining the meaning behind them to Ashley. Kiki told Ashley that a dear friend back in Scotland made the art on those cards. The images came from dreams, and Kiki has had similar images in her own dreams.

Ian was beaming. He wore a giant grin and was conspicuously in a terrific mood. He stood off to the side, conversing with Adam in an animated way, sharing the last of the whisky. Juliana flipped through the photocopied pages of the wagon train diary. After another half hour of tarot lessons, Kiki and Ian declared it time to leave. They had an early morning at the river. The actors were going to film a scene in the water. They would be able to see the whole thing from the top of the mound on the edge of Gram's property.

After the door finally closed, Ashley turned her big brown doe eyes on Janine.

"Oh, my goodness, Aunt Jaja. Doctor McNally is totally trying to date you!" Ashley exclaimed.

"Where in the world did that come from?" Janine laughed.

"He gave you flowers. Did that not clue you in?" Ashley said.

"He gave Gram flowers too," Adam pointed out.

"Dad," Ashley rolled her eyes. "What do you think long-stemmed red roses mean? Love. Love, Dad. Doctor McNally is such a dreamy romantic with a cool accent. Are going to go for it, Aunt Ja? You should. All my friends will be so excited." Ashley did a little jump.

"Yes." Juliana laughed. "Do it for Ashley's friends. They will be so excited."

Janine just waved them away and went into the den to help Gram clean up. Gram sat on the piano bench looking at the photographs lined up on the baby grand. She inspected the old tin type of Christopher Williams. She motioned for Janine to sit near and handed the tin-plated photo to her.

"That Kiki is a character," Gram said. "I enjoy her company. She went out of her way with Ashley, you know."

Janine studied the photo, grainy and dark, a boy stood stiffly. He was dressed in a plain shirt, string tie and short pants. There were buckles on his shoes. His hair was slicked to the side in an unnatural way. Most likely, he had an unmanageable cowlick, like Jack, and they used a lot of hair grease, or water, to try to tamp it down.

"She knows all about me, everything," Janine confided in hushed tones. "Last night. She saw some of my scars and guessed, *Jane Doe from Chicago*. On her first try. She instantly knew who I was."

"It's a scary story, Janine. And Kiki makes a lot of good guesses. She's a real spiritual medium. Kiki is someone who can see things other people can't. I don't think anyone else would be able to guess. I also don't think Kiki is the type to talk about it. Gossip about it."

"I agree with you," Janine said. She held the tin plate photo. "So, is this Christopher Williams or George Lumen?"

"I think Christopher Williams," Gram's said. "This boy looks blond, and Christopher Williams, our Christopher, George, had brown hair."

"Hard to tell in this photo, a grainy black and white. Plus, hair often darkens with age. But it could still be our Christopher, George."

Chapter 11

River Girl

Janine's family enjoyed the morning sunshine on the top of the small hill that separated Gram's house from the calm Rio Linda River and watched the film crew set up along the small sparse beach. The boulders responsible for so many deaths jutted out of the water reflecting the morning light with sparkles of different colors. A small group of actors dressed in old-time clothes were gathered in a group drinking coffee and chatting.

"I see Kiki!" Ashley said. Kiki turned at that moment and waved. Her sixth sense?

"What are they doing with those huge tripods?" Juliana wondered.

"Looks like their rigging a cable across the river. Maybe they're going to suspend a camera," Adam said. "Anyone want to get a closer look?"

"Me!" Jack could barely sit still.

"Me too." Ashley stood up.

"You're not going to get past those two guys," Juliana said. "Plus, Gram wants to go to the market up in Roseville."

Two policemen stood on the outer edge of the roped-off area where they recently turned a dog walker away. Adam stood up and motioned for Ashley and Jack to start moving toward the river. Sammy sat in Janine's lap, humming and blowing on dandelions. Janine was in absolute heaven cuddling her.

"Well, okay. We'll see you three later. Stay away from the water!" Juliana yelled after them.

Ashley turned and waved. They watched as the policemen stopped Adam, Ashley, and Jack at the perimeter line. The small group talked a bit, then Kiki strolled toward them. She reached over the line and hugged Ashley. The trio crossed over with Kiki and joined the group of actors.

"They got in." Juliana smiled. She nodded to Janine and Sammy. "Come on, girls, let's take Gram to that farmer's market. Somebody told me we can get some local almond butter there."

There was a close call at the river. One of the actors, a little kid, went beyond the safety zone placed in the water. He purposely waded toward the center of the river and then slipped into the quick rip stream along the bottom. The river grabbed him and swept him quickly toward the rocks. For a couple of terrifying moments, the water forcefully pressed his body against the boulders as the current tried to pull him under. Thankfully, rescue personnel were standing by for just such an event. Two men with air tanks moved fast.

"The water seemed absolutely calm," Adam said. "You'd never imagine it could sweep someone away that fast, but apparently there's a drop-off and a narrow slip stream where the water rushes by. It can knock a grown man off his feet, they say."

Juliana handed a sleeping Sammy to Adam.

"Can you put this one to bed?"

"Sure." He lugged Sammy away with Jack following.

"And where were you and Jack during this near-drowning?" Juliana crossed her arms over her chest. "Were you scared? Are you okay?"

"Oh mom," Ashley said. "We were sitting on the beach. We hung out with Kiki and the director. But it was pretty scary, I mean, it didn't look like there was a current at all."

"Just stay away from that river bend," Gram told her. "You heard the history of drownings. There doesn't need to be a ghost to make it dangerous."

"We definitely saw that," Ashley said. "One of the rescuers got stuck in the rock during the rescue. When he came out, he told us that the water pushed his foot into an opening. He had to fight the current and twist his foot to get out."

Juliana shook her head. "They should remove those rocks if they're so dangerous."

"Well, there's no swimming in that part of the river. You've seen the signs," Gram said. "A while back the city looked at giant boulder removal and it would cost a pretty sum. The city planners argued that moving the rocks would shift the placement of the river downstream. They figured it would flood Marysville Boulevard at least once a year, all the way down to where it connects to Elverta Road. Kind of a busy place. There are houses down there. Lots of people live down there."

Early Tuesday morning Ian McNally came round in a BMW rental car with an extra warm latte from Starbucks. Janine carried the lost diary pages under her arm. They were stowed inside the old Bible again and strapped together with a narrow leather belt. She double checked the equipment in the trunk to ensure they had everything needed to film an impromptu interview at the museum. Everyone in the house was still asleep when they left and the sun peeked just above the horizon. They talked and joked on the drive. Ian filled her in on what was keeping him occupied.

"I've been pretty busy with the underground stuff. I've been working with the satellite trackers to see if we can detect anything in the deeper layers of earth. There's too much high-frequency wave action to write off as ambient. They're directional. I want to rule out anything that could have caused the low frequency spikes we got."

Ian met with tech geeks from UC Davis and borrowed their ELF dish antennae. The folks at the university were very pleasant and accommodating. One professor urged him to consider being a guest lecturer in the future. He thought he'd give it a go between the seasons, what did she think of that? Ian and a few graduate students spent all day drawing lines of flux around the river and Caroline's old orchard. Something emitted, or reflected, signals with similar energy to a LORAN navigation station. It might be the river rock. Those rocks were slightly magnetic and their magnetic field did not match the direction of the earth's magnetic field. Janine found it amazing, the lengths Ian went to disprove something he wanted to prove. If he could find the source of the low-frequency electromagnetic waves, then they couldn't come from a ghost. Ian missed the reenactment shoot, so he missed the excitement.

He heard the same basic story Ashley told, but with an extra bit of information. Kiki's internal radar detected a strong presence at the river. It was similar in feeling to when Janine heard the whisper, but much stronger. Kiki claimed the river ghost was there, watching the film crew, interested in somebody.

"Kiki's worried there's something missing in her interpretation of the ghost story." Ian said. "We know plenty of spirits hang out in a familiar spot, but Kiki believes this one is getting stronger. She felt more energy than with the Mary spirit."

"She's changing the story?" Janine asked.

"Not really, just running through it again. She mentioned hypnotizing you again. Afraid we didn't ask the right questions. She's going through all her notes and pondering another séance but isn't sold on it yet. Kiki has always been a fantastic receptor for paranormal energy, but she can't summon a ghost at will. She would like to contact the river spirit, but doesn't think that particular entity would respond to an adult."

"Did you tell her about what happened out on the lawn?"

He gave her a sly smile. "You mean what almost happened?"

"Not that." She punched his arm. "I mean that I may have felt something out there. Something watching, or listening."

"I didn't say anything," he said. Then, after a moment, "I want you to know that I meant what I said out on that lawn."

"I did too," she told him. "Do you really think we took things too fast?"

"Not too fast for me. This feeling I have for you, it's not out of the blue, or a flighty fancy." He confessed, "I fell for you the first time you looked at me. Do you believe in love at first sight? Truthfully, this is something I've been carrying around for months." Ian seemed deep in thought. "When we first met, you definitely grabbed my attention, but I didn't want to be unprofessional. Who knew if there'd be more than one show? Then you got that boyfriend you seemed very serious about. You were always running off with him. I was trying to be very cool about it."

"A boyfriend? What are you talking about?"

"Back in Austin, at the end of the first season. You know, that guy you were with at the end of last season. I was certain he's the reason you didn't want to come to the after party. I was a very disappointed because…because I was going to woo you away from him."

"I had Sammy's birthday," Janine reminded him. "I told everyone that. But who is the guy you think was my boyfriend?"

He stared at her. "Oh, come on, Janine. I watched him drop you off every day at work and then come back to fetch you. It seemed like he never let you out of his sight."

"Did he drive a blue Toyota?"

"Yes, that's the one. He had that little goatee. Very hip." He looked annoyed with her. "He showed up right about the time I was working up the nerve to ask you out. You know, after the cemetery in Savannah. I thought we finally connected and you might consider socializing with me, away from the show, I mean. You don't have to laugh about it, that guy showing up is not a fond memory for me. I thought maybe I missed my chance."

Janine laughed so hard she could barely breathe.

"I'm glad you're having fun at my expense and I'm glad he's out of the picture. When I asked about an old boyfriend on our dinner date, he's the one I was worried about. Who was he anyway? Is he totally out of the picture now?"

She caught her breath. "My Uber driver."

He was stunned. "What?"

"He was my Uber driver for a couple of weeks. My car was in the shop. It finally completely died and I didn't have the money for something else." Her amusement finally calmed down. "Not until our final checks came through. He lived in my building, Mike, very nice. Only charged me one way. I felt silly sitting in the backseat because we were neighbors and quite friendly. I guess, he did hang around a lot, but we never dated or anything."

Ian shook his head. "Crikes. No kidding? I'm such an idiot."

"You're not an idiot," Janine said softly, becoming serious. "You're actually pretty terrific. You're romantic and sweet. The flowers, thank you. And I want to make sure to tell you, that night at the party, wanting to go upstairs and announce your feelings for me, any normal girl would think that was pretty romantic. A normal girl would have been pleased with you. The problem is me. I'm making things hard."

"No, no. You're perfect," he said.

"I wish that was true," she said.

"I wish you told me you were leaving that party. I was very worried."

"I didn't know I was going to leave," she said softly. "I only went outside to make a phone call. The truck seemed like a good place for the call I needed to make. I was upset at how I was reacting to you, so I called my shrink. It's been a while since I talked to him. This relationship has triggered some deep buried fears, automatic responses. Things I can't control."

"It's PTSD. Post-traumatic stress disorder." He nodded. "Kiki believes that you must suffer terribly from PTSD from time to time. She said I needed to be patient and—"

"You're discussing me with Kiki?" Just like that, her anger button was pushed. "You're discussing me with Kiki Mellow? Really?"

"We, no! Not really. Not everything. But Kiki guessed."

"Did you fill her in on the details of our trip to Donner Lake? Just how much does she know? Did you tell her the things I told you about… Did you tell the things I shared about… What did you tell her about me? How long have you been discussing my personal life with another woman? What kind of details did you discuss, Ian?" Her heart pounded in her chest, in her ears.

"I didn't discuss any of those things with her. I just told her about my feelings for you. You don't understand, Kiki knows me like a book. She can see right through me. There's no pretending around her."

She recalled a vivid image of Kiki stumbling in the Biltmore Hotel basement and falling into Ian McNally's arms. His overly concerned face flashed into her mind. She remembered being disappointed, thinking, there's no use competing with Kiki Mellow. Kiki always gets her man. Didn't it always seem like Ian was Kiki's man? He has always been very protective of Kiki, shooing off guys who got too chummy with her, almost punching that fellow who cornered her in New Orleans.

"Why is that, Ian?" Janine asked. "Is there something you haven't told me? Is there some history I don't know about? I opened up my past up to you, Ian McNally, I spilled my guts out to you and you're hiding something from me. What is it? You and Kiki are both from Scotland, Ian, what is it that you're not telling me?"

"Crikes," he said, eyes blinking. "Look, we wanted to keep it under wraps. You know, for the show's sake."

Kiki's hand on Ian's leg flashed into her mind, a gesture so familiar to him that he didn't even notice. The way they bent their heads together in private intimate discussions. The way they always seemed to understand what the other was thinking, laughing together with their cryptic inside jokes. Picking up each other's tabs or dry-cleaning. Kiki and Ian drinking whisky together, buying whisky for each other. They were so familiar with each other they could have been married.

"Keep what under wraps? What are you hiding? Do you keep all your past girlfriends a secret? Were you and Kiki an item? Is that it? Were you engaged or even married? What is it?"

"Janine, Kiki is my cousin."

"Kiki is your cousin?"

"Aye, my cousin. You know, our mothers, sisters," he said.

"Kiki is your cousin."

"Yes, my cousin," he repeated. "We're cousins."

They were cousins. It was her turned to be stunned. She would never have guessed on her own, but suddenly it seemed obvious. Ian's mother and aunt belonged to the same coven. Kiki and Ian spent their young summers on the island of Skye in a community of pagan women of the arts. That is, until Ian's father had enough. His father disliked the influence from his mother's side of the family. Too many spirits, faeries, and witches in their history. Regular people wondered why he allowed his son to intermingle with such nonsense. He forbade Ian and his mother from further visits to Skye as Ian grew older. So, while Kiki continued being instructed in a world rich in mysticism and spirituality, Ian got shut out. He pursued his interest in a scientific manner after finally breaking with his father.

Kiki still belonged to the same community of spiritualist. They consider themselves a coven of witches, but not like Janine might think. It's more like an ancient school of learning, where mothers pass down an old philosophy and crude science to their daughters. Ian's mother had been an important leader in the group and had a following of young lassies. Ian always felt a bit teased by the girls, because as a lad, he found the teachings very sexist. Of course, many of those girls turned out to be his very best friends. Did Janine notice, he got on with girls very well? She may have noticed that.

Ian and Kiki didn't advertise their family bond because they wanted to approach ghosts from two independent perspectives. They wanted to prove that the opposites, science and mysticism, could support each other in the middle, with proof of spiritual energy. They believed it would distract from that message if people knew they came from the same roots. Their main goal was to find authentic, paranormal activity and document it.

Steve's backers were more interested in ratings. When the fans responded to the doctor catching Kiki in that hotel basement, they latched onto the possible romance as an ongoing side narrative. It boosted the numbers and made the sponsors happy. It's what got them the funding to keep the show alive. To reach their goal of researching hauntings, they were willing to include some harmless acting here and there.

"You and Kiki. You two truly believe in these ghosts. This is not just another ghost story to you?"

"Well, yes." Ian glanced at her. "Aren't you beginning to believe? You're the one who heard them. You saw them. What are you telling me?"

"If I had to swear on a stack of Bibles, I'd say I heard and saw everything that happened," Janine said. "And I did. But even though I did, I can't help feeling a little unsure. I mean, ghosts? Spirits? Could it be something else? A trick of the mind?"

"You mean like that PTSD you mentioned."

"Yes. My therapist, Doctor Crisper, told me I might have some reactions. Spontaneous memories, flash backs, as this, our relationship, progresses. Deep buried emotions might be triggered. I'm sorry about this, but…"

"It's okay," he said.

"This is hard for me to say. Especially to you. I don't want you to take this the wrong way because you're very important to me," Janine said. "But you need to know. I loved him. Rick, I mean. It was a head over heels, passionate, euphoric love, and this, with you, feels similar. Different, but basically the same out of control feeling. Doctor Crisper says it could trigger psychosomatic delusions."

"Like a ghost?"

"Like deep buried flashes, repressed memories, or something. Deep fear and denial creating protective impulses. I'm sorry, but this feeling I have for you is mixed with… It's mixed with real fear. You saw a little of that," she reminded him. "Maybe my mind has played tricks on me. Think about it. Every time I started thinking about you, like at the river, in the backyard, in the orchard, one of these encounters occurred. Maybe my mind distracted me out of fear. It makes more sense than a ghost, doesn't it?"

Ian stared straight ahead. His eyes were rapidly blinking. She continued, quietly,

"Mary Miller, the ghost. She looked exactly like Caroline Govant in that photo of her as a kid. I saw the photo before the séance. Kiki held it up for us. I went back to look at it again. The girl in the orchard stood in the exact same spot, in a similar pose. *Heed the dictum?* Caroline said that to us in the interview. I reviewed the tape."

"What about the event at the river? You heard, *why did you leave me?* No one said that to you first," Ian argued.

But someone did say that to her. She turned away.

Should she dare to tell him what she thought of those old people, Henry and Caroline, that they were hiding something? That they were part of a secret group, a lingering variation of the city committee that once existed. *Somebody needs to accept her message and be responsible.* Caroline had said. *I pass the responsibility to you.* And lately, Janine remembers seeing a man on the back lawn, a young Henry Webber. He had encouraged her go look at the river. *What nonsense did he think he was participating in?* She was certain those two old people had been tangled in more than just a scandalous love affair in the past.

No, saying all that would make her sound paranoid as well as crazy.

They drove in silence for a time. Ian finally spoke up.

"Maybe so, but I've recorded real, unexplainable energy out there. Measured energy. We taped a faint voice that had no apparent source and Kiki feels these spirits. I totally believe in Kiki. Sure, she will embellish a story now and again, but Kiki has an inherent gift. Most of the women on my mother's side have it. Goes back for generations."

Janine agreed that Kiki had a gift. "She told me I had a dark aura."

"She just meant she can see something dark surrounding you. When we first met, she didn't know if it was in your past or future or what. She was a little scared about it, you know."

"You talked about me?"

"We're cousins! We discussed everyone at the beginning. Brainstormed what a good team would look like. We needed a neutral backup team, people with doubts, not easy believers. It was your dark aura that sold Kiki. She found it fascinating. Fascinating and scary because it can mean so many things."

"Did Kiki also tell you she figured out my past?"

"No," he said. "Did she? How'd she do that? She figured out everything?"

"The knife marks. My scars. The dress she insisted on. I thought I was going to shock her into backing off on that dress, but instead, she knew exactly who I was. She pretty much knows everything that happened to me, everything. Did she tell you about that?"

He shook his head. "What do you mean everything that happened to you? Obviously, you took a knife in the back, but Kiki was able to figure out all the rest?"

"Jane Doe from Chicago," she said quietly. Finally, all her cards were on the table. "It was a pretty big news story four, five years ago. Kiki instantly knew it was me." She watched his eyes grow wide as he remembered the story.

"Crikes, I am a complete idiot. You told me the whole story and I didn't put two and two together. Wait…" He looked at her. "Wasn't Jane Doe from Chicago with child?"

She nodded and said softly, "Sammy."

He took it in. "She's a cute one, that Sammy."

The California History Group in San Francisco housed an extensive collection of photographs and documents chronicling California's history. The archive section of emigration to the Wild West was on the basement floor. They needed to go to that level of the museum to find the Hansen Ledger diary. Doctor McNally and Janine greeted the museum guide, a tall, lanky man with an overly large mustache. He led them down a narrow staircase to where they kept documents unfit for display. He rambled as he walked.

"We have more than fifty thousand volumes of books and pamphlets, four thousand manuscripts and in excess of five hundred thousand photographs. The library is home to five thousand other works of art, including paintings, drawings, and lithographs. The most popular items are upstairs for easy access." He quoted right from their website. "But your diary is down here due to the fragility of the binding."

They entered an extremely small room. A large table dwarfed the room even more and created narrow aisles on all four sides. Three tall stools were placed randomly about and a dissecting microscope and a handheld magnifying glass sat on top of the table with the Hansen Ledger resting next to them. Their guide's name was James Monroe, like the president. His large handlebar mustache called to mind the Old West. James Monroe pushed a box of disposable rubber gloves their way and they each donned a pair. Ian quickly took a closer look at the ledger and started flipping through the pages. The ink-paper contrast on the actual pages made them harder to read than the photocopies. The ledger paper was a bit oxidized and matched the lost pages Gram found in color and texture. Ian turned to the middle of the ledger and found the torn-out section. Janine pulled out the old Bible and unstrapped it. She handed loose pages to James and Ian.

"I think it's absolutely crazy fantastic that you found these lost pages in some basement somewhere," James said. "I never really looked at this one before, but when you ordered a copy, I got very curious. Hansen was a colorful personality, to say the least."

"Wait till you read the removed pages," Janine said.

"More good stuff?"

"It's going to blow your mind," she told him.

"Look at this, Janine. It's a perfect match." Ian pointed to the line of tear marks in the binding of the diary and a page from Gram's collection. "Is it all right if we take a little video clip of this?" he asked James.

"Oh, yes." James nodded. "We got an okay for your project. Film and snap away. We're at your disposal. If you need us to copy or officially document something, we're ready."

They spent the next few hours matching each page in Gram's pile with torn edges in the ledger diary. Janine snapped pictures of each match. They also filmed a nice fifteen-minute interview session with the museum guide. James pulled out other historic documents from the wagon-train era. He showed them a letter that suggested witches from the east traveled to California and settled in Santa Cruz. Ian thought Kiki would find that letter interesting. James also spread out a large, hand-drawn map that traced possible routes over the mountains. By the time they emerged from the museum, it was midafternoon.

"I hope you don't mind, but I made reservations at the Bix restaurant for dinner. They have live jazz and it's a little fancy." Ian grinned. "It's a very pleasant setting, and it'll just be the two of us, no one to bother. We could explore other places, but we could dance together at the Bix." He turned his expressive eyes on her and smiled shyly. "Remember that night in New Orleans with the street musicians and that old guy that claimed you right away? You were nice enough to play along. You were very sweet. You danced to that slow jazz with him. You don't know how badly I wanted to be that old man. What do you say?"

She watched the muscled chords in his neck flex as he glanced up and down Market Street. She loved his height. Ian obviously hoped for a romantic excursion in the city. She felt a surge of happiness staring at him. Apparently, Ian McNally might truly be in love with her. He wasn't put off by her scars, or her muddled emotions, or her dark past.

"How fancy is this place? Will we go dressed like this? If I agree to another date with you, I want to be dressed nicely."

They happened to be very near the fashion district on South Market Street and decided to splurge on fancy new outfits for their dinner date. They also made a pact to turn off their cell phones and spend the evening offline and off the grid. Their planned few hours turned into the rest of the night. They stayed at the Hyatt Fisherman's Warf and did not leave San Francisco until well into the afternoon on the next day. Janine reactivated her phone when they entered I-80 heading east toward Sacramento.

The sky glowed reddish orange and the sun hung low in the sky behind them. Multiple messages from Juliana, Gram, and Kiki immediately popped up in her alerts. She read a few out loud to Ian.

"Juliana is done with all the ghost talk. Gram is driving her crazy. They're taking a road trip back to Texas, probably starting tomorrow. I don't know what happened."

"Oh no, sorry I monopolized you," he said.

"This is normal Juju-Gram behavior. After a couple of days of bliss, they start attacking each other. Two hardheaded women who like to be in charge."

Yet, there was something in the wording of Juliana's messages, worry? Should she call? She checked Gram's message first.

"Gram says you got some sort of FedEx package from a lab called ALS. It came to the house by currier."

"Oh yes," he said. "Rock sample results. Curious to see what's in there."

"Gram is wondering when we plan on returning. She says Juliana needs to be convinced of the facts."

"What does that mean?" he asked.

"Not sure," she told him. "Kiki says the filming in the orchard went well. The grave is very near her séance site, just east of it. And the headstone is definitely magnetic. Says Carlos blathered on and on about his compass? She also says that Timothy was adopted."

"Who's Timothy?" Ian asked.

"A grandson, or something, of Christopher Williams," Janine continued reading. "She double-checked the records. He was adopted from a neighbor. You remember, he was one of the drowning victims Kiki mentioned the other night."

Timothy was their Christopher Williams link. If he was adopted, then his death would have no effect on the dictum or any curse. There were no riches with his death. Kiki assumed his death continued some other windfall.

Apparently, she was having second thoughts about that conclusion. Janine called her sister.

"What's going on?" she asked.

"Gram and her ghost again," Juliana told her. "We were having a very nice visit for once in our lives and now she wants to ban us from Rio Linda. She insists the ghost may go after one of the kids. Kiki Mellow called her and said the curse may not be complete after all. What a loon, what a complete loon! She got Gram in a fit. Plus, Gram found the drawings the kids did on the back porch. All of a blond little girl."

"They drew the ghost! They saw her?"

"No, Janine," Juliana said calmly. "They copied your old drawings. Jack said they liked the painting you did of your imaginary friend and they each copied it pretending to have an old-fashioned imaginary friend. Kids do that sort of thing, pretend. Gram about had a fit when she saw the pictures. Don't worry, we're not going anywhere till you get back."

"Good grief, I can't believe this," Janine said. "We should have come back yesterday."

"No, Janine, you did exactly what I hoped you would do," Juliana said softly. "I'm happy you stayed in the city with that nice man. I hope you had a very pleasant time. You can tell me every single detail when you get here. I feel like you're finally, finally coming back to us now. All of you. Ashley's friends are going to be so thrilled." She laughed softly.

Janine didn't know what to say. Ian gave her an anxious look.

"Is Gram there?" She asked.

"At the zoo, with Adam and the kids. I'm stuck here, packing stuff. Gram is pretty adamant the kids are in danger and wanted them away from Rio Linda during the day. Afraid some ghost is going entice them to the river. If I see Kiki Mellow anytime soon, I may just give her a nice, sharp, slap to the face. I know everyone loves her, but really, does she need to play an old lady like that?"

After they broke the connection, Janine called Kiki.

"It's the only thing that makes sense," Kiki said. "These spirits, they're too strong to be echoes. They still have purpose. Why else would she seek you out that afternoon?"

"But she never asked me to go to the river," Janine reminded her. "Under hypnosis, we determine that she never even mention the river. And the drownings have stopped."

"I'm not trying to be mean, Janine," Kiki told her. "Every part of my being tells me that these two spirits are strong and active. This is my curse, Janine. I can't help feeling the wants and needs and desires of the spirits I encounter. In the orchard, I got a very strong sense that Mary was urging us to complete the dictum and annoyed the hell at you. Probably for not completing the dictum when you were young. Out at the river, I got the very strong feeling that Linda was trying to take that boy. It was unnatural. He said he felt something urging him to go out further into the water. I felt her there! That feeling was not an echo."

Janine gave Ian a worried look.

"*You can be the last one*," Kiki quoted. "Remember that. Caroline Govant told us the spirit said that about you. *She can be the last one*, remember that? We have it recorded, regular speed, clear as crystal. Who said it? Who said those words? They were whispered right into the condenser microphone. To you, Janine. Who do you think Mary was talking about?"

Janine felt her blood start to race.

"We're worried about the same little girl, Janine. Your gram thinks she knows a way to end the curse. I don't know what she was talking about, but she started rambling about someone named Bertha."

Janine relayed everything to Ian. He decided to pull off the road and call Kiki himself. They hit the next exit and coasted the car into an Exon station then parked in one of the empty spaces. Janine called Gram.

"Are you coming back today? We have some bad news about the curse."

"I spoke with Kiki," Janine said, "And Juliana."

"Juliana will never believe us about the river ghost," Gram told her. "Even when her own children drew pictures of her. She didn't listen. We are not going to tell anyone that they drew those pictures. No one. And I have an idea. A terrible idea, but it might be a solution. For more than one problem."

Janine waited for Gram to continue.

"Remember Bertha. I told you about her DNA test and what Leone did. Bertha has decided to stop her chemo. It isn't working anyway and she just feels tortured by it all. They say with or without chemo, she only has days, a month at most. So, she left the hospital. They won't help her out there. Oh yes, they give her stuff for the pain, but they won't really help her do what she wants to do."

"Gram, what the hell are you talking about?"

"She's considering it," Gram said.

"She's considering what?"

"Going willingly. Like Mary Miller did. To the river," Gram said.

"You're trying to talk this woman, Bertha, into drowning herself in the river?"

"Better than a child," Gram said. "Better than one of those beautiful children. And no one is talking anyone into anything. I told Bertha about George Lumen. She was grateful to find out she wasn't living a lie. I told her about everything days ago, and Bertha wants to die. She begged the doctor to give her something to end her life. She's already decided that she wants to die and was looking for help. It's just cruel that they insist on making her suffer out her last few days. She's in pain!"

"Gram, you stay out of whatever it is Bertha wants to do," Janine said in hushed tones.

Gram begged off at that point. She said something about being needed and ended the call. Janine looked at Ian. He came round to hug her.

Bertha walked to the river. It wasn't too far from her worn-down armchair, only a couple of blocks away. She waited until just after her TV show and for her nurse to run an errand. One last game of Jeopardy, one last iced tea with crackers. She couldn't drink the tea and she could barely stomach the crackers. It was no way to live out her last few days. The river could offer her a better purpose. All her life she knew she was destined for something great. She lived years and years of disappointment, never seeing or knowing what it could be.

Then Martha told her the story again. It was all so simple. They always wondered if they really saw a ghost in the orchard when they were young girls. A ghost who urged Bertha to *heed the dictum*. When Caroline dared her take a dip in the river to see if it was true, she called Caroline crazy. But maybe crazy Caroline always knew something the rest of them didn't; that Bertha was meant to go into the river and join the ghost. She could have altered everyone's lives by going to the river. The financial woes her family suffered could have been eliminated. They can still be eliminated. She could redeem them all, save their souls, pay their bills, and end her pain with one decisive event. Perhaps the cancer was God's gift to make her sacrifice easier.

Bertha removed her slippers at the river edge and stepped into the water. She waded slowly and did not notice the ice-cold temperature until she got waist deep. The cancer not only took her fear away, it took the feelings in her legs as well. She admired the metallic luster of the large rocks. She inched further into the water and felt the slip stream. She willingly slipped under that surface.

The current swept her rapidly to the boulders. Water pressed her firmly against the rocks. She couldn't move. She was weak from chemotherapy. Water flowed over her head and washed her scarf away. She gasped for breath but could neither move up to breath, nor down to drown.

An old man walking his dog spotted her in the water. He called 911 on his cell phone and then waded in to get closer. The current pushed him over and he stumbled. Luckily, he regained his footing and made it back to shore. His dog jumped up and down, yelping at him. The dog knew better than to go into the water. Then others gathered around. A human chain was made to reach Bertha.

They got to her! Bertha was pulled to the safety of the shore. The witnesses heard her say something as she laid soaking wet on the pebbles. Soft and woeful and broken.

"She didn't want me."

An ambulance took Bertha away. The human chain dispersed to share the story of the woman they saved and the heartbreaking thing she said. Poor old lady. Shameful that the old and sick are no longer wanted by the young. Whoever *she* is, she should be ashamed.

Traffic through Davis made them very late getting back to Rio Linda. Ian dropped her off at Gram's and greeted her family again, this time as her boyfriend. The smaller kids were already asleep and Gram was mysteriously missing. Ashley and Juliana seemed very approving of Ian. Ian retrieved the FedEx package and turned to head back to the hotel. He needed to pack to make an early morning flight. They were flying back to the main studio in Texas to start putting the movie together. Janine walked him out to the porch to say goodbye.

"Please let your Gram know I said thanks."

"I will. I wish I knew where she was. I'm a little worried about her," Janine held his hand. Even though they were due to see each other by the end of the week, she didn't want to let him go. She had an uneasy feeling about parting with him.

"Are you sure you don't want to fly back with us?" Ian hugged her tightly. "Five days is a long time. I miss you already."

"I need to drive back with Juliana and the kids," Janine told him. "I've got more catching up to do. But I know how you feel. I'm going to miss you too."

Back inside, Juliana stood waiting for her. They went into the study to talk. Piles of ghost research laid conspicuously stacked next to two of Gram's attic boxes. Adam must have lugged the other boxes to the attic. Janine put the Bible with the torn-out diary pages on top of one of Gram's paisley boxes.

"You have no idea where Gram is?" Janine asked.

"We had a little tiff," Juliana said. "She won't answer my phone calls."

"She doesn't answer her cell phone often," Janine told her. "She accidently mutes it a lot."

"There was another near-drowning at the river today. All the neighbors were talking about it. Adam got the story from the man next door," Juliana told her. "They made a human chain to reach an old lady at the rock. She was very lucky."

Two near-drownings in less than three days.

"Do you know who it was?"

Juliana shook her head.

"Are you going to tell me about this doctor of yours?" Juliana asked.

In the midst of telling Juliana about her San Francisco adventure with Ian, her phone pinged with a text from him. Gram and Kiki were both at Caroline Govant's house. The three of them planned an impromptu séance in the orchard at midnight. That's probably why Gram didn't answer the phone. Juliana became visibly agitated at the mention of Kiki Mellow.

"I'm going to try calling Kiki," Janine said.

"You go right ahead," Juliana told her. "I'm going to bed. I am so done with Gram's ghost nonsense."

Kiki picked up on the first ring.

"Gram is fine," Kiki assured her. "She called me this afternoon. These ladies are both very anxious to summon Mary again. Gram seems to believe that Caroline speaks for

Mary. Don't worry about anything, I'll drive her back myself after our thing. We'll give it a go and see if the spirit will answer any questions. Three is a very good number for contacting spirits. Now that we have a better idea of what Mary was trying to tell us, we may be able to ask the right things. These two women seem to be insisting."

Juliana was right, that did sound looney. What was Gram up to? *Janine's suspicions about Caroline and Henry popped into her head.* Was Gram trying to convince the ghost or Caroline?

Janine stole through the kitchen and checked the enclosed patio. Jack and Sammy snored in the rollouts. Janine quietly snuck in to check the lock and bolt on the door. The inside kitchen door was propped open, as always, and Janine eased between the two sleepers where the rollouts met in the middle. They looked so much alike, Jack and Sammy. Same color hair, same pink lips, same little nose. Jack stirred. His eyes fluttered.

"Aunt Jaja. You're back."

"Shh, Jack. Yes, I'm back," she whispered.

"Did you fall in love? Ashley said you were out falling in love."

"I guess I was." She petted his head. "Do you mind if I sleep in here with you for a bit?"

He nodded and closed his eyes again. Janine reminisced about the day Jack was born. Her father allowed her to ditch high school to visit her new nephew. Her sister had been exhausted in a hospital bed, radiant with happiness, and Adam beamed with pride. Ashley, who only turned five years old, made it very clear to everyone that the new baby belonged to her. Janine smiled at that memory. Ashley sitting between her parents, clutching the swaddled baby and making that loud declaration to everyone in earshot. There was so much love welcoming baby Jack into the world.

Very different from the day Sammy was born. Janine turned to the little girl. Her hair was wild and loose across the pillow. Janine touched a stray curl. Sammy took a deep breath. Once again, Janine couldn't believe that beautiful little girl was the baby she gave away; the baby she refused to hold; the baby she refused to acknowledge with more than one brief glance; the baby Juliana and Adam saved from being lost to the unknown. Deep down, Janine wanted her back. She wanted to take Sammy home and love her. She knew that she didn't deserve Sammy after abandoning her at birth and it was wrong to even imagine disrupting her family like that. Juliana was Sammy's real mother. Janine should just be grateful to get a chance to be her aunt.

Sammy shifted and Janine settled down next to her. Janine closed her eyes and cuddled the little girl. A silent tear trickled onto the pillow they shared. What would life have been like if Sammy's father had been the man she first met, and not the one she constantly tried to forget? Sammy's breaths came deep and regular and soon put Janine into a deep sleep.

She woke to Sammy's grey eyes boring into hers. There was a burst of giggles. By the light from the window, it was just after dawn. The porch felt cold and damp. Sammy held Janine's face firmly between her two little hands. Sammy was inspecting her. Janine blinked and stretched, sore from the thin roll out bed.

"You snore, Aunt Jaja," Sammy said.

"I do?"

"Yes. I knew you would sleep with us, but I didn't think you would snore."

"Really, and how did you know that?" Janine asked.

"I heard you last night," Sammy said.

"I thought I was being quiet. Did I wake you?"

"You were being silly."

"I was?" Janine noticed Jack had gotten up. He was not in his rollout.

"You said to follow you home. We are home."

Janine sat up and stared at Sammy's laughing eyes.

"What did I say?" she asked.

"You said to follow you home, silly."

Did she say that? Last night. Did she say something out loud? She didn't think so. Janine felt her pulse start to pick up. *Follow me home.* Where had she heard that before?

"I said that last night?" Janine asked. "Right here?"

"You were outside again," Sammy said. "Out on the lawn, like always."

Janine suddenly felt weighed down, sinking.

There is no ghost. There is just a ghost story!

"You heard me on the lawn, last night?"

"Are you okay, Aunt Jaja?" Sammy asked.

Heed the dictum.

Janine's eyes shot around the room. The back porch door was cracked open and cool damp air trickled in. Janine stood up too quickly. She was instantly dizzy and put a hand out to catch herself. Sammy giggled at her.

"Jack?" Janine called.

She pushed the door open a bit and looked out into the backyard. "Jack?"

She turned to Sammy. "Where's Jack. Did he go outside?" She called into the house, "Jack!"

She looked back at Sammy.

"I don't know," Sammy said.

Janine flung the back door wide and ran outside. "Jack!" *Where was Jack?* Janine turned to Sammy. "Stay inside. Go upstairs and wake your mom and dad. Tell them Jack's missing. Can you do that, Sammy?"

Sammy nodded.

One each for redemption.

"Now go. Go! Tell them. I'm going to the river."

Sammy disappeared into the house.

She can be the last one.

She or he? Janine started running toward the mound and the river. She never, ever thought it could be Jack. Not Jack!

The grass felt cold and damp on the manicured lawn. She reached the edge of the cut lawn, her old boundary line, and crossed over into the rough where smooth grass became prickly weeds. Then she was atop the mound and looking at the river. The water sparkled in the light of a beautiful morning. The shoreline appeared deserted. She kept moving, head swiveling right, then left.

"Jack! Jack!"

Janine could see tire marks on the pebbly beach where someone drove up to the water's edge. She ran to the water and searched all around. Nothing. She ran toward the large boulders at the bend in the river. It was impossible to see under the rippling water.

"Jack! Jack!"

She looked up and down stream. No one, nothing. She waded into the water, knee deep. The freezing snow melt assaulted her legs. Her toes curled in protest. She hesitated and strained to see into the water. Something was down there. Something colorful moved under the water near the rock. Something flowed with the current. *Oh my god, Oh my god, Oh my god,* she thought, *Jack.*

Janine waded further. As she neared the large boulder, the current flowed against her, pushing her around. Her hand passed over a flattened section of rock and she immediately thought of Mary Millers' headstone. The river fought hard to kick the feet out from under her, but she took sure steps, she kept a flat palm on the rock for support. The water was up to her chest and she began to shiver from cold and fright. The sun was not yet high enough to cast any direct light on the river bend. She reached out to grab the flowing object. She had to completely submerge to reach it. She pulled and pulled and got it loose.

Juliana was yelling behind her. Janine slowly backed out of the river. She turned her head and saw Juliana running down the mound toward the shoreline. Cold wet hair hindered her tunnel vision. Juliana, wrapped in a housecoat, looked just out of bed and furious.

"What in the world are you doing!" Juliana yelled. Janine only waded back to waist deep. She thought she might go for another look. "Janine, get out of there!" Juliana demanded.

"Jack's missing," Janine shouted through chattering teeth. "Jack's missing. What if he's in the river!"

"Jack is not missing," Juliana fumed. "Get out of there right now!"

"Jack could be in the water! The door was open and he could be out here!"

"Jack is not in the water! Jack is fine!" Juliana confirmed again.

Janine moved toward shore. She was freezing wet and confused. She shivered. Scowling, Juliana removed her robe and covered Janine with it. Scowling, Juliana took the soaking wet cloth Janine recovered and held it up. A blue-and-orange head scarf. Not Jack's.

"Jack is with Adam. They went out to get us donuts and bagels for breakfast," Juliana calmly told her. "They're at Raley's right now. I just spoke to Adam *and Jack* a moment ago on the phone."

Jack was all right and Janine was all wet. Juliana no longer scowled, but her eyes screamed *complete moron*. Poor Juliana, always dealing with her crazy sister.

They walked back to the house silently. Janine felt a little guilty for using her sister's robe on that crisp morning, but it was too late to give it back now, the robe was soaked through.

Gram stood at the kitchen door with a large beach towel. She seemed in an awful mood with Juliana. Both ladies glowered at each other. Juliana silently implied that Gram should accept some blame for Janine jumping into the river that morning. Janine just wanted to disappear into a warm bath before Jack and Adam returned. She was too embarrassed to face her brother-in-law just yet. She truly believed the river ghost had gotten young Jack.

Though she was sopping wet, Juliana hugged her and said not to worry about it. Ashley hugged her and said she was her hero. Gram hugged her and said everything would be all right. Sammy hugged her and giggled at her silliness.

Then, Janine slunk upstairs to draw a warm bath and hide. Gram disappeared into Misty's room to complain about her granddaughters. Juliana and Ashley strolled to the front room to organize the luggage. Ashley pumped her mother for information regarding her aunt and the dreamy Doctor McNally. What did she find out about their wild adventure in San Francisco?

Nobody noticed when Sammy slipped out into the backyard. Nobody saw her go to the edge of Gram's cut lawn, talking to the air like children do. Nobody observed Sammy run up and over the mound, giggling to no one in particular. Nobody watched her pick up the blue-and-orange head scarf and swing it into the air. Nobody witnessed her drag it into the water, going deeper and deeper and deeper. And nobody ever saw Sammy again, alive or dead.

Most of the town helped search the river and trails around Gram's house. People stayed out all day and night looking for Sammy. The police brought in dogs who scented Sammy's clothes and led them right to the river edge, barking. Lots of voices began to whisper about the River Girl Ghost. Most locals agreed that the small girl probably went into the river and got washed away. Someone saw a man at the river that morning and thought he might know something. Downstream in Sacramento, they dredged areas of stagnant water and found nothing. All the usual catches for miles down the river were searched to no avail.

Janine kept reviewing that first afternoon on the river shore. Henry Webber stood inside the police tape with his dog on a leash. He pointed to some discarded slippers with an angry frown. Why had he walked his dog so far from home? Why had he assumed those slippers meant a small child had drowned? Was he the man someone had mentioned? Why did he purposely avoid turning in her direction.

She suddenly recalled when Henry stood there before and her heart pounded manically. She noticed who he kept glancing at in the small crowd at the river, Caroline Govant. The white-haired old woman watched the action with an expressionless face. Her head swiveled around as she listened to murmurs in the crowd. At one point, Caroline faced Janine and stared right into her eyes. Caroline mouthed something, something that looked like, *heed the dictum*. Janine rushed down the pebbly shore but was stopped by one of the policemen just prior to reaching Henry Webber.

"What did you do!" she screamed at him. "Did you tell her to go into the river!"

Henry Webber turned away and someone dragged Janine off. A tight-lipped frown twisted Henry's face as his eyes refused to meet hers. The police ordered Janine to stay away from Henry Webber.

When Ian called, she finally revealed the theory formed in the back of her mind. They needed to include it in the documentary so that no one would get away with anything. It made more sense than a ghost, didn't it? *A secret cult simmering in Rio Linda, a cult of people who believed in the dictum.*

"It isn't a ghost luring kids, but a human cult of the ghost!" Janine insisted into the phone. "We cannot let them get away with this, Ian. We need to flush them out and expose them if no one else will. The police think it's crazy talk, so we need to include it in the documentary. It all makes sense now. Henry Webber and Caroline Govant and who knows who else!"

There was a very long pause before Ian spoke. His voice was calm and soft.

"Janine, be careful. You're really emotional right now, and, and you're reaching wild conclusions in an attempt to come to grips with what happened."

Oh no, no. He did not just say that. She went completely cold. Her vision began to tunnel as his soft, rational voice, continued,

"It's not uncommon to become hysterical or even irrational as your mind tries to cope with something like this. This is your grief working on you, misplacing blame. We can't blame innocent people of…"

All the soft rational voices came flooding back.

"*…enhanced by pregnancy hormones, combined to cause her hysteria. Plainly, her mind altered the images to cope with what happened to her. She spent a week acting normal, before she became irrational with these wild conclusions and falsely accused an innocent man. Why didn't she speak up sooner? Her mind is misplacing the blame because of their argument, spurred on by a surprise pregnancy…*"

Rick and his legal team nearly convinced everyone with those words, even herself.

She let the phone drop from her hands.

A dark omen.

Janine could barely breath. Her gut tightened into a tense knot. She was dizzy. She would never be able to look at Ian McNally again. She felt so incredibly stupid.

Epilogue
The Riches

The boulders in the river turned out to be mostly made of quartz, feldspar, hematite, and magnetite. Yet, they contained a significant mix of neodymium and the rare earth metals europium, terbium, and dysprosium. The cost of removing the boulders was less than one percent of their net worth on the world market. The town of Rio Linda and all the local citizens would share the wealth of the boulders. Under the mound between Gram's house and the river, another pocket of the same mineral mix lay buried. The rare earth elements alone were estimated to be worth millions.

The extraction of the boulders removed the dangerous catch that trapped so many victims in the past. The river flattened out and grew wide, slowing the rip current in the center of the stream. The predicted flooding of Marysville

Boulevard never happened. Instead, the river bend became a popular cooling-off spot in the summer and an unlikely place for a water emergency. Tourism boomed in Rio Linda, sparked by the film documentary on ghosts. People flocked to the pebbly shore to get a glimpse of the river ghost and the orchard ghost. Séances became regular events in Caroline Miller's orchard. A popular walking tour visited the river, the orchard, the grave site of Mary Miller, and a couple of the streets named for drowning victims. Plans for a museum to highlight the history of wagon trains were discussed at a city council meeting.

Janine sat stiffly in the back of a stretch limousine with Kiki, the doctor, Steve, Ted, and Carlos. She sat right across from Ian but was still unable to completely meet his eye or even to speak to him. She felt furious, ashamed, and sad at the same time. *Doctor Crisper had been right after all.* The car picked them up at the Ritz-Carlton and they followed a long line of limos to the theatre in Los Angeles. Although the February clouds were holding their water, the air felt quite cool outside and anything could happen. Unfair that the guys were fully clothed in tuxedos and protective footwear. The girls wore glamourous heels and fancy dresses designed to expose as many of their scars as possible. Don't worry about it, Kiki told her. A million eyes could stare directly at you and never guess what is in your head, or your heart. This time Kiki wore the light-blue angel color and Janine wore the dark-red devil.

Their documentary proved to be a huge financial success, grossing in the twenty-million-plus category even before the end of the rushed initial run. By the second weekend, the film topped the box office in cities across the country. It grossed even more in theaters in Asia and the European market. People love a good ghost story. The Rio Linda Ghost film earned a nomination for best documentary feature film. Steve laughed about the sheer success of a film thrown together in a single room studio and in the back of a van on a shoestring budget. His main goal from film school had been met. He became a hero in his personal circle and favored to win the Academy Award. He wore a superhero T-shirt under his tuxedo coat and grinned constantly.

The rest of crew, as on-screen stars of the film, experienced an entirely different form of attention. Photo shoots and talk show offers came their way. Their images mysteriously popped up in magazines. The WB considered picking up the rights to the *Spectral Analysis* TV show with a rumor that the production might be moved to a giant new facility in Arizona and flooded with money. A new managing producer would fill in as Steve stepped away. Max Colliers with the black glasses wanted to step in.

Those old people back in Rio Linda always knew the elements of the dictum, she realized. Poor Gram never wanted to accept it or admit it. Gram's denial led to her animosity with Caroline Govant all those years ago. There were still lots of unanswered questions but nobody was talking. Janine felt completely cold about all of it and about everyone. It was karma, she realized. She did not deserve a second chance with anything.

Once again, Kiki suggested the mantra, *I am a badass*, to get across the red carpet. But Janine no longer needed that mantra. For the past months, she went through the motions expected of her under a bright spotlight instead of hiding in the shadows and she realized that it worked just the same. Kiki was right, no one could guess what was in her heart or in her head. Only an intimate few knew how she really felt about their success. It had been in the tea leaves…

The return was not worth the investment.

The End?

Not quite

The following exert was originally written as a prologue for SA.

Deleted Prologue
Rio Linda River~1949

Nobody warned her about the curse, so, when the mercury crept over one hundred degrees, Ashley didn't think twice about taking her young girls to river. It was the fastest way to cool them down. On a recent morning walk, she had spotted a very nice beach near some large rocks. It stayed shallow and gentle for a good fifteen yards before growing deeper. Everywhere else, the river ran much too swiftly for little kids. As long as the girls stayed near the shore, there wouldn't be a problem. Five-year-old Emily and four-year-old Erica were always mindful, careful girls. That river bend fell very convenient too. It was only a scant jaunt down the street and through the prickly blackberry brambles and a large oak. Ashley hoped no one claimed the shade from that oak, she could read under that tree while the kids played on the pebbly beach.

Her small family had recently relocated from Mississippi with her military husband. Peter received orders to PCS to the McClellan Air base in California after completing boot camp. Ashley had no idea what PCS meant until Peter laughed at her and said,

"It means permanent change of station."

Not everyone knew the military lingo, but she kept herself from responding. She planned to be happy instead. Didn't he look nice in his new uniform? Didn't it promise a steady paycheck with a decent job? What did she care if Peter taunted her now and again. At least he finally took responsibility for their little family and began providing for them. It had been a very rough start for the both of them. She dropped out of school with the first baby. Then took a job after the second baby because Peter's wise mouth kept getting him fired. But now they were beginning to behave like real grownups and things were going to be different. Peter's love of airplanes outweighed his disdain for authority, and he signed on with the army air corps to work as a mechanic. They sent him TDY three days after she arrived in California with the kids. TDY meant temporary duty, and the TDY's would happen quite often, he said. Pete was not the nicest man, so maybe the time apart would help them. That is how Ashley consoled herself as she navigated the unfamiliar house and town. There she sat on a very hot day, with two small daughters, in a rural area flanked by neighbors she did not know. On hot days in the southland, they always found a river.

The shady spot under the oak was miraculously free. Ashley found it funny how California folks avoided the shade. The old tree stood several yards up the rocky beach from the water and she could keep a steady eye on the girls as she read her novel. She wondered why more folks weren't cooling off in the heat. There were a few older teens further down river, but nobody else. Ashley brought a picnic basket of treats and small water toys for her girls. Emily and Erica sat on the river's edge, splashing happily in the water. Down the beach, Ashley noticed the teens staring at them with their arms akimbo.

"Are you crazy?" One of the teen boys yelled. "Aren't you afraid of the river ghost?"

Were they addressing her? They appeared very agitated. Were they delinquents?

"You shouldn't be down here with those little kids!" One of the other boys yelled over.

Ashley stood up. Her young daughters eyed the boys and she knew the girls wondered if they should be frightened. They witnessed their own father behave quite nasty at times. Those teens were certainly impertinent. Did the teens think they could keep the river to themselves by being rude? Is that why she found the river bend practically deserted on that very hot day?

"Good day young man, be careful now." Ashley admonished them. "You would be wise to be respectful. These kids need cooling off and we are not going anywhere."

"Meaning no disrespect," the first one's voice carried cleanly through the dry air. "But there's an undercurrent stream in there. Little kids get lured into it by the ghost."

The ghost? Ashley anticipated the move to California might result in bits of the Wild West with cowboys and Indians, movie stars and gold miners. But ghosts too? Backwards and brash, that's how these California folks came off. And they had a halting, mundane accent to their speech, paired with vulgar public behavior that she never expected in a million years. Where was the "good day, ma'am" or the "yes, ma'am" from these fine fellows?

"Thank you, young man, for informing me about the danger, we'll be careful."

The boys still appeared upset. Terrible, those youth trying to scare her away so they could enjoy an exclusive river. Did they desire privacy so they could shout obscenities or something? Maybe they expected young girls to wander along and a grownup would hinder whatever behavior they planned. Regardless of their motive, Ashley was determined to keep her daughters near the cool water. Her children were not used to such dry heat.

Emily meandered to her blanket and shared the shade. Such a sweet girl, always gravitating close to give her mother quiet morale support. Ashley fed Emily a bite of cheese and crackers. They both watched young Erica splashing and laughing. Erica recently turned four and just started speaking in real sentences. Her newest fascination was nonstop chattering to everyone she met. At the moment, she didn't seem to notice she chattered to the empty air. What a funny little girl.

"Who does Erica think she's talking to?" Ashley laughed.

Emily smiled at her mother and giggled with her. "She's talking to Linda."

"Linda? Who is Linda?" Ashley laughed.

"I don't know, but she's very pretty."

Had they met another girl already? The house next door was very large but Ashley didn't notice any children running about. Was Erica pretending to chat with a new friend?

"Mommy, can I go pick some blackberries? I'll put them in a dish for us."

Ashley hunted around for a small dish. "Be mindful of the spiders." She delivered the dish to Emily and watched her older daughter run off to the brambles. Then she turned back to Erica. Erica continued chatting happily. It was a beautiful day. Ashley ignored the teens downstream. From the corner of her eye, she saw them sunbathing on the rocks. Those large boulders had such a nice shiny metallic luster in the afternoon sunshine. Could there be gold in those stones? Peter said they were moving to the gold rush area of California. Wasn't most of the gold found right in the rivers?

"Who are you talking to?" Ashley called over to Erica.

Erica giggled and turned to her mother. "Nobody."

Ashley smiled. "Well, it certainly looks like you're talking to somebody."

Erica smiled. "She's shy."

"Ouch! Mommy!" Emily screeched behind her, near the blackberries. Ashley turned to see Emily hopping around, terror in her eyes. "Mommy! It hurts so much!"

Ashley jumped up and quickly made her way over. She should have told Emily to put her shoes on. The dish of picked blackberries lay on the ground. Berries were scattered everywhere. Emily's fingers were stained red, but it wasn't blood. On the bottom of her foot a very large torn protruded on her heel. Oh careful, Ashley told herself. Get that whole thing out in one pull, please. Wow, she really shoved her foot onto it. A little pearl of blood oozed out along with the thorn. Ashley was a terrible mother, letting her small daughter go near a bramble without shoes. Ashley wiped the tears from Emily's eyes.

"There, there, sweet pea." She cooed. "All will be well in the blink of the eye."

But the smile Emily began was interrupted with a shrill cry coming from the three teenaged boys. They each yelped and screamed at the same time, each with different words, all with high pitched anxiety.

"Lady lady lady lady!" One voice stood out. "Get her get her get her!"

Ashley stood up instantly angry, and scared. The nerve of those hooligans! She turned to glare at them, but in her brief glance across the shore, she saw that something was missing, Erica. Then she spotted her. Erica's small head bobbed in the water and the child was already neck deep. Ashley could tell by the tilt of Erica's head that the girl was giggling. Her small daughter moved further into the water toward the deep drop off.

"No! Erica, come back here!" Ashley abandoned the one daughter to run after the other. OUCH! Her heel took a bramble in the hard steps, but she kept moving. She went into the icy water and felt every muscle from her ankles down instantly lock. She forced herself faster while calling on Erica to stop and come back. Erica turned her sweet face to her mother, she was having so much fun. A smile stretched across her lips as she inched further from the shore. Ashley splashed indelicately toward her child. She stumbled closer and closer. She reached only a hands length away before Erica disappeared underneath the surface of the water. Ashley screamed. "Nooooooo!"

Where did she go? Ashley spotted the small head bob to the surface down river before going under again. The three teens stood on the shore watching, horror on their faces. One boy turned round eyes on Ashley as she splashed down stream toward her submerged daughter.

"Help me! Help us!" Ashley begged them.

But there was nothing to see except the water and the brilliant light reflecting off the crests of the ripples. One teen quickly waded waist deep to search for the missing girl. Another teen turned a face full of sorrow upstream toward Ashley. Then his face of sorrow turned to one of terror. He raised an arm and pointed at Ashley.

"She's going in! Stop her!"

Ashley spun around in time to see her older daughter slip through the barrier that separated breathable air from a drowning death and her heart completely sunk into the abyss. As the amorphous image of her daughter drifted toward her, she dove in to capture her. Two of the teens watched the river from a waist deep perspective. The third ran to the house over the hill to get help.

The water swallowed them all that day. The only person the river spit back out was the mother, Ashley. They found her a mile downstream in an eternal sleep. A woman that no one could identify. When Peter returned from his temporary duty, after that first hot summer month, he naturally assumed his wife had left him. Good thing too, because he actually hated authority more than airplanes and was on his way to getting fired again.

Reviews Help Authors

Thank you for reading. If you enjoyed this story, consider leaving a review on Goodreads, Amazon, B&N or your favorite bookstore. Reviews help Indie Authors!

Spectral Voices

Part 2

As fate forces her to face some startling mystic abilities, Janine grapples with how she fits into the greater scheme of things, all while facing unresolved feelings for the man she scorned.

From across the void, faint whispers tease the paranormal investigators of *Spectral Analysis*. Could one of them, perhaps skeptical Janine, actually be speaking to spirits? Spiritualist and self-proclaimed witch, Kiki Mellow, thinks yes. As the ghost hunting crew seek out paranormal activity in the windy city, they stumble upon an ancient curse linked to a charm necklace, a coven of witches, and to Janine Stinger. As Ian McNally shares his scientific theory on paranormal energy, Janine becomes emotional entangled all over again; with the doctor, the paranormal, and her violent past. Will she take the leap of faith and embrace Kiki's pagan philosophy? If she does, it could lead to her own demise, or, to her happily ever after… who knows the dangers that manifest when reaching across the void?

Spectral Redemption

Part 3

An ancient curse, reeking of passion, betrayal and murder, force Janine and Kiki to question the men they love, all while ominous events send them spiraling towards a deadly conclusion.

Spectral Analysis enters into a research stage to develop new devices for recording paranormal energy. This gives Kiki Mellow an opportunity to return to Scotland and reconnect with her pagan coven where it's soon revealed that the trilogy curse is bigger than imagined and that Janine Stinger may be a key player in resolving that ancient mandate. As dark forces swirl, bending their actions toward a pattern of love, betrayal and death, Kiki wonders who will succumb next? Kiki? Janine? Or both? The trilogy concludes when *Spectral Analysis* lands in Scotland to investigate ghosts on the island of Skye in a glen near the birth place of a curse spawned centuries ago. The twelve Comba charms reunite and a demon spirit is summoned in the hopes of ending things for good. Messages from each part of the trilogy become clear as the final dark act is at hand. Love, betrayal and death mean that someone must kill and someone must die. Someone will be the last to fulfill the dictum, but who will it be?

About the Author

Joanne Alain Cook is a mother, wife, sister, teacher, artist, officer, and writer. She retired from the USAF after serving both in the active duty and reserves as a C-130 navigator, executive officer, and maintenance officer. Joanne is of Korean/American heritage and has lived in Texas, Japan, Georgia, and California. Her adventures have taken her to every hemisphere on Earth, and she has spent many hours flying in the air and scuba-diving under the sea and lounging on her sofa while reading. She lives in Sacramento with her very handsome husband of twenty-plus years, beautiful brainy daughters, goofy Labrador, angry bearded dragon, frightened chickens, and clueless fish.

Author Drawing by Alaina Grace Batten